THUNDER
IN THE
DAWN

Tor Books
by
Earl Murray

Song of Wovoka
Free Flows the River
High Freedom

THUNDER
IN THE
DAWN

EARL MURRAY

A TOM DOHERTY ASSOCIATES BOOK
NEW YORK

THUNDER IN THE DAWN

Copyright © 1993 by Earl Murray

This book is printed on acid-free paper.

Maps by Victoria Murray

Design by Lynn Newmark

A Tor Book
Published by Tom Doherty Associates, Inc.
175 Fifth Avenue
New York, N.Y. 10010

Tor® is a registered trademark of Tom Doherty Associates, Inc.

Library of Congress Cataloging-in-Publication Data

Murray, Earl.
        Thunder in the dawn / Earl Murray.
                p. cm.
        "A Tom Doherty Associates book."
        ISBN 0-312-09706-9
        I. Title.
        PS3563.U7657T47 1993
        813'.54—dc20   93-11522
                                                                    CIP

First edition: October 1993

Printed in the United States of America

0 9 8 7 6 5 4 3 2 1

To Karen, Dan, and Michael,
my wonderful sister and her family

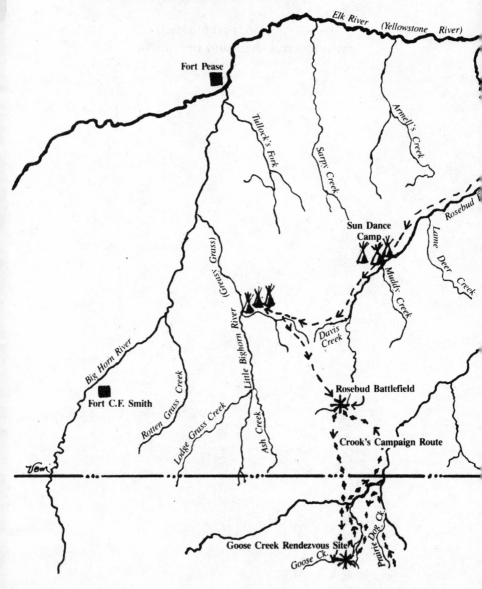

Indian Movement/
Crook's Rosebud Campaign
March-June, 1876

Elk River   (Yellowstone River)

Fort Pease

Tullock's Fork

Sarpy Creek

Armell's Creek

Rosebud R.

Sun Dance Camp

Lame Deer Creek

(Greasy Grass)

Little Bighorn River

Muddy Creek

Davis Creek

Big Horn River

Fort C.F. Smith

Rotten Grass Creek

Lodge Grass Creek

Ash Creek

Rosebud Battlefield

Crook's Campaign Route

Prairie Dog Ck.

Goose Creek Rendezvous Site

Goose Ck.

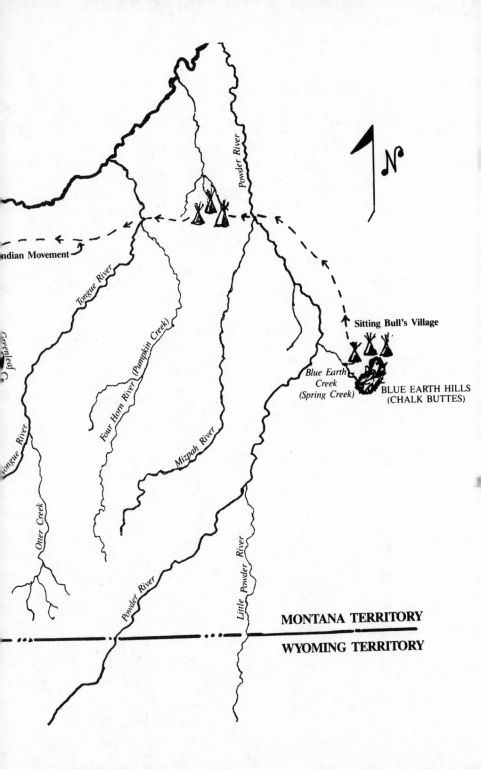

N

Powder River

Tongue River

Indian Movement

Greenleaf C.

Four Horn River (Pumpkin Creek)

Sitting Bull's Village

Blue Earth
Creek
(Spring Creek)

BLUE EARTH HILLS
(CHALK BUTTES)

Tongue River

Mizpah River

Otter Creek

Little Powder River

Powder River

MONTANA TERRITORY

WYOMING TERRITORY

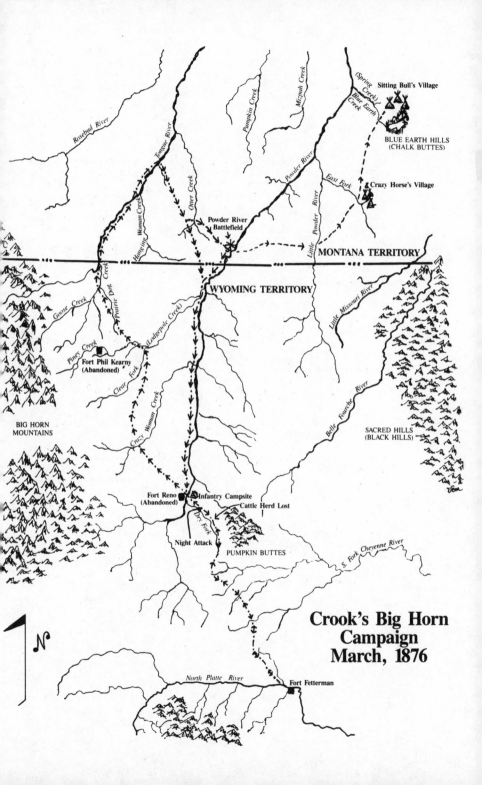

Rosebud River

Pumpkin Creek

Mizpah Creek

(Spring Creek) Sitting Bull's Village

Blue Earth Creek

BLUE EARTH HILLS (CHALK BUTTES)

Tongue River

Otter Creek

Powder River

East Fork

Crazy Horse's Village

Hanging Woman Creek

Powder River Battlefield

Little Powder River

MONTANA TERRITORY

WYOMING TERRITORY

Little Missouri River

Goose Creek

Prairie Dog Creek

(Lodgepole Creek)

Piney Creek
Fort Phil Kearny (Abandoned)

Clear Fork

BIG HORN MOUNTAINS

Crazy Woman Creek

SACRED HILLS (BLACK HILLS)

Belle Fourche River

Fort Reno (Abandoned)
Infantry Campsite
Cattle Herd Lost

Dry Fork

Night Attack

PUMPKIN BUTTES

S. Fork Cheyenne River

Crook's Big Horn Campaign March, 1876

N

North Platte River

Fort Fetterman

PART I
Winter, 1876

ONE

Private Mathew Dolan was dead. Mason Hall pulled his hand away from the young soldier's face and sat up in the darkness of the rickety ambulance. Surely Dolan had been alive just moments before. Hall couldn't believe the young soldier was gone.

Outside, a February moon rose over the deserted plains of eastern Wyoming Territory. Ten companies of the Second and Third U.S. Cavalry and two companies of the Fourth Infantry formed shadowed columns across the expanse of deeply drifted snow, patterned in waves, like sculpted, frozen sand. Four difficult miles farther lay Fort Fetterman, the last outpost along the southern route to the Black Hills.

Privates Hall and Dolan were among the forces under General George Crook, headed into the region east of the Black Hills and west of the Big Horn Mountains. Hall had been told that Montana and Wyoming territories were running wild with Sioux Indians who had refused to return to their reservations. The government had given the Indians until January 31, 1876, to comply with the directive, or be hunted down by the U.S. Army.

Private Hall touched young Dolan's face once again, then shook him. No response. Now he was certain; Dolan was gone.

"This isn't the proper way or place for a man like you to die," Hall said. "Damn this army, anyway!"

Hall turned and gazed out across the frozen night. He removed his gloves and blew on his hands, thinking that this was a fine way to spend his twenty-sixth birthday, or any night of any man's life, for that matter.

Earlier, Hall and Dolan had been talking about their lives to pass the cold hours. Private Dolan had become a soldier at his father's insistence. "You must learn what it is to become a man," his father had told him. "I served my time, and now it's your turn."

Dolan had confessed to Hall that he was just a month past sixteen. He had told the Army he was nineteen, and that he could use a rifle. He had shot himself in the right side while learning maneuvers at Fort Laramie. The bullet had fragmented against his ribs, but the post surgeon believed all the shards had gone through him, and Private Dolan was pronounced fit for duty.

"All I can really do is play me whistle," Dolan had told Hall upon leaving Fort Laramie. "Can't carry a gun, so I'll carry a tune."

Dolan could certainly play his whistle, his penny whistle, as he called it. During the train ride to Cheyenne and the march onward to Fort Laramie, the soldiers had often cheered at the Irish jigs and ballads that Dolan deftly coaxed from the whistle.

Hall continued to blow on his hands. Dolan lay in the front of the ambulance. He had talked about his mother at sundown; but after the last stop to feed the horses he had seemed content to ride in silence. Hall hadn't said much, had just listened to the young soldier's stories about the days before his mother had passed with the fever, and how it had been in Ireland as a boy.

Hall could stand it no longer. He scrambled out the back of the ambulance, tumbling into the snow, yelling, "Stop! All of you, stop!"

The troopers riding behind the ambulance fought to control their horses. Others in the ranks broke formation to keep their horses from spooking. The ambulance driver pulled the mules to a halt.

Hall got up and limped to the front of the ambulance. His voice came through a cloud of condensed breath. "Dolan's gone," he told the driver. "Colder than stone."

"You stopped this army for that?" the driver asked.

"I'm not riding with a dead man," Hall said.

The driver shrugged and drank from his flask of whiskey. "Take it up with your sergeant."

Sergeant Arlan Buckner had already arrived to investigate the disturbance. He took a quick look into the back of the ambulance. "Why didn't you keep talking to him, like I asked?"

"It's not my fault, sir. He should have been left back at Laramie. It's too damn cold out here."

Sergeant Buckner glared down at Hall. "You don't like your orders, soldier?"

"Don't ask me, Sergeant. Ask Dolan."

"Dolan doesn't care much now, does he?" Buckner snapped. "Get back inside."

Hall balked. "I said I'm not riding with a corpse."

"You can't march or ride either one, soldier," the sergeant said. "Get back inside. That's an order."

Hall gritted his teeth and pulled himself back into the ambulance. He contemplated an escape into the darkness. But even if he eluded the soldiers, he could not survive. He had no food, nor the proper clothing for such a place at such a time of year. He might have been able to overcome these if it weren't for a third problem: his leg was still badly swollen from the knife wounds that had exposed the bone, sustained in Leavenworth Prison three weeks past.

Hall had killed a guard and two inmates one night in his cell. Another guard had been badly wounded. Hall would have hanged, had he not provided convincing evidence that the men had been plotting to have the warden killed.

Hall had overheard the two guards in a latrine. They had recruited two inmates to help silence him. Instead of the promised parole, the inmates had received death. Hall had then turned on the guards, killing one and knocking the other unconscious before more guards pulled him off. Once Hall had told his story to the warden, the wounded guard, under torture, had confessed to his part in the plot.

Private Hall had been inducted on crutches. After being rejected by the infantry, he had been assigned to the Second Cavalry. They reasoned that he would not be able to walk well for some time to come, but he would be able to stay on a horse. By the time they reached Fort Fetterman, the Army figured, his wounds would be close to healed and he would be ready to fight.

The column began to move again, and Hall settled himself into the ambulance. He stared at Dolan's body through the darkness. It was lying at an angle and was already getting stiff. Hall removed his gloves and laid the young soldier on his back. He pulled his eyelids down and straightened his legs, but he could not get Dolan's hands to clasp over his breast and had to leave them at his sides.

Hall sat back and spoke to Dolan. His voice was filled with bitterness.

"This isn't right. Neither you nor I gives a damn about this army's ambitions out here. We had to come. The difference is, your father's back in the States and he don't know what's happened. My father's out here someplace, and he for damn sure don't *care* where I am."

Dolan lay motionless on his back. "You hear that?" Hall repeated. "I haven't seen my father in a lot of years. He left me! He just ran off and left me!"

From outside came the sound of horses snorting frozen breath. All else was silent but for the creaking of leather and the crunch of hooves and wagon wheels through crusted snow.

Hall rubbed moisture from his eyes. "I came home from school one day to find him gone. Ma said he'd left for the mountains, that he'd gone back out to trap and live. She always said he'd go back. I didn't want to believe her. He never could settle down to farming. He used to keep me up late at night telling stories about the mountains. Said he couldn't get them off his mind. My mother used to get so mad. I guess I should've known he'd go back, but I thought he'd wait and take me."

Hall blew on his hands. "I was twelve when he left, and he'd already taught me a lot about hunting and living off the land. He could just as well have taken me with him."

When Hall reached for his gloves, his hand bumped Dolan's penny whistle. He moved over to Dolan.

"Then Ma died of scarlet fever," he said as he stuffed the whistle under Dolan's uniform, next to his heart. "I was alone, no kin closer than Philadelphia, and I wasn't going back there. I wanted to go out to the mountains, but nobody would take me. Pa should have taken me. I wouldn't have been any trouble."

Hall moved once more and settled himself as best he could. Outside, the men were cheering. A dispatcher was riding the length of the column, announcing their arrival at Fort Fetterman.

"I wouldn't have been any trouble," Hall repeated as he took a deep breath. "It would have worked out just fine."

* * *

The troops were told to bed their horses at the stables before pitching their tents for the night. Many fell asleep in the hay and had to be rousted by the officers. Some were leaning against their horses, asleep on their feet.

Private Dolan's body was taken to a tack shed, where he lay with three soldiers from the fort who had recently died of pneumonia. In the spring, the four and any others who might have joined them would be buried down by the creek. They would be given wooden headboards.

Hall was taken to the post hospital. Two cast-iron stoves were ablaze, one at either end of the room. Patients filled both ends of the hospital near the stoves, leaving the center virtually empty.

Hall had to settle for a bed directly in the middle, where frost had already seeped through cracks in the adobe. He lit a lantern resting on the small nightstand at the head of the bed and placed his gear at the foot.

After rubbing his hands for a time over the lantern, Hall removed his uniform and crawled under the woolen blanket. He couldn't complain; anyplace was warmer than the ambulance. His hands and feet, his cheeks and nose all tingled from the change in temperature. He knew he could expect some frostbite, but was relieved that no fingers or toes had frozen.

Hall was rubbing his injured leg when he noticed a stirring in the bed across from him. A slim man of medium height with long, thinning gray hair slipped out from under the covers, naked as the day he was born, except for a small claw necklace and a thick silver bracelet around his left wrist.

The man pulled a buffalo robe out from under his bed and spread it over Hall.

"That ought to thaw you out some," he told Hall. "A man can't sleep good when he hears teeth chattering."

Hall stared at him. The man had a large bruise on his right ribs.

"I don't want to take your blankets," Hall said.

"Ah, I'm plenty warm. This is like summer in here."

"You're sure?" Hall couldn't help staring at the bruise.

"Don't give it no thought." He climbed back into his own bed.

The robe was heavy and warm. Hall thanked the man and introduced himself.

"I'm Jordan Kincaid," the man said. "I hired on to pack mules for Crook. He's taking damn near as much stock up the trail as he is soldiers. He's going to be taking one less mule, though, when I get out of here."

"One less?"

"Hattie kicked me in the ribs. I don't take to that. I'll make stew of her for the wolves."

"How bad is your injury?"

"The doc ain't seen me yet. He'd best get here, though. I'm tired of listening to these sniffling blueboys. Ain't nothing wrong with most of them that a dose of salts wouldn't cure."

"I still feel as if I robbed you of this robe," Hall said. "I don't really need it."

"Don't fret so much," Kincaid said. "When I need it, I'll just rob it back."

The post surgeon, his graying hair disheveled, entered the hospital and poured water into a pail from a pot boiling on one of the stoves. He came toward Hall with the pail and a satchel, and set both down on a table near Hall's bed.

"I see you found a warm robe to lie under."

Hall pointed across at Kincaid. "Yes, due to the kindness of that gentleman."

The surgeon grunted. "He's no gentleman."

"Well, he was here ahead of me," Hall said.

"He was in here earlier and refused treatment," the

surgeon said. "He finally decided that cracked ribs are no laughing matter and came hobbling back. He'll live. I know your leg to be serious, so I'll look at you first."

"There's nothing wrong with me," Hall said. "My leg's healing fine."

"You've been talking to Kincaid, I see. You've taken on his attitude."

"I'll make it," Hall said.

The surgeon studied Hall's stern features. Though Private Hall hid it well, agony had carved tight wrinkles at the corners of his blue eyes. Most men would be crying out.

The surgeon opened his satchel, noting Hall's sharp glances that took in everything at once, the thick head of dark hair that hadn't seen clean water for a good long time. Though not heavily built, this man carried strong muscles, and was likely very fluid in movement. It was easy to see why the prison board thought hanging him would be a waste. He was a good candidate for Crook's march against the Sioux.

"I hear you're a fighter," the surgeon said. "Let's have a look at that leg."

The surgeon lifted back the robe and blanket. Hall lay still. The right leg of his long underwear was stained with dried blood from hip to ankle.

"Pull those off," the surgeon said. "I'll see you get a clean pair."

Hall slipped the underwear down. "Where did you hear that I was a fighter?" he asked.

"Your commanding officer told me about you," the surgeon replied, snipping the old stitches from the leg and jerking them out. "He said you were once a trick shooter with a circus. That right?"

Hall nodded, grimacing with pain.

"The word around the fort is that General Crook has

his eye on you. He thinks you'll kill five times the Indians anyone else will. He's glad you're in the outfit."

"I didn't have a choice," Hall said. The surgeon washed away the dried pus and blood, and tested the wounds with his thumbs. Hall's face was bathed in sweat.

"You don't want to be here?" the surgeon asked.

"No."

"Would you rather have died on a gallows?"

"It wouldn't have mattered. I don't feel much alive, anyway."

"I understand you were sent to prison for attempting to kill the circus owner."

"It was either him or me. He wanted a brand-new rifle I'd won in a shooting contest. I didn't want to give it to him. He was going to bash me over the head with it."

The surgeon continued to wash Hall's wounds. "Five years in Leavenworth can harden a man. You don't seem all that hard to me. Where's your family?"

"You ask a lot of questions, don't you?"

"Maybe I do, at that." The surgeon began probing into the deepest cut with a scalpel.

Hall sucked air. "If you'd just leave me be, I'd heal properly."

The surgeon grunted. "Have you had that leg treated since Leavenworth?"

"No. There wasn't time. We moved right in and out of Cheyenne City. We didn't stay at Fort Laramie all that long, either."

The surgeon looked up. "Surely you must have had time. You don't like doctors very well, do you?"

"Doctors keep you in bed. I expect to be walking in a few days."

The surgeon spoke matter-of-factly. "I tell you, if you and I were back in civilization, I would take this leg."

"No, you wouldn't," Hall said.

The surgeon laughed. "At least you and your commander think alike. I heard you're going to be one of Egan's white-horse boys."

"I told you, I don't care what kind of horse I get. I didn't ask for any of this."

"Well, they think you're a dandy," the surgeon said. "Maybe even officer material someday. They want me to care for you like a baby."

"I don't need that," Hall said.

The surgeon probed a while longer, spreading the wound open with his thumb and forefinger. He reached into his bag and pulled out a tin container. "Hold on," he said, pouring tincture of iodine into the cut. Hall bit his tongue to keep from screaming.

The surgeon put the iodine back and snapped his satchel shut. "I'll sew in new stitches in the morning, when I've got better light."

When the surgeon had left, Kincaid wrapped himself in an old blanket and came over to Hall's bed. "I won't bother you if you don't want," he said.

"No, I don't mind," Hall said. "Sit down."

Kincaid was smiling. "I've been watching you. I figure you're going to make it out here. And I think I figured out why."

"What do you mean?" Hall asked.

"You said your name was Hall. Are you related to that lieutenant in the Second Cavalry, Christopher Hall?"

"No," Hall answered. "We're not related."

Kincaid's eyes sparkled. "Then I bet my hunch is true. I used to trap beaver with a man who had your eyes, and your set ways. His name was Ingram Hall. He said he had a boy back in Missouri that someday he was going back to get. Would you by some wild chance be him?"

Hall stared hard at Kincaid. He hoped the shock didn't

show on his face. He didn't want to know about his father, about the man who had hurt him so deeply.

"I'll bet you're Ingram's son. Sure you are!"

Hall shook his head. "No. I don't know any Ingram Hall. I never knew my father."

"Damned if you don't look a sight like Ingram," Kincaid said.

"I said, that man isn't my father."

"Then, by the gods, he's not," Kincaid said. "I just thought I'd ask."

Kincaid got back into bed and pulled the blankets over him. Hall blew out his lantern and settled back under the buffalo robe, reeling with conflicting emotions.

He fought the urge to get up and go over to Kincaid's bed, to learn about his father and possibly understand why he hadn't taken him along.

After consideration, Hall decided he would never know why his father had left him behind. In his own mind, there was no good excuse. There was no reason to dwell on it. As far as he was concerned, he didn't have a father.

Hall closed his eyes, exhausted. He hoped that when he awakened in the morning Kincaid would be gone.

But he knew Kincaid would not be gone. He knew Kincaid would always be somewhere close by during the entire campaign, packing his mules, watching him, and knowing that, by some strange quirk of fate, he had met the son of Ingram Hall.

TWO

She sat alone on a hill above the village, wrapped in a buffalo robe, singing sacred verses to the midnight sky. Broken wisps of clouds drifted across the frigid heavens, curling around the moon like silken fingers. She fanned a fire of sacred sage with a raven's wing while her songs, high and melodic, drifted up with the smoke.

A woman both loved and feared among the northern Cheyenne people, Ghostwind would soon count her twenty-fifth winter. Though happily married to a strong warrior and the mother of two healthy children, she felt a deep void in her life. She had no memory of anything before coming to the Cheyenne at the age of eight. She only knew that she was part Cheyenne and part *Wiheo*, part white.

Ghostwind had come to Old Bear's village of Northern Cheyenne during a raging blizzard. No one knew where she had come from, or how she had found their village. When she had drifted in like a small shadow through the swirling snow she had been mistaken for a wandering spirit. The villagers had scattered, watching her with their hands over their mouths. Finally, a woman named Mountain Water was brave enough to touch her, and cried out that she was a live person, not a ghost.

But not everyone believed. At the same time that Ghostwind arrived, a snowy owl had appeared in a cottonwood at the edge of the village, followed by three more. "The owls have brought me to you," Ghostwind had cried out in Cheyenne. Her eyes had been wide and vacant. "I have an important message for you. You must stay here and not go to the Washita to camp with Black Kettle and his people. You must not go!"

The owls had hooted in the tree, and the people had again backed away from her, for they believed that the owl foretold death. It was said that owls contained the dispossessed spirits of those who had not successfully crossed over to the Other Side. Whenever owls appeared, it meant that the unquiet dead had come to claim victims among the living, and force them into the wrong side of the Spirit World.

Some insisted that Ghostwind be sent back into the storm. "Send the ghost away!" they cried. But the woman named Mountain Water, first wife of a warrior named Five Bulls, took her into their lodge. There they learned that the ghost girl borne on the wind was a mixed-blood. Though her face was dark, her hair was light and her eyes blue.

Ghostwind collapsed in the lodge. When a large lump was found on the right side of her head, a healer named Horned Bull was called in to help her. All the people knew that such a blow could knock out the memories of life in this world.

Horned Bull brought Ghostwind's eyes back to life. She sat up in her bed and listened while he named her for the storm and for the way she had come to their village. From then on she was called Woman-Who-Comes-Like-a-Ghost-on-the-Wind.

She had suddenly lain back down and curled up in fear. Her eyes had come back to this world, but her memories had not.

"She has had a bad accident," Horned Bull had said. "Who knows what is happening in her head? She cannot remember who she is or where she came from."

Throughout the day, Ghostwind would arise in her robes and talk in trance. "Everyone in this village must live. No one must go to the Washita. Not yet."

After another day of the warnings, Horned Bull said, "I believe we should not move our camp down to the Washita with Black Kettle. The spirits are speaking through her, warning us not to leave here."

This raised many arguments. On the third day after Ghostwind's arrival, Old Bear called a council to decide the matter, for Black Kettle and his people were expecting them within two days. Members of the council adjourned to the lodge where Ghostwind lay in her robes, and they heard the words for themselves. The council agreed that the village should not be moved down to the Washita, not until Ghostwind said the time was right.

The following morning, in the Washita camp, Black Kettle and his people were attacked at dawn by Bluecoat soldiers. The hated Bluecoat leader, Long Hair Custer, swept through their village, murdering many in their beds. Black Kettle and his wife met their deaths. The Bluecoats did not care if their bullets and sabers cut down women and children. They killed indiscriminately. The Washita ice was covered with blood.

That morning, Ghostwind walked from the lodge, still speaking in trance. She told the people that they could now move their village. Though they were both angered and sorrowed when they learned what had happened to Black Kettle and his people, they were thankful to Ghostwind for saving many lives. She came out of her trance during a feast in her honor.

Now, as then, Ghostwind was both feared and respected. Owls still remained around the village, leading many to believe that she was a prophet from the dead. She had entered Five Bulls' lodge and had become a daughter to Mountain Water, who said she looked like her only child, lost to sickness. Five Bulls, a Minneconjou of the Lakota Sioux, was a respected warrior. He promised to provide for Ghostwind and make her life happy again.

The owls stayed with Ghostwind, but her memories refused to return. She learned the Lakota tongue of her father and, during walks alone, spoke English to herself, never knowing why but realizing there must be a reason. She never questioned her intuition, or the signs that came to her so clearly. After all, they had saved her life and the lives of the people she now dwelt with.

As she grew to be a woman, Ghostwind kept mostly to herself. She remembered the storm that had brought her to the village and the time thereafter. But this was not enough for her. She wanted to know who she had been before the blow to her head.

When the passing of the winters did not bring back her memories, Ghostwind was forced to leave that part of her life behind. She was now a wife and mother and had turned to learning her life's pathway. Since she could not know her past, it was fitting that the owls teach her how to read the future.

Ghostwind had learned much from the owls, many things that others could only wonder at. The owls had taught her how to read the darkness, so that she might know the omens that spoke of change. It was the night that brought the talking winds; their flow of secrets came only after the sun fell. The winds' direction and their speed, their intensity and pitch, told many things about the weather, as well as changes coming to the land. She had learned to hear the winds' words, and often the silence told her just as much.

Though she did not know the reason, Ghostwind felt that on this particular night she must read the signs very well. A hill just above the creek had called to her and she had climbed it to listen to the darkness.

In the old days, before the reservations, the creeks that fed the upper Powder River were a favorite place to spend the cold moons. Game of many kinds could be found there in abundance, and the water was always fresh. Now, when the people were without food on the reservation, Old Bear had decided to move his people and join Two Moon in winter camp, hoping that they could save themselves from starvation.

Not long after, messengers had brought news that the Great Father in Washington wanted them back on their reservations by the end of the January moon. They were told that if they did not go, the Bluecoat soldiers would come out from the forts to hunt them.

The people had done no wrong. They had left the reservations to hunt, as the treaty provided. There was no other choice, as the rations that were supposed to have come had been delayed. Now, with the daily winter storms, there was no way to comply with the order. It would be suicide to go anywhere, for this cold season was as bad as any the people could remember.

Old Bear and Two Moon held council with the important men of their villages and decided they would move back to the reservation after they had hunted to provide for their families. By then the weather would be open and the traveling easier. They sent a messenger back to the reservation with this decision.

Shortly after, the village received smoke signals telling of a massive buildup of Bluecoats to the south, at Fort

Fetterman. Two Moon and Old Bear had been joined in camp by He Dog and Crazy Horse with their village of Oglala. The camps had joined in hunting and had brought in large amounts of game. The village was ready to go through the worst part of the winter, but moving would be impossible.

Now it was certain the Bluecoats would come. The people felt great concern. No one would ever forget that day on the Washita, and many feared that Long Hair would come back to kill again.

Ghostwind hoped that signs would come this night, so that she could advise the people, as she had sixteen winters past. So far this night, nothing had happened. But she continued to watch the sky, singing and fanning the smoke skyward with a raven's wing.

The rest of the village lay sleeping, bedded tightly in family groups against the cold. Ghostwind's husband, Kicks-the-Fox, slept in the lodge with their two small children. Early in the first moon of the new year he had fallen with his horse, sustaining a serious groin injury. He did not walk for days.

Now he seemed to be improving. He went into the hills alone and had even gone hunting. But his temper had not improved, and the children had noticed the distance between their parents widening.

Young Horse had seen eight winters and Talking Grass just three. They longed for the day when their parents would again hold one another and share low talk. But they were not certain if this would ever happen. They believed this distance might be why their mother had taken to speaking with the spirits so often. They had come to believe that she belonged more to the night than to the day. She seemed more like the wild ones the elders told stories about, the people of old who could become like the creatures of the night that survived because of the shadows. The wolf and the fox, the tawny mountain cat and the small bobtailed cat of the brushy bottoms all gathered most of their food after the sun had fallen. The people of old could become just like them; the stories had been told many times.

Both children believed their mother was akin to the silent winged warrior, the owl. This was the creature that she talked of most, so silent and deadly, with eyes so well suited for seeing into many worlds.

Young Horse and Talking Grass knew many owl stories, told often to children in their lodges at night, to keep them from wandering. The stories were frightening.

Young Horse, now lying awake in his bed, thought about these stories. His mother had been watching the northern skies for a number of days. Light had flashed in the night, the light that comes when changes are being made. Young Horse knew that his mother had been watching the light and looking for the white owls that flew in with the blizzards. The birds were an omen of frozen death.

Talking Grass awakened and leaned over to see if her brother was awake.

"I haven't been asleep for a long time," Young Horse said.

"Are you worried about Mother?"

"Why should I be worried? She has done this before."

"But she's never been so serious before," Talking Grass pointed out. "She hasn't laughed in a long time. Not since Father hurt himself."

"What does that have to do with it?" Young Horse asked. "They didn't laugh together before that happened."

"But tonight, Mother has been gone longer than usual," Talking Grass said. "Why do you think she is out so late?"

"I think she went to meet the owls," Young Horse replied. "She's going to try and talk to them, to learn what is to come. Then she wants to send them back where they came from, so the people do not see them and become alarmed. But I know the people will become alarmed. I'm going to try and find her."

"Don't do that," Talking Grass said. "She has told us both not to go out at night looking for her."

"I think she would like to have me with her," Young Horse said.

Talking Grass sat up in her bed. She checked to see if her father was still asleep. He had been hunting all day. It would take a lot to wake him up.

"If you're going, I'm going, too," Talking Grass said.

"No! It's much too cold."

"I'm going!" Talking Grass said, and stood up.

"Oh, all right, if you have to," Young Horse said. "But be quiet."

The two slipped into deerskin tops and leggings, and covered their feet with deerskin moccasins. They wrapped themselves in cut-up blankets and eased quietly from the lodge into the frigid night.

The sky greeted them with bursts of light. The north was alive with streaks of white that shimmered against the black distance. Overhead, the full moon shone brightly through floating crystals of ice.

Young Horse took Talking Grass by the hand and whispered, his breath a cloud, "We have to keep moving until we find her. It's colder than I thought."

The two bounced through the snow toward the creek. The lodges were set up within an open stand of cottonwoods, in the bottom of a gorge. The slopes above camp were rocky and steep.

Young Horse studied the climb ahead of them. Their mother often settled on top of a hill, where she could unite with the Powers from above. Young Horse looked to where a main horse trail worked its way up from the bottom. He hurried Talking Grass across the ice and onto the slope.

A short way up Talking Grass jerked her brother's hand. "I'm tired. Let's stop and rest."

"Just for a short while," Young Horse said. "We have to find her soon."

"What if she went clear up to the top?"

"Just let me worry about finding her."

Talking Grass breathed heavily and shivered in the cold. "Why don't we go back? She'll come back to the lodge when she is ready. She always does."

"I feel that she wants us with her," Young Horse said.

"But I don't like it out here," Talking Grass insisted. "I feel the way I do when somebody dies."

"You're right," Young Horse said. "Something has come this night. Smell the wind. Mother is burning sacred sage, trying to drive it away. Hear her singing? She wants to talk to the Ancestors."

Talking Grass continued to catch her breath.

Something was happening in the darkness around them, for over the sounds of his sister's breathing Young Horse could hear whispers.

Talking Grass said, "The Ancestors are out here, aren't they? I can hear them whispering. Can you?"

"Yes." Young Horse looked into the trees at the top of the slope. The heavy shadows seemed to shimmer. He didn't want to think he saw figures moving. The whispering grew louder.

Talking Grass stamped her feet against the cold's creeping numbness. "I want to go back."

"No, I see Mother," Young Horse said. "There she is! See her, on top of that hill?"

Talking Grass peered through the darkness. "I don't see anything."

"There, on that pointed hill, just to the side of those

two trees. You can barely see the smoke rising from her fire. She is sitting right there."

"I see her now," Talking Grass said. "You have night eyes, like she does."

"Let's hurry," Young Horse said. "I know something is troubling her very deeply. I think that she needs us."

Ghostwind saw the two small shadows making their way up through the rocks toward her. Perhaps she was dreaming, or perhaps the strange night was teasing her. Everything was changing. The moon in the middle of its circle had turned a lucid blue. The smoke from her fire began a lazy, twisting ascent, spiraling skyward in a thick loop of gray.

Ghostwind felt herself, to be certain her body was still with her. She had to be dreaming. Even the arrival of Young Horse and Talking Grass seemed unreal. Never before had they come out into the night to find her.

When they took form in the light of her fire, their small faces alive with concern, Ghostwind felt deep fear creeping through her.

Talking Grass fell into her mother's arms. Young Horse pointed into the shadows. "The Ancestors are here," he said. "We both heard them. What is going to happen?"

"I am glad to see you," Ghostwind told her children. "But it is late and very cold."

"Tell us what is happening," Young Horse persisted. "I don't like the feeling out here."

"I can only say that what you both feel is real," Ghostwind replied. "I don't know for certain what is coming, but it is very bad."

"Will we all die?" Talking Grass asked.

"No, we will not all die," Ghostwind answered. "If I can understand what is being said tonight, maybe no one will die. But so far I am unable to make connections."

"Look!" Young Horse pointed to a dead pine silhouetted against the sky. "Owls!"

Ghostwind stared in surprise. They hadn't been there just moments before. Now four of them sat in the branches, the flashing northern lights behind them, staring across the hill at her and her children.

"Make them go away," Talking Grass begged.

"Calm yourself," Ghostwind said. "Rather than turn away from them, we must look and listen. We must understand what they are here to tell us."

"I feel strange and afraid," Young Horse said. "I heard whispering before. Now I hear crying."

"He's right," Talking Grass said. "We heard it coming up the hill."

"For some time I have been trying to understand my bad feelings about what is to come," Ghostwind said. "Tonight I hope to find the answer."

Young Horse said, "Why did I feel I should come up here?"

"Maybe someone was calling you," Ghostwind suggested.

"Did the owls call me?"

"Maybe. It is hard to know," Ghostwind replied. "But you have been called before. Do you remember?"

"Was it a night in the middle of the warm moons?" Young Horse asked. "Was it at a lake below the mountains of the Big Horn?"

"Yes," Ghostwind said. "You were but four winters. You talked like someone else that night. Do you remember? Your voice changed, and you said there were buffalo to hunt at the north end of the mountains."

Young Horse remembered asking to go up on the hill with his mother. And he remembered her telling him about the ceremony and the voice that had come through him. But he could not remember talking.

"Is that what I am supposed to do tonight?" Young Horse asked. "Am I supposed to talk with another's voice?"

"Do you feel the way you did that night on the hill above the lake?" Ghostwind asked.

"Yes, I do," Young Horse answered. "Maybe that's why I was called up here."

Talking Grass clutched her mother. "I'm frightened."

"You have nothing to fear," Ghostwind told her daughter. "Let us all hold hands in a circle. Maybe the spirit will come and speak through Young Horse."

Talking Grass whimpered.

Ghostwind squeezed her hand. "Be calm. It does no good to cry at a time like this."

Talking Grass bit her lip and trembled in silence. Young Horse held his mother's hand tightly. He felt his body relaxing. His head bowed against his chest, and Ghostwind began a song, letting her eyes travel up the spiraling smoke. Before long, Young Horse fell into a deep trance. His body began to shake.

Ghostwind released his hand and stood back. When Young Horse was calm again, he no longer seemed like a boy.

THREE

"I want to speak through your son," said a voice that came from Young Horse. The voice was far deeper than Young Horse's own. "Will you allow this?"

Talking Grass whimpered again. Ghostwind took her daughter in her arms. "Yes, it is well that you talk through my son," she said to the voice. "I believe I have heard you speak through him before. Is that true?"

"Yes, it is true," the voice said. "I do not do this often. Only through the chosen."

"Did you come to warn us about approaching danger?" Ghostwind asked.

"You are already aware of the coming danger," the voice said. "You must understand that the foretold time of great change is upon your people. Stay above what is happening, and do not close your heart."

"Do not close my heart?"

"The foretold changes are coming," the voice repeated, "but there are changes coming for you that you are not aware of. Do not be swept away by personal feelings, for now you must act for the good of your people as a whole."

"Personal changes for me?" Ghostwind asked.

"Yes. They will reach into the very core of your being. But you must be strong."

Ghostwind was overwhelmed. "If all this is coming, how do I keep focused on what I must do?"

"Now, of all times, it is most important to hold onto love," the voice replied. "Do not give in to fear or anger. Otherwise you will not think straight. You will not be able to see clearly. And you must see clearly."

"I feel the same as I did when our people were killed on the Washita," Ghostwind said. "It makes me afraid, and also angry."

"Push it all away," the voice said. "Speak to the silence as much as you can. Do what you must, but maintain your wisdom. That is important."

"What must I watch for?"

"Keep the sacred sage burning, day and night. Watch where the smoke goes. There and only there will you be safe. The land is filling up with evil. Your people will look to you for guidance. Give them that guidance."

"Will you talk with me again?" Ghostwind asked.

The voice did not answer. Instead, Young Horse suddenly stood and raised his arms to the sky. He yelled and his body jerked. Then he said, "It is over!" in his own voice. The owls flew from the dead pine into the darkness, and Young Horse collapsed into Ghostwind's arms.

"Young Horse is himself again," Talking Grass said. "My fear is gone."

"Good," Ghostwind said, holding both children next to her. She was glad for Talking Grass, but her own fear had suddenly grown stronger. Added to the terror of knowing that the Bluecoats were coming was the fact that she had been handed a great burden.

Ghostwind stared out into the night, wondering. As she did so, an image materialized from the darkness. At first,

Ghostwind believed the voice that had been within Young Horse had decided to take human form. But Young Horse was pointing.

"Look—the Strange Man of the Lakota, the one called Crazy Horse."

"Your eyes are truly those of the night," the man said, moving closer. "I am indeed who you say I am."

Crazy Horse came forward from the shadows, dressed in blue leggings and wrapped in a red blanket. He was of medium height and build, with a narrow face and a high, sharp nose. His hair and complexion were both lighter than those of his people. The blanket was open at the neck, revealing an Iroquois shell necklace that gleamed in the light of the fire like his dark, unsettling eyes.

Talking Grass and Young Horse were both staring at him. The sky above the warrior was alive with light. Talking Grass said, "Look into the light! There is a pony running in the wind!"

Young Horse said, "Maybe it has come to carry us away to another campsite. Something is wrong with this place."

Crazy Horse looked across the fire at the children and smiled. "No matter the power of those who are older, it is always the children who can see the truth."

"Why do you honor us with your presence?" Ghostwind asked.

"It is I who am honored," Crazy Horse said. "I've been in these hills fasting for three days and nights, to learn what is to come. I've been able to learn nothing. But the spirits have come to your son. Perhaps my anger is so deep that I can no longer hear the spirits."

Ghostwind found it hard to believe that Crazy Horse would worry about messages from the Spirit World, for he had the power to live in two worlds simultaneously—the "known" world and that of the spirits. Among his people, there were few who were as highly thought of, or who could make the people listen so intently to his occasional words.

Though he was born of two Lakota people, his light hair and complexion made some believe that the spirit of a white man, a *Wasichu,* had come to live within him.

Crazy Horse had proved his heart to be pure Lakota. He was a respected leader greatly feared by the Bluecoat armies. No one fought more bravely. He had, in fact, become a legend even before his twentieth birthday, fighting bravely in a battle against the Arapaho.

The Bluecoats interpreted his name to mean that of a horse with a shattered mind. But the name described a vision of a warrior on a spirit horse, with a hawk riding the wind above him, a special warrior who painted himself like a hailstorm and took no scalps. It had been his father's name.

Now in his mid-thirties, Crazy Horse had reached a high degree of power. He needed startlingly little food to survive and very few articles of clothing to maintain warmth. No one could understand him, and all had stopped trying. It was best to stand back and watch, and hope this strange man would bring as much power to the people as he could.

"Perhaps my life has become tainted," Crazy Horse continued. "If I could but return to the ways of a child."

"What causes you to come to us?" Ghostwind asked.

Crazy Horse pointed to a rock that stood a short way distant. "The rock spirit put words in my head, saying that the Cheyenne woman Ghostwind and her children would hear the words of a Wise One from the Other Side. Perhaps it was the Wise One speaking through the rock. I cannot say. I wish to learn the words, if you would share them."

"The words came through my son," Ghostwind told him. "The voice said that the time of the prophecy is near, and that I am to help my people. I am sure you have heard similar words yourself."

"I'm having a hard time knowing what to do," Crazy Horse confided. "I hear many voices these days, and not all of them are good. I cannot bear what is to come."

"You are a great leader," Ghostwind said. "You will be shown the way."

Crazy Horse turned back toward the rock. "Maybe if you went back to the rock with me, the voice would return. We could learn more about what is to come."

Ghostwind stared into the fire. Crazy Horse might have a good idea. Perhaps she could learn more at the rock. Together, Crazy Horse with his powers and she with hers, they might be able to learn a great deal more about what was to come.

She did not want to take the children, for they were both very tired. She knew that the voice would not speak through Young Horse again. If she was to go, she would leave them by the fire. She turned to Crazy Horse.

"Are you certain the rock spirit will not be angry with you for taking me there?"

"No. I think you should stand there with me. Perhaps together we can call the Wise One back."

Ghostwind put more wood on the fire and sat Young Horse and Talking Grass down. "Stay here and keep yourselves warm," she instructed. "I will go to the rock with Crazy Horse and try to understand more about what this night means."

Talking Grass held her mother's arm. "Don't go. I'm afraid."

"She's right," Young Horse advised. "It would not be good to go."

"I'm not going far," Ghostwind said. She pointed. "You'll both see me right over there. I won't be gone long."

Ghostwind walked with Crazy Horse into the darkness. Crazy Horse took off his red blanket and handed it to her, saying, "I only offer this to you for warmth, not as an admirer."

Ghostwind took the blanket. "Thank you. I have become chilled for some reason."

Ghostwind hurried toward the rock, looking back occasionally to check on the children.

"Do you fear me?" Crazy Horse asked. "Is that why you find it hard to speak to me?"

"I do not find it hard to speak to you, nor do I fear you," Ghostwind said. "For some reason I feel very strange. It is unusual for this conversation to take place."

"You know that I am unusual," Crazy Horse said. "And I know that you are unusual as well. I only wish to learn with you, if that is possible. It is for the good of the Cheyenne and the Lakota. Though you are mixed with *Wasichu* blood, the spirits favor you."

"They did not come to me, but to my son," Ghostwind said. "You will have to thank him for what we've learned."

"True, they have chosen him tonight," Crazy Horse said, "but they have come to you often. I have heard the story of when you saved Old Bear's people from what happened to Black Kettle and his people on the Washita. I know that owls stay around you, and that you do not fear them."

"They've always helped me," Ghostwind said. "But they have yet to tell me about my early life, my years before my head was hurt."

"It's important that you are alive and respected by your people," Crazy Horse said. "If the years you have lost are important, they will return to you."

Ghostwind recognized the truth in his words. It did no good to worry about the time she could not remember. And she could not complain: the time she had spent with Old Bear's people had been very good.

And now she felt good that this kind of respect came

from Crazy Horse himself. Even if she were not married, though, she would not think of trying to attract him. There was much sorrow in Crazy Horse's past, and many said his future would be sorrowful also.

All who knew him believed that he had already found the love of his life and had lost her. Though he was now married to a woman named Black Shawl, many believed he could never care for a woman again as he had cared for Black Buffalo Woman. He had fought a man named No Water for her, had been shot in the face, and finally had been disgraced by his warrior society. Still, he had given her up to keep his people together.

His wife, Black Shawl, now lived with her parents, fighting the coughing disease. Their baby had died of the fever, and it was said that Crazy Horse had spent three days lying with her on the burial scaffold.

Many said that all this had made Crazy Horse unpredictable. He would go on rampages, killing the miners who came into the Black Hills for gold, then yearning for peace so that his people could be left alone.

But he had finally concluded that peace could never be; the white race were too many and wanted too much. He now believed that the only way to maintain dignity was to live in the old way and die when that way ended.

"Your son is a chosen one," Crazy Horse said. "In manhood, he will become a great leader."

"It's my hope that he will grow to manhood," Ghostwind said. "I feel that death has talked through him tonight."

"Death has told you how to keep him safe," Crazy Horse said. "It is a fact that the Bluecoats are coming soon. I cannot understand why they would be so foolish as to do anything in this weather, much less make war. But they are coming."

"Death came to the Washita during the cold moons. It

can happen at any time," Ghostwind said. "I fear for all the people. I can only hope we will learn more of what is to come at the rock."

"I believe we will," Crazy Horse said. "But if the Wise One will not come, we will not have lost anything."

Crazy Horse stopped in front of the huge sandstone ledge that outcropped near a line of trees, on the edge of a canyon filled with deep shadows. Ghostwind stood beside the rock, wondering if she should climb upon it or not.

"What do you feel?" Crazy Horse asked.

"I feel very strange," Ghostwind said. "I see many shadows moving. I don't know whether I should climb the rock."

"I only brought you here so that we might learn together," Crazy Horse said. "Perhaps the rock is giving you a message. Maybe you don't want to see."

"No, I need to see," Ghostwind said. "I have to."

Ghostwind was starting to climb the rock when she heard a voice calling to her. She turned, with Crazy Horse, to see a man approaching them. He was angry and out of breath. It was Kicks-the-Fox, Ghostwind's husband.

"So, this is why you come out at night," he said. "I thought you were talking with the spirits. You could at least have sent the children back down to the lodge."

"No," Ghostwind said. "I have not come up here to be with Crazy Horse."

Kicks-the-Fox pointed. "Why are you wearing his blanket?"

"I offered it to her against the cold, nothing more," Crazy Horse said.

"Yes, I'll bet you did," Kicks-the-Fox said. "I've heard that you are good at this kind of thing. Is your own wife not enough for you?"

"I am telling you that your anger is not justified," Crazy Horse said. "We've done nothing."

"I know better!" Kicks-the-Fox blurted. "Why can't you keep your mischief among the Oglala and leave the Cheyenne people alone?"

"That's not fair!" Ghostwind cried. "Crazy Horse is telling you the truth. Besides, when have I ever looked toward another man?"

"Maybe I just haven't noticed," Kicks-the-Fox said. "I've been too busy hunting, providing meat. All the while you have been away from the cooking fire, doing other things." He turned and hurried down the hill.

"Kicks-the-Fox! Wait!" Ghostwind ran after him, leaving Crazy Horse at the rock. When she caught up with him, he would not listen, but turned and started down a steep draw where he knew she would not follow.

Ghostwind watched him working his way down the treacherous slope. She called him back, but in vain. She looked back up to the rock, but Crazy Horse was gone. Finally she went back to the fire.

"What's the matter with Father?" Talking Grass asked. "Why did he go down into the canyon?"

Ghostwind took the children by the hand. "Let's go back down to the lodge."

"I heard him shouting," Young Horse said.

"Everything will be fine," Ghostwind said. To make better time, she carried Talking Grass and told Young Horse to run with her. She worked her way down the hill and back into the village, wondering what would happen with her husband. He had never before accused her of being unfaithful. She could not understand why he would think such a thing.

Kicks-the-Fox was not in the lodge. Ghostwind put her confused and tired children to bed and told them their father would be back soon. She crawled inside the robes she shared with her husband, tears rolling down her cheeks. She tossed and turned, trying to fall asleep, wondering where he was.

If only she had not gone up on the hillside! If she had stayed in the lodge, her husband would not have come up the hill and found her talking to Crazy Horse.

Kicks-the-Fox knew full well how much she loved him. He had taken her as his wife just three winters after she had come to the people, and she had never been with another. He knew also that she had never wanted another. He had talked before of bringing another wife into the lodge, when the time was right, and she had not argued against it. She had felt she would always be his most important wife.

She thought that possibly his groin injury had something to do with it. She had snuggled up to him in bed often enough; it had been he who had told her he needed to wait before he tried making love again. Perhaps he had become worried that she was longing to make love with someone.

Finally, Ghostwind could stand it no longer. She left her bed and again dressed for the cold. Outside, a gray light had invaded the eastern sky. Ghostwind hurried to her parents' lodge and awakened them.

"Would you go and stay with my children for a short while?" she asked her mother. "I'm going to look for Kicks-the-Fox."

Mountain Water was a big-framed woman, a buffalo woman, as such were called. Though she was well into middle age, her hair was as dark as the day she had been born. Her eyes were bright and penetrating and her motions quick.

She sat up in her robes and frowned. "Kicks-the-Fox is gone? Where?"

"It's hard to explain," Ghostwind said. "I was out on the hillside and the children came up to find me. Crazy

Horse saw us and came to talk. Kicks-the-Fox thought we had met to be together."

"He accused you of adultery?" Mountain Water asked.

"Yes, and he was very bitter. I tried to tell him. He wouldn't listen."

Ghostwind's father, Five Bulls, raised himself on an elbow. "He'd better come to his senses. There's no time for foolishness."

"I'll find him soon," Ghostwind said. "He can't have gone far."

"Why should you go after him at all?" Mountain Water said.

"He's not thinking well lately," Ghostwind said. "I don't want anything to happen to him."

"It's good to care about your husband," Mountain Water said, "but there is only so much you can do."

"I have to find him," Ghostwind insisted. "He has to know that I have not been unfaithful."

"Don't stay out long," Five Bulls said. "The cold does not care if you love your man or not."

Ghostwind left her parents' lodge and hurried to the edge of the village. The sun's rim had topped the horizon, sending its gold through dense frost crystals that hovered in the air. At the river, horse tenders were taking the herd to drink. Fresh water ran in a stream from the hillside onto the ice of the river. Steam rose in dense clouds. The horses snorted and pawed in the slush.

Ghostwind stood on the bank, studying the herd. The horse tenders watched her, and finally one rode over.

"I am looking for Kicks-the-Fox's best horse, the black stallion he calls Shadow," she said. "I do not see it."

"Shadow is not here," the boy said. "Kicks-the-Fox took the horse late in the night."

"Did he leave the village?"

The horse tender shrugged. "He came out and got the

horse and took him back into the village. Maybe he rode out the other side. I don't know."

"Help me catch one of my husband's other horses," Ghostwind said. "The buckskin mare named Dancer."

The boy threw a horsehair lariat over the buckskin's neck and brought the horse to Ghostwind. She thanked him and led Dancer back into camp. Her father awaited her with a blanket and saddle. Her mother made certain she had enough clothes to ride without getting frostbite.

"The children are still sleeping soundly," Mountain Water said. "Do not worry about them."

While her father saddled the buckskin, Ghostwind hurriedly rubbed charcoal mixed with grease under her eyes. She did not want snowblindness, for it might not go away until the winter season ended. She took the reins from her father and climbed on.

"Do not go too far looking for Kicks-the-Fox," Five Bulls advised. "He should not have ridden away."

"Father, he's not thinking straight," she said.

"Ah, but the cold will clear his mind," Five Bulls said. "If you don't see him before the sun climbs to its highest, turn around. If he loves you, he'll come back and talk about it."

Ghostwind turned the buckskin and rode from the village. She could not understand what her husband was doing. Surely he couldn't be leaving the village, riding off, not with his injury. Perhaps he simply felt he needed to be off by himself. Whatever the reason, Ghostwind wanted to find him and settle the issue once and for all.

Ghostwind urged the mare up the trail that led out of the steep canyon and onto the rolling country above the river. The sun had risen fully over a frozen land, making it visible for a long distance. There were many horse tracks, for the herd ranged all over the area. Finding a lone rider would be nearly impossible.

She rode to a high hill and looked in all directions, thinking that it was impossible to know which way he would go, or why. But she did not want to think she wouldn't find him. She wanted her children to have their father with them again, and she wanted her husband to know that she loved him and would never want another, not even Crazy Horse.

FOUR

It was well after dark when Ghostwind returned to the village. She had not found Kicks-the-Fox. Her tears were still fresh as she dismounted and gave the pony over to a horse tender, turning her face from a gusty wind that promised snow.

Few noticed her, as the village was alive with alarming news. Messengers from a Lakota camp to the south had come to report that Bluecoat soldiers were gathering at the fort called Fetterman. It was believed the Bluecoats would soon march north in search of Indian villages.

Ghostwind's friend, Day Lily, approached her and told her that the day had been filled with speeches and emotion. Though everyone realized the danger, most thought that the Bluecoats were after Crazy Horse and the Oglala. Word of Crazy Horse's medicine had spread among the Bluecoats long ago, and everyone knew of the feud between Crazy Horse and the Bluecoat leader, Three Stars Crook.

Crazy Horse had warned Three Stars not to cross the Tongue River, or there would be war. Three Stars knew that young warriors competed with one another to follow Crazy

Horse. It was he who had the power to lead the Sioux nation against the incoming whites and secure a victory, no matter the odds.

In council, Two Moon and Old Bear had decided that with the coming of the first spears of grass they would lead their people back to the agency. Staying out in the hunting grounds, whether or not a right legally ceded to them by treaty, was not worth risking lives over.

The council was still in session, addressing a group of warriors who wanted to go and steal the Bluecoat horses. The debate was raging in the center of the village.

"Much has happened since you left this morning," Day Lily said. "Everyone is afraid."

Ghostwind had expected to hear that Bluecoats were coming, for her dreams had told her. But her mind was on Kicks-the-Fox.

"It is difficult to think of anyone but my husband right now," Ghostwind said. "I couldn't find him, and I don't know where to look."

"He's with the warriors who are forming a horse-raiding party," Day Lily said. "I saw him talking to my husband."

Ghostwind frowned. "No. He left camp last night and hasn't returned."

"You are wrong," Day Lily said. "I told you, I saw him."

"I don't understand," Ghostwind said. "How can he steal horses with his injury? And why didn't he tell me he was going?"

"Let's go into the village," Day Lily suggested. "Everyone is there, listening to Crazy Horse."

Ghostwind walked with Day Lily through the center of the village. Crazy Horse was standing on the back of his red pinto pony, talking to the people in sign, the blustery wind spreading his long hair. The pony stood motionless as Crazy Horse gestured to the crowd.

"I will move my people from this village to another, along the Little Powder River. It is I who Three Stars wants to kill. Let him come after me and leave my brothers, the Cheyenne, alone."

"We will fight beside you!" a warrior shouted from the crowd. Other warriors whooped and cheered.

Crazy Horse raised his hands. When the crowd had quieted, he said, "Those of you who wish to help, join the horse-raiding party. Many of them are already catching their best ponies. The council has decided to let them go. But there will be no fighting, just horse-stealing. The elders believe that there should be no bloodshed, or the Bluecoats will be able to say that we started the war."

Again the Cheyenne warriors voiced their support. Ghostwind studied the crowd, looking for Kicks-the-Fox. He was nowhere to be seen.

"I don't see Red Bear, either," Day Lily said. "He gathered his things and said good-bye to me earlier. He told me he would be leaving, whether or not the council approved."

Warriors went into their lodges and returned with bridles and clothes for winter riding. They continued to cheer until Crazy Horse quieted them again.

"There is much strength in our two people combined. And it makes my heart glad to know that the Cheyenne people would help keep the Bluecoats from attacking us, even though they do not wish to have war come to their lodges either. The brave Cheyenne are taking a great chance exposing themselves. The Cheyenne need not risk their people to get involved, but they are doing so to show their love for the Lakota people."

"I'm not sure that the Bluecoats aren't after all of us," Ghostwind told Day Lily. "The death owls do not give any signs that the Cheyenne people are safe."

"I believe as you," Day Lily said. "No one is safe."

"The Bluecoats are very worried that I will lead many warriors into the Black Hills and drive the invaders out," Crazy Horse continued. "They have taken the most sacred of our lands. We cannot go into the *Paha Sapa*, the Sacred Hills, to pray any longer. The mountains are covered with whites who dig for the yellow metal, and these men are very cruel.

"But if I go after these men anymore, it will not happen until the snow has left and my Cheyenne brothers have reached the agency. I will make no war until the Cheyenne are safe. That is why we are moving downriver. If the Blue-coats do come, they will go after my village and not this village."

When Crazy Horse had finished, he wrapped himself in his red blanket and sat down on his horse. Warriors ran from the village to join others already mounted. Then from the edge of the village came a chorus of whoops and yells as the horse-raiding party rode into the oncoming storm.

"Many mothers and wives will worry," Day Lily said. "I will be among them."

"I had no idea Kicks-the-Fox was healed," Ghostwind said. "That puzzles me." She stared out from camp, looking for her husband among the riders. But it was too dark.

Someone then asked Crazy Horse if he would preside over a ceremony meant to secure the horse-raiders' success.

"I will do this," Crazy Horse said. "Everyone must sing and pray together, so that the horse-raiders may turn the Bluecoats back before they reach any of our villages."

"You will stand beside me for the ceremony, won't you?" Day Lily asked Ghostwind. "Your medicine is also powerful. The night could be filled with great power."

"I'm very tired," Ghostwind said. "I don't think I could do much good in the ceremony."

"But you could!" Day Lily insisted. "Please."

"Very well, I'll come back for the ceremony," Ghostwind promised. "First I must see my children and my parents."

By the time Ghostwind had reached her father's lodge, the breeze was filled with snow. She found her mother sewing moccasins for the children and her father smoking a small pipe. Young Horse and Talking Grass were asleep.

"They've been sick with worry about you," Mountain Water said. "They finally ate something and just collapsed."

"Did the council let the horse-raiders go?" Five Bulls asked.

"Yes," Ghostwind said. "Kicks-the-Fox was with them. I can't understand that."

Young Horse and Talking Grass awakened and jumped up to greet their mother. She hugged them tightly.

"Grandmother said you would return," Talking Grass said. "She said the winter spirits care about you."

Young Horse spoke up. "Father returned, but left again. He didn't talk to us very much. He was in a hurry. He said he would steal a pony for me from the Bluecoats."

"I'll take the children back to your lodge," Mountain Water told Ghostwind. "Talk to your father for a while. Then you can come to your children."

Ghostwind hugged Young Horse and Talking Grass again and assured them she would be right along. When her mother had taken them from the lodge, she turned to her father.

"I don't understand. I went to look for Kicks-the-Fox and he was here all the time?"

"I don't know where he went," Five Bulls said angrily. "He wouldn't even talk to me. But he must not have gone far."

"But what about his pony?" Ghostwind asked. "I saw that Shadow was gone this morning."

"I think he wanted to trick you," Five Bulls said. "He

wanted you to go and look for him. He knew you would."

"I don't understand him anymore," Ghostwind said. "Maybe it's his injury."

"His injury is no reason for his rudeness," Five Bulls remarked.

"What did he do?"

"When I told him you had left to search for him, he ignored me," Five Bulls replied. "He didn't even go to look for you, or wait for you to return. I don't know what is wrong with him, but he shows little respect for you. And that angers me."

Ghostwind thought a moment. "Why would he ride off with the horse-raiders if his groin is still bothering him?"

Five Bulls puffed on his pipe. "That's something you should ask him. In fact, there are many things you should ask him."

Ghostwind got up. "I need to spend some time with the children before the ceremony. They must be confused."

"They are also hurt," Five Bulls said. "Their father's actions bother them. His disregard for you makes them sad and angry at the same time. Something is wrong with your husband."

Ghostwind left the lodge. The people were forming circles within circles in the center of the village, while snow swirled all about them. Many were singing.

Ghostwind hurried to her lodge, but the children were not there. Her mother was sitting by the fire.

"I sent them off to spend the night with cousins in another lodge."

"Why?" Ghostwind asked.

"It's best that they stay elsewhere tonight. Sit down. We must talk."

"What is troubling you?"

"Please, sit. I cannot make this easy."

Holding her breath, Ghostwind took a seat.

"Kicks-the-Fox was in another's lodge last night," Mountain Water said. "I heard some other women talking while getting water at the river, but I did not tell your father."

"Are you saying he was with another woman?"

"Yes."

Ghostwind felt as if a large club had struck her in the lower stomach. The pain rose, and tears flooded down her cheeks.

Mountain Water's eyes filled also. "I'm sorry," she said, hugging Ghostwind. "I'm so sorry. But you have to know."

"Whose lodge?" Ghostwind asked. "Do I know her?"

"No, she is one of Two Moon's people. She's a young woman who lives with her grandmother, who is very old and cannot hear."

"I don't understand," Ghostwind said. "I thought Kicks-the-Fox had injured himself. I thought that was why he didn't want me for so long."

"Perhaps he did injure himself, perhaps not," Mountain Water said. "Who will know for certain? But that doesn't matter now."

"I will not stay with him," Ghostwind said, slamming her fist into a robe. "I do not deserve this!"

"You have every right to leave him," Mountain Water said. "If he had done this according to the law, and had wanted another wife, it wouldn't be so bad. But he's shamed you."

Ghostwind began to cry again. "But why?"

"No one can answer this," Mountain Water said. "It happens and cannot be explained. It's painful, I know, but time will heal you, and another will take you for his wife."

"What if he doesn't want me to leave him?" Ghostwind asked.

"It's not his choice to make now, is it?" Mountain Water said. "That's the law."

Ghostwind's pain again turned to rage. "To think of the things he said to Crazy Horse and me last night." She drove her fist into the robe again. "He is a man without honor."

"It is best to put all of it behind you," Mountain Water said. "It will be difficult for the children, but they will understand. You can move back in with us. I'll help you with your belongings."

"Not yet," Ghostwind said. "I will wait until he returns."

"It would be better to do it now."

"No, I want to wait. I want you and Father to be there, outside the lodge. I want Father's friends to be there. I want Kicks-the-Fox to try to stop me."

"There is enough trouble without causing more," Mountain Water insisted. "And the children, it would cause them even more pain."

"It is *he* who has caused the trouble, and he will pay for it."

"No, daughter. Think of your little ones."

Ghostwind knew her mother was right. She cried for a time and said, "I will move tonight, right now."

"Move tomorrow," Mountain Water suggested. "The storm will be bad very soon. Besides, Kicks-the-Fox is gone with the horse-raiders and they will not have returned by morning. You have plenty of time to move."

"Then I had better sleep now, and get well rested. The ride in the cold made me very tired."

"What about the ceremony?" Mountain Water asked. "I thought you promised Day Lily you would pray alongside her."

"I don't feel like praying for Kicks-the-Fox."

"You should pray for him anyway," Mountain Water said. "He is in need of prayers, and it will make you stronger."

"Pray for him so he can return and cause me more pain?"

"You will have more pain if he doesn't return and you didn't pray."

Ghostwind hugged her mother again. She rose and stepped out into the storm, snowflakes mixing with her tears. Firelight filled the center of the village, where Ghostwind joined Day Lily. Crazy Horse was just beginning the ceremony.

Crazy Horse lit a pipe and offered it to the earth and sky, and to the four directions. Snow swirled about him as he smoked and passed it in a circle to the other men present, those who had stayed behind to protect the village.

When the men had smoked, Crazy Horse said prayers and passed the pipe again. Ghostwind noted the sadness in his face and how he stared toward the south for a long time.

Everyone began to move in rhythm with a large drum near the main fire. Eight young men sat around the drum, singing and pounding. Ghostwind held Day Lily's hand and that of an older woman on her other side. She closed her eyes and began to sing. Day Lily noted her tears, but said nothing.

The ceremony was intended to direct thoughts of conquest toward the horse-raiders, to give them power from afar and let them know that everyone in the village wanted to help. Like the others in the ceremony, Ghostwind envisioned the warriors returning triumphantly, driving the Bluecoat ponies ahead of them. She saw them circling the village while the people sang praises and admired their loved ones.

In her mind, Ghostwind viewed the returning raiders with excitement. She saw them pounding through the new snow on their ponies, whooping and yelling, both Cheyenne and Oglala. She saw their faces clearly, the brightly colored blankets that they whipped over the horses' backs.

Ghostwind envisioned many different warriors before thinking about Kicks-the-Fox. She fought the pain as she started to visualize her husband. She did not know what she would say to him, but she realized she would have to confront him and tell him she had moved out and why.

As Ghostwind tried to visualize her husband, her pain quickly turned to concern. She could not find his face among the others. Then her vision changed. The warriors on horseback began to swirl and fade into the air. The entire scene reversed itself, and Ghostwind saw no more horse-raiders.

Instead, she saw Bluecoat soldiers driving the Indian ponies out from the village. There were no returning raiders, glorious in bringing back horses, just the Bluecoats, who had won a victory.

Ghostwind broke from the circle and stumbled off by herself. Day Lily followed, asking her what had happened. Ghostwind fell to her knees, shaking her head, but the new vision would not leave.

As the Bluecoats drove the herd of ponies into the steep bluffs above the village, a lone horse turned from the herd and galloped onto a hill. It was Shadow, Kicks-the-Fox's black stallion. Huge tears rolled from the horse's eyes, while on his back lay empty buckskin clothing. The clothing belonged to Kicks-the-Fox.

Ghostwind felt herself being lifted to a sitting position, snow melting against her face. She had no idea that she had fallen, or how long she had been on the ground. The entire ceremony had gone wrong. Dancers had converged around her, their hands over their mouths. Many were weeping. Day Lily had her by the arm and was speaking.

"Are you back with us?"

"Yes," Ghostwind acknowledged. "I'm back in this world."

"What did you see?" Day Lily asked. "You were scream-ing loudly, something about Bluecoats."

"I want to go back to my lodge," Ghostwind said. She climbed to her feet.

"But what did you see?" Day Lily persisted. The others joined her, pressing Ghostwind for information.

"I must consider what I saw before I can discuss it openly," Ghostwind said. "My vision was both confusing and terrifying. Once I know for certain what I saw, I will come forth."

The dancers started for their lodges, speaking to one another in fear. Ghostwind was living up to her name again. Everyone believed that her vision could only be a bad omen.

"I shouldn't have come to the ceremony," Ghostwind said. "I've ruined everything."

"It's right that you came," Day Lily said. "Perhaps what you've seen is a warning to our people. I'll help you to your lodge."

On the way, Ghostwind could not contain herself. "I'm afraid for the horse-raiders," she said. "And especially for my husband. I saw Shadow returning with Kicks-the-Fox's clothes hanging on his back."

Day Lily put her hand over her mouth. "Did you see anyone else's pony with only the rider's clothes?"

"No. Just Shadow."

"You were screaming that the Bluecoats were here," Day Lily said. "Did you see Bluecoats?"

"They were driving our ponies away," Ghostwind said. "I saw Shadow run up to the top of a hill, without my husband. The pony was standing alone, and his eyes were filled with tears."

"You have been given a message," Day Lily said. "Maybe you should tell Two Moon. He will want to hold a council."

"I need the night to decide what I must do," Ghostwind said. "This cannot be hurried."

"Perhaps you will dream and learn more," Day Lily said.

Day Lily left as a crier approached Ghostwind and said, "Crazy Horse would like to speak with you, if you would."

Ghostwind followed him through the storm to the edge of the village. Crazy Horse awaited her with five other warriors. He held the halter ropes of his two best ponies, including his favorite red pinto.

"I've not asked you to talk about your vision," Crazy Horse assured her. "That is yours alone, to share if and when you wish."

"I have frightened the people," she said, "both yours and my own."

"It is a bad time," Crazy Horse said. "I want to make things good by your husband. I wish to talk with you in the presence of He Dog, my friend, and four Cheyenne brothers. This way it will be known that my intentions are honorable."

Ghostwind acknowledged the presence of the warriors. The three Cheyenne men were prominent, including Horned Bull, the healer who had saved her life as a girl and had named her.

"I do not question your honor," Ghostwind told Crazy Horse. "I've never had reason to do so."

"I want no trouble with my Cheyenne brothers," Crazy Horse said. "And I want no trouble with your husband, who is also a Cheyenne brother, so I will present you with my two best ponies, which are now his."

Ghostwind took the horses. She wanted to tell Crazy Horse about her vision, but remained silent.

"When your husband returns, he will know where these ponies have come from," Crazy Horse continued. "I want him to know that I respect him and would never try to steal his wife. My four Cheyenne brothers who have watched this tonight will tell him."

The warriors passed a pipe among them. Ghostwind held the ponies and, when they were finished, told Crazy Horse that when Kicks-the-Fox returned, he would ride the ponies with pride. She hoped the darkness and the storm hid the tears that streamed down her face.

Crazy Horse left with He Dog, while Horned Bull and the other warriors walked silently back to their lodges. Ghostwind led the ponies to her lodge and tied them to a picket pin driven deep into the ground. The two ponies were the finest presents Kicks-the-Fox had ever received, from anyone. Ghostwind feared that if he ever got to see them, it would be from his place in the Spirit World.

FIVE

Private Hall sat on a wooden bench at the south end of the stables, testing the new latigo a workman had sewn to his saddle. Three days remained before the command would begin the journey north. At dawn on the first of March he would be atop a dappled gray-and-white gelding, riding in formation after the notorious Sioux, a people he did not know and had never seen.

Hall had made it no secret that his heart was not in the campaign. For this reason, none of the other troopers had approached him to make friends. The only one he had talked with was Kincaid, the frontiersman who had known his father, who had taught him a great deal about the Sioux and Cheyenne.

Hall had learned that the Black Hills, long a sacred site and now the destination of thousands of gold-fevered prospectors, was the last bastion of the Plains tribes. General George Armstrong Custer had led a column of troopers and explorers through the region two years earlier, in defiance of treaty terms. News of their gold findings had reached every major newspaper in the country.

The result had been a crazed rush of humanity, scaring game and ruining hunting grounds already under stress from the encroachment of large cattle herds. Although scarce, buffalo were shot for both food and sport, while other game animals migrated north to the Yellowstone to escape the influx of people. Miners had been killed and their bodies mutilated by young warriors bent on driving the invaders out. Now a major war had begun, designed to end the Indian problem once and for all.

Hall had overheard a lot of soldiers discussing the upcoming campaign. Few of them seemed as well informed as either the scouts or the civilian contractors. All they knew was that the Sioux had to be stopped, or the country would be overrun and every civilized soul butchered and left for the wolves.

They all knew their regimental songs and made their bets as to which unit would shine the brightest in the upcoming campaign. More than a third were Irish, ruffians longing to prove themselves. The rest were French, German, English and Italian immigrants, taking their own pride in being soldiers protecting the interests of the American people.

Among the troops, Hall had become more than an outcast. There were those who thought him a traitor. But no one cared to accuse him and arouse his anger. Fighters though most of them were, they had heard rumors that he was more dangerous than the Indians themselves. They had heard he couldn't be stopped by a half-dozen men.

That was the story, though some said that Hall had fought more than six men—that he had subdued as many as eight in his cell that night. It didn't matter that his leg had been cleaved to the bone, he couldn't be put down. Someone said he had been shot as well, but no one could prove that. But sure, Mason Hall was dangerous and shouldn't be provoked.

At first, Private Hall had trouble getting used to the stares from wide-eyed soldiers, making the motions of intense fighting while pointing him out, telling their tales of him as they had heard them, or would like to have heard them. Everyone watched him carefully, for it would be interesting to see how well he fought Indians.

Hall realized he would soon have to face that test. Though he was still recovering from his wounds, he felt as capable of fighting as any of the others, for the leg had healed considerably during the past ten days. The two lesser knife wounds were now long scars. The deepest wound still ached near the bone, but it had closed over and would not reopen.

He had spent his time doing pretty much as he pleased: making friends with the scouts and mule skinners, walking the grounds, watching his fellow soldiers drilling in the cold, and resting in the hospital. He had been moved to the barracks just two days ago, to make room for a man who had broken his leg when his horse fell on him.

Hall himself had ridden only twice, more to test his leg than to get used to the back of a horse. Hall wasn't concerned about riding. He had grown up on horseback and could stay atop anything the Army had to offer. It was the weather that bothered him, as it did each and every soldier in Crook's command.

It was general knowledge that the mercury had congealed in the bulb three times during January. On each of those nights the temperature had dropped below minus forty degrees Fahrenheit. Hall had thought the night he had arrived at the fort the worst of his lifetime. But the temperature had reached only minus fifteen that night. Though the weather had opened up again, the word among the veterans was that the cold would certainly return, and likely during the campaign.

Hall wondered how any army could operate in such

extreme cold, even though General Crook had ordered special clothes to outfit the troops. General Crook, who had previously fought Ute and Shoshone Indians during a northern winter, had replaced regulation dress with wool and heavy blue flannel under double-breasted Minnesota blankets. Uniform insignias had little use when the weather was below zero. By now Hall had gotten used to the feel of his new uniform and was grateful for its warmth.

Hall had secured three pairs each of woolen low and high socks, the latter reaching above the knee, and had insisted on just the right fit of knee-high buckskin moccasins. The troops had been issued the moccasins to be worn under a buffalo-hide overboot made with the hairy side inward. Hall found them bulky, and they would be difficult to ride in, but they covered nearly the entire length of the leg and would certainly ward off cold.

He had tried on a half-dozen buffalo greatcoats before deciding on the one he now had. His head would be covered by a woolen cap with a fur border, ear flaps, and a fur collar that covered the neck. For his hands, he had woolen gloves to be worn under gauntlets of beaver fur. At least he had the best protection possible against the cold.

Hall had finished work on his saddle and was checking its fit on his horse when a large, dark-complected man dressed in furs came in and walked up to him. He looked Hall over carefully and introduced himself.

"I'm Frank Grouard," he said. "The general sent me. He wants to talk to you."

Hall stared at the man. "General Crook wants to see me?"

"Don't be alarmed," Grouard said. "I'm certain it will be a friendly discussion."

Hall was puzzled. He could think of no reason for the general to send for him. It also seemed odd that a scout

would come for him, and not one of Crook's commanding officers.

But Frank Grouard was not just an ordinary scout. He was Crook's head scout. He was an imposing man, six feet tall and more than two hundred pounds, and the heavy furs made him look even larger. His complexion was that of a light-skinned Indian, with high cheekbones and large, dark eyes. But his manner and speech were those of an educated man, making him an oddity among veteran frontiersmen.

Everyone talked about Grouard, many with misgivings. It was said that Grouard had been born somewhere in the South Sea Islands, the son of a native mother and a French missionary father. It was said he had come to the States as a small child and had lived with a Mormon family, who had taught him the manners of society. But he had no love for civilization and, as a young man, had come west as a freighter and mail carrier, only to be captured by the Sioux.

Rumor had it he had lived among Sitting Bull's people and later as part of the Bad Face band, and that he was a special friend of Crazy Horse himself. There he had taken a wife, but had soon after left the band.

"Grouard can't be trusted," Hall had heard a soldier say. "Once a Sioux, always a Sioux. He's apt to lead us into a trap and get us all killed." Another soldier had argued, "You have no right to say that. I know him to be the best and truest of men. We can't go wrong with him."

Hall had no reason to take sides either way; he hadn't expected ever to have any dealings with the man. Yet Grouard was now standing beside him, holding out his hand.

Hall shook with Grouard and introduced himself. Grouard's smile broadened. "I think everyone knows who you are," he said. "They say you are a hard one. Is that right? I heard you killed nine people in Leavenworth."

"Tomorrow it will be ten," Hall said. "It doesn't matter."

Grouard shrugged. "No, I suppose it doesn't. After but a few more days, you will have killed many more."

Hall pulled the saddle off his horse and set it over a railing. "I'll tell you what I've told the others. I didn't come out here of my own accord, and I don't look forward to shooting at people I don't have any quarrel with. So I don't believe I will be the battle-crazy soldier everyone expects."

"It sounds like you don't care about fighting," Grouard said. "That's too bad. If you did, you could become somebody."

"I have no problem with who I am already," Hall said. "I don't need to kill Sioux to prove anything."

"No, you aren't listening," Grouard said. "The soldiers talk about you, and say you are nothing but a street fighter. But the general tells me that he knew your uncle, and that he fought well in the Rebellion. He thinks maybe you have what it takes to be an officer."

Hall took a deep breath. "It seems to be awfully hard to make anybody understand me around here. I don't *care* about soldiering. I'm here because I have to be."

Grouard shrugged again. "Yes, but why not make the best of it?"

Hall studied Grouard. "Is there some reason you would like to see me kill a lot of Sioux?"

Grouard was thinking of an answer when two other scouts hurried through the stable to his side. Hall had seen them around a number of times. They were the two called Big Bat and Little Bat.

The bigger one, a French-Indian named Baptiste Pourier, said something to Grouard in French. Grouard frowned and looked at Little Bat, Baptiste Garnier, who nodded quickly.

Grouard turned to Hall. "I've got some business. Maybe I'll see you."

Grouard turned and walked out of the stable with the other two. Hall watched him with curiosity, wondering why Grouard had singled him out for a mission against the Sioux, and why the general might be interested in him. It was true that Crook had known his uncle, Jackson Hall, during the Rebellion. But that didn't seem enough of a reason to push him toward an Army career.

Hall fed his horse, left the stables and began the half-mile walk back to the main fort grounds. He had walked this distance, back and forth, for the past six days, in varying weather, making certain his horse was fed and watered, and giving his leg the exercise it needed before he could ride any distance.

At first the pain had caused him to pause often. Now he barely limped. If the riding wasn't too hard for the first couple of days, he would be able to stand the journey.

The sky was hazy and overcast with scattered clouds and a raw southwest breeze that bit through his greatcoat and underclothing to the bone. Still, the view was spacious and, in spite of the cold, attractive to the eye.

Fort Fetterman stood on a plateau that overlooked the North Platte River. Hall looked into the west, where the Laramie Range rose jagged and bluish white. In the sky an eagle circled higher and higher on the wind, seeming to drift into the clouds without effort. Far out, a small herd of buffalo grazed the open hillsides, brown lumps against the streaked and patchy snowfields of the windblown valley. Closer in, antelope browsed the tops of sagebrush plants, leery now of the fort and the men who had come there.

Hall had noticed a number of antelope hanging from cottonwood limbs near the river. The general himself had accompanied some of the men on a hunt, telling them that they should get a taste of the wild before venturing into it.

As he approached the fort grounds, Hall could feel the mounting excitement. Everyone was making final preparations for the campaign. In addition to the fourteen companies of soldiers, a large number of contractors, like Jordan Kincaid, had signed on to take care of a beef herd and a pack train of some four hundred mules. Nearly nine hundred men would follow Crook into the Big Horn country.

Hall wondered whether Fort Fetterman had ever seen this many men gathered at one time. During the middle sixties, when the Sioux and Cheyenne had closed the Bozeman Road, the fort had seen a lot of use. Since then, the post had fallen into disrepair. Of the heavy plank fortifications that once surrounded the main grounds, only a section around the barracks and a log gateway remained.

With the sudden presence of so many men, the fort overflowed. The barracks and mess halls could accommodate but a small fraction of them. As a result, long rows of tents had been set up along the river, below the plateau.

Down along the river, packers busied themselves checking gear and sorting the mules into categories. The younger, less experienced animals were getting their manes and tails shaved, so that they would stand out. On the trail, they would be mixed in with the older mules, in hopes that outbursts of temper could be kept to a minimum.

Elsewhere, companies of infantry were drilling. Some were taking target practice with their Springfields, shooting into sidehills at cans and boxes. Many of the soldiers had a difficult time even holding their rifles steady, much less hitting the targets.

Hall, amused by the scene, awaited the presence of Captain Egan himself, who rode toward him, flanked by two subordinate officers.

Egan dismounted and Hall saluted. "I trust you're on your way to see the general?"

"I am, sir."

"I don't intend to hold you, Mr. Hall," Egan said. "But I promised you the best weapons I could find. Unfortunately, I couldn't get you one of the new Colt's forty-five-caliber revolvers. A Colt Army forty-four and a Springfield will have to do. I apologize for that. Your weapons await you in the general's quarters."

"From what I hear, the Indians are armed better than we are," Hall said.

Egan was watching the soldiers training down below. He turned to Hall and smiled crookedly. "That shouldn't bother you, not the way you handle a firearm—any firearm, I'm told."

"How could you know how well I shoot?" Hall asked.

"You've left a good long trail of records to follow," Egan replied. "If I recall, you became a trick shooter in a circus at the age of thirteen. Likely the youngest of your kind on the road, wouldn't you say?"

Hall was dumbfounded to know that the Army had traced him that far back. A month after his father had left, his mother had died of influenza, and a year later his only uncle had enlisted in the Union Army to fight the Rebellion. Young Mason Hall had been left to fend for himself.

His second week on the road had brought him to a traveling circus. Hall had convinced the drunken owner to hire him as a trick shooter, for his meals and a nickel a week. He had opened the circus owner's eyes with a number of trick shots; for three full months he had doubled and tripled the crowds.

During that time the meals had been sparse and the nickels rare. After a bitter argument, Hall had left the circus and had taken up work helping traders and steamboat woodcutters along the Missouri. In the next five years, Hall had come in contact with every kind of character, as well as remnants of the Kansas and Missouri Indian tribes.

He had tried to learn their culture; but the tribes had been totally subdued, and cared little about their past.

"I learned to shoot well," Hall said. "I make no apologies for that."

Egan laughed. "On the contrary, Mr. Hall. You stood out among your contemporaries. You still do. The problem is in your judgment. You should have stayed away from the circus."

Hall couldn't argue. Yearning for the active life again, he had taken to working for circuses and medicine shows. Just after his twentieth birthday, he had taken a job with the same circus owner who had first hired him at the age of thirteen. It had been a mistake.

Four months later, during a show in Kansas City, Hall had won a brand-new Henry repeating rifle offered by a wealthy admirer. In a drunken fit, the circus owner had demanded that Hall hand the gun over. Hall had refused. The man had wrenched the rifle from Hall and had broken the stock over his back and head, trying to kill him. Hall's fists and a round from the circus owner's Colt Dragoon had ended the fight in Hall's favor.

The authorities had come immediately. Hall had tried to run, but had passed out from his head wounds. He had awakened behind bars, and hadn't seen the outside until the Army called him for duty.

"Maybe I should have just given him the rifle," Hall remarked to Egan. "I would have starved to death with that man, but I couldn't be any worse off now."

Egan mounted his horse. "Just think of that circus owner when we reach the Sioux. Make each shot count." He rode off, with the other two officers following.

When Hall reached the officers' quarters, Crook and the other commanders were studying a herd of horses milling around in a rope corral. Five frontiersmen had come to the fort that morning with nearly a hundred head they hoped to sell to the Army. The ponies milled and tossed their heads, while the frontiersmen lassoed them for closer inspection.

The frontiersmen, dressed in furs and moccasins, all looked to be in upper middle age. All had long hair, covered with wolf- or fox-head fur caps, but none had a beard. Three wore eagle feathers and the other two wore dried birds, tied or pinned into their locks.

Hall thought them to be more Indian than white, except for the way they addressed Colonel Joseph J. Reynolds of the Third Cavalry, designated by Crook overall commander of the campaign. They all spoke English well, one of them in a clipped British accent.

The Briton did most of the talking, selling Reynolds on the fact that the ponies were already acclimated to the area and would have no difficulty withstanding strenuous duty in the Big Horn country. Reynolds, with long muttonchop sideburns and collar-length white hair, listened with his hands behind his back. He declined assistance from Frank Grouard and two other scouts in choosing the best horses.

"I know horses as well or better than any of you and will lead this expedition in all aspects," Reynolds told Grouard. "See to it that you don't bother me again until I send for you."

Grouard backed away and now stood off with Pourier and Garnier. Pourier smiled behind a large hand as Garnier gestured emphatically to Grouard in sign language. Hall stood fascinated, watching Little Bat ridicule Reynolds to the other two scouts without uttering a sound. Both Grouard and Pourier laughed out loud several times.

Crook was giving Reynolds a chance to assume full command and gain the respect of the men under him. Reynolds, oblivious to the mockery, rubbed his chin and ordered ponies separated, seemingly on a whim.

In the end, Reynolds rejected nearly a quarter of the

herd. Hall knew that many of these horses were superior to those that had been selected. He had no idea how the price had been decided upon, but he could see that the frontiersmen were more than happy with the bargain.

Crook ducked back inside his quarters while the other officers went about their duties. Hall hesitated, trying to decide what the general might say to him. None of this made sense. But nothing so far in his life had, and this might as well be taken in stride. Whatever happened couldn't be any more senseless than his being here in the first place.

SIX

In front of the general's quarters, Hall saluted a wiry
lieutenant named Bourke who announced Hall's arrival
to the general.

General Crook was seated at a table, going over a map.
On the edge of the table rested a large felt hat, burned
around the edges. The general was casually dressed in
scuffed field boots, a blue flannel shirt, and soiled brown
corduroy pants.

"At ease, Private Hall," Crook said after Hall had
saluted.

Hall waited for the general to say something, but Crook
seemed intent on the map. He was a square-faced and wiry
man somewhere near fifty years of age, with close-cropped
blond hair liberally streaked with gray. His beard, more red
than blond, was also heavy and graying. It forked at the
base of his chin, giving the impression that a portion in the
middle had been cut away, leaving two individual beards on
either side of his face.

Resting at Crook's feet was a collie, a beautiful sable
well into maturity. The collie studied Hall and in a moment
was at his side, one paw up on his leg.

Crook looked up, revealing sharp blue eyes. "Go ahead and pet him if you'd like," he said, looking back down at the map. "He certainly likes you."

Hall reached down and scratched the collie's ears. He realized Crook was studying him even as he studied the map. The man seemed an intense sort, someone bent upon his own convictions, yet something about him made Hall believe he could be kind and understanding. The way he studied the map, though, left no question of his determination.

Hall folded his arms in front of him. The collie leaned against his leg, tail wagging, awaiting more petting. Crook called the dog back over to his side and looked up at Hall.

"Do you know much about maps?"

"I can read them pretty well," Hall said. He stepped over to the table.

"Tell me what you think," Crook said, pointing to a segment that showed the upper Powder River country. "I want to get us up into the country around the Big Horn Mountains. My scouts tell me the Wolf Mountains are actually steep hills, mostly rock. What do you think?"

Hall studied the map. He knew Crook had hired Grouard and the other scouts for this very purpose. Hall concluded that the general was testing him.

"Sir," Hall said, "if those relief lines are accurate, we will have some tough going in that area. Is that where you expect the Indians to be?"

"That's where they've wintered for many generations," Crook said. "My scouts tell me that it's good game country. If that is the case, there's good reason to expect them to be somewhere in the area."

"Yes," Hall said, "I've heard they were starving on the reservations."

"I won't comment on the management of the reservations," Crook said. "Even if I did approve of it, I couldn't let my opinion interfere with my command."

"If I may be so bold, sir," Hall said, "I don't believe the Indians are being treated fairly."

Crook glanced up from the map. "How much do you know about the Sioux?"

"I don't know anything about them. I just know what it's like to go hungry."

"Are you in sympathy with them?"

"I don't have anything against them, if that's what you mean."

Crook rose to his feet and strolled to a window, his hands behind his back. The collie stayed on the floor but followed him with his eyes.

Crook stopped at the window and looked out over the fort grounds. "I will say, Private Hall, that I've never met a more honest-spoken man. I know you live your life as you see fit, and do the best you can. But you have made some mistakes. I hope you don't believe that will cost you a future in this army."

"I hadn't thought about a future in this army, sir," Hall said.

"That's what I've been told," Crook said. He turned from the window and looked directly at Hall. "I knew your uncle, Jackson Hall, very well. I wept when I learned of his death."

"I did, too," Hall confessed. "A lot."

Crook turned back to the window. "He rose in the ranks very quickly. Every time I turned around he had earned another brevet promotion. I always believed he worked hard because he got a late start."

"I wish he had never enlisted," Hall said.

"He talked a lot about you," Crook continued, as if he had not heard the remark. "He often said that he believed that with the right chances you would grow into a great man someday. You two must have been pretty close."

"I saw him a lot before the Rebellion started," Hall said.

Crook looked hard at Hall. "I think you're cut from the same mold, son. You can *be* something in this army. This is your chance. I know you had to kill that circus owner, and you had to pay for it. Can you put that behind you?"

"It's already behind me."

"Good! That's the spirit! Hold your head up from now on and someday you'll lead men. I know you can."

Hall stared. Crook's eyes were wide, his brow bathed in sweat.

"Well?" Crook said. "What say you? Can you rise to this challenge?"

"Why are you picking me, General?" Hall asked. "It can't be just because of my uncle. Did you think that much of him?"

Crook blinked. "I thought more of him than you'll ever know, Private Hall. There's few men who know this, but that man saved my life, more than once. When I see Jackson Hall in you, that means you are special to me. Can you understand that?"

"Yes, sir, I believe I can."

"Can you understand that I would want the best for you, then?"

"Yes, sir."

"Don't ever question that, Private Hall. I know you got here under unusual circumstances, but that's all behind you now. Look ahead. Tell me you will."

"I will, sir."

Crook pointed to a table, where a Springfield rifle and a Colt Army .44 lay next to a holster and a box of ammunition. "Those arms are yours. I've inspected them myself. Keep them oiled and ready for use at all times."

Hall walked to the table. "I will do that. Thank you, sir."

Crook leaned over his desk and put his forefinger on the map. He drew a circle that encompassed the region around the Black Hills, to the Canadian line and down the Rocky Mountains to Colorado.

"These are some of the best mineral lands in the whole of these United States, and possibly the world," Crook said. "Our people can develop this area and build an economy second to none. Can you see that the Sioux are standing in the way of that, our future peace and happiness?"

"Did you ever stop to consider that maybe they think the same of us, sir?"

Crook cleared his throat. "Private Hall, how would you have it? Should we propose that all the emigrants who have moved into this country pack up and return to their previous homes? Should we go backwards?"

"I would propose that the government allow the Indians to keep the lands they are entitled to," Hall suggested. "Just keep settlers and miners off that land. There's plenty left for the emigrants. That should make the Indians happy. Isn't that all they've ever asked for?"

"What the Sioux ask for, Private Hall, is something that is no longer available to them. The Black Hills can no longer be home to wild tribes, for they cannot exist side by side with the people who are moving there."

"I have been led to understand that the Black Hills are a sacred ground to the Sioux and Cheyenne," Hall said. "There's not much respect being shown to them, would you say? I don't believe many white folks would be gracious if their churches were suddenly turned into saloons and hotels."

"That is a point well taken, Private," Crook said. "But it is not for us to argue. Certainly the towns there now are on the wild side. But those small towns are now growing into cities, where respectable citizens live."

"With all due respect, sir," Hall told the general, "I understand that your 'respectable citizens' are primarily miners and gunfighters who shoot Indians for the bounty on their scalps."

"They are not the majority, I can assure you," Crook said. "In any case, it is our duty to see that this nation grows. That is why we're here. That is a job not to be taken lightly."

"I guess we're back where we started, General," Hall said. "I don't agree with that philosophy, and I don't care for the job."

"Perhaps the job does not meet with your tastes or your philosophy," Crook said with an edge to his voice, "but you do understand, Private Hall, that you are now a member of this army, and your commitment is to obey orders. Do you understand, Private Hall?"

"I understand that a commitment was made for me," Hall said. "Not by my own choice."

"Nevertheless it is a commitment," Crook said, "a commitment that you *will* honor."

"I have no choice, sir."

Crook walked around the table and Hall came to attention. Crook clapped him on the shoulder. "Perhaps in time you will understand that our cause is just. I can see that there is a lot of your Uncle Jackson in you, and that you have a keen eye for detail, just as he did. Again, I tell you that as far as I'm concerned, your past will not cloud your future. Just don't do anything in the present to change that."

Hall stood rigid and silent.

"You do understand me, don't you, Mr. Hall?" Crook said.

"Yes, sir, I do, sir."

"In just three days you will gain the opportunity of a lifetime."

"Yes, sir."

Crook turned back to the table and looked down at the map. "Very well, then. You are dismissed."

Hall stepped out of the office and onto the parade ground. Why did Crook care enough to push him as he had? Even insults hadn't affected the general's attitude. Hall concluded that the general must have told his uncle that, if it were ever possible, he would help his nephew out.

Whatever the general had in mind, Hall wanted no part of it. He realized that any number of other soldiers would jump at the chance to be taken under General George Crook's wing. All Hall wanted was a life where he could decide for himself what was right, and what he wanted to do. He wanted it in the worst way, and one way or another, he was going to have it.

Kincaid found Hall eating his evening meal on a small knoll just off the fort grounds. He had carried his plate up to be alone; and though the air was cool, he seemed content to sit and watch the sun descend toward the west.

"By the gods, you're hard to find!" Kincaid said. "If I didn't know better, I'd think you were a loner."

Hall wiped the last bit of bacon grease from his plate with a piece of biscuit. "I've got nothing in common with the others."

"Maybe not," Kincaid said. "But just the same, you'd better come with me. I'll show you something."

Hall followed Kincaid to a knoll with a better view of the river. Kincaid pointed into the distance. "Do you see what's coming?"

A long column of Indian riders were making their way along the river. The riders were followed by women and children, afoot and on horseback, and a number of horses dragging travois laden with lodge skins and other camp supplies.

"Are those Sioux?" Hall asked. "Have they given up?"

"No, they're not Sioux," Kincaid replied. "They're Arapaho. The Sioux ain't about to come riding in here like that, not unless they're painted for war."

Kincaid said, "The leader is Black Coal. His village has some forty-five lodges."

"What are they doing here?" Hall asked.

"They don't want no war, so they're coming to the fort."

Hall had seen Indians before, Kansas or Osage in small groups on the outskirts of Kansas City, but he had never seen any of those tribes who still warred among themselves and hunted the remaining herds of buffalo. As he watched the Arapaho he wondered how much they resembled the Sioux, or if the Sioux looked even wilder.

Down by the river Frank Grouard and two other scouts were leading Crook and Reynolds out to meet the column.

"Look at old Black Coal pointing to the north," Kincaid said. "You can bet he's talking about Sioux and where they're camped."

After the scouts and officers left, the Arapaho leaders began to point and talk to the women.

"They'll make camp there," Kincaid told Hall. "The leaders will come and ask Crook to go down later and smoke with them. I'd sure like to hear what goes on."

"How can you tell them from Sioux, or the other tribes out here?" Hall asked.

"You've got to learn their differences," Kincaid replied. "It's not all that easy sometimes, even for a man who's lived out here. But after a while you can tell, although the Arapaho aren't so different from the Sioux or the Cheyenne, and they're all allied at times." He added, "Likely some other members of the Arapaho nation'll be fighting instead of going in to the agencies."

Hall gaped.

"You've got to remember that all these people out here

live independently," Kincaid explained. "A certain chief speaks for his own people, those in his village, and for no one else. If they come in and say they won't fight, that doesn't mean the next village won't. The Army don't seem to understand that."

Hall and Kincaid walked past the main fort grounds and to the bluff overlooking the river, where they joined a number of other curious onlookers watching the Arapaho women erect camp. The sun had reached the western horizon, spilling gold across the valley. The women went about their business eagerly and efficiently, working in groups to beat the darkness, while horse tenders and warriors drove the pony herd onto the flats across the river. Soon the lodge poles were in place and the coverings were being sewn together.

"I've never seen anything like it," Hall said. "Unbelievable."

"They get things done in a hurry," Kincaid said. He was watching a group of women preparing fires for cooking. "From the looks of it, they don't have a lot of provisions. I'll bet they've recently killed some buffalo and will offer tongues to Crook and his officers tonight."

"What you're saying," Hall said, "is that this village of Arapaho is extending an offering of peace."

"Black Coal wants no part of what's coming up," Kincaid said. "He's going to make sure his people are out of the line of fire. They'll likely stay here by the fort all winter, no matter how bad the hunting becomes."

Still fascinated, Hall studied the village. Kincaid suggested that they go down so that Hall could get a closer look.

"Maybe they don't want us in the way," Hall said.

"They won't mind us," Kincaid insisted. "They want peace, so they'll welcome us."

Hall followed Kincaid down the steep trail from the

bluff. They crossed through the army camp and downriver into the Arapaho village. The women went about their work, paying them no mind, but scolding the dogs if they became too aggressive. The children stared and pointed.

Already a number of curious soldiers and frontiersmen were in the village, talking with the warriors, pointing to the north. Hall was not interested in hearing about the Sioux. Instead, he was curious about the paintings on the lodges. He wanted to see them before total darkness fell.

"The buffalo is very sacred," Kincaid said, running his finger along a design. "They pay homage in a lot of ways and ask the buffalo spirit to stay with them."

There were many animal and bird designs on the lodges, giving Hall the sense that the symbols might actually have some kind of life.

"I feel these paintings are staring at me," Hall said.

Kincaid laughed. "By the gods if you ain't right about that. And I'd say the spirits look on you with favor. I believe you'd do just fine out here."

The remark made Hall think about his father. He wondered again where his father was and if he was still alive. No doubt he had seen many villages such as this, and perhaps had lived in one. He followed Kincaid around for a short while longer and suggested they leave.

"There's a lot left to see," Kincaid said.

"Maybe tomorrow," Hall said. "I think I'll go back and work on my saddle."

Kincaid stared at him. "What's eating you?"

"You don't have to come. Join some of the others."

"Oh, I'll go along with you," Kincaid said. "I need to check on my mules."

Hall and Kincaid walked out of the lower end of the village, along the river. Hall noticed movement in the cottonwoods just back from the trail and walked closer to investigate.

"Where are you going?" Kincaid asked, seeing the same movement.

"That doesn't look right to me," Hall said. "Isn't that a soldier pulling an Indian woman's hair?"

Kincaid took Hall by the arm. "Don't go over there."

"That's not right," Hall said, pulling away. "He's pushing her head down on him."

"Let it go, Hall," Kincaid said. "Just leave it be!"

Hall ignored Kincaid and hurried into the cottonwoods, Kincaid still warning him from behind. Seeing Hall's approach, the soldier pushed the woman away. Hall recognized Sergeant Buckner hastily buttoning his pants.

Buckner glared at Hall and ran the other way, into the shadows. Hall found the Indian sitting against a tree, crying. She couldn't have been more than thirteen.

"Do you need help?" Hall asked, not even thinking that she likely knew no English.

The girl stared at Hall with blank eyes. He offered to help her up, but she shook her head violently. From behind came footsteps. Hall turned to see four frontiersmen.

"What's going on here?" one of them demanded.

"I was trying to help her," Hall said.

"I'll bet you were," another one said.

Two of the men tried to grab Hall, while a third threw a punch at him. Hall ducked the punch and exploded, smashing his fist into the man's face. The frontiersman, his jaw smashed, tumbled backward, unconscious, to the ground.

Another frontiersman tried to wrap an arm around Hall's neck. Hall took the man's wrist and twisted the arm around into a hammerlock, then jerked hard. The shoulder popped from its socket.

The other two came at him, their knives drawn. Hall pulled his Colt Army and had the hammer drawn when Kincaid yelled. "Stop! Hall, don't shoot them!"

The two had dropped their knives and were backing away. Hall followed, the barrel of his pistol in one man's face.

"Hall!" Kincaid yelled again. "Don't shoot!"

Hall lowered the pistol, and the two frontiersmen circled around him and stopped beside Kincaid. "That man's crazy," one of them remarked.

"It wasn't him that bothered the girl," Kincaid said. "It was a trooper."

"It wasn't just a trooper," Hall said. "It was a sergeant. It was Buckner. Why don't you men go and use your knives on him?"

"Go on," Kincaid told the two. "He won't do nothing more to you. Get them other two up and out of here. Just be certain who you attack next time."

The frontiersmen went to the aid of their friends. Neither of the two injured men could stand, and one of the frontiersmen went for help. Hall walked away, with Kincaid at his side.

"I told you to let it be," Kincaid said. "Now look at what happened!"

Hall turned angrily to him. "Are you saying I should have just let Buckner go ahead with what he was doing?"

"What difference does it make?"

"Damn!" Hall said. "That kind of thing's not right. Besides, we'll have her people at our throats."

"That's crazy," Kincaid said. "She won't tell a soul. It don't matter at all."

"What are you talking about?"

"Hall, you've got a lot to learn," Kincaid said. "Even if she said something, them Arapaho won't think twice about it. They came here to get away from war with the Bluecoats. They don't want the Army hunting them. Do you think they'd want to start trouble over a girl?"

"What will her parents say?" Hall asked.

"They'll get after her for being out from camp alone," Kincaid said. "The women learn to go in big groups around the forts. Either that, or find themselves with a trooper breathing heavy on top of them."

"I'm still glad I stepped in," Hall said.

"You won't feel so noble when that sergeant starts in on you," Kincaid said. "To my notion, you're going to have a hard trip up the trail."

SEVEN

Private Hall sat near one of the campfires along the river, cleaning his pistol. He and all the troops now slept in tents or out in the open, to get used to the rigors of the upcoming campaign.

Though the cold was foremost in everyone's mind, the enemy ranked a close second. Hall had heard that the Plains tribes were the best horsemen in the world. Even as Hall worked on his pistol, another story about Sioux horsemanship was being told, this one by a veteran who had fought with the command at Fort Phil Kearny against the Oglala chief Red Cloud in the late sixties.

"They come at us up at the Wagon Box," he was saying, "well over two thousand of them, painted like devils and screaming like their asses was afire. They had better rifles than us and they could shoot them. I never saw anything like it. They can ride just as well agin a horse's belly as on its back. Or either side, for that matter. You couldn't see them to shoot.

"But me and Frenchie Melot and Zeke Calamote was up front, and we commenced to knocking them off their horses. Didn't think they was going to stop coming, though. That renegade Crazy Horse came down at us with a bunch and we had to fight for our lives. I nearly got Crazy Horse that day."

One of the younger soldiers asked how that happened, and the veteran started in to tell him. Hall got up, pulled on his overcoat, and walked out to the edge of the frozen river, where a snappy breeze drowned out the camp noise. A major snowstorm wasn't far off and light flakes were already finding his face, melting into running drops of water. He turned when he heard someone behind him.

It was the scout, Frank Grouard, laughing as he approached. "What's the matter, Hall? You don't like the story?"

"I've heard too many of them," Hall said. "I've yet to hear one I can believe."

"That old geezer never got within a mile of Crazy Horse, or he'd be without hair, and his head as well," Grouard said. "You afraid of what they say?"

"I've got nothing to be afraid of," Hall answered. "I should have been dead long before this. If they get me, then I'll just have run out of luck."

"You speak like someone who's lived out here awhile," Grouard said. "The general told me you had a hard side to you."

"Does the general tell you everything?" Hall asked.

Grouard laughed again. "He tells me nothing. He expects me to give him all the information. But he has high hopes for you, and he wanted me to keep an eye on you."

"I'll get by without a nursemaid."

"No, you don't understand. I'm your friend, and I want to help you any way I can."

Hall felt the wind bringing more snow to his face. He turned toward Grouard.

"The general knew my uncle very well, so I can understand his concern for me. But what's in this for you? Is Crook going to up your wages or something?"

"Oh, come now," Grouard said. "I am only saying that men like you aren't common among the ranks. I want to fight beside somebody like you, not the others. You could do a lot during this campaign. Think what they would say if you killed Crazy Horse himself."   ·

"Do you want to see Crazy Horse killed?" Hall asked.

"Oh, listen," Grouard said, "I just believe you could make a new life for yourself if you were brave enough to get Crazy Horse. That's all."

Hall took a deep breath. "I'll tell you what my new life would be, if I could make it," he said. "If I had my horse right now, I'd just ride out into the storm and let the rest of you bastards go for the glory."

"And what if you ran into Crazy Horse?"

"He wouldn't keep me from going back to Missouri."

Grouard laughed. "Oh, so you're not afraid of Crazy Horse?"

"I'd take my chances."

"You'd have no chances," Grouard said. "That man is a ghost. He's a fighter beyond compare. He rides the best horse on the Plains, but he can travel just as far on foot. He's not like you and me. He doesn't need food to live, and he can stand in the cold for hours and never freeze. He is something. You do not understand."

"You make him sound invincible."

"Nearly so, but only to men who are afraid to die. If you are not afraid to die, he will respect you."

"You sound as if you know him."

"I do, very well," Grouard said. "Surely you know I was taken as a child by the Lakota. I know Sitting Bull and all the leaders. But I know Crazy Horse better than any of them. I lived with him and his people for a good long time.

I ate with him, hunted with him. I was the same as a brother."

"If that's so, then why are you hunting him?" Hall asked.

Grouard looked into the north and let the incoming storm cover his face with snow. "Everything has changed," he said. "Crazy Horse has changed. He was once as close as a brother, but no more. He took one of my horses, my best horse. It wasn't right."

"He took *your* horse?" Hall asked. "I thought you said he already had the best horses."

"You aren't listening." Grouard pounded his gloved hands together. "He has the best horses because he took mine."

Hall laughed. "I like the stories the old-timers tell. They're more credible." He started back toward the tents.

"You aren't a fighter, Hall!" Grouard yelled. "You're a coward!"

Hall turned. "What's the matter with you?"

Grouard caught up with him. "I am telling you, *I* can't kill Crazy Horse myself. Someone else has to do it."

"This doesn't make sense," Hall said.

"It does if you know the pact we made," Grouard explained. "We swore that we would never kill one another, even if our friendship died. Even if we became bitter enemies. If we could get someone else to do it, that would be fine. But we could never harm one another."

Hall stared. "So why are you picking me?"

"You're the only one among these men who I believe could do it. You don't do things by the book. You never have. You're the kind that could get Crazy Horse, if any white man could."

"Why would I want to?" Hall asked.

Grouard threw up his hands. "There you have it. Maybe you aren't the man who could do it. Maybe you really are a coward, like I said." He turned and walked back toward the camp.

Hall stared after him, deeply angered. He wanted to give Grouard a chance to see who the real coward was, but realized that it would do no good to provoke trouble. Grouard was a big man and would be hard to put down. He would probably have to be put down for good in order to end the fight. Risking his own life to satisfy his anger would be more than foolish.

Besides, Grouard enjoyed higher status than many of the officers. As far as the general was concerned, Grouard was the most important man on the expedition. Though many of the other mixed-breed scouts knew the country just as well, it was Grouard who was the master tracker and interpreter, and it was Grouard whom Crook had come to depend on to find Crazy Horse.

Hall's temper cooled with the increasing snowfall, and he walked back into camp. He saw Buckner watching him and wondered if the sergeant intended to quiz him about the meeting with Grouard. If so, he would say nothing.

Instead of advancing toward him, Buckner moved away. Hall stopped trying to understand the behavior of anyone and everyone, and joined the other soldiers, who were all making last-minute preparations for the campaign. He made certain he had everything assigned to him, and that all his equipment was in good order. His horse and gear would be all he could depend on to keep him alive for what now seemed to him a long time to come.

The sun broke into a clear and frozen sky. Private Hall, his face turned against a biting wind, heeled his horse into formation. The sweeping landscape rolled on forever in a sea of dazzling white, interrupted only by jagged breaks where the land dropped off into the winding river.

Hall worked to steady his gelding. The smell of grain in

the eighty-six wagons and four ambulances made all the horses hard to handle. Behind the wagons, five divisions of eighty mules each composed the pack train of tents and supplies, followed by more than forty head of cattle.

General Crook rode by to the front of the column. His Army overcoat had been altered to include a high collar with wolf fur sewn around the inside. His beaten felt hat bore the insignia of his rank, but other than that his dress was much the same as that of the men who served under him.

Hall was interested to note that the general did not ride a dashing horse that would make him stand out. Instead, he rode a large, dark mule named Apache, brought up with him from the wars in the desert southwest.

Crook's collie was absent. Hall wondered if the general missed the dog. There would be no dogs allowed on the campaign, as the general thought the weather and the traveling would be too harsh for them.

The orders were given to move out, and the column eased into motion. The long procession of wagons and heavily laden mules would keep the pace slow. Hall rode next to a young trooper who looked into the north with trepidation.

"It's supposed to get colder than this, even," he said. "I can't hardly move my fingers as it is. How do they expect us to shoot at Indians?"

"They not only expect us to shoot *at* them," Hall pointed out, "but they expect us to *hit* them as well."

"We'll get it done, and it'll all be for glory," a trooper behind them said. "We'll see our names in print come Christmas."

Despite the heavy clothing, the biting wind soon made every man miserable. What had been little more than a breeze would suddenly erupt into a whistling torrent that whipped the air with stinging blasts of snow, only to settle back again into a whisper. Those who had weathered the northern territories before said that this was a certain sign of the most unsettled weather, and that the worst was on its way.

Hall adjusted his weight in the saddle to ease the tension against his injured leg. It didn't help much.

The column advanced up the old road to the Montana goldfields—many called it the Bozeman Road—across rolling, snowbound plains that swept off into eternity. Hall could not understand the reason for the mission against the Indians. Though Crook had told him the land was filled with riches, Hall saw instead a vast open wilderness he could not imagine being habitable, much less worth fighting over. Certainly this could not be the gleaming land his father had spoken of so often. There was nothing here. Such a place could never be filled.

The open bottoms that broke up the surrounding plains, now packed with drifts, held pools of alkali water, unfit for human consumption. Crossing these bottoms was treacherous. The ice was soft, and wagon accidents and other delays caused worry. The trails that were snowbound had to be opened by the civilian labor force, who dug through large colonies of bottomland grasses. Cordgrass and giant wild rye clogged the watercourses, their stalks often rising eight to ten feet.

As his horse fought its way with the others, Hall became increasingly angry. He was being forced to fight for something he had absolutely no stake in. The men who would profit from this folly were seated in comfortable offices where no bullets or arrows would ever harm them. They did not have to sleep on frozen ground or eat in a biting wind. Yet they would reap profits from this, just as similar men had in times before, while those who died for this cause would lie in forgotten graveyards covered with bunchgrass and sage.

As the morning progressed, Hall began thinking that he should have taken to farming, as he had been advised. That way he would never have collided with the law and ended up in prison. He would never have been forced to choose between the Army or a hangman's noose. Both, he decided, offered death. He had picked the worse of the two.

Hall shook his head. He could never have stayed in one place, much less on that farm. Too many memories remained that had kept him from sleeping at night, and from enjoying the sunlit days. The memories had forced him away, to go somewhere, anywhere, just so he didn't have to feel the pain that came when he stood in the house his father had left. The very sod had reminded him of laughter on his father's knee, and late-night stories of high peaks and painted Indian warriors, and mountain men who had conquered it all.

Back then Hall had felt the urge to go and see it. He had asked his father many times to take him out to the mountains. "Once you go out, you won't come back," his father had said many times. "You're smart, and you take to schooling. You could buy up a lot of land around here and do something for yourself. You'd best stay where a good future lies, so that you don't waste your life a-wandering, like I did."

Hall had been disappointed by his father's words, and he could never understand why his father had considered his own life wasted. If the mountains had given him such joy, how could he blame them for the life he had chosen?

Certainly, Hall realized he was more like his father than he wanted to admit. He had found it difficult to stay in one place very long. Being held in prison had nearly cost him his sanity, until he had learned to allow his mind to take him where he wanted to go, no matter that his body could not follow.

During his time in prison, he had sworn never to go

anywhere that his father had been. He had blamed his father for all his unhappiness and never wanted to be reminded of the man again.

Yet, he could see, the memory of his father held him so fast that he was being carried into the very lands his father had loved. In Jordan Kincaid he had even met someone who had known his father. By some process he did not understand, he was being swept by the wind toward the very world he had wanted to see with his father, and had then shunned because of his father's leaving.

As noon approached, Hall settled into a lighter frame of mind. He had fought his situation during his first weeks in prison, but had found peace of mind through acceptance. Now he was again in a circumstance that he had no control over. Fighting it would do no good. He would accept whatever came, until such time as he could change things. And he would leave his mind open to know when that time came.

In early afternoon, Crook ordered that camp be made, though the column had gone just twelve miles. Hall did not understand why they were stopping so early, but he was glad; it gave him an opportunity to rest his leg. Kincaid explained that Crook did not want the men or the horses tiring early in the campaign. Traveling too fast at the outset would take its toll later on in the more rugged country to the north.

The tents were erected along a nearly level bottom filled with greasewood, a large shrub resembling sagebrush but much rougher in texture. The general, who had learned the grazing preferences of stock animals, allowed the horses and mules, as well as the cattle herd, to eat what they wanted of the greasewood tops.

"They get their salt from that plant," Kincaid told Hall.

"You let them animals eat what they want and they'll survive just about anything."

Though the livestock browsed the greasewood with relish, they preferred eating snow to the brackish water that seeped along the drainage, making it difficult to keep them bedded down. There was fresh water not far to the north, and the stock could smell it.

Half of the herders and packers stayed busy throughout the afternoon, while the rest slept. Come nightfall, those in their bedrolls would roust out and spend most of the night with the stock. The soldiers set up their tents and sleeping gear, then gathered around fires to await the evening. Those selected for night guard duty slept, while the rest talked about Sioux Indians.

Sergeant Buckner found Hall at one of the wagons, collecting his sleeping gear.

"Don't get too comfortable, Hall," Buckner said. "I want you on guard duty right away. Don't leave your post until somebody comes to relieve you. I don't care if it's all night, you stand your guard. Do you understand, soldier?"

Hall saluted. "Yes, sir."

Buckner left, and Hall replaced the buffalo robe and canvas ground cover in the wagon. Kincaid had said Buckner would take revenge for disturbing him with the Arapaho girl. He would likely have no need for sleeping gear now; Buckner would keep him on guard duty all night.

Hall took his post and marched his segment of the guard. He knew Buckner was watching closely, looking for an opportunity to cause him serious trouble. The evening meal came and went, and darkness fell with the sentries around him getting their relief, but no one came for him.

Under cover of darkness, Hall sat down to rest his leg. The exercise might have helped it, but the seeping cold increased the pain. Hall thought about Buckner and wondered if this harassment would continue throughout the campaign. Maybe he should just get it over with and take Buckner from his bedroll at gunpoint, out away from camp, and throw him a pistol. They would both be armed and Buckner would have to face him with even odds. No rank or any of that kind of thing—kill or be killed; that would settle things one way or another.

Hall could see it in his mind. Buckner wouldn't stand a chance. He could see the flash of flame from the muzzle of his Colt Army, and Buckner tumbling head first into the snow.

Hall shook his head. He realized that would be foolish. It wouldn't be the end of it, but the beginning.

He could see the circle of rifles around him, the arrest being made. Crook would be shaking his head, wondering how a man could go so bad and remain so bad, when his uncle had been such a great man. He could plead self-defense; but no one shoots an officer, not even in self-defense.

They would put him under guard, with everyone talking, until he could be taken back to Fort Fetterman. Then he would be transferred back down to Fort D. A. Russell, the command headquarters at Cheyenne City. There he would waste away in the stockade until General Crook returned and a court-martial date was set.

It would be no different from Leavenworth and most likely far worse. Though the cells he had known had been cold and dank, the stockades at Fort Russell afforded little more shelter than being outdoors. It was no alternative to his present circumstance. He lowered his elbows onto his knees to wait out the night.

EIGHT

S till sitting, Hall continued to consider his situation, trying to decide what he would do the next time Buckner assigned him to guard duty. He certainly wouldn't allow himself to be given unrelieved duty. Maybe it would come down to whether Buckner or he survived the next few days.

Hall heard crunching in the snow behind him. He jumped to his feet and leveled his rifle.

"Whoa! You don't need to shoot me," Jordan Kincaid said. He stood in the shadows, wrapped in a heavy trade blanket. "I'm damn harmless these days."

Hall took a deep breath. "I guess I shouldn't be so quick."

"Everyone's edgy," Kincaid said. "Don't give it no more thought."

The two sat down together. Kincaid, who couldn't sleep, was looking for some good conversation and didn't believe he could get it with any of the soldiers. He admitted that he would feel a lot better with a few experienced men, or else alone, out away from the main camp.

"There's not a one of them Sioux that don't know right where we are," Kincaid said. "They'll come in one of these nights and stir up a mess. My hair'd feel a lot safer someplace else."

"I can understand your point," Hall said. "I think I'd just as soon take my chances with the Indians. They can't be more insane than some of these men."

Kincaid laughed. "Yes, except the Sioux got their backs to the wall. They're apt to do anything."

"I don't even understand this campaign," Hall said. "Why doesn't Crook wait until spring and let them come back peacefully?"

"There's nothing peaceful about this army," Kincaid said. "They aim to get the Sioux one way or another. If they can roust them in winter camp, it will make things a sight easier. Steal the horses. Burn the lodges. Shoot all they can. They figure the Sioux'll be easier to kill in the cold."

"White men die just as easily in this weather," Hall pointed out. "Especially when they're not used to it."

"You don't get anywhere is this army if you've got any decency," Kincaid said. "Men like that sergeant, Buckner, put me on edge. He'll do anything to get some stripes. And now that he's got you in his sights, he'll think more about how to get to you than he will the Sioux. That will put a lot of men in danger."

"I can't apologize for what I did," Hall said. "That Arapaho girl wasn't having all that good of a time. If I had it to do over again, I'd shoot Buckner and let someone else try and figure out how it happened."

"Likely you would at that," Kincaid said. "But it happened the way it did, and you'd best figure you owe me for coming along and saving your hide from those buckskinners when I did."

Hall turned to Kincaid and laughed. "Maybe they'd

ought to thank you," he said. "If I remember right, I was about to shoot one of them between the eyes."

"That you were," Kincaid said. "If you had, this world would be less one Ingram Hall."

"What?" Hall said. "That man was—was the one you told me about in the hospital?"

"The very same. I figure he was curious about you, but you said you didn't have no kin out here, so that's what I told him."

Stunned, Hall tried to remember the man and the face he had shoved his pistol into, but could not. He had been so angry that he hadn't noticed anything.

"He was curious about me?" Hall asked.

"Later, after I called you off them and you went to bed, he wanted to know about you. He heard me calling you by name and wondered. I told him you said you didn't have no kin out here, and he left with the others. Didn't ask no more about you."

"Why didn't he say something when I had the gun on him?" Hall asked. "If he heard you calling my name, why didn't he ask?"

"He can't speak no more," Kincaid said. "I didn't know it until I saw him later. He took a bullet through the throat last winter. I figure he'll be talking in sign language until they put him under." He stared at Hall. "I thought you said you had no kin out here. You seem pretty curious, to my way of thinking."

Hall was so overwhelmed he could not speak. Finally, he said, "Maybe my father is still alive, and maybe that was him. But I don't want to talk to him. I don't want to know him."

"Why wouldn't you want to get to know him?"

"He left me back there in Missouri," Hall said. "I'll never forgive him for that."

"How do you think he'd feel if he'd brought you out here and you got killed somehow?" Kincaid asked.

"I wouldn't have," Hall said.

"Well, you can't say that, either," Kincaid told him. "When a man lives in a wild country, he don't know what's going to happen next. He can't hope to know what will happen to a kid."

"I wasn't a kid."

"For this country, you were a kid."

Hall thought for a moment. Kincaid had a point: living in this country at the age of twelve would have been very difficult. It would not have been impossible, but very difficult.

"If I were to change my mind someday and decide to look for him, where do you suppose he would be?" Hall asked.

"I figure he and the others are with the Sioux," Kincaid replied. "He used to have a Sioux woman. Maybe he still does."

"My father married an Indian?"

"Lots of men did. You see something wrong with it?"

"Well, no. I just can't picture that. Besides, I thought the Sioux hated white men."

"Not if they're family," Kincaid explained. "He's married into them now, and he'll do what it takes to protect them. And they'll protect him. That's how it works."

"So why was he selling horses to the Army?" Hall asked.

Kincaid broke into a crooked smile. "He and the others bring horses in to Army posts to sell and then buy guns and bullets with the money. Before long, the Sioux come along and steal the horses back. Then they have guns and horses both. Pretty clever game, eh?"

Hall stared at Kincaid, unable to speak.

Kincaid said, "Now you can see that this army don't know nothing about who they're fighting."

"You mean there are a lot of men like my father siding with the Indians?" Hall asked.

"A good many of them," Kincaid said. "I'd likely be doing the same, but I've got a score to settle."

"What kind of score?" Hall asked.

Kincaid took a deep breath. "Back in the beaver days, I was married to a Shoshone woman. The village was moving camp when we got caught by a Sioux war party. Most of the village got away, but I got caught out in the open with my wife and son. I told them to kill me and let them go, but they wouldn't. They tied me up and made me watch while they skinned them both alive."

Hall's breath caught in his throat. "You saw that happen to your family?"

"I won't forget it," Kincaid said. "They skinned them and drug them behind their horses." Kincaid had his head bowed, reliving the horror. He trembled with pain and rage. Hall wished he had never asked.

"That war party rode off and left me there," Kincaid continued. "Just rode off and didn't look back. Since then, I don't care for the Sioux."

Hall looked toward the east, where the sun was rising into a deep pink horizon. "I'm sorry," he said. "I'm truly sorry."

"My son would have been about your age now," Kincaid said. "I can tell you, when a father's got a son, he wants to see him. I miss my wife and son every day. I think about them. I see my son riding in my dreams. He's got a fast horse. Then I wake up, and the sky is empty."

Kincaid got up and hobbled out to get his mules ready for the day's journey. Hall began to march his sentry duty again. The camp came to life, and Buckner finally appeared from his tent. He watched Hall for a time, then sent a soldier to tell him he could join the others for breakfast.

Strangely enough, Hall didn't feel hungry, although he

had missed two meals. He walked to the edge of camp to get his horse, watching a small pack of wolves that trotted in single file, just under the crest of a hill.

From the top of a distant butte, a ball of dark smoke rolled into the air. Then another, and a third. Hall watched with fascination. He noted that Grouard and the other scouts had already gathered and were pointing. The general was summoned from his tent. He mingled with the scouts, listening to them, turning an eyeglass on the smoke.

Hall saddled his horse and rode into formation with the others. Already they had encountered the enemy and couldn't even see them. He couldn't worry about his leg or that he hadn't gotten any sleep. He had a lot of things on his mind. Kincaid had told him more than enough to think about.

During the day Hall fell into short lapses of sleep in the saddle, while the troops around him worried about their lives. The signal smoke hung in the bitter cold like dark clouds of doom. Everyone stared into the surrounding hills, awaiting the cries of attacking warriors on horseback.

During the noon meal, Hall's thoughts centered on his father. He still couldn't believe that the man he had nearly shot was the same who had held him on his knee. Although it had been a number of years since he had last seen his father, he couldn't believe he wouldn't have recognized him. Still, it had been a long time.

Try as he might, he couldn't clearly remember the events of that night he had nearly killed his father. Nor could he bring back his father's looks and features. Too much had happened: the shock of finding Buckner with the Arapaho girl had blurred his thoughts.

The idea that his father now lived among the Sioux and sided with them was no less overwhelming. They could easily meet again on some frozen battlefield near the Big

Horns, where one or both of them could die in the snow. The possibility seemed highly unfair. Though Hall had sworn he would never again admit to having a father, the knowledge that he had actually seen the man made his oath impossible.

The column made another sixteen miles, and in late afternoon stopped to camp along the upper reaches of the Cheyenne River. Hall fell asleep immediately. To his surprise, Buckner did not bother him. Hall slept through the evening meal, until well after dark, when the call to arms awakened him.

Shots were coming from the direction of the cattle herd. Word came that Sioux and Cheyenne warriors had come in the dark to chase off the cattle and horses. The troops were told to take positions all around the camp and ordered to fire only when an enemy was in close range. No one heeded the command, and several shots were aimed at shadows in the darkness.

Hall took his position with others of the Second Cavalry protecting the horses. They formed a tight line around the eastern edge of camp, waiting, their rifles at the ready. To the south, the sounds of shooting continued as a detachment left to try to recover the stolen cattle.

Hall knelt on one knee, wondering whether a horde of warriors was nearby and whether a bullet might come at him from the darkness. He could hear horses running through the snow just a short way out. The hoofbeats drew nearer until a line of whooping warriors appeared, riding low over the backs of their ponies.

A volley of rifle fire echoed through camp. The horses jumped and squealed in fright, but could not break free of their picket ropes. Then, as if they had never come, the warriors were lost in the darkness.

Hall had not gotten a clean shot and had held his fire. He now waited for more to come, his rifle leveled, while others around him reloaded, yelling about having them on the run.

Behind him, one of the commanders shouted, "Stay put! Do not break your ranks!" But a number were already running into the shadows, shrieking and waving their rifles overhead.

"They think they're back in the Rebellion," a soldier next to Hall commented. "Damned fools! Them Sioux will pick them off one by one."

The soldier then ran into the shadows himself, yelling at another soldier named Jonas to come back. Commanders shouted and went after them, some on horseback. Hall stood his ground with the remainder of the command.

Suddenly another group of raiders emerged, riding directly for the horses. Hall and the others leveled their rifles. Upon seeing this, the raiders turned and rode back into the night.

A big soldier next to Hall laughed. "They thought they could decoy us away. I've seen that one before."

One of the warriors hesitated. Hall saw what he believed to be a rifle aimed toward him. He fired and watched the warrior fall to the ground. The big soldier clapped Hall on the back.

"A fine shot!" he said. "If I do say so, a very fine shot."

Hall was reloading his Springfield when another warrior rode back to pick up the fallen one. The soldier next to Hall aimed quickly and fired. He missed, cursed and reloaded.

The returning raider kicked his pony into a dead run, the wounded warrior holding on behind him. Hall considered shooting again, but saw soldiers in his line of fire. One of them was trying to control a black stallion.

Hall watched while a group of soldiers tried to subdue the stallion. He rose on his hind legs and kicked violently, scattering men in every direction. With a toss of his head he was lost in the night.

Hall hurried to the spot where the warrior had fallen and picked up a four-foot length of pole, painted and topped with feathers. He carried it back to camp, where everyone examined it.

"Got yourself a coup stick, I see," Kincaid said. "You'll want to hold on to it."

Hall felt the feathers. "A coup stick? What's it for?"

"A warrior touches his enemy with it," Kincaid explained. "It brings him honor, makes him a stronger warrior."

"I thought it was a rifle," Hall confessed. "I couldn't tell in the dark."

Kincaid winked. "You're the one who counted coup tonight. Don't take that away from yourself."

Kincaid left to watch the mules. There would be a double guard for the remainder of the night. The cattle were gone, and the herder had suffered a bullet wound through the left lung, but there had been no casualties among the officers or enlisted men. The Indians had been routed, as the talk went, thanks mainly to Hall. He had shot the only raider to fall.

Though the warrior hadn't died outright, the big soldier told everyone that it would only be a matter of time.

"I seen him jerk, big as you please," the soldier said. "He's as good as gone now."

Hall was a celebrity. The whispers and stares began once again, but not in the same vein as they had back at Fort Fetterman. They might still fear him, but he was one of them. Now he was proven, a soldier who had drawn the first enemy blood in the campaign against the Sioux and Cheyenne.

* * *

Soldiers asked questions throughout the night. Hall answered flatly that he had gotten off a lucky shot. In the circus, he had felt the same. Admiring spectators had asked him endlessly about his marksmanship, wondering at a young man with such a keen eye. It had finally gotten to be too much.

Now, in the same fashion, the soldiers all wanted to hear the story of what had happened. Over and over he told it, to a new group each time, letting them all touch the coup stick. At last, to get away from it all, he bundled himself in his heavy buffalo coat, took the coup stick and his rifle and relieved a man on guard duty.

This brought Sergeant Buckner out to check on his sanity. Hall saluted in silence.

"I didn't order you to stand guard," Buckner said. "Do you think maybe another Indian will show and you can make yourself bigger?"

"I don't care about that," Hall said. "I just need some time to myself."

"I know you," Buckner said. "You're so noble, aren't you? But really, you'd rather just run away from all this. You're not really the man you want everyone to think you are."

Hall stood silent and expressionless.

"I'll have you standing guard for the rest of this campaign, Hall," Buckner continued. "You won't get even a little sleep."

"I don't think so," Hall said. "Otherwise you would've put me on right away when we camped. Who told you to lay off me?"

Buckner was suddenly beside himself. "If it were up to me, I would have you sent back to Leavenworth," he snarled. "But the general believes you have what it takes to make an officer. Preposterous! If it weren't for him, you'd be gone."

Buckner, like the other officers, knew that Crook's feelings for Hall's deceased uncle were still strong, so strong they were clouding the general's attitude about Hall. It seemed that the general wanted to elevate Hall as high as he could, much as he was working to make Colonel Reynolds a name among leaders.

It was common knowledge that Crook had given Reynolds command of the campaign so that Reynolds might prove himself as both an officer and a gentleman. Reynolds had made some miscalculations during his career and was not in good stead with many of his superiors; it was obvious to all that Crook hoped to bring Reynolds's career back in line.

There were still others, including Kincaid, who believed that the general was treating Hall as if he were a son. "I can't say for certain, but I don't think the general has a boy," Kincaid had once told Hall. "Maybe he'd like to have someone he could bring along in this army, someone he could be proud of like they were kin."

Hall didn't feel comfortable with the idea. It was known that Crook had a wife in the East, and that he never partook of women or strong drink, as most of the officers were prone to do, but no one knew of any children. If he had a son, the general hadn't talked about it.

There was one good thing about the general's high regard; it had pulled Buckner off his back. But as for aspirations toward a career in the Army, Hall would never change his mind.

"You hear me, Hall?" Buckner continued. "I'd like to see you out of this army."

"Sergeant Buckner," Hall said, "aren't you wasting your time out here?"

"Hall, I won't stand for any insubordination," Buckner said.

"I'll make you a deal, Sergeant," Hall said. "You leave

me alone, and I won't complain to the general. Is that fair?"

Buckner took a deep breath. "This little moment of glory won't last long," he said. "And when it's over, you're going to pay. You're going to pay dearly."

Buckner stomped off without bothering to exchange salutes. Hall watched him enter the camp and disappear in the maze of tents and equipment.

Overhead, a cut moon graced a cloudless, bitterly cold sky. Hall realized the night had made him a celebrity. He wished he hadn't fired. Yet he knew he couldn't blame himself: in the darkness, he couldn't have told the difference between a rifle and a coup stick.

Crook would be asking to see him soon, to offer his congratulations. The event would further strengthen the general's resolve to make him a good soldier and, eventually, an officer.

Hall thought about what he would say: "Thank you, General. I appreciate your kindness, but I don't feel qualified to become an officer. I haven't been in the Army that long." He knew Crook would have an answer for everything: "Now, Private Hall, don't be so modest. You've proven yourself a brave man! Stand up and accept it! I knew you had it in you. Didn't I tell you that?"

Hall felt his heart pounding. Any other soldier would be celebrating. Hall believed he had made a wrong move. He had trapped himself.

Hall decided he would listen to the general's praise. He would nod a lot and say a lot of thank-yous. When it was over, he would salute the general and leave. Then, with the next break in the weather, he would saddle his horse in the dead of night and ride as fast and as far away as he could.

PART II
Late Winter, 1876

NINE

Through the following days, the smoke signals continued and Hall began to see mirror signals, bursts of flashing light, like daytime stars embedded in the hills, coming from along the column's right flank. During the stops, Kincaid would comment on what the signals meant and point out pony and travois tracks in the snow, showing that Indians were keeping on the move.

"They've been roaming around a lot," Kincaid explained. "Maybe game is hard to find. Or maybe they're all planning to group into one main village."

The temperature stayed below zero, even at midday, and at night they crawled under piles of buffalo robes as soon as the evening meal was finished. Hall was never ordered to stand guard again, ever, nor did he see Sergeant Buckner for more than fleeting moments. He knew, however, that Buckner was hard as stone. That envisioned gunfight would eventually have to take place.

Hall was transferred into the front ranks of Egan's company, a move designed to show advancement without an increase in rank, proving to the other men that acts of bravery were rewarded. Hall knew that should he perform well in any more engagements with the Sioux, he would certainly be given a promotion.

Crook still hadn't called for him, but Hall knew that the general was informed of his every move. He carried the coup stick tied to his saddle and thought often about that instant when his rifle had bucked against his shoulder and the warrior had toppled off the black stallion. As a result of that moment they all had their eyes on him. It would be virtually impossible to desert.

Moreover, they had gotten deep into the Indians' hunting grounds, and any move away from the column would be fatal. Warriors often showed themselves in small groups, fur-clad horsemen tempting the eastern and southern sectors of the column. Strict orders had been given not to shoot at or pursue any Indians, under any circumstances, unless so instructed. Anyone who broke these orders was subject to court-martial.

During a stop to water the horses and mules, Kincaid explained to Hall that the Indians were becoming braver and more eager to cause disturbances. This meant the column was getting closer to their villages.

"The mirrors are a-flashing like crazy, and the smoke is rising from more and more hills," Kincaid said. He pointed into the distance, where four buttes rose above the snowbound plains. "Those are Pumpkin Buttes. That's a good place for them to watch us from. You can tell they're flashing toward their camps, which look to be down in the rough country ahead of us."

In a few days the rolling country they now traversed would turn into a land carved deeply by time itself. Out from the Bighorns, the lower edge of the foothills met with a broad expanse of steep ravines and rock cliffs where horses and men could stay hidden for days at a time.

"That country's wilder than any dream you ever had,"

Kincaid told Hall. "There's miles of rock walls and scrub timber, and some of the hills look to be red as fire. There's smoke and fire itself in them hills. It comes out from coal that's been burning underground for a long time. Strangest thing you ever saw."

Hall was intrigued by the notion of burning hills. As a child, he had listened to his father's stories of underground fires that sent up bubbling gases and boiled out spitting masses of mud and water on the surface of the ground. Yet this didn't sound the same.

"You're thinking of the place they call Colter's Hell," Kincaid explained. "That's a good piece west of here, in the high country of the Yellowstone. The fire that I'm talking about here is caused when lightning strikes the coal that's above ground, then burns back into the hills."

"It burns all the time?" Hall asked.

"That's right. A trader once told me that all the red rock is from giant coal fires that started thousands of years ago and burned so hot they cooked the rocks. Can't say if that's true or not. That trader told some big ones, and you couldn't tell when he was jawing you."

"How did he know so much about it?" Hall asked.

"He went to college, believe it or not. Then he came out with Major Henry to trap beaver in 1823. I met him at a rendezvous down on Green River. That winter the Blackfeet killed him and cut him up for the wolves."

Hall turned to the hills. To hear Kincaid talk, the odds were against anyone living long in this country. Obviously a college education didn't guarantee that a man had the right kind of sense to stay alive among Indians. It made him wonder what Kincaid and his father must know to have survived thus far.

"How have you managed to stay alive out here?" Hall asked.

"I should have been dead more times than there are

fingers on both hands," Kincaid replied. "There's been somebody upstairs watching out for me, that's all I can say." He laughed. "My mother always said that I was too hard on my guardian angel. When I was a little shaver she'd tell me, 'Jordan William, you've got to use some sense. You can't ride wild cows and stay in one piece. The good Lord sent you a good guardian angel, but there's a limit.' "

Hall laughed nervously. Anyone who came into the West was looking at life day-to-day. He believed that Kincaid and his father must be among the smarter ones. They hadn't kept themselves alive, though, by riding through endless snowbound miles of frozen country.

A short way to the east, a dozen horsemen appeared, waving blankets in the air.

"They're going to try and get somebody to chase them," Kincaid said. "They won't give up."

Hall turned his face away from the bitter cold breeze. "I can't see why they would even be out in this weather."

"They wouldn't be if we weren't," Kincaid replied. "There's not a lick of sense to it."

On the afternoon of the fourth day, the scouts killed a number of antelope and a few old buffalo bulls wintering together. The column halted for the night, and Kincaid secured a cut of buffalo hump meat. Just before sundown, as he prepared to cook it, columns of smoke rose against the horizon. Hall asked if the Indians were planning an attack.

"They won't take us on," Kincaid said, carving pieces of buffalo. "There's too many of us. If the general was to split the command, that would make things different."

"Do you think the general will do that?" Hall asked.

Kincaid produced two willow sticks and jabbed a chunk of meat on each of them, then gave Hall his choice to hold over the fire.

"I figure the general will have to," Kincaid replied.

"We're moving too slow. At this pace we won't have supplies enough to last until we reach the Sioux villages."

"You mean he ordered too many men into the field?" Hall asked.

Kincaid laughed. "Crook wants a whole passel of men to fight with, but I'd bet he leaves the wagons and the mules at old Fort Reno. We'll be there tomorrow."

Hall watched how Kincaid roasted his meat at the edge of the fire, over the coals, instead of directly in the flames.

"What about you?" Hall asked. "You won't be going ahead with us, then."

"I aim to go on, one way or another," Kincaid said. "I haven't figured yet how I'll swing it, but the general needs men who know the country. He puts too much stock in Grouard. There's talk that Grouard might turn against us."

"I don't know if I believe that," Hall said. "Grouard tried to talk me into going after Crazy Horse, to get revenge for him. He told me that he and Crazy Horse made a pact never to kill one another, so he wants me to do it. I think Grouard hates the Sioux as much as you do."

Kincaid turned to Hall. "Grouard wanted you to kill Crazy Horse?"

"That's what he said, the night before we left the fort."

"Why did he pick you?" Kincaid asked.

"I asked him the same thing. He said I was a good fighter. When I told him I wasn't interested, he called me a coward. I don't know why he picked me, I never got a straight answer."

Kincaid turned his stick thoughtfully. "Maybe he thinks you're crazy, with your fight in prison and all. I figure he would want you to go straight on at Crazy Horse while he slips up from the back."

Hall noted the resentment in Kincaid's voice. "Did Grouard do something to you?"

"I just don't trust him," Kincaid said. "He never says

the same thing to anybody. He always has a different story. All anybody knows for sure is that the Sioux call him The Grabber. He always puts his hands up when somebody gets the best of him."

"If there's so many who don't trust Grouard," Hall asked, "then why's he the head scout?"

"Grouard talks a good line," Kincaid said. "He likely told the general he's killed a thousand Sioux already, and knows just how to get rid of the rest. Crook likes to hear that kind of thing." He pulled his cut of buffalo from the fire and studied it. "You don't figure to do what he asks and go after Crazy Horse, do you?"

"I'm not going out of my way, one way or the other," Hall said.

"You see him coming, you go the other way," Kincaid advised. "Crazy Horse lives in a different world than you and me."

"Grouard said the same thing," Hall said. "He went as far as to say that the man is part ghost."

"That's the truth of the matter. He's more than a man. I can tell you that for sure." Kincaid was chewing, looking at Hall sternly. "You hear me? Stay away from Crazy Horse."

Hall took his stick from the fire. He bit off a small piece of meat and chewed it. "Is buffalo always this tough?"

Kincaid chewed another piece free. "Old bull won't cook no matter what you do, but there's better to be found when the spring comes. I figure it's certain you'll be around then, if you don't do something foolish in the meantime."

"I've done some foolish things," Hall said, "but never in a country I know nothing about."

"Good," Kincaid said. "I wouldn't want you to change your ways now."

* * *

Ghostwind sat on a hill with her two children, feeding wood to a fire and awaiting the return of the raiders. She now made it a practice to pray every night and early morning on a hill above the village. The sun was just rising through a heavy fog that had settled along the river, blending a gold light into the crystalline frost that hung thickly in the air.

A messenger had arrived in the village late the night before to announce that some of the raiders were near the village, while others had chosen to remain in hopes of stealing Bluecoat horses. The first attempt had failed. One of the warriors, Kicks-the-Fox, had been badly hurt and was near death.

Ghostwind's children had heard the news and were in shock. She had said nothing to them about her decision to leave their father, and her parents had told them nothing, either. She knew with certainty that her vision of his death would quickly be reality. What would she say to him should the chance come to speak with him? There would be no confrontation about the other woman. He would die, and she would go on with life as best she could.

The sun rose above the horizon, and more light swelled through the fog.

Talking Grass shifted herself nervously. "When will they be coming? Shouldn't they be here by now?"

"Be patient," Ghostwind said. "All we can do is wait."

"You know that Father will die, don't you?" Young Horse said. "I know he will."

"That is in the hands of the One Above," Ghostwind said. "We can only hope that Horned Bull will help him recover."

"Horned Bull cannot help him," Young Horse said sadly. "I feel that it is too late."

The fog slowly began to lift, and the sound of horses coming down the trail into the village brought Ghostwind and her children to their feet. Young Horse pointed.

"There they are. Where is Father?"

Ghostwind stared through the fog, holding her breath, but could not make out any of the warriors.

"I see a black horse at the end," Young Horse said. "Whoever is riding him is bent over and covered with a robe. That has to be Father."

Ghostwind and her children hurried down into the village. The raiders' return was neither glorious nor cheerful. In the middle of the subdued column, Kicks-the-Fox rode doubled over his pony. He was wrapped in skins, with a buffalo robe over him, and tied to his stallion.

"Father!" Young Horse ran to the black stallion and took hold of his father's leg. "Father, can you hear me?"

Ghostwind carried Talking Grass, who was sobbing against her mother's shoulder. She reached Young Horse and pushed him back from the stallion. Kicks-the-Fox looked unconscious.

"The horse might step on you," she explained to Young Horse. "Wait until he's taken to Horned Bull's lodge. If any medicine man can help him, Horned Bull can."

Young Horse yelled in anger and tried to pull away, but she held him fast.

"You'll be able to talk to him soon," Ghostwind promised. "But you have to wait."

Ghostwind's mother and father hurried from their lodge. Mountain Water's face was filled with pain for her daughter. Five Bulls looked on stoically for a short time before returning to his lodge.

Ghostwind stood back with her children and her mother while three warriors took Kicks-the-Fox down from his horse and carried him into Horned Bull's lodge. Day Lily came and offered apologies.

"Let me fix food for you until the moon changes," she told Ghostwind. "Come to my lodge when you're ready."

"I'll stay outside with the children," Mountain Water told Ghostwind.

"I want to go with Mother," Young Horse said.

"Wait, please," Ghostwind said. "Your father and I must talk. I will send for you."

Ghostwind entered the lodge, choking back tears. Despite everything she still loved him. The love and anger tore at her. She did not know what to expect from him. Would he even be able to talk? The warriors who had brought him in were leaving, and Horned Bull was getting his paints and medicine articles ready for a healing ceremony.

Kicks-the-Fox opened his eyes and Ghostwind knelt down beside him.

"I'm shot through the side," he told her in a raspy voice. "My days in this world are over."

Ghostwind bit her lip. "Horned Bull is preparing for a healing ceremony. He can help you."

Kicks-the-Fox shook his head feebly. He called for Horned Bull, who knelt beside him, his face half painted.

"There will be no ceremony," he told Horned Bull. "It will do no good. I can already see the Other Side. I must talk to my wife now."

"Are you certain of this?" Horned Bull asked. "Maybe you are supposed to stay in this world."

"No, the spirits talked to me all the way back to the village," Kicks-the-Fox said, "while my life drained out of my side. I'm called to cross over for good."

Horned Bull left the lodge. Kicks-the-Fox beckoned Ghostwind to move closer, for his voice was giving way. "I'm sorry for what I did to you," he managed, his eyes wet. "You have been the best wife anyone could want. Please forgive me."

"I forgive you," Ghostwind said. "You don't have to talk about it."

"And I feel bad for the words I said to Crazy Horse," Kicks-the-Fox continued. "I was wrong."

"He brought his two best horses for you," Ghostwind said. "You must recover and ride them."

Kicks-the-Fox gasped in pain. "I will never ride again," he said. "Keep one for Young Horse and give Crazy Horse his best pony back. I don't deserve good horses. I wronged you."

"Don't talk," Ghostwind said. "Save your strength."

"I've none left to save," Kicks-the-Fox said. "I see my father." His father had been killed by the Crow when Kicks-the-Fox was ten. "He has come for me. My grandfather is with him. They have come to take me across. It's almost time for me to go. Let me talk to the children."

Ghostwind stepped out of the lodge and brought Young Horse and Talking Grass back. "Father, when will you get better?" Young Horse asked. Talking Grass had already fallen on top of him and was sobbing on his chest.

Kicks-the-Fox held out his hand. "Take my hand, son, and tell me you will learn the ways of a warrior."

"You will teach me," Young Horse said.

"I cannot," Kicks-the-Fox said. "You must learn from someone else. That's the way it must be."

"I don't want you to leave us," Young Horse cried.

"It is my time to go," Kicks-the-Fox said. "Be strong. Someday I will come for you."

Young Horse rubbed his sister's back. She continued to cry on her father's chest, holding him tightly. Kicks-the-Fox's eyes began to glaze over.

"Take care of them," he told Ghostwind. "Someday I will see you again, if you want me to see you."

"Certainly I will want to see you again," Ghostwind

promised. She trembled as she touched his face. A small rush of air came from his lungs and he lay still.

"Is he gone?" Young Horse asked.

"Yes, he is gone." Ghostwind leaned over and kissed him on the forehead. "I will miss you, my husband."

TEN

Daylight was fading rapidly and the temperature was falling as the column reached Crazy Woman's Fork of the Powder River. Frank Grouard and a select group of scouts were already in camp, their fires glowing against the snowbound twilight. They had traveled ahead of the column three days before to search out Indian villages and find the best attack routes.

Orders to bivouac carried down the line and Hall began working with the others to establish camp. Small detachments were sent to the surrounding hills as guards while horses were unsaddled and hobbled for grazing and mules laden with wood for cookfires. Others were assigned to collect water in large pots for cooking and for coffee.

During the evening meal, the talk among the men centered around the country they were approaching and where the Indians might be camped.

"I'd lay any odds that Grouard's found Crazy Horse, or thinks he has," Kincaid said. "He's likely figuring we'll catch them in camp now that the cold and snow have set in."

There was good reason to believe that might happen. Two days before, a group of Sioux warriors had attempted another assault, sneaking through a grove of cottonwoods at the Dry Fork campground. The assault had been repelled easily. Since then there had been little or no sign of Indians.

"They might have gone back to their villages," Kincaid said. "They'll be back, though. The Sioux have beat this army before and they won't give up."

The ruins of old Fort Reno lay a half day behind, bleak remnants of the failed attempt to subdue the Sioux and Cheyenne ten years before. The images of the old fort hadn't yet left Hall's mind. He could still see the wall and chimney fragments jutting from the snow, together with nearly a dozen twisted headboards that marked forgotten gravesites.

Hall was reminded of Mathew Dolan, the young soldier who had died in the ambulance. Maybe Dolan was better off, Hall thought as he turned his face from a north wind filled with blinding snow. He could almost hear Dolan laughing, saying, "If you'd had any sense, you'd have left this world with me that cold night. You knew it wouldn't get better, and it's bound to get worse."

Hall and Kincaid dropped their mouths in astonishment as new orders came to prepare for departure. After conferring with Grouard and the scouts, Crook had called his officers together for a meeting. He ordered that the wagons return to Fort Reno and set up a base camp, and that all cavalry and pack-train units leave immediately, following a northwest course toward the hostile villages.

Advancing officers and men were to travel light: they would be allowed only those clothes they were wearing and the choice of one buffalo robe or two blankets for bedding, a small shelter tent, and half rations of bacon, hardtack, coffee and sugar. The trip would last fifteen days, unless the hostiles were discovered first.

Kincaid was overjoyed to be going along with his mules. "I didn't think he'd take the whole cavalry," he told Hall, oblivious to the bitter weather. "Grouard must have found them. We'll be in a fight soon. This is what I come for."

"You don't seem to mind the fact that we could freeze to death out here," Hall said.

"I've seen worse," Kincaid said, "and there wasn't but our buckskins to eat."

"What we've got isn't much better."

Kincaid laughed. "Count your blessings, boy, just count your blessings."

Hall rode just behind the officers of Teddy Egan's column. The storm had abated and a heavy stillness lay over the land. A three-quarter moon hung overhead, throwing off a foggy light that seemed suspended in the frigid heavens. Horses and men breathed vaporous clouds, and the squeak of cold saddle leather became a monotonous chorus up and down the line.

The terrain was rough, the trails across the broken hills steep and difficult to negotiate. Moonlight caught saddle and gun-barrel steel as the column moved in single file like a giant gleaming serpent, slithering up and down and across a vast and ragged white wilderness. The horses had trouble keeping their balance and slipped often. Hall's leg bothered him. Staying in the saddle now meant continuously shifting weight from one stirrup to the other.

During a stop to water the horses and mules, Hall discovered that they were headed for the Tongue River, a major tributary of the Yellowstone. Grouard and three or four of the top scouts all favored the upper Tongue. Rough and secluded, the area offered myriad locations for hidden campsites in the deep depressions and watercourses.

The column continued through the cold, the steepness of the terrain exacting great effort from the men and the animals. To Hall the rocky slopes seemed heaved up from the very bosom of the earth, only to be smothered by an endless blanket of ice. The scattered stands of yellow pine and both low and upright juniper that dotted the slopes cast eerie shadows across the snow, as if many things lived in this land that couldn't be clearly seen or understood. Only those without concern for their future would dare venture here.

At the top of the Clear Creek divide, the Big Horn range came into view. Hall, with the others, stared in awe. Through the frozen distance, jagged peaks laden with snow gleamed in the moonlight like polished marble. Highest of all rose Cloud Peak, the summit that was a sacred place to all Indians of the region.

They made camp in the predawn hour. The creek was frozen solid in many places, but they got water from a warm spring that left one large area open and steaming. There was no timber for fires, however, and little grazing for the horses and mules.

Hall and Kincaid spoke little as they cared for their animals and dragged their bedrolls into camp. After finding a suitable location, they both wrapped themselves in their buffalo robes and fell asleep immediately upon the frozen ground.

Shortly after sunrise another storm swept in, and Hall awakened to a blizzard. He could barely see Kincaid or any of the other men. Grouard had suggested moving camp. Without any breakfast fires, Hall chewed a stick of frozen bacon while he saddled his horse.

The column halted five miles farther down Clear Creek, in a stand of old cottonwoods. Hall and Kincaid and another mule packer named Zack Morgan huddled with the others around fires, their backs to the blowing snow, turning their faces from the smoke and ashes that billowed up with the raging wind.

That night Crook ordered that the men use horse and mule blankets, as well as their buffalo robes, to secure them against the weather. Hall got up often to exercise his leg. The lean-to held back the wind, but not the cold.

Up for the third time, Hall considered his chances for deserting. The men posted on guard duty at the edge of camp would likely be fighting the cold rather than remaining alert. Food wouldn't be a problem, for he had stuffed his pockets with frozen beans and bacon and had stolen a butcher knife when one of the cooks had turned away. Anything he shot along the way he could butcher.

If he was going to do it, tonight was the night. Though deep in Indian country, he felt he had a better chance of escape now than he might have had before. The Indians would likely be in their villages, away from the storm, and certainly no one from the command would come after him in this weather.

Hall figured his chances of survival would be just as good as, or better than, his chances with the campaign. They were headed into certain battle with the Sioux, if the weather didn't get them all first, and he would be in the front lines. He liked neither the odds nor the cause.

Getting back south would be difficult, but with the wind at his back, he believed he could survive the weather. He could make good time alone and knew the country he had come through. He would just avoid Fort Fetterman and find his way back down to Cheyenne before anyone could stop him.

Making certain that Kincaid and Morgan were asleep, Hall collected his bedroll and saddle and started for the horses. He looked back once; he would miss Kincaid. The old packer had taught him a great deal. But there was no time now for sentiment. The Army just wasn't for him.

Hall turned his face away from the wind and snow, more determined now than ever. Just before reaching the horses, he thought he heard someone talking a few feet ahead. He stopped and dropped his saddle, thinking that Sergeant Buckner had flanked him and was now going to arrest him. He thought about running, but knew he had no chance without a horse.

Hall stood rigid, holding his breath, while the blizzard lashed his face. Through the darkness he heard the talk turn to laughter. Then a half-naked soldier walked right into him.

The soldier screamed in fright. Hall jumped back, staring at the soldier, who now began to cry, "I won't run away again, Pa, I promise. Don't whup me again. I'll stay home."

The soldier had covered his face with his hands and was sobbing. He wore only long woolen underwear, without the top, and stood barefoot in the snow.

"What are you doing out here?" Hall asked.

"Please, Pa, I won't leave no more," the soldier said. "Don't whup me. Just let me go to bed. I won't eat tomorrow if you don't want me to. Just don't whup me."

Buckner and three other soldiers arrived. "There he is," one of the soldiers said, pointing through the storm. "Someone's found him."

"I knew he'd snap," the other soldier said. "He was talking crazy this morning already. He just got out of bed and took off, mumbling crazy talk."

"Take him back into camp," Buckner ordered. "Get him next to the fire, and get the surgeon."

The sobbing soldier began to wail louder and fought the others trying to help him. "Hold onto him!" Buckner yelled. "Don't let him run off!"

The three soldiers continued to have trouble. Buckner pulled his pistol.

"Hold him!" Buckner ordered. "Hold him still!"

Buckner slammed the barrel of his revolver into the sobbing man's skull. The soldiers let him go and he slumped, groaning, into the snow.

"Don't drop him, you fools!" Buckner yelled. "Take him back to camp. Hurry up! We can't afford to lose a man to the weather."

When they were gone, Buckner holstered his pistol and Hall picked up his saddle. Buckner walked with him back toward the fires.

"What were you doing out here with your saddle?" Buckner asked.

"I was exercising my leg and remembered I had left it out by my horse," Hall replied.

"You left your saddle out by your horse?"

"I was tired. I just forgot it. Others do it, you know that."

Buckner stopped Hall by one of the fires and stared hard at him. "Are you telling me you got up from your bed to go out and bring your saddle back in?"

"I got up to exercise my leg," Hall said. "I remembered my saddle and heard the soldier yelling. He obviously needed help."

"Obviously," Buckner said. "What's the matter with your leg? That should be healed by now."

"Hard riding in weather like this doesn't help the process."

Buckner continued to stare at Hall. "If it were anyone else, I wouldn't be suspicious. But I can certainly imagine you trying to desert, even on a night like this."

"Imagine anything you want," Hall said. "It's a good thing I found that soldier."

Captain Egan and Colonel Reynolds suddenly appeared and Egan extended his hand. "I understand it was you who discovered Private Grady."

"Yes, sir," Hall replied.

Reynolds then extended his hand. "You've done a good job. Had he gotten away from camp, he might have wandered far enough to alert the enemy."

"I thought it was best to help him, sir," Hall said.

Reynolds turned to Egan. "I'm going back to bed. I will carry the news to the general in the morning. You may all carry on."

The three saluted. Reynolds returned the salute and disappeared among the fires and bedrolls. Hall noticed that the storm was easing up.

"You have again proved yourself a fit and capable soldier," Egan told Hall.

"Thank you, sir."

"How's your leg holding up?"

"I'll make it, sir," Hall said. "I just have to keep it loose."

"This weather can't last. Are you ready to fight?"

"Always, sir."

"That's the spirit." He turned to Buckner. "We need more like him."

Buckner's teeth were clenched. He managed a faint smile. "We do at that, sir."

"Very well. Carry on then," Egan said.

Hall and Buckner saluted as Egan left. Buckner headed toward his own bedroll, stamping his boots. Hall carried his saddle back to the lean-to and set it down in the snow. The storm had lessened considerably, and Hall thought Egan was right about the weather. It made him wish he hadn't run into the crazed soldier.

Hall was certain Kincaid and Morgan were both sleeping soundly, but as he laid his robe back down and crawled under it, he heard Kincaid roll over.

"No matter what, you can't help but be a hero, can you?" Kincaid said in a harsh whisper. "It's a good thing that crazy bastard was wandering around out there. You wouldn't have lived through the night."

"You knew I was leaving?"

"A man don't take his saddle on a walk. But you're old enough to do what you want. I wasn't about to stop you."

Hall could hear the rage in Kincaid's voice. He was acting the same as when he had talked about losing his family to the Sioux.

"Why are you so angry?" Hall asked.

"I ain't angry, boy. Just disappointed."

"Why?"

"Get some sleep. This army won't feel sorry for anyone who falls out of his saddle."

"We'll talk about this tomorrow," Hall said.

"Hell we will," Kincaid said. "It ain't worth my time."

Hall settled into his robe. Though he tried to fall asleep, he kept hearing Kincaid's harsh, uneven breathing. It seemed as if Kincaid might never talk to him again.

The sun topped the horizon, bathing the snowbound hills in a golden light. Ghostwind, her hair chopped to shoulder length and her lower legs bloody from superficial cuts, knelt over the body of Kicks-the-Fox. She had been with him since the previous morning, after the storm had ended, when his body had been taken by four warriors and placed, naked, atop a hill a good distance from the village.

Kicks-the-Fox would not rest in a scaffold or in a tree. He had died as a warrior and was honored by being left for the wolves and the coyotes, the eagles, magpies and hawks. That way his remains would be scattered by his wild brothers, as was meant to be for a fighting man.

As the sun grew brighter, Ghostwind knew she would soon be leaving her husband for his final journey. Day Lily would be coming to take her back to the village. Her place among the Northern Cheyenne now would be entirely different. She would be in mourning for a long time.

Soon after Kicks-the-Fox had died, he had been carried to the edge of the village, where a buffalo robe had been placed over him, so that his spirit would not interfere with those still living. When the storm had ended, the warriors had placed him upon a travois and had taken him to the top of the hill. After they had told Ghostwind of his whereabouts, Five Bulls and Mountain Water had begun the task of supervising the giveaway of everything Ghostwind and Kicks-the-Fox had owned together.

Their lodge had been given to another family whose own lodge had been damaged by fire. Kicks-the-Fox's weapons had gone with him to the hilltop, and all his clothes had been burned during a ceremony performed by Horned Bull.

Young Horse and Talking Grass would live with their grandparents and extended family until Ghostwind was given a new lodge. Ghostwind had accepted an offer to live with Day Lily and her husband. Since Ghostwind had no brothers or uncles, the chances were good that she would have to wait until she remarried to have her own lodge again. Her new husband would then have the responsibility of providing buffalo skins for her use.

All these things passed through Ghostwind's mind as she waited for Day Lily. She knelt in the bitter cold, wrapped in a buffalo robe. Besides the robe and the deerskin dress and leggings under it, she had kept none of her clothing. She would have to make new ones and rely on gifts from others.

Her children and her parents were likely very worried about her. Though the night had been as bad as any during these cold moons, she had remained with her husband's body until the proper time to leave. Had she left earlier, his journey across might have been much more difficult.

Ghostwind now looked to the sky and thanked *Maheo* for giving her strength against the cold. She knew the weather would have at least taken her fingers and toes, and also the skin from her face, had she not refrained from eating and drinking. She had also offered a thin piece of flesh from her right leg, to show that her pain for her husband was real.

Ghostwind looked down the hill and watched Day Lily making her way up a snow-packed trail. No one could ask for a better friend than Day Lily. She had no children of her own and adored both Young Horse and Talking Grass, often remarking that she hoped to give her husband, a warrior named Stands Alone, a child very soon. Stands Alone had become unhappy with her and she feared they would part if a child did not come soon.

Ghostwind stood up and hugged Day Lily. Careful not to speak Kicks-the-Fox's name, Day Lily told Ghostwind that she hoped her husband had had a good journey to the Other Side. Ghostwind thanked her, and the two started down the hill.

"I believe now is the right time to tell you this," Day Lily said. "Crazy Horse is in the village. He came this morning with He Dog and some of the Oglala warriors who were on the raiding party with your husband. They have brought meat for you, and some cooking utensils that their wives donated."

"That is very kind," Ghostwind said. "I will have them leave it at your lodge. Since I am staying with you, we will share everything."

"But it is for you."

"No, it is for *us*," Ghostwind insisted. "You have offered to share your home with me. I want you to share in my good fortune."

"There is more good fortune, for all of us," Day Lily said. "Crazy Horse says that two large herds of buffalo have been spotted up on the Elk River. Our brothers among the Oglala wish for us to make two hunting parties together."

"That is good news," Ghostwind said. "There will be plenty of meat to see us through the remainder of the cold moons."

"Yes, and we'll need it," Day Lily said. "Word has also come that some Northern Cheyenne from the agency who have been camped east of here will move to join us. They have some supplies of their own that they brought from the agency, but there isn't enough to feed everyone until the snow leaves."

"Will they come in time for the hunt?"

"Not unless they start soon," Day Lily said. "Crazy Horse wants to go as soon as the weather opens. A dreamer among his people has said that the cold will leave for a time, and it will be good hunting weather. He will lead his people, and He Dog and some of the Oglala will remain with us, so that we can all hunt together. The women are moving their lodges now, so that they will be here to help with the hunt."

"What about the Bluecoats?" Ghostwind asked.

"The scouts say that Three Stars Crook has stopped at the old fort place far down Powder River. They believe he will turn around and go back where he came from."

Ghostwind frowned. She walked on without speaking.

"You don't believe the Bluecoats will turn back?" Day Lily asked.

"They started up here to find us in bad weather," Ghostwind replied. "Why would they turn back now?"

"But they stopped because of the severe cold," Day Lily said. "They will surely run out of food soon."

"You and I have both heard the men talking," Ghostwind said. "Three Stars Crook has brought Crazy Horse's enemy, The Grabber, to scout for him. And it is said that there are scouts along with them who once lived at the agencies. They are mixed-bloods, like me, but they are our own people."

"Our own people would not hunt us," Day Lily said.

"Everything is changing," Ghostwind said. "The *Wiheo* money and whiskey makes even those with good hearts think differently than they once did."

"I hope you are wrong and the scouts are right," Day Lily said. "For the first time, I hope you're wrong."

ELEVEN

After a morning of sunshine, another storm closed in. The column plodded through two more days of heavy snowfall, the men alternately riding and walking by day and huddling around campfires by night, while the thermometer never once registered above zero.

Grouard had set the course, leading Crook and his command through narrow ravines and along switchback trails over steep divides. On occasion he left with some of the other scouts to check the country ahead for Indian camps. Often they returned with news of Indian movement or an abandoned village, but never was the column very near the enemy.

During these trips, Grouard and the others often killed deer and antelope, and brought the meat back as a supplement to the regular rations. This kept the morale higher than it might have otherwise been. Traveling through the wild and frozen land, awaiting battle that might happen at any time, had drawn deeply from their emotions.

The only change from snow-covered rock and timber came in the form of a prairie-dog town nestled along a creek which bore their name. Resembling large gophers, they stood on their hind legs, yipping at the column, running back and forth between their burrows, their squat, furry bodies alive with energy.

The troops argued as to whether or not these animals ordinarily hibernated. Some said the animals had already completed their ordinary hibernation period and it was time for them to come out. Others argued that no self-respecting prairie dog would ever gallop around in snow and sub-zero temperatures, no matter what time of year it was. Only the U.S. Army did that.

Though the men had gradually hardened to the weather, there was no getting used to the traveling. Paved into glare ice by the pounding of hooves, the trails were miserable. The men had severe sprains and bruises from frequent spills and accidents. A corporal in D Company of the Third Cavalry was badly injured when his horse fell on him, and he had to be transported on a travois made of two small pines and a blanket. The surgeon feared that he would suffer additionally from frostbite, and possibly even freeze his hands and feet, since he could not move around as the other soldiers did.

Though there was little complaining now, many were suffering from the cold. Black and swollen fingers and toes were common, as was peeling facial skin. Noses and cheeks were especially vulnerable to the wind, and many would have lost their ears had it not been for the issued scarves and fur-lined caps.

Hall was glad for the rough country. Had this weather set in while they had been traveling out in the open, the entire command might have become frozen lumps under the blowing and drifting snow. The steep ravines and canyons offered shelter against the constant wind and kept the warmth from the fires in, to a degree.

The troops had learned to first build fires on the spots

where they would be laying their bedrolls, to thaw the ground and heat the soil enough to provide warmth for most of the night. More fires were built for cooking and additional warmth. Thus the day's travel was made easier by the knowledge that the night would be more comfortable.

When the snow finally quit, the cold settled in ever deeper. Night temperatures fell past forty below zero. More than once the mercury congealed into a solid button in the bulb of the thermometer. Though the surgeon was kept busy dealing with frostbite, there were no complaints of lung disorders.

"Too cold for bugs of any kind," Kincaid told Hall during a night meal. "You can snore as loud as you want and nothing will come in through your mouth."

Hall and Kincaid had spoken little since the night Hall had tried to desert. Hall had not slept near Kincaid and Morgan, but with each new camp had found a spot by one of the fires. This attempt by Kincaid to resume their friendship made Hall uneasy.

"What's the matter?" Kincaid asked. "Don't you know when a man is saying he's sorry?"

"Yes, I guess I do," Hall said, putting down his plate. "I just didn't figure that you'd pass judgment on me like that."

"Judgment? Hell, I was angry at your mule-headed stupidity," Kincaid said through a mouthful of beans. "Where'd you get the thought that you could make it back out of this country alone?"

"I would have made it."

"Didn't you figure to build no fires?"

"I guess I thought I could do without."

Kincaid laughed. "Even if the weather would've broke, there'd have come the time when you'd have built a fire, just to see the light of it and feel the warmth. Then the

Sioux would have found you and there'd be nothing left of you a'tall."

Kincaid turned away, but Hall was certain he had seen moisture in Kincaid's eyes. He hadn't realized how much Kincaid thought of him. Not being used to kindness of any kind, or even open to it, Hall hadn't recognized Kincaid's awkward attempts to befriend him.

"I just don't like what I'm doing here," Hall said. He used the tip of his fork to play with the beans. "I don't believe in this cause."

"You shot straight enough the other night."

"I thought he had a gun! I didn't know it was a coup stick. I was just trying to stay alive."

"What's done is done," Kincaid said. "You can't change it. And you can't run away from this, or you'll be running to your grave. You understand?"

Hall stared into the fire. "I guess it was a foolish thing to do. It just seemed like the only way out."

"Promise me you won't do that again."

"I'll wait until it warms up," Hall said with a smile.

Kincaid returned the smile. "You'll be waiting till you're older than me."

The Big Horn Expedition moved ever deeper into Indian hunting grounds along the Tongue River. Hall was so used to riding now that he felt himself part of the horse's back, although his leg ached from early morning until he wrapped himself in his buffalo robe next to the fire. He had begun to believe that Kincaid was right: the country was forever locked in ice and snow.

The days began to run into one another; the country remained rough and hard, the weather nearly unbearable. The rations had begun to dwindle, and if it hadn't been for the numbers of older bison found wintering in the draws, the food supplies might have become exhausted.

Though tough and stringy, the meat was welcomed without complaint.

Yet the suffering among the men increased. Despite plenty of wood and water, and warming the ground with fires, no one could ever get a good night's rest or a meal that filled and satisfied. Half the men were now missing fragments of skin from their lips and tongues, having forgetfully placed forks and spoons in their mouths before first thawing them out.

Meals were difficult to prepare. One of the cooks had broken an ax trying to chop frozen bacon, and the large kettles of water had to come to a boil before the beans would even begin to thaw.

Hall's thoughts went once again to his father, for they had entered a region where coal seams ran thick along the sides of the hills. "We're in Montana Territory," Kincaid had told him. "If we don't find them Sioux before long, we'll find ourselves on the Yellowstone. Then we might as well talk to our Maker, for there's no relief trains anywhere up there."

Grouard and the other scouts went out almost daily, returning each time with no certain leads. The men began to grumble that the Sioux and Cheyenne had all gone back to their reservations and that the Army had sent them out into this frozen hell for no reason.

"I'll have to agree with Grouard, the Sioux are out here," Kincaid said. "But it's a big country. It's hard to find them with just our bunch alone."

The men grumbled that the other two factions of the campaign, Terry's division from Fort Abraham Lincoln and Gibbon's division from Fort Ellis, had chosen not to march. Was Crook crazy, or what? Kincaid remarked that no one, not even Crook, could have forecast this type of cold in mid-March.

There was also the complaint that Crook was in direct

competition with other commanders for honors and commendations.

"The general's not about to be outdone," Kincaid commented. "He figures he can strike at the Sioux first, and maybe even push them back to the agencies. He'd like to have his name down for having stopped both the southern and northern Indian tribes. Then he'll want a star for each tribe he's fought. He'll be the first dozen-star general."

Hall found little humor in the observation. "How many men will lose their lives in this effort?" he asked Kincaid.

"As many as it takes," Kincaid said.

"And you don't care, as long as you get to drop some Sioux from their horses."

"I don't care if they're a-horseback or standing flat-footed," Kincaid said. "I'm just after Sioux."

"Why didn't you get this out of your system a long time ago?" Hall asked. "Why wait until you're this age?"

"I tried back in the mid-sixties, when the Bozeman Road opened up," Kincaid said. "But there wasn't a commander out here who knew a whit about fighting Indians, and none of them wanted to learn. A lot of men died because of that, and we never got close to the Sioux."

"Do you see it as any different now?" Hall asked.

"You could do a lot worse than to be under Crook's command," Kincaid said. "He listens to his scouts. He won't take the chances with his men that some others do."

Hall scoffed. "You're saying Crook's not taking a chance with eight hundred men out in this weather?"

"I'm talking about when it comes to leading men, and sending them into battle," Kincaid said. "There's one in particular you couldn't get me to work under for all the gold there is. Maybe you've heard the men talking about him. His name's Custer."

Hall had indeed heard the men talking about the lieutenant colonel they referred to as "Hard-ass" George Armstrong Custer.

All the men, no matter what company, had heard of Custer. He had made a name for himself in the Rebellion fighting for the Union, and had come out a brevet major general. Everyone knew he drove his men beyond any human limits, while he himself traveled with a private cook and other luxuries. There were some who had managed to transfer out of the Seventh Cavalry to get away from him.

Custer was a difficult man for his superior officers to control. But one thing the Army liked about him: he killed his enemies.

Yet Custer had a reputation for being just as harsh with his own men. Anyone under his command who spoke against him was in for a hard time, they said. Hall thought of Buckner and wondered how anyone could be worse than him. Apparently Custer was.

It was a well-known fact that, during a campaign against the Cheyenne in 1867, Custer had sent out an assassination party against a group of deserters. Begging for mercy or not, they had been shot.

"Custer is one who'd do anything," Kincaid continued. "It don't matter what the scouts say. They can warn him, but he don't listen. Crook's different. He sets things up first. He gets a lot of men together when he goes out. A man don't often get the chance to fight in a crowd this size. No one goes after the Sioux in small numbers. You would have learned that, had you managed to sneak off the other night."

Hall realized that Kincaid would never let him forget that he had tried to desert. Likely he would never forgive him, either. Men like Kincaid lived by an odd code of honor: You finish what you start, no matter how you find yourself there, no matter who forced you. When it's over, you forget about it and go ahead with life.

The following evening Grouard returned with news of an abandoned village not far ahead. The column made camp at the site, a broad bottom along the river where enormous cottonwoods grew. The trees were filled with Indian burial platforms arranged across the limbs, the bodies wrapped in blankets and robes, faces to the sky.

Hall and Kincaid sat next to a cookfire built near one of the cottonwoods. Enormous and old, the tree was dead but for a few branches near the top. Zack Morgan and a number of packers, together with a few soldiers, had gathered, waiting for their plates.

A gust of wind hit the fire and a flurry of burning sparks rose and flew in all directions. Hall and Kincaid piled away from the fire. One trooper began to scream as his coat caught fire. Kincaid and Hall helped him from the coat before he was seriously burned. Zack Morgan rubbed snow over the red blotches along the soldier's back.

Meanwhile a big trooper named Jess Blye laughed until he could barely stand.

"What do you find so funny?" Hall asked him.

"I aim to laugh at whatever I choose," Blye said, his small eyes narrowing in his puffy face.

"Maybe you'd like some coals down your neck," Hall suggested.

"You aim to try?" Blye asked. He spread his legs slightly and doubled his hands into huge fists.

"This should be fun," Hall said. "Not much of a challenge, but fun."

A ring of men formed. Kincaid took Hall by the arm. "Let it go. You won't do no good with the likes of him."

"Maybe he needs to learn some manners."

"Let it go," Kincaid insisted.

"Listen to him," Blye told Hall. "Keep yourself in good health."

Hall had decided to ignore Kincaid and was starting

toward Blye when Morgan yelled and pointed to the huge cottonwood. Flying embers had somehow gotten inside the hollow trunk, and flames were leaping into the sky from the top of the tree.

Everyone scattered as fragments of burning robes and weapons fell from the limbs into camp. Ribs and leg bones, and a number of skulls, fell from the tree.

Soon the tree was reduced to charred wood and ashes. The cookfire was put out and another one started a distance away.

"This is an old burial ground," Kincaid said, as everyone settled around the new fire. "They've used this place a long time. It makes my skin crawl. We shouldn't have camped here."

Blye still wanted to fight Hall. He glared across the fire and began to laugh at Kincaid.

"You just heard too many nighttime stories is all. You're too old for this kind of thing."

Kincaid said nothing. Morgan and the other packers merely stared at Blye. Kincaid put his hand on Hall's arm and held him down.

"Anyone want to get something started?" Blye asked, staring at Hall. He stood up and doubled his fists again.

Zack Morgan was younger than Kincaid, of medium height, and built like a bull. "You ain't big enough to stop all of us," he told Blye. "How'd you like to end up in this fire, nose first?"

Morgan stood up, as did the packers and even the other soldiers. Hall and Kincaid stood with them. Blye looked from man to man, then turned and left.

"There's a greenhorn for certain," Morgan said, dousing the fire. "And a bad one. Maybe we'd ought to educate him."

Kincaid and the others agreed. Morgan volunteered to

be the "teacher" and promised to rouse anyone who wanted to watch when the "lesson" was to begin.

Late into the night, Hall felt Kincaid shaking him.

"Come on, if you want to see this."

Hall sneaked quietly through camp with Kincaid and the others to where Private Blye was sleeping in his robes. They stood back while Morgan—wrapped in an old blanket, his face blackened with charcoal—bent over Blye and yelled into his ear. Blye awakened with a start and upon seeing something with a black face wrapped in a blanket, began to yell and kick his way out of his robes.

Morgan dropped his blanket and fell to the ground with laughter. Kincaid and the other packers clapped one another on the back and hooted.

By now a number of soldiers were sitting up, wondering at the commotion. Blye had recovered from his shock and was enraged. He began to kick Morgan in the ribs, and Kincaid hurried over to stop him.

"It was only a joke," Kincaid told him. "No need to get riled up."

"I don't find it funny," Blye snarled. "And you were a part of it." Blye swung and caught Kincaid a glancing blow across the forehead. Kincaid staggered back.

"Nobody meant you any harm," Hall said. "But you've been pushing for this."

"Come on, then!" Blye charged Hall and swung wildly. Hall ducked and landed a savage blow to the trooper's solar plexus. Blye doubled up and toppled to the ground, gasping for air.

Hall stood back, waiting for Blye to get up. The circle of soldiers began to break, and Sergeant Arlan Buckner appeared.

"That's enough!" Buckner yelled. "Hall, what are you doing beating up on that man?"

Hall had no chance to answer before Buckner went on: "You're a troublemaker! You—"

Kincaid interrupted. "I'm to blame for this," he said. "A few of us figured we'd have a little fun with Blye, that's all."

"It looks to me as if Private Hall is doing more than having a little fun," Buckner said. "I would say that he wants to kill him."

"Now, Sergeant," Morgan said, "that's really going too far."

Buckner turned on Morgan, his eyes flashing. "You listen to me, mule packer. You have no right interfering in regular Army business. You were hired to tend mules. I suggest you do that and keep your mouth shut." He turned back to Kincaid. "That goes for you as well. Understood?"

Kincaid and Morgan glared at Buckner. The circle again opened as Captain Egan and Colonel Reynolds approached.

After saluting, Buckner said quickly, "We have a problem here. It seems Private Hall is causing considerable trouble. I suggest he be placed under arrest."

"What say you, Hall?" Reynolds asked.

Hall had never talked to Reynolds before, and had never been near him but for that afternoon when Reynolds had been selecting horses back at Fort Fetterman. He knew that Reynolds now acted as the main commander of the campaign, directly under Crook. Reynolds had the power to make things very difficult.

"Well, I'm waiting," Reynolds said.

"I would say, sir, that a practical joke got out of hand," Hall said. "I'm sorry for the trouble."

Buckner leaned closer to Hall. "A practical joke?"

Reynolds cleared his throat. "Sergeant, if you will, I'm handling this."

Buckner bowed his head and took a step back. Reynolds stared at Hall. "Continue, Private Hall, if you will."

"It was thought, sir, that Private Blye needed to learn respect for the fighting ability of Indians," Hall said. "It was decided that he should understand how an Indian might sneak up on you if you were not careful."

Some of the men began to snicker. Reynolds cleared his throat again, and the snickering stopped.

"Did you play the part of the Indian?" Reynolds asked.

"No sir, but I thought the event quite funny. Private Blye's sense of humor is suffering from frostbite."

The men broke into laughter, but Blye was seething with anger. Buckner kept his head down, grinding his teeth.

Reynolds turned to Egan, who had been listening with a smile on his face.

"What do you think, Captain?"

"I think that Private Hall is telling the truth. We all know that Private Blye is a bit quick-tempered. I can see no real harm done."

"Very well," Reynolds said. He then addressed the men as a group. "I know it's been a trying campaign thus far. But we will meet the foe, and we will meet them soon. I suggest we all save our aggressions for that moment. Then we can go home with pride and dignity, and let civilization take its course."

Then Reynolds and Egan were gone. Hall started back to his bedroll with Kincaid and Morgan, but Buckner called from behind and insisted that Hall stand at attention.

"What is it, Sergeant?" Hall asked.

"I suppose you feel that you've won again, don't you?"

"Won?"

"Yes. You feel you've beaten me again. Isn't that true?"

"I'm in no competition with you, sir," Hall said. "There's nothing that I care to win."

"You just pulled a practical joke and got away with it," Buckner said. "I believe you're trying to test me."

Hall fought to hold his temper. "I told you before, Sergeant, things would be fine if we stayed away from one another. Can't we leave it at that?"

"I can't have you making me look like I can't control my troops," Buckner said. "Tonight was a mockery!"

Hall put his face in Buckner's. "This whole campaign is a mockery, Sergeant. Everything that's happened up to now has been insane. It won't get any better. The best thing for us to do is stay away from one another, and get through it. Otherwise, one of us is going to die."

"Are you threatening me, Hall?"

"I'm telling you a simple truth, Sergeant. You'd better think about it. You see, you're tied up with this army. It's your whole life. Me, I don't care one way or the other. That gives me the edge."

Hall stared, and Buckner took a step back. A gust of wind blew snow through the camp. Hall smiled and said, "I'm going back to bed and dream of ways to get rid of you, Sergeant. Why don't you do the same? Maybe soon we can see which one of us had the best dreams."

TWELVE

Crazy Horse stood with Ghostwind at the edge of the Cheyenne village, watching Young Horse bring the two ponies he had given Kicks-the-Fox. Young Horse rode Hail Stone, the red pinto pony, and led Big Spot, the black-and-white pinto, behind him. Because Kicks-the-Fox had been killed, the horses were to be returned to Crazy Horse.

As he watched, Crazy Horse remembered the many times he had raced the ponies after buffalo and had ridden them proudly into battle. Of the two ponies, Hail Stone was the best he had ever ridden. Before giving it to Kicks-the-Fox, he had rarely been without the horse.

As Young Horse drew nearer, Crazy Horse smiled. "He rides Hail Stone as if he had been born on him."

"Yes," Ghostwind said. "Young Horse has been caring for both ponies daily. He waters them in the morning and feeds them cottonwood bark, then watches them as they roam the hills. He's never home. He wanted your ponies to stay in the best possible condition."

Though he was too young to become a regular horse

tender, Young Horse had insisted that he be responsible for both ponies. He had even fought an older boy to show his determination. Though he had lost the fight, he had gained respect from the regular horse tenders. One had told Young Horse that he could enter one of their honor societies in two winters, something many older horse tenders would never achieve.

Young Horse got down from Hail Stone and handed the halter ropes of both horses to Crazy Horse. He blinked back tears. "My father has gone to the Spirit World. He did not wish to take these ponies with him, so they are yours again."

Crazy Horse took the halter ropes. "Thank you, Young Horse. Now that you have returned them, I wish to give them back, as a present to you this time."

Young Horse's mouth dropped. "You're giving them to me?"

"Would you like to have them?"

Young Horse thought a moment. "I can't ride two at once. I'll keep Big Spot and you take Hail Stone. I know he's your favorite."

Crazy Horse smiled. "Thank you. You've given me back my best pony. But I know you will be happy with Big Spot."

"Big Spot is a fine horse," Young Horse said. "I will water him morning and night and see that he stays fat. No one is happier than me."

"You're a fine young man," Crazy Horse said.

Young Horse smiled. "I know that you give many things to others. I want to do that when I'm grown."

Crazy Horse took a small feather from under his blanket and handed it to Young Horse. "This is from a hawk just before it left the nest. Wear it in your hair."

Young Horse's eyes enlarged until it seemed they would burst from their sockets. "For me?"

"You have the heart of a warrior," Crazy Horse said.

"You can give to others freely. Some day you'll have many different feathers, and you will hold a place of honor among your people."

"You don't know how happy you have made me!" Young Horse said. "Thank you!"

"You're welcome," Crazy Horse said. "You're a son that any man would be proud of."

"Go now and show your grandparents," Ghostwind said. "I'll be along soon."

Young Horse jumped on Big Spot and rode off at a gallop, whooping and yelling. Crazy Horse patted Hail Stone's neck. "He has eaten well," he told Ghostwind. "Young Horse has done very well by him."

Ghostwind smiled. "You know how he feels. It isn't every day that a boy gets to care for ponies that Crazy Horse once rode."

"You have a fine son," Crazy Horse said. "It's too bad your husband couldn't see him become a warrior."

"My husband died with a heavy heart," Ghostwind said. "He felt very bad about his words to you. He wished he had never said them."

"I can understand why he became angry on the hill," Crazy Horse said. "It must have looked as if I wanted you. I wish it hadn't happened. I only wish he was still in this world."

"Things happen that we cannot explain," Ghostwind said. "No one will ever understand the ways of the Great Mystery."

"Your words are very true," Crazy Horse said. "But at least there will be no mystery in the hunt up on the Yellowstone. Thanks to your son, my pony is fat. I will make many kills."

Crazy Horse and a number of warriors had come from downriver to visit He Dog and the Oglala who were camped as guests of the Northern Cheyenne. As the weather had remained open, there was continuous talk of the upcoming hunt. All had cleaned their guns and sharpened their arrows in anticipation.

There was talk that a group of frontiersmen, Long Knives who had once hunted the beaver, were bringing more guns and ammunition from Sitting Bull's village. They had brought horses into Three Stars Crook's fort to the south and had gotten money. Then they had bought rifles and bullets at the trading posts in the Black Hills.

White men who had married Indian women were living in various camps among the Lakota, and even among some of the other Cheyenne bands. These men were helping to fortify the Indian people against the Bluecoats. The Lakota people already had many guns with much ammunition. The Cheyenne had some, and would be getting more before long. No one wanted to use the guns for anything but hunting, but those whites with Indian wives said they knew the Bluecoats all too well.

Most of the powder and pig lead in the Cheyenne village had come from trading. Both the Lakota and Cheyenne people had learned how to make bullets over the years from traders and Long Knives. Everyone hoped that there would be no fighting. That way there would be ammunition enough for many hunts.

Everyone's mind was on reaching the Elk River. Though herds usually stayed in one place longer during the cold moons, it was possible that once the weather broke they would move again. There was already a good supply of meat in all the camps, but a large herd of buffalo so close offered added security against hunger once the people returned to the agencies. Hunting songs and dances had already been offered. Everyone was ready, but the deep cold had yet to lift.

"The seer who spoke of change is still certain the warm

winds will come," Crazy Horse told Ghostwind, "but the Cold Maker has a strong fist."

Though the snow crunched underfoot and their breath fogged heavily, Crazy Horse seemed comfortable in his red blanket with a buckskin top and leggings underneath. His high-topped moccasins reached no higher than his ankles and were no thicker than those he wore in warmer weather.

Ghostwind, like everyone else, wore heavy furs. "The weather does not concern you," she said, "but I believe the Bluecoats do."

Crazy Horse looked to the south. "It is said they have gone back to their fort. But who knows this for certain? Everyone is preparing for the hunt. No one has been out to look around."

"It would be foolish for them to ride such a long way in this weather," Ghostwind said. "It would take a lot of wood for fires, and a lot of food."

"The Bluecoat leaders do not care about their men," Crazy Horse said. "The *Wasichu* as a people think only of themselves and how they can gain by using one another."

Ghostwind had heard others say the same thing about the whites. Each time she would wonder about her childhood. No one seemed to think she was being insulted, though; and Ghostwind had no reason to think she was. She still had no conscious memories of her white parent.

Still, there were people in the village who, after all these winters, wondered about the white blood in her and the way she had come to them. There were those, mostly elders, who would never forget that day, and who still looked at her strangely, as if wondering whether she was really a human being.

But most of them considered her to be like them, one of *Maheo*'s people, a Northern Cheyenne, true to her native blood. And a good many thought of her as very special, someone with strength who would be needed one day when the people's spirit was tested greatly.

Crazy Horse continued to speak of the Bluecoats and of the various leaders who had come over time into the buffalo grounds to fight his people. He saw them all as brazen and ignorant of either honor or Indian ways. One commander in particular struck him as the worst. Though he had not yet faced Long Hair Custer in battle, he had heard much about this Bluecoat from other Lakota people and from the Cheyenne.

"If there is any one leader to whom I will not give my respect, it is the man called Long Hair," he said. "I know from my Cheyenne brothers that he is a man who cares about nothing, not even himself."

Ghostwind wondered at Crazy Horse's observation.

"How can a man not care about himself?" she asked.

"Any man who treats those who fight with him like so much dirt cannot care about himself," Crazy Horse explained. "A leader must respect everyone. He must rely on those who fight beside him for support. He who cares nothing about his men will have no support in the end."

"But they all do what he says," Ghostwind said, remembering how the Bluecoat soldiers had followed Long Hair through the winter cold to Black Kettle's village on the Washita. "They all follow him into battle."

"They follow him out of fear, not out of respect," Crazy Horse pointed out. "The Bluecoats fight differently from our people. They're told they must fight, and are then told how to fight. Though we encourage it, we've never forced any of our men to fight. Theirs is a personal choice."

"Are you saying that the Bluecoats are told to fight, that they aren't out here because they seek honor?"

"Honor among the Bluecoats goes only to the leaders," Crazy Horse replied. "The leaders tell those under them what they must do. Each one of our warriors fights in his own way, according to his own medicine. The Bluecoats must listen to those who lead them, even if they know inside that it's wrong. A Bluecoat will even die without honor."

Ghostwind noticed that Crazy Horse did not say that all Bluecoats and their leaders were without honor. She knew there was a single Bluecoat leader whom he respected.

"I say these things about the Bluecoats and about the *Wasichu* people as a whole, yet the chief called Three Stars Crook, the Gray Fox with the red beard, isn't like any other," Crazy Horse continued. "His word, among all of them, is the only one to be trusted. If he says he will do something, he will. If he says he won't, then you know he won't. Still, he wants to claim victory over our people, and it will be he who pushes the hardest."

"Three Stars is the leader of those who are coming?" Ghostwind asked.

"Yes, he's the best Bluecoat leader. He will stop at nothing."

"If he has honor, why would he want to lead his fighters in this weather?"

"Because he knows our people will not think he would do this," Crazy Horse said. Then he smiled. "I heard you say that he *is* coming. So you believe, like me, that he did not go back to the fort?"

"I know he did not go back. I saw many Bluecoats in a vision the night you spoke to our people. After you went to your village, I joined the ceremony for the raiders. It was then that I knew my husband would die, as would others. But I don't know when."

"Three Stars is coming for us. He is coming for me. He has no quarrel with your people."

"I do not believe he knows the difference," Ghostwind said.

"But The Grabber does," Crazy Horse said. "The one named Grouard, you know of him?"

"Yes, I've heard much talk of this man. I know of no one who likes him."

"It's The Grabber who works hard to find my village," Crazy Horse continued. "He doesn't care about anyone but me. He'll know when he's found a Lakota village, and then the fighting will begin."

"Would Three Stars come if he didn't have The Grabber with him?"

"Three Stars has other scouts with him," Crazy Horse replied. "They are all good trackers, but it's The Grabber who wants badly to find me. He wishes to see me dead."

Ghostwind stared at Crazy Horse. "But it will not be so. I do not feel death coming for you."

"That is good to know," Crazy Horse said. "I feel I must help my people through the difficult times to come."

Ghostwind turned her face to the southwest, feeling a slight change in wind direction. She saw that Crazy Horse felt it also. Within a day, the cold would break up.

Crazy Horse turned his face into the wind that was developing and held up his hand to feel it. "I, like you, fear for our people. There was a time when the Bluecoats would come to council and would listen to talk. I believe those times are gone now. The Bluecoats want to fight. Among my people and yours as well, many innocents will die."

"You want to know how the general can shoot?" Captain Egan asked Hall. "You just watch."

It was late afternoon. The column had camped at the mouth of Pumpkin Creek, a major tributary of the Tongue River. Grouard had taken half the guides with him to the Yellowstone the previous morning and would return to meet Crook and the command the following day. A wind that Kincaid called a chinook had begun at midday and was blowing from the southwest, bringing the temperature well above zero.

"You see where those pin-tailed grouse just landed?" Egan continued, pointing to a small knoll. "The general will ease over there from downwind and you'll see some marksmanship."

Hall watched while Crook dismounted from his mule and stepped lightly toward the knoll. The grouse rose, and Crook opened fire. Remarkably, he shot three times and downed three before the grouse flew out of range. Nearby another covey rose and the general emptied his rifle, shooting four more times. Three more birds fell.

"Did you ever see anyone shoot that well before?" Egan asked Hall.

Hall knew that at one time in his life he could have done so. He wasn't certain about it now, after being out of practice in prison.

"No," Hall told Egan, "I can't say that I have. That was truly remarkable."

"Had it been warm weather," Egan concluded, "he wouldn't have missed a one."

During the evening meal, Kincaid told Hall that word was going around that Crook had shot six out of seven grouse, all from one covey.

"I can't believe a man could shoot that fast, even if they were to stay in range," Kincaid said. "You were up front. Did you see it?"

"I saw it," Hall told him. "He shot six birds, but from two different coveys. Still fine shooting."

"Very fine," Kincaid said. "I've heard stories about the general's skill, but I'd never heard that even he could down six birds at once."

Hall finished his meal thinking about the general. Crook seemed to relish his role as an outdoorsman.

It seemed to Hall that Crook might secretly wish to be one of the scouts rather than the commander. The general preferred the company of Grouard and the others to that of the enlisted men and stared with envy at the deer and antelope they frequently brought in. It seemed to Hall that Crook enjoyed hunting above most other pastimes. He wondered if the general felt any different when he had Indian warriors in his sights.

Everyone slept well that night, owing to the rise in temperature, and they were allowed to sleep until well after dawn. Grouard and the other scouts had still not returned by midmorning. Everyone rested and explored the surrounding area.

A short way downriver lay another abandoned village. There Hall got his introduction to the ways of warring Indians. A flock of magpies burst from a large cottonwood, where they had been feeding on something. As he drew closer Hall saw that it was the remains of a warrior. The detached arms and legs hung from the branches, and the head had been tied to a limb by the hair. The trunk, devoid of internal organs, was impaled upside down on a branch near the ground.

"Though it's hard to tell, I'd say he was a Crow," Kincaid told Hall. "The Crow and Sioux and Cheyenne all hunt this area. The Crow aren't friends with either of the other two. Like as not he was trying to steal horses."

Hall studied the remains. It appeared the captors had not been content with merely cutting him up. They had shot the fingers off his hands and had filled his arms and legs with bullet holes. An arrow hung from each eye socket, and the sexual organs, or what remained of them, had been stuffed into his mouth.

"Do they normally do that kind of thing to a body?" Hall asked.

"That might have happened before he was dead," Kincaid replied.

Hall stared. "Not a good joke."

"Nobody's joking," Kincaid said. "You get caught by the Sioux, you're apt to be cut up."

"Do they do that to all their captives?" Hall asked.

Kincaid laughed. "Just the lucky ones."

The camp hadn't been abandoned long; two horses and a mule were wandering in the hills nearby, left behind. Hall followed Kincaid around the area.

Kincaid said that this particular campsite was used often, as evidenced by the numerous paintings on the inner bark of the cottonwoods. The designs in yellow, red and black depicted various hunting and war feats by both Sioux and Cheyenne warriors.

"The two tribes are pretty close," Kincaid said. "They hunt and have ceremonies, and even go to war together. They don't fight just the Crow, but the Blackfeet and the Assiniboine to the north, and the Shoshone to the south and west. And to the east there's the Pawnee. The Sioux and Cheyenne have got nobody but each other."

Hall studied one of the drawings. "You mean they fight against every other tribe?"

"And every other tribe fights them. It's been that way for a long time, since the horse came. And that goes back awhile, from what I hear."

Kincaid started up out of the bottom. Hall followed him, trying to envision a man on foot, keeping up with the game, and couldn't make himself believe anyone could survive. He said as much.

"I've heard stories from the Shoshone," Kincaid said, stopping on a hilltop that overlooked the country. "Their people go back a long time without horses. When they first saw one, they thought they were seeing an elk-dog." He laughed and sat down. "They ate them before they started riding them. I don't know if they traded for them, or what. They came from the south, as I remember the stories. The Spaniards brought them in, and the southern Indians

started using them. Then the northern tribes started stealing them. That's what the Shoshone told me. That's how
the tribal fighting really got started."

Again Hall lost himself trying to imagine how these
Indians could have lived so long without horses. He looked
across the country and said, "It seems to me that if all these
tribes out here ever quit fighting each other and got together, the U.S. Army wouldn't have a chance. Everyone
would just have to stay out of here. Forever."

"You sound as if you think that wouldn't be a bad
idea," Kincaid said.

Hall shrugged. "A lot worse could happen than leaving
this country alone."

"It's too late for that," Kincaid said. "When your pa and
I came out here for beaver, it was already too late. Others
had been here, and they went back to the States and told
everybody else. This was bound to happen. Can't say as I
like it, but a man can't stop it."

"Didn't you say that men like my father are living with
the Indians, fighting against soldiers?"

"It won't make a difference," Kincaid said. "They'd best
get out of the way."

"What would you do if you met my father on a battlefield?" Hall asked. "Would you shoot him?"

"I've thought of that," Kincaid said. "I told you, I'm
after Sioux. I don't hanker to shoot my own kind."

"What if he shot at you?"

"He wouldn't."

"Why not? If you're with soldiers, why wouldn't he
shoot at you?"

"We go back a long time," Kincaid argued. "We're not
about to take sides against one another now."

"But don't you see? You already have," Hall said. "If
you follow Crook into a Sioux village, and my father's

there, he'll fight to protect himself and his family. Maybe he won't look where he's shooting."

Kincaid studied an arrowhead he had found near one boot. "Maybe you're right. Maybe we'd just open fire on one another. After all, he's married to a Sioux woman, and my wife and son were Shoshone. I guess we took sides then. And how about you?"

"I'd try and tell him who I was," Hall said. "I've been thinking. Even though I'm angry that he left me behind, I don't want us shooting each other."

"How are you going to let him know who you are?" Kincaid asked. "You don't speak Sioux."

"I've seen Grouard and the scouts talking with their hands," Hall said. "I guess it's called sign language."

"Sign talk," Kincaid said. "Most Indians use it outside of the village, so as not to make any noise."

"I've seen you use it, too," Hall said.

Kincaid laughed. "You want me to teach you, is that it?"

"Yes, if you would," Hall said.

"It's not something you pick up in a day or two."

"I know that," Hall said. "I could pay you something."

"I'm not asking for pay," Kincaid said. "I want you to know it won't stop what could happen in a fight. There's not a lot of time to use sign if you're shooting a gun."

"Maybe not," Hall said. "But at least I'd feel better knowing I could try to talk. I may never see him again, but at least I want him to know that I made it out here, whether he brought me or not."

"That's really important to you, isn't it?" Kincaid said. "You've got to prove a point to him."

"He should've brought me out a long time ago," Hall said. "Maybe then things would be different."

THIRTEEN

Grouard and the other scouts returned in late afternoon with a half-dozen deer and news that there had been a hunt somewhere to the north and east along the lower Yellowstone. The scouts had seen considerable dust, no doubt from stampeding buffalo. All trails and signs they had crossed showed that the villages were along the Powder and not the Tongue.

Storm clouds blotted the setting sun from view, and a cold wind brought snowfall into camp. Hall ate in silence, while Kincaid and the other packers argued about Crook's next move. They all agreed he would take the column west, but how could he maneuver without detection?

"We can't just ride over to the Powder and not expect to be seen," Zack Morgan said, chewing a piece of fried bread. "I can't figure why they ain't tailing us now."

"They have to think we've given up and gone home," another packer said. "I'd bet we get into a row with them before another sundown."

"You've got to figure they'll put us to the test," Kincaid said. "With guns and meat, they'll be hard to beat."

Morgan noticed Hall listening intently. "For a fighter like you," he said, "you've sure got a sour face."

"He didn't care for the looks of that Crow we found today," Kincaid said.

Hall had seen men die more often than he cared to, but Kincaid was right. "That's a terrible way to die," he said. "His screams must have echoed up and down this river."

"I doubt he uttered a sound," Kincaid said. "Most of them take whatever's given without so much as a flinch."

"Is that your idea of a joke?" Hall asked.

"No joke," Kincaid replied. "When I lived with the Shoshone, they did the same thing to captives. I saw them cut open a Blackfoot once and jam a burning stick into his paunch. His eyes rolled plenty, but he never so much as whimpered."

The other packers then shared stories of their own experiences watching torture. Women and children often tormented a captive enemy with rocks and pointed sticks. If the captive showed any sign of discomfort, the treatment got worse, and the death was slow and calculated. On the other hand, if a captive said nothing and took pain without flinching, his death was usually quick. On occasion he was even granted his freedom.

Kincaid explained that warring Indians did not want their dead enemies coming back to haunt them. An Indian's view of the afterlife included the use of everything that was afforded him in this life, everything that he used in love and war. If the weapons were destroyed and the body mutilated before the final departure of the spirit, the chances were good that the warrior wouldn't enjoy himself in the next world, nor could he come back to exact revenge.

"I still feel sorry for that Crow," Hall said. "I think I'd rather hang."

Morgan dipped his bread into the last of his beans.

"That the first time you ever saw a man butchered like that? Better get used to it."

"How could anybody get used to that?" Hall asked.

"He's right," Kincaid said. "We should think a whole lot more about how we'd feel if it was one of us."

The other packers laughed. One of them said, "Kincaid's afraid they'll laugh at his witzel."

"Yeah, Kincaid," Morgan added, "you don't have to worry. If they looked in your pants, they wouldn't find near enough to stick up your nose, let alone stuff into your mouth. They'd feel sorry for you and send you on your way."

The laughter continued. The packers began to brag on their endowments, and how they had made women everywhere moan with delight. Hall quickly tired of hearing all the alleged commendations from dance-hall girls and hog-ranch beauties.

As Hall crawled under his robe, he wondered how the Crow warrior had reacted to being caught, and what it must be like to be butchered alive. He couldn't imagine taking that kind of torture stoically.

Hall didn't sleep well that night. He tossed and turned while odd and scrambled visions flashed through his mind.

Suddenly he saw himself in another world, standing alone in the vast open below the mountains, surrounded by a large ring of mounted warriors. It was late summer, and a curiously mottled sunset flamed the sky behind the peaks, streaks of scarlet swimming like enormous snakes in a darkening sea.

Hall looked around him. The warriors rode in single file, the dust from their ponies' hooves swirling in small whirlwinds above them. He tried to move. Nothing but his head felt alive. His arms hung like lead and his feet held fast to the sod, planted as firmly as the bunchgrass that topped his knees.

The warriors ran their horses around him, closing in, waving weapons and screaming from faces alive with glistening paint. He saw that besides a weapon, each warrior carried a human body part, taken from a freshly killed victim.

"No!" Hall screamed. But the sound was a dull echo within his head.

The warriors closed in and slowed their ponies. One of them, painted entirely in red and black, rode toward him from the circle on a blue horse and thrust a severed head into his face. Hall gasped. He couldn't move. The head was upon him, the dark hair tangled and matted, the mouth gaping. Hall couldn't turn away. The lids were open, the eyes rolled back in their sockets.

"Pray to your God for him," the warrior commanded, and rode off.

Hall choked with horror. Another warrior, painted blue and white, was approaching, holding another head. Hall tried to close his eyes, but the lids stayed open. He could not turn his head, or his body. He would have to watch.

The dead man's hair was red this time, the eyes and the mouth grotesque. The warrior said the same thing: "Pray to your God for him."

A third warrior arrived, painted entirely in dark yellow, his eyes and mouth ringed with black. Hall forced his eyes closed and breathed a sigh of relief. He would see no more of this horror.

But his respite was short-lived. With his lids closed, his eyes burned like fire. Only when he opened his eyes did the pain stop. He had no choice. He would have to watch.

The yellow warrior approached in a different manner from the other two. Instead of coming straight on, he rode in a zigzag, the other warriors chanting behind him. The head he carried was much larger than the other two, and covered with hair the same color as the warrior. The head began to spin in circles as the warrior drew ever closer.

"Stop!" Hall cried. The echo was a dull thud within his mind.

The warrior was upon him, the head spinning. Hall stared. The yellow hair flew from the head, leaving an exposed skull covered with blood and gore. The head suddenly quit spinning and Hall screamed within his mind.

Staring out at him from the head were the largest eyes he had ever seen, grayish blue, the pupils burning like gleaming black coals.

The eyes were nearly touching him when Hall awakened and sat up. Kincaid and Morgan were sleeping soundly, as was the rest of the camp. The storm had passed and the sky was deep and dark, glistening with stars, nothing like the scarlet horror of his nightmare sundown. It had seemed so real that he still couldn't believe he wasn't there.

Hall lay back down but could not shake the strange, gut-churning feeling left by the dream. He rose and walked toward a large cottonwood at the edge of camp, wretchedness gnawing at him. He raised his arms to the sky and kicked his legs freely. He closed his eyes, feeling no burning pain.

Hall ran his fingers over the cottonwood's huge trunk. It felt rough and cool. Somehow, it soothed him. He placed both hands on the bark and closed his eyes. The power of the tree coursed through him, and he knew that what he had seen in his dream had, in some unexplainable way, been just as real as what he was now feeling.

He realized that he had received some form of communication. Something had spoken to him in a way both strange and mysterious. He had no way of understanding it. Though he had dreamed all his life, and usually thought little of it, he knew the mystery would bother him until he could understand the vision's meaning.

Feeling utterly drained, Hall started back to his bedroll. From the large cottonwood behind him came a low hooting sound. Hall turned and looked up. At first he could see nothing. He shifted position and found a huge bird silhouetted in front of the moon. The bird hooted again. It was an owl.

Hall stared. The strange feeling of his dream returned, rising from deep within, bringing a primordial fear that overwhelmed him. The owl took wing and sailed directly over him and along the edge of camp, huge and white, floating out into the darkness without a sound.

After returning to his bedroll, Hall was afraid to close his eyes. The feeling he now had was worse than when he had first awakened from his dream. He realized the owl must have something to do with the nightmare. He felt he needed to know immediately. This couldn't last until morning. He shook Kincaid.

Grumbling, Kincaid asked him what he wanted.

"What do owls mean to Indians?" he asked.

"Owls?" Kincaid was groggy, talking though still half asleep. "Owls what?"

"I want to know what an Indian would think if he saw an owl."

"Owls are bad medicine."

"Bad medicine?"

Kincaid was almost asleep again. "Death. Owls mean death."

Hall lay back in his bed. What he had seen in his dream was certainly death, in the most horrible fashion imaginable. He wished he had waited until morning to ask Kincaid. Now he was afraid to close his eyes for fear they might not open again.

The hunters had been straggling in since sunrise, their ponies laden with meat and hides. The weather wasn't as mild as the day they had left, but it still seemed almost balmy compared to the earlier deep cold. The women who had gone along to butcher were already hanging meat over hot coils to cook, singing and laughing among themselves.

Crazy Horse was now downriver with his people. Their hunt had also been very good. He Dog had remained with the Oglala to wait until their meat was ready to pack. Then they would rejoin Crazy Horse and the others. In the meanwhile, there would be much visiting and sharing of good fortune back and forth between the Oglala and the Cheyenne.

With no lodge and no husband to hunt for her, Ghostwind had stayed behind. She would have to rely on donations from others, something she had no concern about. Her father had gone, as had the medicine man, Horned Bull, and both would give her more than enough meat to last her through the remainder of the cold moons.

It wasn't the meat that worried Ghostwind, for she knew her people now had more than enough to sustain them. She felt that no amount of food would do any good if the people fell to Bluecoat rifles.

During the nights the hunters had been gone, she had prayed on the hill, burning a fire of sacred sage, watching the smoke as it spiraled skyward. Always the smoke rose straight up, becoming lost in the vastness overhead. The big white owls had not returned, but she knew they were somewhere nearby, watching her and waiting for the right time to speak to her again.

Besides her concern over the Bluecoats, she had been worrying a great deal about Young Horse and Talking Grass. The children hadn't adjusted to living without her. They loved their grandparents dearly, and liked the others who took them in on occasion, but the changes brought about by the loss of their father had been difficult for them.

Even today, as the hunters continued to come into

camp, Young Horse and Talking Grass showed no excitement. Try as she might, Ghostwind couldn't get them to join their friends and have some fun. They weren't acting like children anymore.

Ghostwind took them up on the hill and built a sage fire. After they had begun to turn pieces of fresh buffalo meat over the flames, Ghostwind spoke.

"Are you not grateful for the fresh meat?" she asked them.

"This is the first time Father has not been with us after a hunt," Young Horse said. "It doesn't feel right."

"I can understand that," Ghostwind said. "But your father wouldn't want you to die along with him."

Young Horse and Talking Grass cooked their meat in silence.

"What can I do to help you both learn what happiness is again?" she asked. "You act as if the world has ended."

"It might as well have," Young Horse said. "Everything is changed."

"Do you expect things to remain the same?" Ghostwind asked. "Have you not been told by your grandparents and the elders that nothing remains the same, just the earth and sky?"

Talking Grass leaned into her mother's arms and began to cry. "I miss Father. I miss him a lot."

"I know you do, my child," Ghostwind said. "But we know he is still with us when we want him. All we have to do is think of him and we can see him in our minds."

"But I want him to hold me, as he did when he was alive," Talking Grass said.

"And I want him to take me riding, and hunting, as he promised," Young Horse added.

"Those things are no longer possible," Ghostwind told them. "You can dream about it, but you can't make it happen as it once did."

"Didn't he want to be with us any longer?" Talking Grass asked. "Did I make him angry in some way?"

"No, of course not," Ghostwind said. "Neither you nor Young Horse made him angry in any way. Please, don't think it was your fault. *Maheo* wanted your father to be in the Other World. It had nothing to do with either of you."

"I don't want *Maheo* to have him," Young Horse said, tightening with anger. "It isn't fair. I want my father to be with me."

"That is not for us to decide," Ghostwind said. "What happens is not up to us. Things do not remain the same."

Young Horse became angrier. "Maybe things would be the same if it hadn't been for that night up here on the hill."

"What do you mean?" Ghostwind asked.

"You know what I mean," Young Horse said. "You and Crazy Horse were together. That made Father angry and he ran away. Then he died."

Stunned, Ghostwind told him, "That night had nothing to do with your father's death."

"I don't believe you," Young Horse said. "Maybe he wouldn't have gone with the raiders if he didn't think you wanted to be with Crazy Horse."

"Oh, Young Horse, I loved your father, you know that. Crazy Horse just came to talk, that's all."

Tears filled Young Horse's eyes. He threw down his meat stick and ran down the hill toward the village, with Ghostwind calling after him. He would not stop, but ran as fast as he could. He fell twice, sliding a good distance the second time. But he did not let that stop him. When he got to the bottom, he ran to his grandmother's lodge.

Talking Grass cried all the way down the hill. Ghostwind carried her, trying without effect to soothe her. By the time they reached the bottom, Ghostwind's cheeks were also wet with tears.

Mountain Water met Ghostwind at the doorflap. "He's very upset and won't listen to you, no matter what you say. I'll talk to him and take care of him, as well as Talking Grass."

Shattered, Ghostwind left Young Horse and Talking Grass with her mother and returned to the hill. She placed more sage wood on the fire, praying for her children. She would not speak to anyone, not even Day Lily, who walked up the hill twice to comfort her. *"Maheo* is angry with me," she told Day Lily. "He must be. Everything is going wrong. I must spend time in prayer. I must be alone."

Ghostwind did not care that the Cheyenne band from the agency had arrived, nor did she care that a feast was being offered in their honor. She continued to pray over her fire long into the night.

Near dawn, the wind changed and a frigid breeze began to blow from the northeast. *Hoimaha,* Winter Man, would soon return. In late morning, Day Lily came up with exciting news: Ghostwind's children wanted to see her.

"Young Horse told me he feels bad for the things he said," Day Lily told Ghostwind. "He says he no longer feels worthy to come upon the sacred hill to be with you. But he hopes you will come be with him and Talking Grass."

Ghostwind's eyes filled with tears. "When is he going to learn that he's not to blame?"

Ghostwind and Day Lily hurried down the hill. At the same time, ten more lodges of Lakota arrived in camp to visit and celebrate the great hunt. They were Unkpapa, from Sitting Bull's camp.

Day Lily waved gleefully to an older woman who had once been married to her uncle, before he was killed in a battle with Bluecoats at the foot of the Big Horn Mountains. Now she was married to an older Long Knife, one of the white men who had come out many winters past to trap beaver.

Though Ghostwind was anxious to see her children, she agreed to meet Day Lily's aunt out of courtesy. She would talk a short while and leave to see her children. However, she was not eager to have anything to do with the Long Knife.

"I cannot feel anything but anger in my heart for anyone with white skin," Ghostwind said.

Day Lily explained that the Long Knife was not like other whites, but supported the Indian cause. He often sold horses to the Bluecoats to get money, and then bought rifles and ammunition for the Lakota people.

"He wishes to see the Bluecoats driven away," Day Lily said. "He and my aunt have a child together, a boy not much older than Young Horse, who stayed back in Crazy Horse's camp with friends. And they lost an older son in a fight with the Bluecoats. This man's blood no longer runs white, but has changed to Lakota blood."

Day Lily's aunt, a short, round woman named Pine Woman, hugged Day Lily and met Ghostwind with a broad smile. "I have heard about you from Day Lily, and also from others," she told Ghostwind. "You are the prophet woman of the Cheyenne people who speaks to owls, yet is not harmed by them." She touched Ghostwind lightly and laughed. "My hand doesn't go through you, and you didn't bite me. You are nicer than Day Lily said you were."

Ghostwind smiled. "It's good that you came to our village. I hope you can visit for a good long time."

"We had intended to go back in a few days," Pine Woman said. "If it is cold and snowing, we will stay."

Pine Woman then introduced Ghostwind to her husband. The Lakota called him Shot-in-the-Throat.

The Long Knife, dressed in furs, stood as tall as most of the warriors. Over his long, graying hair he wore a cap made of ermine skins, the black-tipped tails hanging down the sides and back. His blue eyes sparkled in his slim face, and when he greeted Ghostwind he spoke in sign language, for he was mute.

"It's good to meet you," his motions told Ghostwind. "Like my wife, I've heard a lot about you. I'm glad to visit your people and celebrate the hunt."

"You are welcome here," Ghostwind told him. She felt guilty, for she didn't mean it, and wondered if he could tell by the hesitation in her hand movements. "There's plenty of meat for everyone."

Ghostwind excused herself. She would return to Day Lily's lodge when she had spoken with Young Horse and Talking Grass. It was important that she spend as much time with her children as possible now, especially since many changes were coming.

She felt encouraged that Young Horse had gotten rid of some anger. Perhaps he could now be himself again. As she approached her mother's lodge, she turned her face against the cold breeze coming in from the northeast. Snow and bitter cold would certainly be back.

With so many things on her mind, Ghostwind had not completely doused her fire up on the hill. She would always remember the night when Crazy Horse had come to talk, but she had forgotten the voice that had spoken through Young Horse. She had certainly forgotten the warning.

Now her fire burned brightly, and the warning showed plain in the cold afternoon air. Though no additional wood had been added, a thick column of smoke curved out in a strange pattern like thick strands of dark rope, twisting in a northerly direction, directly into the wind. Just above the smoke line a snowy owl flew northward, on a direct and silent course toward a distant camping site far down the Powder River.

FOURTEEN

Hall turned his face from the blustering wind and snow that slashed along the rocky slopes. The deep cold had returned, and after nearly twenty-four hours in the saddle, he felt like screaming. The country was far rougher than any they had previously crossed and his arms and shoulders ached from pushing himself up in the saddle, trying to relieve the pressure against his throbbing leg.

Hall thought back on the previous morning and wondered how their fortunes could have changed so quickly and so dramatically. Everyone had been looking forward to St. Patrick's Day, when they would have substituted remnants of deer and antelope for corned beef. Instead, with the coming dawn, they would be engaging in the first action of the campaign.

Late the previous afternoon, Big Bat Pourier had spotted two young warriors watching the column from a high hill. They would have gone undetected, but Pourier had noticed the erratic flight of a raven over the warriors' position and had spotted them hiding in a stand of yellow pine.

Crook had ordered the column to advance, to make the

two warriors believe it was going on to the Yellowstone. Near sundown, however, Crook gave Reynolds orders to take six companies of cavalry and ride behind Grouard and the scouts as they tracked the two warriors back to their village. He allowed the news correspondent, Robert Strahorn, to accompany them. The general wanted all possible documentation of their success. He himself would advance with the pack train and the remaining four companies to a rendezvous point at the mouth of Lodge Pole Creek and wait for Reynolds.

Kincaid had been furious at being left behind with the pack train. Hall would have eagerly given him his uniform in return for a chance to wrap himself in his buffalo robe. Now there would be no stopping until the battle was finished, for Grouard, even in the dark, had discovered the trail of at least forty warriors, probably hunters, headed back toward their village.

As dawn approached, Hall dismounted with the others and worked to bring feeling back into his hands and feet. He held the muzzle of his horse while the officers convened at the front of the column. Egan returned with news that Grouard had discovered Crazy Horse's village just ahead.

"There's no doubt it's Crazy Horse!" Egan told Hall. "Grouard said he saw ponies that belonged to Crazy Horse. We're in luck!"

"So this will end the campaign?" Hall asked.

"When we get Crazy Horse, the rest will go in with their heads bowed," Egan said. "And this company will be the one to do it! We're going into the village first, while Captain Noyes and his men drive the pony herd upriver. The other companies are splitting up to cover all directions into the village and lend us support as needed."

"It sounds like we'll have them boxed in," Hall said. "It should be a quick fight."

"That it will!" Egan said. "We'll ride in with pistols

drawn and get them coming out of their lodges. We'll take our victory to Crook on Lodge Pole Creek."

As the divisions separated, the order to remount was given. Hall swung into the saddle, his bad leg still dulled with cold and pain. Two soldiers behind Hall had lain down on the ground and were asleep. Sergeant Buckner dismounted and kicked both of them awake, slurring oaths at them in a harsh whisper. "If this happens again, to any man," he told the rest of his command, "he'll find himself on report."

Buckner turned back for his horse and, in passing, slapped Hall's bad leg. "This is the day I've been waiting for, Mr. Hall."

Hall's face tightened with the pain. Buckner grinned broadly and remounted.

Grouard, certain of the village location, led one of the companies supporting Egan's advance. Pourier and Garnier, Big Bat and Little Bat, led Egan's company down off the top through a deep ravine they believed overlooked the village. Here the wind quieted, and the advancing daylight revealed a dense fog along the bottom.

The slope into the bottom was a nightmare of glare ice. The troops were forced to lead their horses over the treacherous footing, falling frequently and scrabbling to remove rock and deadfall from the trail. Hall struggled to keep from sliding under his horse, gritting his teeth against the pain in his leg.

Near the bottom, the horses became almost unmanageable. There had been no stops for water since the previous day, and the horses could hear the Powder River gurgling under the ice.

"That is a sweet sound," one of the soldiers said. "But I'd sooner be drinking Indian blood than water."

At the bottom, it was discovered that the village was farther ahead than anticipated. Some of the scouts grumbled that Grouard had been wrong. "He's good at the scouting," Big Bat said, "but he's not always good at the judgment."

Divided into two columns, the command pressed ahead as fast as their weary horses could carry them. The sun would be fully risen soon, and already the fog was beginning to lift in places. The village would be awake, and all efforts toward a surprise attack would be lost.

As they rode, Hall noticed various groups of soldiers afoot in the distance, making their way over the rough country. The scouts had not anticipated how long it would take to move through the steep rock and timber. None of the divisions would be in position at the same time, making it impossible to fight the battle as planned.

Hall stuffed a chunk of frozen bacon into his mouth. Each man had been given one meal's rations to last until they met Crook late that evening. It would not appease the hunger he felt, but it might keep him from getting any weaker.

When they finally reached the edge of the village, the sun was up and dogs were barking, but a small patch of fog yet to lift obscured their view of the lodges.

The order was given to draw revolvers and return to single file. Hall's stomach tightened. The order to charge would be given at any second. The time had come for his first battle, and he wanted nothing to do with it.

Young Horse patted Big Spot on the neck and talked to the pinto in a soft voice. This morning had started like all the others since Crazy Horse had given him the pony. Just before dawn, he had taken Big Spot to water, and now looked forward to riding the pony to the hill where his mother always prayed.

There Young Horse would again give thanks to *Maheo* for sending such a good man, Crazy Horse, into his life. He would also ask blessings for Big Spot, so that the pony would always be strong and healthy.

Though the weather had gotten cold again, he rode the pony daily. When the weather warmed, he wanted to surprise Crazy Horse and show the great leader how well he could ride. He wore the hawk feather proudly and wanted to remain worthy of such a gift.

Young Horse led his pony from the river up through a ravine. He took this trail often, as it led to the bluffs above the village. From there he could watch the fog lift from the surrounding valley.

Young Horse stopped to blow on his hands and stamp his feet against the strong cold. "I doubt if Mother will pray very long up here this morning," he told Big Spot. "She'll freeze. Maybe we should go back and tell her it's too cold."

Young Horse started to turn around, but stopped suddenly. He heard the sounds of horses not far away. Riders were coming down the trail toward the village.

Young Horse listened intently. He did not believe them to be Lakota or Cheyenne, for they would not be traveling so early in the morning. Also, they would have first sent a messenger into the village.

Young Horse gasped as the riders suddenly appeared like ghosts in the fog. They wore fur hats and buffalo robes for coats, and held pistols in their hands. Their faces were white and covered with hair.

He stood just off the trail, partly hidden by the stump of a tree. There was no chance for him to get away. They were directly upon him.

"This is the end for me," he told Big Spot. "When they shoot me, run away and don't let them catch you."

Young Horse wrapped his blanket tightly around him and stood as still as he could. The white men were the dreaded Bluecoats. They stopped their horses to point at him and whisper. They were so close that he could have spit and hit any of the leaders.

One of them raised a pistol. Another quickly spoke in a high whisper and put a finger to his lips. Young Horse realized he would not die. They did not want to make any noise. They had come to kill more important people than he.

When the soldiers started to move again, Young Horse mounted Big Spot and rode quickly to the hill. There, he called a warning cry with all his might. It echoed through the valley floor like the scream of a giant bird.

"Charge!" Egan shouted as the echoes died. "Charge the village!"

Hall leaned over his horse as bullets whizzed into the ranks. The Indians had instantly opened fire to protect their homes. Bourke was yelling that he should have killed the boy. Buckner was yelling more loudly, ordering the men to follow Egan into battle.

But the intense fire had driven the column out of formation. Just behind Hall, a horse took a bullet in the intestines and fell, trapping its rider. Another horse was struck in the head, both eyes knocked out.

Egan again ordered the charge, and Hall kicked his horse into a gallop. The column surged into the village as naked women and children ran screaming from their lodges toward the steep and rocky slope behind. Screaming war cries, warriors took cover behind trees and brush and poured rifle fire into the troops.

Still riding low, Hall clutched his horse's mane and rode without shooting. A soldier just ahead of him, sitting upright and firing wildly, took a bullet that shattered his collarbone. Blood and bone splinters splattered Hall's face. The soldier fell under Hall's horse and Hall found himself flying forward, head first into the snow.

The impact set Hall's head ringing. He tried to rise, but fell back. The whole world was swirling, and he felt sick to his stomach. He turned on his side as the remainder of the force galloped past and into the village, yelling wildly and shooting at anything that moved. Hall tried to rise again. This time when he fell back, everything faded away.

Ghostwind had been up and dressed for some time. She had been anxiously awaiting Young Horse's return, for something told her he was in danger. She had been wrapping herself against the cold to go and find him when she heard Young Horse's warning cry from the hill, followed by the charge of the fur-clad Bluecoats.

Now all was pandemonium. Bullets flew in all directions from the Bluecoats and the warriors defending the village. Ghostwind intended to find Young Horse, even if it meant going in the direction of the Bluecoats instead of away from them.

"Run!" Day Lily yelled. "We must all run into the high rocks for safety."

"I cannot go anywhere without knowing about my son," Ghostwind said. She told Talking Grass to go with Day Lily and the others, but the child clung to her and would not let go.

With no time to lose, Ghostwind picked up Talking Grass and ran, ducking among the lodges. She tripped over the body of a fallen child, stumbled and ran on. Everywhere Lakota and Cheyenne were running for their lives, leaving everything behind.

Gunfire echoed in the canyon. The air in the village was thick with bullets, like large angry bees. A Lakota woman and her child were shot down a short way from Ghostwind, while another child fell nearby. Ghostwind decided to seek cover.

After taking a knife from a fallen warrior, Ghostwind

ducked into a thicket of wild plum at the edge of the village. She lay flat, with Talking Grass under her. More Bluecoats entered the village on foot and began raking the camp with pistol and rifle fire, killing anyone who moved.

The shooting finally dwindled to sporadic bursts, but Ghostwind stayed in the thicket. She rubbed her daughter's hands and feet to ward off the bitter cold. Never once did Talking Grass complain. She kept her eyes on the sacred hill and, with a broad smile, whispered to Ghostwind that she had seen Young Horse.

A short distance away a Bluecoat soldier rose from the ground to a sitting position. He held his head in his hands and looked around, turned to his side and vomited. Ghostwind saw blood on his face and thought he had been shot in the head. When the Bluecoat lay back down again, she thought he would soon die.

The Bluecoats ransacked the lodges. They made enormous piles of food and clothing, cooking utensils, ceremonial headdresses and furs that were baled for trade. She saw three of them unfold an elkskin floor covering, beaded nicely on all the borders, and hold it up for the others to admire. One of them shot a hole in it, and the others laughed.

Saddles and halters, tools and pots were all thrown out of the lodges and into piles. Ghostwind noted that many of the Bluecoats chewed pieces of dried meat ravenously, while others stuffed handfuls of pemmican into their pockets and drank greedily from the water bags that had hung from the lodges.

A group of Bluecoats and their scouts began to talk to an older Lakota woman, whom they had propped up against a tree. She was holding her stomach with bloody hands while a large scout interrogated her, no doubt asking where he could find Crazy Horse. Ghostwind knew that the large man must be The Grabber.

One of the Bluecoats pulled the old woman's head up by the hair so that she would speak directly to The Grabber. Ghostwind gripped her knife tightly. She wanted to run from cover and drive the blade into as many of the Bluecoat dogs as possible; but she knew that in the end it would cause her own death, as well as the death of her daughter.

The Grabber turned from the old woman and walked away. The Bluecoat released her hair, then pulled his revolver. Another Bluecoat stopped him. He helped the old woman to her feet and escorted her to one of the lodges.

Dense smoke began to rise from the other side of camp. Ghostwind knew the Bluecoats had fired some of the lodges and would no doubt burn the entire village. Then rifle fire came from the rocks above the village. Incensed by the burning of their homes, the warriors had gathered for a charge against the Bluecoats.

To Ghostwind's surprise, the Bluecoats began to retreat. They hurried into the plum thickets a ways down from her and took position, firing up at the warriors shooting from the rocks.

The Bluecoat who had been lying on the ground began to rise again. He sat for a time, getting his bearings. Then he rose unsteadily to his feet. Overwhelmed with rage, Ghostwind gripped the knife and told Talking Grass to remain under cover while she took a measure of revenge for what had happened in their village.

Hall watched black smoke rising from burning lodges on the opposite side of the village. He felt as if he had reentered a world were many things had happened since his departure. He knew he was in the middle of a pitched battle, but could find no reason for being alone.

The events of the day finally began to return to him. He recalled having entered the village with the other soldiers, then falling from his horse and striking his head. His horse was gone, and all he could think of was how he might find another horse and escape.

The gunfire in and around the village was brisk, and at first Hall thought he had been unconscious only a few minutes. But his hands and feet were numb, and the sky overhead told him it was already past noon.

Alarmed, Hall began to shake himself and stamp the circulation back into his feet. He cared little about the throbbing in his head or the pain in his leg; he did not want to lose his hands and feet to cold.

Hall could see his command a distance away, fighting from cover along the river. Warriors were moving from rock to rock along the hills above, gaining better position with each passing minute. Other soldiers rushed through the village, torching more lodges and piles of goods.

Hall saw his revolver lying nearby. The cold was so intense that the barrel stuck to his fingers. At a noise behind him he turned to see an Indian woman charging him with a knife in her teeth. She was upon him so quickly that he had no time to react, and went down under her small but powerful body.

Hall felt the pistol rip free from his fingers, tearing bits of flesh with it. The woman had taken the knife from her teeth, and Hall blocked her arm as she drove the blade toward his chest. She was screaming at him, her face twisted with the deepest anger he had ever seen. She would not stop until she had killed him.

Hall grabbed the woman's wrist before she could thrust the knife again. In a powerful surge, he twisted out from under her and threw her to one side. She was on her feet in an instant, the knife firmly in her grasp.

Behind her came a small girl, crying loudly. The woman turned and pointed to the brush. The child retreated back into cover and the woman charged Hall again, swiping viciously with the knife.

"Die!" she screamed in English. "Die, you Bluecoat dog!"

Stunned, Hall shouted to her, "I don't want to kill you! Just get away from here! Take your daughter and run!"

"First I will see you die!" the woman said. "I want you to hear this promise I make you, in your own tongue." She lunged toward Hall again.

Hall noticed a Winchester rifle lying a few feet away beside a fallen warrior. If he could grab it, he could make the woman back off. Then he could give her another chance to run and save herself. But she was coming fast.

Hall caught her charge; she tripped him and he again went down. He grabbed her wrist, knowing he had to get the knife away this time, but his hands were too cold for him to hang on for long.

Around him the village erupted into a firestorm. Lodges and piles of goods burned wildly. Explosions hurled entire lodge poles into the air like rockets, and fireballs flew everywhere in a torrent of smoke and flame.

A burning ember blew into the woman's hair. She reached up to put the flames out and Hall grabbed the blade. He worked a handful of snow into her hair to put out the fire, then scrambled over to the rifle.

"Go!" he yelled, pointing to the edge of the village. "Get out of here while you can!"

The small girl burst from cover and rushed to her mother. The woman scooped the child into her arms. Hall waved the woman away frantically, while she stared in disbelief. As she turned to run, two mounted soldiers appeared from the smoke in front of her.

Upon seeing the woman and child, Sergeant Arlan Buckner cocked his pistol. Hall brought the rifle to his shoulder and fired. The blast tore through Buckner's left shoulder, hurling him backward off his horse. The other soldier, Private Jess Blye, stared momentarily at Hall, then fired on him.

The first shot rang off the rifle barrel, nearly knocking it from Hall's grasp. Hall levered in another round as another blast whizzed past his cheek. He fired before Blye could shoot again.

The bullet entered Blye's left side, under his arm. Roaring with pain and rage, Blye dropped his pistol and fought to stay in the saddle. He coughed mouthfuls of blood onto his overcoat and clung to the saddle horn with both hands while his horse pitched and bucked. Hall carefully fired another round into Blye's head.

Blye tumbled from the horse, kicking violently. Hall ran to the woman, who was bent over her screaming daughter. "Take your child and go," he ordered her. "More soldiers are coming."

The woman carried her child into the thicket as Hall heard the retreat being played. More troopers emerged from the smoke, kicking their horses as hard as they could. Hall hurried over to catch Blye's horse. Blye lay still on his back, his eyes staring into the frigid afternoon sky.

Buckner lay a few feet away, his eyes closed. He still clutched his revolver, and Hall pried it loose. Buckner suddenly opened his eyes and lifted his head.

"Damn you, Hall!"

Hall stared in shock. He stood up and backed away from Buckner. Soldiers continued to ride by, and Hall decided he would have to shoot Buckner again. But the surgeon appeared and reined in his horse.

"I'll take care of him," the surgeon said as he dismounted and knelt over Buckner.

Buckner was pointing and yelling that Hall had tried to kill him.

The surgeon stared at Hall. "What's he talking about?"

Hall quickly mounted Blye's horse. Buckner sat up,

holding his shoulder. "Stop him! He shot me, and he killed Blye. I'm placing him under arrest."

Two more soldiers stopped. Buckner yelled for them to level their guns on Hall, but Hall had already kicked the horse into a full run and was lost in the smoke and flames of the village.

FIFTEEN

Ghostwind knelt in the thicket at the edge of the village watching a number of Bluecoats helping the wounded one onto a horse. She held Talking Grass tightly, thinking of the Bluecoat who had saved her life. She could still not believe it had happened, or understand why, but she could see that he had gone against his own kind and had ridden into the village to escape.

The village was burning wildly, creating a dense cloud of smoke and ash that rose high into the early-afternoon sky. Warriors streamed down from the rocks to shoot at the fleeing Bluecoats. The Bluecoat who had been shot in the shoulder was now in the saddle and was being held by another Bluecoat who rode alongside. They all rode as fast as they could toward the trail that would take them out from the village onto the flatlands.

Ghostwind watched the last of them disappear into the distance, leaving their dead and wounded behind. She thought about Crazy Horse's remarks regarding honor: these men had chosen to leave without those who had fallen; they could have no honor.

The only Bluecoat who had shown any decency had been the one who had shot his fellow Bluecoats. Though Ghostwind felt a sense of obligation to try to save him from being killed, she did not run into the village after him. Her family came first. She carried Talking Grass toward the hill, where she met Young Horse riding down on Big Spot.

She hugged him tightly, tears streaming down her face. "I was very worried until Talking Grass saw you on the hill. I'm glad you stayed up there."

"I wanted to come down," Young Horse said, "but I knew I could do no good against so many. I felt good when I saw you duck into hiding, and Grandmother and Grandfather got up into the rocks without harm."

Ghostwind was relieved to hear that her parents were safe. She put Talking Grass on Big Spot behind Young Horse and instructed him to take his sister and go find them. Now she could see if there was still time to save the Bluecoat who had helped her.

Ghostwind hurried into the village. Men and women were working frantically to save as many goods as possible from the flames. Some mourned over the fallen, while others assisted the wounded. Somewhere in the smoke and flame a man was screaming. If it was the Bluecoat, he was surely being killed.

But it was not the same Bluecoat. Ghostwind found the Bluecoat who had helped her along the northern edge of the village. He stood with blood streaming down his right leg from a bullet wound, holding a knife, yelling defiantly at three warriors with rifles coming to finish him off.

Ghostwind stepped in front of him and held up her hand to stop the three warriors. One of them was Horned Bull, the healer.

"Please, do not harm him further," she said to Horned Bull. "He saved me from the others. He shot two of them so that my daughter and I would not be killed."

"He saved you and your daughter from death?" Horned Bull asked.

"Yes, or I surely wouldn't be here now."

"That is a strange thing," Horned Bull said. "Why would he do that?"

Ghostwind turned to Hall, who had dropped to a sitting position, and asked in English, "They want to know why you aren't like the other Bluecoats. Why didn't you kill me and my daughter?"

Hall held his right leg. The bullet had passed through the knife wound. He was close to passing out.

"I've got nothing against you people," Hall said. "I was made to become a soldier. I didn't come to kill anyone, especially women and children."

Ghostwind relayed the message to Horned Bull and the other two warriors. At first they didn't want to believe Hall's words, but they knew Ghostwind had to be telling the truth. If anyone had reason to hate Bluecoats, it was Ghostwind. If she wanted to save one from death, there had to be a special reason.

Horned Bull and the other warriors nodded to each other and set their rifles down in the snow. Ghostwind assured Hall that no one intended him harm. Hall gritted his teeth as Horned Bull knelt and cut through his pant leg. The bullet had passed through cleanly, without hitting bone or a major blood vessel.

Horned Bull reached into a bag around his neck and brought out a handful of herbs. "The spirits are with him," he said, stuffing the wound. "But it looks like someone once cut him badly with a knife, and it hasn't fully healed. What are we to do with him?"

"He saved my life, and the life of my daughter," Ghostwind said. "He can travel to Crazy Horse's village with us, if that is his wish. If Crazy Horse will not welcome him, I will care for him someplace else. When the cold moons are gone, he can go where he chooses."

Horned Bull stared at her. "Are you sure you want to do this?"

"Yes. I tried to kill him myself with a knife. He did not hurt me, but told me instead that he didn't want to see me die. He said he didn't believe in what the other Bluecoats were doing."

"No matter how you feel, you can't be surprised if the others try to kill him," Horned Bull said. "Another wounded Bluecoat was left behind. Some of the people cut him to pieces."

Ghostwind had heard the terrible screaming. "I understand," she said. "The Bluecoats have done a bad thing here today. The people are angry and will remain angry. There will be war with the Bluecoats."

"They have taken our ponies and burned all our food and clothing," one of the other warriors said. "We will be lucky if we make it to Crazy Horse's village."

"I will ride ahead and take the Bluecoat with me," Ghostwind said. "That way Crazy Horse's people can come back and help us."

Old Bear, Two Moon and He Dog had already called a council at the edge of the village. Horned Bull took Ghostwind's message to them and returned to say that the council wished to see her and the Bluecoat. Ghostwind had been talking with her mother and father, who both agreed with her decision to help the Bluecoat, if that was what she wanted. Her father especially had decided that nothing was what it appeared to be any longer.

"Everything is crazy," Five Bulls said. "I have much anger toward the Bluecoats, but I feel this man is not a true Bluecoat. He doesn't seem like a Contrary, but a true white warrior. Yet he isn't angry at our people. This doesn't make sense. Did you find out why he came with them?"

Ghostwind explained that Hall had been forced into the Bluecoat army against his will. Five Bulls understood. All the people knew how the whites made soldiers of everyone they could, including many who did not wish to fight.

Mountain Water had been listening. "I have mixed feelings about this man," she told Ghostwind. "He might not be angry at our people and might have no quarrel with us, but still he is an angry man, very angry inside. What if he harms someone later? How will you feel about keeping him around?"

"I believe he would rather fight other Bluecoats than us," Ghostwind said. "Otherwise he wouldn't have ridden into our village to escape them. He would rather have died by our hands than be with them any longer."

"I believe you," Mountain Water said. "But you're going to have to explain it to the children. They just lost their father to the Bluecoats, and now you are saving one of them."

"Talking Grass saw him save me, though I tried desperately to kill him," Ghostwind said. "She knows he is an unusual man and shouldn't die in this village."

"I hope you can talk to them," Mountain Water said. "A great many things have happened to them lately."

Young Horse and Talking Grass were staring wide-eyed at Hall. Talking Grass had already described to Young Horse how the Bluecoat had saved her mother and her, even though her mother had run at him with a knife.

"He even shot two Bluecoats who were going to kill Mother and me," Talking Grass said. "He must be a spirit who has come with the Bluecoats to help us."

"Yes, he may have come dressed as an enemy, but he is not really against us." Young Horse turned to Ghostwind. "Does *Maheo*, the Father, test us in strange ways?"

"We have many tests," Ghostwind replied. "This man's

coming could be one. I only know he does not want to see us die. Otherwise your sister and I would be dead now."

Young Horse walked up to Hall and touched him quickly, then stepped back and studied his hand. "He doesn't feel any different from one of our people. Why are they different? Why do his people want to kill us?"

"There is no simple answer," Ghostwind said. "Maybe in time you can talk to him about this. But now you must stay with your grandparents and do what they say."

Young Horse protested, "Won't you be with us? I don't want you to go anywhere without us."

"You don't have to worry," Ghostwind said. "The Bluecoats are gone. We are all going to go to Crazy Horse's village. Stay here and keep as warm as possible near the fires. I'm going to take the Bluecoat ahead with me and tell Crazy Horse what happened."

"Why don't you let the warriors and young men do this?" Young Horse asked. "Why do you have to go?"

"Because I don't want more harm coming to this man," Ghostwind answered frankly. "If he stays among the villagers, someone will surely want to kill him."

"Maybe Crazy Horse will want to kill him," Young Horse suggested. "Then what?"

"I'll tell him what happened," Ghostwind said. "He's a fair man. He'll respect my wishes. Then I'll return to bring you and your sister, and to help others who are coming along the trail."

Though Young Horse continued to protest, he realized his mother had made up her mind. He went with his sister and grandparents to gather with the other villagers.

"I don't understand all that's going on," Hall told Ghostwind, "and I don't want you to put yourself in any trouble. Just leave me. I'll take care of myself."

"I cannot do that," Ghostwind said. "I've never liked Bluecoats, and after today my feelings have deepened. But you showed me kindness. I will not turn my back on that."

"How did you learn to speak English?" Hall asked her.

"It's a long story that I may tell you later," Ghostwind said. "But maybe I won't. Now we must meet with the council."

The council greeted Ghostwind with respect, but stared at Hall and pointed. The majority wished to kill him outright. But this was forbidden. Ghostwind was asked to speak on Hall's behalf.

"You all know that my husband was killed by Bluecoats not long ago," she said. "So you know my feelings for the white race. Though this man is a Bluecoat, he stopped others from killing me. I don't understand it, but I know the spirits do not wish his death."

"The spirits tell me he should die!" one warrior spoke up. "And it is I who should finish him."

Ghostwind stepped in front of the warrior. Some members of the council laughed, and one remarked, "The Bluecoat cannot be a man if he needs a woman to protect him. Maybe Ghostwind wants to be the man and the Bluecoat can be the woman."

The laughter hushed when Hall stepped up behind Ghostwind and moved her aside. Though he couldn't understand the language, he knew the council was laughing at his expense. He used what sign language he had learned from Kincaid and told them he did not want them making fun of anyone.

"Talk to me and not to the woman," he said. "She does not deserve to be laughed at."

The council members murmured. The warrior who wanted to kill Hall pointed to him and asked Ghostwind, "Where did he learn to sign?"

"I don't know," Ghostwind said. "Maybe he knows Indian people somewhere. Maybe that is why he didn't want to fight us."

"Or he may have learned to sign from the Crow," the warrior suggested. "They are fighting with the Bluecoats. This Bluecoat and all the others should die. I want to kill this one."

The council discussed the warrior's wish. Eagle Wing, who had just that morning lost both his wife and young son, was justified in wanting revenge. He was a respected member of the Red Shields warrior society and had led many successful raids against enemies. His voice was prominent among the council members. It was decided that if he so wished, he would fight Hall.

"The Bluecoat has a badly injured leg!" Ghostwind protested. "That isn't right."

"It isn't right that the Bluecoats killed our people in their beds!" Eagle Wing yelled. "Now I have no family! You say he did not shoot anyone, yet he rode into our village with them. He is no different from any of the others!"

Ghostwind argued further, but got nowhere. She told Hall what was about to happen and that she could not stop it. To her surprise, he showed no fear.

"If I'm to die today," he told Ghostwind, "then at least I'll take him with me." He removed his boots, then struggled to his feet and began to strip. He asked that if he was killed, she might tell his father, who had an Indian wife among the Lakota.

"He's a man who was shot through the neck," Hall said. "He can't speak, but uses sign language. I was told he's married to a woman in Sitting Bull's village."

Ghostwind stared. She remembered the man named Shot-in-the-Throat, married to Day Lily's aunt. She remembered disliking him just because he was white. They had left for Sitting Bull's village just two days before. Otherwise this Bluecoat might have met his father, or might have seen his father die.

"I know who this man is," Ghostwind said. "Did you once live among the Lakota?"

"No. But my father has been out here a long time. Just tell him that I didn't want to come out here to fight. Tell him I wanted to see him when I learned he was still alive."

"If Eagle Wing kills you," Ghostwind said, "I will be sure your father learns about you."

Hall stared hard at Eagle Wing and began to breathe rapidly, bringing his mind and body together for the fight. The council watched with interest. He seemed to be ignoring the pain in his body, intent only on fighting a good fight. He was naked, except for thin briefs he had been wearing beneath his long underwear. He slapped himself all over to loosen the muscles and took a knife that was thrown to him.

"There's going to be a bad fight," he told Ghostwind. "Nobody will win this one. We'll both die." His injured leg was swollen and covered with blood, but he stood defiantly before the crowd and shouted into the air.

Ghostwind relayed Hall's words to Eagle Wing. The warrior stared at Hall with narrowed eyes. "Does he have a crazed spirit inside him?"

"You're the one who challenged him," Ghostwind said. "I already warned you about the spirits."

"He's certainly a strong one," Eagle Wing said. "He doesn't even know that he's injured."

"He has a strong mind," Ghostwind said. "If he was one of our people, he would already be an honored warrior."

Hall said to Ghostwind, "Tell him to make up his mind. I'm not going to stand around in this cold for very long. Either he comes after me, or I go after him."

Ghostwind turned to Eagle Wing. "He says that he is

tired of waiting. He wants to show you what it feels like to die."

Eagle Wing stared at Ghostwind. "He said that?"

"You can see that he has fought bravely many times before," Ghostwind said. "He believes that if he must die, then he will take you across with him. I believe nothing will stop him from doing that."

Eagle Wing gripped his knife in frustration. He realized that Ghostwind was right; the Bluecoat who faced him had great medicine. If they fought, the Bluecoat would kill him. He could feel it. It would do no good to kill the Bluecoat and forfeit his own life at the same time.

The council members began to talk among themselves. Two Moon approached Eagle's Wing. "Do you still believe you're supposed to fight him?"

"He will not die easily," Eagle Wing said. "And he may not die at all."

"You're right," Two Moon said. "I have never seen a Bluecoat so defiant. He's a great fighter, one who's not afraid to die. He is more like one of us than one of them. Do you think you might be killed?"

"I'm very angry about losing my family," Eagle Wing said. "And I want to kill as many Bluecoats as possible. But today is not a good day for me to fight. I was foolish to challenge him."

Two Moon studied Hall further. "He's steady and determined. He has nothing to lose by fighting you with all his might. He's very dangerous."

"That's true, and it will work against me," Eagle Wing said. "I want his life because other Bluecoats killed my family. But I believe Ghostwind is right: the spirits are with him. I'll save my anger for another day and other Bluecoats. This one is not supposed to die."

Eagle Wing told Ghostwind his decision and she relayed it to Hall, who took the news with surprise.

"What made him change his mind?"

"It's not a good a day for him," Ghostwind said. "He knows you would kill him. He will never challenge you again."

"He's still staring," Hall said.

"He does not know what to make of you," Ghostwind explained. "Our people have seen no Bluecoats like you. It is ended. There will be no fight."

Hall started to dress. "He won't try to shoot me in the back, will he?"

"Eagle Wing is a very honorable man," Ghostwind said. "He wouldn't do such a thing. Maybe that is common among your people, but not among mine."

"I just thought he might have lost face by backing down."

"No one among my people will ever lose face by using his head," Ghostwind explained. "Things happen that make a warrior decide not to fight. He can gain honor by fighting, but he won't lose honor by deciding against it. Life is far more precious than that."

As Hall dressed, he decided he didn't know enough sign to make his thoughts easily understood. He asked Ghostwind if she would take a message to Eagle Wing. "Tell him that I'm sorry for what happened here today. I know it won't make him feel any better but if it were up to me, there would be no wars between the races. It serves no purpose but to spread hatred."

Ghostwind told Eagle Wing what Hall had said. Eagle Wing watched Hall, wondering. Ghostwind had told him that he had shot some of his own kind to keep them from killing her and her daughter. Yet he had ridden into the village with them. None of it made any sense. But many things that happened could not be explained.

Eagle Wing began to wonder if there weren't honorable men among the *Wiheo*. Even if Ghostwind hadn't spoken in his behalf, this man would likely have saved himself. The other Bluecoat had pleaded for mercy and had died screaming. This one would have never allowed them to torture him without fighting.

Eagle Wing gave Ghostwind a message for Hall. "Tell the Bluecoat that he has proved his honor. Maybe, if he were not a Bluecoat, I could consider him a friend."

The villagers dispersed and Hall finished dressing. Ghostwind watched him, talking with her son and daughter. They were amazed, yet no more amazed than Hall himself. He had succeeded once again in keeping himself alive.

Hall struggled to get his boots on. As his determination to fight ebbed, the pain in his head and body took over once again and he began to feel dizzy. In fact, he began to have trouble holding onto his consciousness.

"What's happening to you?" Ghostwind asked.

Hall looked at her, hazy and indistinct before him. The children appeared to be floating.

"You should lie down," Ghostwind said. "Your spirit is rising from your body! Lie down and be still, or you will surely die!"

Hall felt Ghostwind's hands. He heard her voice, fuzzy and distorted, calling for Horned Bull's help. He closed his eyes and felt himself sinking, as if falling through the ground and into a long tunnel. He didn't know that he had slumped sideways and now lay still upon the snow.

SIXTEEN

H all continued to fall through the tunnel, twisting and
turning, out of control. He feared he would meet the
Indian warriors again. He resisted the fall as much as possible, but found he could not stop his descent.

But the tunnel did not lead to a grassland at the base
of the mountains. There would be no warriors on horseback. Instead, he found himself floating out of the tunnel
and into a soothing white light.

The light seemed much whiter and softer than anything
he had ever experienced. He could feel himself loosening
and healing, so that his entire body felt relaxed, the most
relaxed he had ever been in his life.

Then the light dissipated, like the fog over the river that
morning as they had entered the village. He found himself
looking into a meadow filled with flowers and rimmed with
oak. It felt like his childhood home in Missouri.

People were gathered at the edge of the meadow, setting a picnic table for a Sunday meal. He found a trail
leading along under the oaks and began to hurry toward
the people. But he was stopped by a beautiful young

woman who stepped out from behind a tree and held up her hand.

"Please, Mason, don't come any farther."

"Mother!" Hall cried.

The woman smiled. "Not yet," she said. "In time, but not yet."

"I don't understand," Hall said. "You're my mother. I want to hug you."

"You can feel me hugging you without touching me," she said. "Can't you?"

Hall did feel as if she were holding him, sending a warm love through him. He had known this love as a small child and had been without it since her death. It filled him with warmth. He still wanted to touch her physically, but found he couldn't move.

"Why can't I walk toward you?" he asked.

"You must listen. It is not time yet," she said.

Hall looked at his arms and legs, but could make out no clear definition of form, although he could see his mother perfectly. "Am I a child again?"

"You're no child," she replied. "There are childhood issues that you must resolve, and I will help you. But you cannot do it here."

"But I've missed you so."

"Please, don't make this harder. You must turn around and leave the meadow. It's not time for you to be here yet."

Hall thought he should feel sadness, yet that emotion didn't come to him.

"When will the time be right?" Hall asked.

"That's not up to me," his mother replied. "And you cannot take it upon yourself to decide the time. That will only bring you misery. You will remember this moment with me, but only barely. It won't interfere with your life."

"But I like it here," Hall said. "I don't want to leave."

"You must," she said. "Just remember, all you have to

do is close your eyes and I will hold you and give you the love you have wanted for so long. When the time is right, we will see each other again."

Hall's mother turned and walked down the path toward the picnic. Happy laughter floated through the trees. Then she was gone.

Hall turned around and found himself back in the tunnel. The turbulence of the day again overwhelmed him, and he wanted to go back to the meadow. No matter what his mother had said, he did not want any more of the life he now knew. But he could not stop his forward progress.

The mental and physical pain became almost unbearable. His whole body ached, and he was full of anger and despair. Why had he not allowed the warrior, Eagle Wing, to kill him? Had he not been so defiant, he would now be with his mother at the picnic, and all this would be behind him.

He realized that he was moving, his fingers and toes first, then his arms and legs. He heard himself groaning, arching his back with pain. His right leg felt twice its normal size and burned like fire at the slightest movement. He would open his eyes and face this world once again, but he understood that it would be some time before he knew comfort of any kind.

Hall swung his bad leg over the saddle, struggling to keep from passing out. Though Horned Bull had cleaned the wound and repacked it with herbs, the pain would not recede. Nor would the throbbing in his head. He would ride the horse, though. He would not be put on a travois.

"You'll fall off and die," Ghostwind told him. "After all the trouble I went through to save you, you're bent on killing yourself."

"I'm not going to die for a while, no matter how hard I try," Hall said. "I'll freeze my arms and legs on a travois.

I'm not going to let that happen." Though he felt colder than at any other time in his life, he didn't want to complain; already two babies and an old man among the villagers had frozen to death. Many were suffering from frostbite.

"We have to hurry," Ghostwind said. "A number of warriors have gone after the stolen ponies, but it will take several days to find them. My people don't have long. They must get to Crazy Horse's village or die."

"I don't feel right about taking this buffalo robe," Hall said. "Give it to someone who's going to be walking."

"You keep it so that you'll live," Ghostwind said. "We must reach Crazy Horse's village tonight. You can tell Crazy Horse all about the Bluecoats and their plans to kill us. We must know the best ways to fight them."

Hall found himself thinking about Kincaid. He wasn't a Bluecoat. All Kincaid wanted to do was get even with the Sioux. Kincaid had made him feel as if someone in the world cared about him.

Hall realized that if he recovered and found his father, there was no doubt he would take sides with the Indians. But he didn't want ever to face Kincaid in battle.

Hall kicked the horse into a trot and followed Ghostwind out of the village. The sky was clear and filled with early stars, the temperature so far below zero that the snow cracked like firewood. It seemed like a new world, someplace far different from the one he had known that morning. He realized he had injured his head and couldn't piece everything together clearly. But he did know he had been somewhere that had changed him.

All he understood for certain was that he had fallen from his horse during the initial charge into the village. Then he had awakened with a buffalo robe over him and Ghostwind's children staring down into his face.

His memories of fighting Ghostwind and nearly fighting Eagle Wing were sketchy. He didn't see how it could be, but he believed with all his heart that he had seen his mother and had been told he would someday be with her again. It seemed ludicrous, but he knew it had happened.

Once when they stopped to water the horses, Hall said to Ghostwind, "I don't remember much about what happened today. But I think I dreamed about my mother."

"You were talking to your mother," Ghostwind acknowledged. "You spoke to her out loud. You probably crossed over to the Other Side and she told you that it wasn't time to be there yet. That's common among my people."

"You mean I was going to die and my mother told me I shouldn't?"

"You *did* die," Ghostwind explained. "But your mother told you that it wasn't time. The Great Mystery wants you in this world. You have things to do."

"I don't understand," Hall said. "What does all that mean?"

Ghostwind told Hall not to think about it any longer, but to concentrate on reaching Crazy Horse's village. He could rest there until his head healed. In time his memory would clear and he would know all he needed to. He was alive, and now he should be certain he stayed that way.

In saying these things, Ghostwind was reminded of her own lost memories of childhood. She realized she had suffered a head injury that must have been worse than his. She believed she had died and crossed over as well, then had come back.

Though Crazy Horse had told her to let the memories come in their own time, Ghostwind wondered now about her childhood and what had happened to her. How long had she spoken English, and with whom had she lived in order to learn it so well? She had had little trouble communicating with Hall, though many winters had passed since she had come to Old Bear's village.

Hall remained confused throughout the journey to Crazy Horse's village. The ride was a blur of pain and misery. His wound was stiff and the cold had bitten deeply through his entire system. It seemed almost impossible now to keep going.

Ghostwind seemed not to be bothered by the weather. Hall saw her rubbing her face and her hands often, but all the while she would be singing, and he couldn't understand it. Watching her, it finally occurred to him that she might be diverting her own attention from the cold by placing herself somewhere else in her mind.

Hall asked her what to do to ward off cold. She explained to him that he was a good man and that his heart would warm him from the inside. "You are not a person who wishes death on anyone," she said. "For this the Creator will reward you. That does not mean you won't suffer. It only means that you can feel good throughout any ordeal you might face. You can be certain that the Creator is holding you in His hands."

Hall could not understand what she meant and found himself angry with his situation. He didn't want to die, and yet it seemed that death would be the only end to all this. As close to dying as he had already come, he wondered why he must continue to suffer. It made no sense.

Ghostwind kept up a strong pace, both on horseback and walking, as they occasionally had to. At times Hall thought he must be dreaming again, for she seemed to be floating on her horse, as if she were not a real person. Completely exhausted, Hall found himself yelling at her to go ahead, that he would catch up as soon as he had rested for a while. But she would not allow it. She kept him either walking or riding, but never did she allow him to stop.

Hall argued with Ghostwind. "Rest is what I need!" he

demanded. "You expect me to do the impossible!" Ghost-wind would only tell him to save his strength, that they would be at the village before he knew it.

They stopped and built a fire once, and both ate pemmican that Hall had salvaged from the ashes of a lodge. Hall wanted to lie down but Ghostwind pressured him until he rose and climbed onto his horse.

Late in the night, Hall slid from his horse and fell to his knees in the snow, yelling at Ghostwind to go ahead.

Ghostwind dismounted and walked back to Hall. "So you want to stay here?" she asked.

"I'm going to rest," Hall said. "That's all there is to it."

Ghostwind knelt beside him and slapped him hard on the back. Hall pitched forward, face first, into the snow.

"I didn't know you were such a coward!" she yelled. "Maybe you are just a weak child. Maybe you aren't strong enough to follow me, a woman who cooks and sews."

Hall pushed himself to his feet. Ghostwind shoved him again. He fell, cursing.

"Stay down there, and cry for yourself. Crazy Horse will not want to meet you, for you are weak and no good to anyone."

Hall came to his feet yelling and watched Ghostwind mount her pony. She rode away without looking back. Hall struggled onto his horse and followed, screaming oaths. He was mad enough to strike her.

Ghostwind kept her horse just far enough ahead of Hall's that he thought he could reach her. He cursed under his breath and even screamed into the frozen black sky once. Finally, he realized that she had saved his life. His anger slipped out with a stream of tears that wet his cheeks. He quickly wiped them away, before they turned to ice.

Dawn brought a streak of scarlet that bled across the horizon, followed by a ball of gold that spread a crisp light along the lower reaches of Powder River. The arrival of morning raised Hall's spirits, but the temperature barely budged. He dreamed of warmth and comfort, and wished to know what it was like to be without a headache and freezing toes and fingers.

A memory came to him of an evening just before the forced march toward the village, when he and Kincaid had enjoyed the balmy weather sitting atop a hill, watching the clouds roll into the distance. As he thought about Kincaid, other memories began to flood over him. Visions of the village in flames. Blye lying on the ground, and Sergeant Buckner screaming at him.

He wondered if Buckner had died, or was still alive. And what about Kincaid? For the first time since the fight and its aftermath, Hall began to feel a deep sense of loss. Kincaid had treated him like a son. Now Hall had no reason to think he would ever see Kincaid again.

"Look!" Ghostwind called to him. "Crazy Horse's village!"

Ghostwind was pointing to a distant line of bluffs, where threads of smoke were rising into the blue. Though tired and weak, Hall felt a surge of energy and raised his fist into the air. His voice cracked as he yelled for joy.

Hall wanted to hurry toward the village, but Ghostwind told him they could not force the horses any faster. They had already been pushed hard by the Bluecoats with little to eat and could give out at any moment.

"We're nearly there," Ghostwind said. "We must save the horses. We will need all of them for fighting the Bluecoats."

Just outside the village, they stopped to water the horses. Ghostwind helped Hall dismount. She took his hands and congratulated him warmly.

"You can be proud that you survived," she said. "You have a great deal of courage."

"It was you who kept me alive," Hall said. "I wouldn't be here now if you hadn't pushed me like you did."

"No, you kept yourself going," Ghostwind pointed out. "I couldn't have said or done anything to keep you alive if you hadn't wanted to survive."

Hall wanted to draw her close to him. In the short and very unusual time they had been together, he had begun to feel something for her, something he couldn't explain. He wanted to think he had always been looking for this woman, but that seemed preposterous. Still, he felt somehow that he had known her for many years and that they had finally come together.

The feelings embarrassed him, and he stepped back from her. Maybe it was his head playing tricks on him. He felt dizzy and disoriented. He wondered where he had come from and where he was going from here. Behind him was a past that had brought grief and misery, while before him was a future that he could have never predicted. He wondered whether it would bring more pain, or the satisfaction in life that he had always desired. At the moment he felt certain that satisfaction would soon be his.

But none of it made sense. Though he knew he should be afraid, Hall realized that deep within was a feeling of settlement. He could not understand it, nor even accept it. On some level he believed he had come home, returned to his roots, from which he had been separated for a very long time.

Despite the intense physical pain, he wanted to shout for joy. Again he blamed the urge on his head injury. He must be hallucinating. How could he be standing just outside a village of people he had never met and feel as if he was one of them? He turned to look at a group of warriors riding out to meet them, his eyes swimming with confusion.

Ghostwind stared at Hall. A moment ago she had

thought that he might take her in his arms. She realized she would have welcomed that. Even though she had just lost her husband and soldiers had tried to kill her people, she felt close to a man who had been with them. It made her very confused. She could not understand what was happening inside her.

This Bluecoat had saved her life, but the feelings ran much deeper than that. She realized that had she met him under any other circumstances, she would have felt the same. She would have felt as if she had always known him and had been waiting a long time for him to return to her.

Something new and wonderful was beginning, she could have no doubt. As strange as it seemed, her feelings were telling her this, and her feelings never lied.

"Are you all right?" she asked Hall, touching him on the arm.

Hall turned to her. "I think my head is really hurt," he said. "Maybe I'm going crazy."

She looked into his eyes. "I see no craziness. I see feelings coming that you cannot explain. I have feelings I cannot explain as well. Maybe it's the cold."

"I feel warm right now," Hall said. "Real warm."

"It is not the weather," Ghostwind said. "Maybe the spirits are touching us."

Hall stared at her, unable to explain to himself the deep feelings that continued to well up from within. It seemed ludicrous! How could it be happening? He didn't even know this woman!

Yet he did know her. He had saved her life in the village and she had saved his in turn. She had endured her own painful night in the cold to ensure that he survived and reached Crazy Horse's people.

Now they would tell Crazy Horse and his people what had happened. Certainly no one among these people would understand how he was still alive. They would listen to Ghostwind and she would tell them all they needed to know. And they would believe her, of this he had no doubt. There had to be something special between them.

SEVENTEEN

H all rode with Ghostwind and the warriors into the village. The people gathered to stare. Crazy Horse greeted Ghostwind and listened intently as she told of the early-morning raid. When she asked for help in getting her people downriver and into camp for food and warmth, Crazy Horse gave immediate permission to any of his people who wished to go and meet them along the trail.

Ghostwind told Hall that she would introduce him properly to Crazy Horse and then join those who were going out to help the Cheyenne. "You can't go back," Hall said. "It was hard enough getting here in the first place."

"I have my children to think about," Ghostwind said. "I must help them get here safely. But first, I will help you speak to Crazy Horse."

Crazy Horse was not what Hall expected. He was not huge and scowling, nor did he carry a giant war club. Of medium height, he had brown hair that hung long and wavy. Had he kept his locks cut and lived among the whites, he could easily have been a dignitary, dressed in a suit, standing before his countrymen, addressing issues that concerned everyone.

No doubt Crazy Horse did just that among his own people. Hall could see how the villagers looked to him for his opinion, watching him carefully to see what he thought of this intruder. As Hall felt Crazy Horse's stare, he realized how deeply this man was inspecting him, and knew that he must be as honest as he could.

Warmed by a fire in front of Crazy Horse's lodge, Hall ate and told in sign how he had come to enter the Powder River country, had been made to become a Bluecoat soldier. He signed that he wanted nothing to do with pushing the Indian people back onto the reservations.

Crazy Horse read his sign with interest. He knew many of his people would like to kill this Bluecoat, but he respected the man's boldness and honesty. And since he had come with Ghostwind, he deserved to be heard.

"He has already died and crossed over," Ghostwind told Crazy Horse. "He came back, as he's not supposed to leave this world yet. Maybe he has been saved by the spirits to help us. He says his father lives with Sitting Bull's people. He's the one they call Shot-in-the-Throat."

"Oh, yes," Crazy Horse said, "he is a good man. Yet his son comes as a Bluecoat and then fights against the other Bluecoats to save you and your child. It is indeed a strange thing to try and understand."

"I only know that I'm alive because of him," Ghostwind said.

"What made you turn against your own kind?" Crazy Horse asked Hall in sign.

Hall did the best he could in sign and told Ghostwind in English, "Tell him that I do not believe in pushing the Indian people back onto the reservations with force. I did not want to fight, but was made to come."

Crazy Horse told Ghostwind to ask Hall if he believed the Indian people should have to live on reservations at all.

"You must tell him exactly how you feel," Ghostwind

warned Hall. "If you say one thing, yet feel another, he will know. Then he will not respect you, and nothing I can say will save you."

Hall dispensed with sign and spoke directly to Ghostwind. He did not want to take the chance of being misinterpreted.

"Tell him this. It's my belief that all people should be able to live together. No one group of people is any different than another. We all breathe the air from the sky and eat from the bounty of the earth. We're all the same.

"But very little I've believed in over the years has ever come to pass. And I can see that the Cheyenne and Lakota people don't live the same way as the whites. For this the Indian people have been persecuted. They can't win. Maybe they should do what is asked of them and save themselves."

Ghostwind translated. Crazy Horse listened and grunted. "He sounds like one of our elders. 'Don't fight. There are too many.' How can he be a wise one and find himself in such a condition?"

"He chose this condition rather than kill me and my people," Ghostwind said. "He believes there is honor in dying for what he believes is right."

"And you believe he has honor?"

"I do. I believe he is someone special."

Crazy Horse knew Ghostwind to be special herself. For her to say such a thing about another had deep meaning. But she had to know that this man's words about doing what the *Wasichu* wanted could never be. The Lakota and the Cheyenne would have to band together to defend their right to life.

"He is far braver than any Bluecoat I have ever seen," Crazy Horse told Ghostwind, "but he does not understand that my people will not lie down and die for the Bluecoat government. Now your people have gotten a taste of this madness. The Cheyenne must fight alongside the Lakota. Does this Bluecoat believe he can live with us and fight against his own people?"

Ghostwind turned to Hall. "He wonders if you would be willing to fight with us against the Bluecoats."

"I will gladly do that," Hall said. "If they ever catch me, they'll shoot me."

Ghostwind told Crazy Horse what Hall had said, and added that he could help fight the Bluecoats in more ways than just with a rifle. "He knows their battle plans and how they think when they fight. He could tell you what to do to gain victories against them."

"Possibly," Crazy Horse said. "I will honor your wish to save him."

"Will you see to it that he gets rest while I go to help my children?" Ghostwind asked.

"I will see to it," Crazy Horse said.

"I thank you," Ghostwind said. "You won't be sorry that the Bluecoat has come to us."

Crazy Horse could see the light in Ghostwind's eyes. She had already come to care deeply for the man. As she prepared to leave, she helped the Bluecoat into Crazy Horse's lodge and told him that he would be well cared for. Crazy Horse saw her squeeze the Bluecoat's hands and he knew that she wanted to kiss him.

Strong jealousy rose in Crazy Horse. He had been able to see a future with this woman, after his present wife died from the coughing sickness that was slowly killing her. He had been able to see himself with her the first time they had met. As he watched her mount a fresh pony to go and help her people, he wished he had never come to know her.

That night on the hill, when he had discovered her and her children praying, he had wondered what it would be like to lie with her. When her husband had showed up and had yelled at the two of them, he had felt deep guilt.

Though they hadn't been together, he would have liked to be, bringing dishonor to both Ghostwind and himself.

As it stood now, he would never be with Ghostwind. Not because of the Bluecoat, but because of a promise he had made to himself after the problems with Ghostwind's husband that night on the hill. He had told himself that under all conditions, he must contain the feelings that had welled up within him. Once before he had brought dishonor to himself and his family because of his desire for a woman other than his wife. Only bad had come of it.

His affair with Black Buffalo Woman and its aftermath had brought a heavy cloud over the Oglala. He had almost been killed, and the people had become divided. He would not allow that to happen again. Though his present wife would certainly cross over before long, he had promised himself that even if Ghostwind, through some measure of fate, came to be without a husband, he would never pursue her. This he would enforce upon himself, for he needed to make amends for past indiscretions.

Crazy Horse believed that perhaps his dishonor was one reason the Bluecoats had come into the country; it could be that *Wankantanka* was punishing him and his people for his bad behavior. He had promised *Wankantanka* that he would do good and walk a very trying road if only his people could be spared.

Now, as Crazy Horse watched Ghostwind leave the village, he realized his promise was going to be tested severely. It would not have been so hard had there not been a raid by Bluecoats, for now the Cheyenne people would be living with the Oglala for a time. Ghostwind would be in his village; he would see her often.

Crazy Horse had already found it difficult not to think of her often. After hearing of her husband's death, his passion had begun to grow. When he had talked with her while receiving his pinto pony back from her son, he had thought he would go crazy with desire. And now, so soon after, she was bringing a Bluecoat soldier into his village with a light in her eyes that proved she cared for him.

But why a Bluecoat? She deserved far better. Crazy Horse believed she deserved him. But he had promised *Wankantanka* he would never have her, and he realized that keeping that promise would be as trying as anything he had ever done.

Kincaid believed he would never get over losing Hall. He thought about him endlessly while the command made a forced march through continuous bad weather back to Fort Fetterman. What had begun as a quest for vengeance had become one of the saddest times in Kincaid's life.

As part of Crook's reenforcements, Kincaid had ridden to the mouth of Lodge Pole Creek, where Reynolds's exhausted command had bivouacked without food or proper shelter. At least six wounded men had made it out of the village, but they seemed in no worse condition than the rest of the command. All the troops suffered from hunger and frostbite. It had been a bitter day for a fight, and even though it seemed that a victory had been won, there was little to celebrate.

For the first few days no one discussed the battle much. Crook was raging about camp, asking questions of those who had fought. Most kept their mouths shut for fear of court-martial, which was certain for Reynolds and possible for others under his command.

In burning the village, valuable powder and ammunition had been wantonly destroyed, not to mention the quantities of meat and stored provisions that could have been used to feed the command. Robes and blankets that could have been used against the cold had been reduced to ashes.

At least four men, and possibly more, were gone. Certainly none of them could have survived. Hall was among those missing. Kincaid felt that something had been torn from deep within him, something that could never be replaced.

He didn't even rejoice with the others when, on the fourth day of the march back, the weather finally broke. Though the temperature reached only ten degrees above zero, it felt like a breath of spring to the men.

Kincaid sat with Zack Morgan near a cookfire, awaiting a cut of horsemeat. The horses that the troops had seized during the fight had been captured back by warriors trailing Reynolds's retreating forces. Grouard and the scouts had managed to recapture nearly a hundred head, which were now being butchered for food and to get rid of the trailing Indians.

"You hear them yelling in the hills?" Morgan asked. "They're mad as hell that Crook ordered them ponies killed."

"I am, too," Kincaid said. "That's a waste of good horseflesh. The Army ought to be riding those horses, not eating them."

Kincaid seethed while he waited for his plate of horsemeat. Around him, the soldiers argued among themselves whether or not they had attacked Crazy Horse's village. Some held that Grouard had found Crazy Horse, while others believed those scouts who held that they had struck a peaceful Northern Cheyenne village, mixed with a few lodges of Sioux.

"It was crazy that we even went into that village," one soldier was saying. "Some of those lodges were built with government-issue canvas, 'G.I.' stamped right on them."

Kincaid stood up and began to slam a piece of firewood against the trunk of a nearby tree. Morgan rose and grabbed him by the arm.

"You gone plumb mad?"

"I've never seen the likes of it," Kincaid said, taking a deep breath. "Grouard leads them to the Cheyenne, not the Sioux, and they go in anyway. They burn meat and robes that they could have used to feed everybody here for a month, and then Reynolds takes them out and leaves the dead and wounded behind. I could strangle somebody!"

"You're thinking about Hall, aren't you?" Morgan said. "You've seen the likes of this before. The Army's always done things this way. It's Hall being gone that's got you so riled."

"I'd at least like to have seen his body," Kincaid said. "As it is, he's likely been chopped limb from limb like that Crow we found a piece back."

Kincaid slumped down onto a log and held his head in his hands. Morgan sat next to him and rested a hand on his back. "I'm truly sorry, Jordan. Hall was a fine lad. We'll all miss him."

"Don't go feeling so sorry for him," a soldier nearby said. "He was a traitor."

Kincaid and Morgan both stood up. "What did you say?" Kincaid asked.

"He shot Jess Blye and tried to kill Sergeant Buckner," the soldier said. "It's all around camp. Hall was a traitor. He deserved to die."

Before Morgan could stop him, Kincaid had jumped the soldier and had him on his back, pummeling his face with both fists. Another soldier jumped Kincaid, and Morgan jumped that soldier. The scuffle was interrupted by a booming voice.

"That's enough! Any more and you'll all go on report. Is that understood?"

No one mistook the voice of General Crook. He stood with his hands on his hips, accompanied by his adjutant, Lieutenant Bourke. The soldiers scrambled to their feet and stood at attention. Kincaid and Morgan simply stood.

"I'm going to ask you the meaning of all this." Crook was pointing at Kincaid, whose face was flushed with rage. "And I want to know it *now!*"

"I don't like the talk about Private Hall," Kincaid said. "These men are rubbing his face in the dirt. He's gone now, and he deserves better than that."

"Mr. Kincaid, what is the talk that you dislike so?"

"I don't believe the talk, General. It's all lies!"

"I didn't ask you if you believed it or not, Mr. Kincaid. I asked you what you've heard."

Kincaid cleared his throat. "They're saying that Private Hall was a traitor. They say he shot some of his own men. I don't believe that."

"Sergeant Buckner claims it was not an Indian who shot him, but Private Hall," Crook said. "The sergeant also says that Hall killed Private Blye, to stop him from shooting savages."

Kincaid stood silent, his rage growing.

"Sergeant Buckner is lying under robes, sick with fever," Crook continued. "He sticks by his story."

"Begging your pardon, sir," Kincaid said, "but Sergeant Buckner isn't fit to lick a dog. He's no leader of men, and I would vouch that, given the truth, any man here who's served under him would just as soon he didn't recover."

Crook looked around from face to face. "Is that true? Is Mr. Kincaid telling it like it is?"

No one would look into the general's eyes. To a man, they looked to the ground or off in another direction. Crook turned back to Kincaid.

"It seems you know my men. But I will have no more fighting. We cannot afford that." He began to pace, addressing everyone. "Whether Private Hall did or did not shoot Sergeant Buckner is no longer the point here. We have not yet completed our mission. We have not yet driven the Sioux back to the reservation. That will come in due time, but now we must fall back to Fort Fetterman."

Crook continued to pace among the men. All stood solidly at attention, their eyes fixed.

"There will be no more fighting," he repeated. "Anyone fighting will be court-martialed when we return to the fort." He looked at Kincaid. "Civilians will be released immediately, out here among the savages, no quarter given, and not allowed to accompany the command back to the fort. I hope that is understood. Now, all of you get some rest."

When the men had dispersed, Crook approached Kincaid. "I want to see you at my tent. I will expect you immediately."

Crook left, with Bourke following close behind. Morgan came over to Kincaid, a troubled look on his face. "You think he's going to dismiss you?"

"I doubt it," Kincaid said. "I suppose he wants to know why I'd fight over Hall's reputation."

"Careful what you say," Morgan advised.

"I'll say any damn thing I please," Kincaid said, and headed toward the general's tent.

On his way, Kincaid wondered if Morgan might be right. What would he do if Crook let him go out here? It would be a death sentence. But he didn't believe the general would do that. It would take another fight for that to happen; but if someone said another word against Hall, there would be another fight.

Bourke stood in front of the tent and announced Kincaid's arrival. Inside, Kincaid was offered a good cigar and a seat on a pile of buffalo robes. Crook lit the cigar for him and sat down.

"So, I guess you thought a lot of Private Hall," Crook began, lighting his own cigar. "I understand he was like a son to you."

"I guess you could say that," Kincaid replied. "I thought a lot of him."

"How did you get to know him so well?"

"I'll level with you, General," Kincaid replied. "I know Hall's father. I saw a lot of the old man in the boy."

"Do you mean Hall's father is out here?" Crook asked.

Kincaid bit hard on his cigar. "He's living with the Sioux."

"Living with the Sioux? Why didn't Hall tell me this?"

"I would think for obvious reasons, sir," Kincaid said.

Crook frowned. "Yes, I suppose you're right. It's little wonder his heart wasn't in the campaign. He told me as much in the beginning. He just didn't say why."

"I don't think he came out here with the intention of finding his father," Kincaid said. "That's just the way it happened. You can't expect a man to want to fight against his own kin."

Crook frowned harder. "Mr. Kincaid, there were a lot of men who didn't want to fight against their own kin. But they did, because they believed in the union of these United States. I see no difference here."

"Maybe not, sir. But Private Hall did. And he was one to call things the way he saw them."

"Private Hall was not one to hold back," Crook agreed. "I must admit, I thought he would come through and that I could recommend him highly for officer school. But not much that I expected has come of this campaign."

"We'll just have to give it another shot come spring," Kincaid said. "Come good weather, we'll get the job done."

"I hear you saying 'we' will get the job done," Crook said. "I infer that you intend to be along then as well."

"Yes, if the general will have me."

"You realize that because of what just happened, you're going to have a lot of troops against you," Crook said. "Even the ones who don't have an opinion about Hall's loyalty will side with the others, just because you're a packer and not a soldier."

Kincaid spit out a piece of tobacco. "I know that, sir."

Crook blew a cloud of smoke. "I don't like bickering in my camps. If you weren't one of my best packers, I'd send you on a hike. And Private Hall liked you, so there must be something you know more than mules."

"I know a lot more than mules," Kincaid said. "In fact, I could do a sight better job of scouting for you than Grouard or the others ever thought of."

"Is that so?"

"I wouldn't have led those men into a Cheyenne camp," Kincaid said. "I know Sioux from Cheyenne."

"The Cheyenne are our enemies as well," Crook said. "You can't separate them any longer."

"Maybe, but you wanted Crazy Horse, and that's the point."

"I want them all, whoever resists," Crook said. "Any man who scouts for me has to know that."

"Yeah, I know that," Kincaid said. "One's the same as the next. I don't know a soul among them."

Crook relit his cigar and blew smoke throughout the interior of the tent. "Maybe you shouldn't be so certain about that. How would you feel about fighting if someone you cared about lived with them?"

"Someone I care about?"

"You understand me, don't you? I speak of kin, or someone you hold as dear as kin."

"I don't follow you, General."

Crook cleared his throat. "How would you feel about fighting against Private Hall? One of my scouts says he saw Private Hall riding with a Cheyenne woman north along Powder River. I find that hard to believe, but the scout is reliable. Big Bat Pourier is one of the best."

Kincaid nearly lost the cigar from his mouth. "What are you talking about?"

"Big Bat was among those who recaptured some of the Indian horses," Crook said. "He went off by himself to scout for more that might be loose in the hills when he saw two people riding along the bottom. He says he's certain it was Hall, together with a Cheyenne woman. He wanted to ride down but he thought there might be more Indians nearby. He didn't want to push his luck."

Kincaid couldn't imagine that Hall had survived. Indians made short work of those who rode into their villages and set them afire. And to be riding out in the open with an Indian woman? Nothing seemed further from probability.

"That's a mighty strange story, General," Kincaid said. "You're sure Big Bat saw things right?"

"I'm not making this up, if that's what you're wondering," Crook said. He settled back and puffed on his cigar. "I liked Private Hall very much. But if all this is true, that he shot Sergeant Buckner and is now living with the savages, I would have to drop him as quickly as I would any other among the enemy. Would you do the same?"

Kincaid realized the wrong answer could cost him his job and thus his chance to get back at the Sioux for the death of his family. That had been his goal in life for a lot of years, and he didn't want to give it up. Life wasn't worth anything else.

But when he thought about Hall, he wondered what he would really do if they came face to face on a battlefield. The general had certainly stated his position clearly. As Kincaid thought, he decided that maybe he hadn't known Hall all that well. Besides, if all that he had heard was true and Hall was now with the Cheyenne, nothing could ever be the same between them anyway.

"Well, I'm waiting," Crook said. "What say you about scouting and fighting with me?"

"I'll take you up on it," Kincaid said. "I've never had any love for the Sioux, and anyone who rides with them is no friend of mine."

"Good," Crook said. "We'll be back at the fort within a week. Keep your mules fit until the snow leaves. Then we'll head back up into this country. And this time we won't fail."

EIGHTEEN

Night fell with no relief from the cold. Fires burned in the camp of Cheyenne homeless headed for Crazy Horse's village. For the first time in two days, the children had something to eat.

Ghostwind had reached her people with the volunteers from Crazy Horse's village, bringing needed food and clothing. For many the protection against the cold was too late. A number of infants had already frozen to death, and many of the smaller children and the older men and women were just waiting to die.

Ghostwind found Talking Grass and Young Horse nestled next to a fire. Both children whimpered from the pain of frostbite, their hands and arms showing patches of white. But they jumped up to greet their mother with enthusiasm.

"You have returned to us," Young Horse said. "We will live now."

"Yes, you will live," Ghostwind said, tears flooding her eyes. "Did you ever think you wouldn't?"

"I knew we would live," Young Horse said. "But I was

worried about you. And where is the Bluecoat? Did he live?"

"Yes, he's alive," Ghostwind replied. "He's in Crazy Horse's village, resting."

Pine Woman and Five Bulls sat nearby, while Day Lily helped her husband, Red Bear, strip the hide off an antelope. Red Bear had been among a number of warriors who had followed the retreating Bluecoats. They had escaped from the village with some rifles, had managed to steal back the pony herd, and had killed what game they could to feed their cold and hungry families. Now, with the food brought by the Oglala, the rest of the journey would be easier.

"You look very tired," Day Lily told Ghostwind. "You should eat something and sleep until we break camp."

Pine Woman and Five Bulls both agreed. Five Bulls said, "When you have rested, Red Bear has some important news for you."

"What news?" Ghostwind asked.

"It's something I want to show you," Red Bear said. "Why don't you eat and I'll go and get it."

Ghostwind shared a strip of antelope loin with her children. She fed them, for their fingers were too sore to hold anything. When they had finished, both children fell asleep immediately. Ghostwind wanted to wait for Red Bear's return, to see what news he had for her. She talked with her parents and Day Lily, but her eyelids wouldn't stay open. Finally, giving in to exhaustion, she lay down next to Talking Grass and closed her eyes.

The dream came to her on a tanned hide of white buffalo. Stick figures with feathered hair came to life, their eyes wide and their mouths open and yelling, holding rifles and bows and lances above their heads, all riding into a long, hard battle on a day as hot as fire.

Swirling in brightly mixed colors, the mass of stick ponies ran full speed, led by various riders from the Sioux and Cheyenne nations. One warrior stood out; he rode a brown pinto pony.

The stick ponies ran among other stick ponies ridden by figures dressed in blue. They swirled and milled about, fighting without much effect. Then the battle changed.

The charging warriors broke their ponies into even groups, each group forming a clean line that bore down upon a faltering column of the blue-colored figures. No single warrior rode alone for honor as in the old style, but all rode together to drive the invaders out, fighting in the same style as the invaders themselves.

The figures churned and turned upon the buffalo hide, while storms of flower petals danced among the fighters. Ghostwind tossed in her sleep as the smell of fresh blood mingled with the pungent odors of wild plum and rose, and the screams of men and horses drowned out the caws of crows gliding overhead. Many blue-colored stick figures broke into pieces.

Then from all the figures emerged the warrior on the pinto, who rode to the top of a hill and raised his rifle into the air. His cry carried across the wind and echoed throughout the valley. A white man with scars on his leg rode up next to him, and his cry also echoed throughout the red hills.

Ghostwind jerked in her sleep as she saw Hall's face. He was painted for war, and he was laughing. He turned his horse with Crazy Horse's pinto, and the two of them became lost among the other stick figures, all rolling themselves together into a swirling mass, rising with the dust of sundown into the flaming sky, borne on a fateful wind that cried out like a thousand eagles.

* * *

Ghostwind sat up. The camp was still. The fire crackled, spreading warmth over the sleepers. Red Bear lay next to Day Lily, sleeping soundly. Ghostwind wondered about his news for her but decided she could hear it later, when they began their journey again.

She lay back down next to her children, content, for the spirits had shown her that the Bluecoat who had saved her life would gain honor among her people. He would help her people fight for their lands, and he would ride proudly next to the strong one, Crazy Horse.

Hall awakened in the shadows of Crazy Horse's lodge to the smell of boiling plants and meat. Startled, he looked around him; nothing seemed familiar. He knew he was in an Indian lodge, but had no idea where. All he could think of was Ghostwind.

A frail-looking woman who coughed repeatedly kneeled over a fire, stirring a pot with a metal spoon. Hall realized he was in Crazy Horse's lodge. He vaguely remembered drinking various herb solutions that had allowed him to sleep almost continuously for nearly four days. His hands and feet itched terribly, and he saw that they were covered with a thick salve that smelled of herbs and grease. The skin was black and swollen. As Hall stared, the woman frowned and shook her head.

"Don't touch or scratch," she told him in sign. "Your skin will fall off."

Hall realized how severe his frostbite had been. He was lucky he hadn't lost fingers and toes. He knew from gently touching his face that his nose and cheeks were also swollen. He was glad he didn't have a mirror.

Hall asked the woman in sign if she was Black Shawl, Crazy Horse's wife.

"I am," she responded. "But I'm not supposed to talk to you."

"Can you at least tell me where Ghostwind is?"

"She and her family are living in a lodge that has been donated. I will go and get her."

"Where's Crazy Horse?"

"He went out to hunt for game. More meat is needed. I can say no more. I will get Ghostwind."

Hall lay back in his robes. Though his leg and head felt much better, he began to wonder if all this weren't some form of dream. His returning to consciousness in the Cheyenne village and the fight with Ghostwind seemed like pieces of memory from a far distant time. His stripping to face Eagle Wing had now mixed with fights he had survived as a child. One desperate struggle for survival had mingled with another, and time seemed to have no foundation.

The painful journey to Crazy Horse's village, though little more than a blur, seemed the only event that he could assure himself had happened. He reasoned that if he could accept the trip to Crazy Horse's village as reality, then the events preceding it must have taken place as well.

As he lay quietly, Hall heard muffled crying and yelling from elsewhere in the village. He sat up, wondering if something terrible had happened over the last four days.

Ghostwind entered the lodge, her face and hands wrapped in blankets and skins. She smelled strongly of herbal medicine. Hall stared.

"I see you've awakened," she said.

"The cold did that to you?" he asked.

"The cold has been hard on everyone," she replied. "I'm among the lucky ones."

"Is that what the crying I hear is all about?"

Ghostwind nodded. "The suffering is terrible."

"What about your children?"

"They are not dead," Ghostwind replied. "The spirits watch out for them."

Ghostwind filled a bowl with stew from the pot. She handed it to Hall with no expression.

"Aren't you going to have some with me?" Hall asked.

"I've already eaten, thank you," Ghostwind said. "This preparation is just for you. There are plants in with the meat that will help you heal."

Hall ate ravenously. The medicinal taste of the herbs was lost in his desire to fill his stomach. When he handed Ghostwind the bowl for more, she told him that he must wait for a while. Eating too much at one sitting would make him sick.

Hall studied Ghostwind. "I know that seeing your people suffer is hurting you," Hall said, "but you've changed toward me. Did I do something wrong?"

"You have a way of seeing through me," Ghostwind said. "How is that?"

"You act much different," Hall said. "I can't help but notice. What did I do?"

"When I returned to help my people I was given a Bluecoat horse," she replied. "I was told it belonged to you."

"Someone found my horse?" Hall said.

"It was wandering out from the village. There was a coup stick tied to the saddle, a coup stick that once belonged to my husband."

Hall tried to hide his shock. The Indian he had shot during the night raid back along the trail must have been Ghostwind's husband. He wished that he had never kept the stick.

"My horse didn't have a coup stick tied to it," Hall said.

"Yes, it did," Ghostwind said. "My cousin, Day Lily, saw you fall from the horse. Her husband Red Bear saw you, also. They remember it vividly, because they saw the coup stick when your horse stumbled. Were you the one who shot my husband?"

Hall saw no purpose in trying to lie again. She already knew the truth.

"I was only saving my own life," he said. "It was dark and he rode into our camp with a number of other warriors. I thought he was going to kill me. I'm sorry."

"You do not hate Indian people, I know this to be true," Ghostwind said. "So I cannot hold it against you for killing my husband. But it gives me a funny feeling inside."

"It doesn't make me feel all that good myself," Hall said. "I didn't intend to shoot anybody, even in battle. I guess a person doesn't know what he's going to do until he's tested."

"It seems so strange that you would kill him and then spare me and my child," she said. "Strange things happen in war."

Hall watched her refill his bowl. "I mean it. I'm sorry that I shot your husband. I don't want you to hate me."

"I cannot hate you," she said, handing him the bowl. "It will be hard for me to sort my feelings out, but I cannot hate you."

Hall started to eat, then put the bowl down. He had lost his appetite.

Ghostwind stood. "I must go to my children. After you finish that bowl, don't eat any more until tomorrow morning."

After Ghostwind had left, Hall stared into his food. He sat up, dumped the mixture back into the pot and looked out past the doorflap. He watched as she entered a lodge not far away, found a blanket to cover his head and face, then wrapped himself in a buffalo robe and limped from the lodge.

It was the dead of night and the stars shone down from a clear and frigid sky. He felt cold both physically and emotionally. After having met Ghostwind and surviving so much, it seemed now that he was adrift by himself in a vast ocean of loneliness.

Ghostwind seemed to have lost all feeling for him. This bothered Hall far more than anger or even violence. That was what he had expected. Instead, she seemed to have totally distanced herself from him.

As Hall limped through the cold, he heard the crying more clearly. The Cheyenne had been given lodges together, and the entire area was filled with suffering. Even the hills above the village resounded with wails, as mothers and sisters and grandmothers mourned those who had died from the bullets and the cold.

Hall stopped and listened. The cries were of anguish, but they brought back to him another kind of cry: the screams of terror that had filled the air that morning now five days past. Visions flooded his head. Flame from gun barrels shot into the cold air, mixing with the rising smoke from burning lodges; people running naked in the snow, carrying small children; dogs barking, falling alongside their masters; warriors offering their lives to save their families. The screams filled his head.

Hall slumped to his knees. He couldn't drive the scene away. Breathing rapidly, he sat back on his haunches and stared up into the night sky. The vast array of stars sparkled through the frost, whirling before his vision. But the scene from the village left him, and finally the stars settled into their places.

Hall took a deep breath and struggled to his feet. He hurried back into Crazy Horse's lodge and got the pot of stew, again stepped into the cold and started through the village toward Ghostwind. Along the way he heard the whimpering of children in nearly every lodge. Often he could hear babies screaming in pain and mothers singing to try to calm them. But the scenes from the village didn't return. He stopped, out of breath, at Ghostwind's lodge.

Hall called and Ghostwind stuck her head out of the doorflap. "What are you doing?"

"I brought food for the children, just in case you didn't have enough."

Ghostwind stared. "That food is for you."

"I've had plenty. I just thought your children might need some."

Ghostwind thanked Hall. She set the food inside.

"Why didn't you take some when you came to Crazy Horse's lodge?" Hall asked.

"That food was meant for you," she said. "You're a guest. It's important that you get well."

"I'm not more important than your children," Hall said. "I don't need the food that badly."

Hall started to leave when Ghostwind stopped him. "Please, come inside. My children want to talk to you."

Hall stepped into the lodge and took a seat. Everyone in the lodge was awake. Stoic faces stared from everywhere.

"That is my friend, Day Lily, and her husband, Red Bear," Ghostwind said. "Five Bulls is her father and Pine Woman is her mother. You will get to know them all very well."

Hall bowed slightly with the introduction. He felt uncomfortable, but knew he couldn't leave until he had heard from the children. They ate clumsily with black and swollen fingers, looking back and forth from Hall to their mother, speaking to her in low tones. Talking Grass's left hand was wrapped tightly. The space where the last two fingers should have been was empty.

Ghostwind turned to Hall. "My children wish to know why it is that you killed their father and now wish to feed them."

Hall cleared his throat. "Tell them I'm sorry I had to kill their father. But I believed he wanted to kill me. I did not want to die, and I shot him to save myself."

Ghostwind translated for the children. They continued to stare.

"Tell them," Hall went on, "that I want them to have the food because they need it worse than I do. I hope they will accept it. That's all I know to say."

When Ghostwind had finished speaking to them, the children nodded. Talking Grass laid her head on her mother's lap, tears streaming down her face. Young Horse studied Hall a short time, then lay down in his blankets and turned away from the fire. There was again silence in the lodge, except for the children's muffled sobs.

Ghostwind held the bowl of food, biting her lip, her hands trembling.

"I'll leave now," Hall said. He turned and slipped under the doorflap.

Outside Hall was again greeted by the cries of suffering children. The wailing from beyond the village seemed louder. He feared his vision of the burning village would return and tried to run. He stumbled on his injured leg and fell.

He forced himself up, thinking that had he any means to catch a horse, he would ride from the village. He even contemplated walking out. Then a voice from behind startled him. He turned to see Ghostwind.

"You should stay off your leg for a time," she said.

"My leg's fine," Hall said. "I'm sorry about your children. I wish things hadn't happened this way."

"They're not blaming you," Ghostwind said. "They have asked me to thank you. They are mourning the loss of their father, yet they believe you have a good heart. So do I."

"Tell them they're good children and that I hope the food helps them heal. I know I don't have much to offer them, but I feel responsible for their situation."

"But you're not responsible," Ghostwind said. "You couldn't stop a whole army of Bluecoats. It's foolish to think that you could."

"But I was with them," Hall said. "Eagle Wing was right. I came along, so I'm as much to blame."

"Didn't you say that you were forced to be a Bluecoat?"

"Yes."

"Were you lying?"

"No, of course not!"

"Then stop blaming yourself." Ghostwind turned back toward her lodge, where two small heads were peeking from the doorflap.

"You'd better go back to them," Hall said.

"They aren't worried about me," Ghostwind said. "They just wanted to be sure I caught up with you."

"I can't believe they don't hate me," Hall said. "I wouldn't blame them if they never wanted to see me again."

"You must understand that the children know what's in your heart," Ghostwind said. "They do not blame you for what happened to our people, and they do not blame you for the death of their father. You were honest with your feelings and they understood that you were saving your own life. If you believe them, then you will not punish yourself any further."

"But it's not fair what's happened to them," Hall said. "They don't deserve this."

"Maybe not," Ghostwind said, "but there's nothing we can do to change what's taken place. We must go on with life and believe that the Creator has a reason for what happens to us."

"I'm having a hard time with the Creator right now," Hall confessed. "I don't understand any of this."

"I don't know anyone who understands life completely," Ghostwind said. "Those who say they do are fools. My people believe we are here to honor the Creator, no matter what happens. That is the only way to live."

"But aren't you angry about what's happened?" Hall asked. "Doesn't it bother you that your daughter lost two fingers and that both children are suffering from hunger and exposure?"

"Of course it bothers me," Ghostwind said. "On the way back to help my people, I shouted at the sky. I got my anger out and now I'm going to care for my children as best I know how. There's nothing more that I can do."

"What about their anger?" Hall asked.

"They will get rid of their anger, as I have," Ghostwind said. "If I choose to always be angry, then they will learn that from me and take it into their adult lives. It is my duty to teach them to forgive and not to hold hatred in their hearts."

"Even after all this? How can they help it?"

"Maybe they understand all this better than we do," Ghostwind suggested. "Children are very close to the Creator. They know truth and can see many things that are lost to us when we grow to be adults. Trust them. They will tell you the way it is."

"I'm glad you talked to me," Hall said. "If you hadn't, I would have tried to leave the village."

"You must not leave," Ghostwind said. "Not now, not ever. Your place is with us. The spirits have told me."

"What do you mean, the spirits have told you?"

"Someday you will understand. Go now and rest. Worry no more about me and my children."

Ghostwind left for her lodge. Hall stared after her, and only when she had slipped inside it did he start for Crazy Horse's lodge, wondering about Ghostwind. What kind of life did this woman live, thinking of spirits and talking to things that couldn't be seen? He thought about Kincaid and Morgan and the scouts, all believing in these things. And he thought about himself, and how he had suddenly become part of a world he had never known existed.

NINETEEN

The remainder of the night Hall tossed and turned, unable to sleep or to keep his mind off the suffering in the village. Black Shawl never returned, and no one came to the lodge. Just before dawn he heard the sound of wind, and rose to find a warming chinook blowing through the valley.

He stepped out, breathing deeply of the refreshing air. The cold had finally loosened its grip on the land.

Hall found Ghostwind at the river, breaking ice with other women. "I need a pony and a rifle," he told her. "I want to go hunting."

· Ghostwind studied him. "Are you going to leave?"

"No. I've thought about it. I won't be leaving unless you or someone else asks me to go. I don't understand it, but I feel I belong here."

Ghostwind smiled. "My father has a rifle that he never uses. Wait back at Crazy Horse's lodge."

When Ghostwind arrived with the rifle, Five Bulls and Red Bear were both with her. Hall stepped out of the lodge, ready to go, and Ghostwind told him they had not come to hunt with him.

"They don't trust me," Hall said. "That's it. I guess I can't blame them."

"No, that's not it. They wonder whether you are even able to use a rifle. They believe that, like the other Blue-coats, you should have shot at our people. Since you didn't maybe you don't know how. They don't want to give a rifle and ammunition to someone who can't use it. There's not enough ammunition to spare."

Hall wanted to laugh. "Didn't you tell them that I shot two of my own people to save you?"

"Yes," Ghostwind said. "They said that is not like shooting game. That was much easier. I can't change their minds."

Hall thought a moment. "Tell them to tie my hands behind my back," he said. "I'll bet them that I can shoot better tied up than they can with both hands free."

Ghostwind stared at him. "How can you do that?"

"I learned to shoot guns very well," Hall said. "Just tell them and see what they say."

Ghostwind relayed the challenge to her father and Red Bear. Both men laughed. Hall insisted they bet on their certainty, and a wager was made.

If Hall could not prove that he was a better marksman than either of them, even with his hands tied behind his back, then he would be required to drag a travois around for two days, giving the village children rides. If he won, then Five Bulls and Red Bear would each surrender two ponies.

Red Bear left to get a length of rope. While he was gone, Hall explained to Ghostwind that he had no concern about losing the bet.

"I have no doubt I will be four horses richer," he told her. "In fact, I feel a bit guilty."

Hall told Ghostwind of his childhood as a trick shooter and informed her that he had frequently shot bottles and cans from the air while riding horseback. He described other tricks and said without expression that he had been able at one time to light a match by aiming a rifle through a mirror and firing backward over his shoulder.

"I'm actually taking advantage of them," Hall said. "Why don't you explain this to Five Bulls and Red Bear, in case they want to call the bet off."

Red Bear stood waiting with the rope. He and Five Bulls listened with interest while Ghostwind detailed what Hall had said. They talked to Ghostwind, nodding and smiling. When they had finished, Ghostwind turned to Hall.

"They want to go on with the bet. They said it will be worth two ponies apiece to see someone shoot that well."

They moved to the edge of camp, with a number of curious villagers following. Red Bear was tying Hall's hands when Crazy Horse and some of the hunters entered the village. Concerned about what he was seeing, Crazy Horse dismounted and demanded to know what Hall had done.

"It's not what he's done, but what he's going to do," Ghostwind said.

She explained to Crazy Horse and the others what was about to take place. At first Crazy Horse was skeptical, wondering if Hall wasn't affected in the head from his fall. He didn't want to endanger his people, and at first forbade the bet. Hall had Ghostwind tell him that it didn't really matter one way or the other: if they didn't want him to hunt, then he wouldn't hunt.

"This all started when he wanted a rifle to get meat for camp," Ghostwind told Crazy Horse. "Five Bulls and Red Bear didn't believe he could shoot, so he bet them he could do much better than either of them. He said he could shoot even with his hands tied behind his back. That's when you came."

"So he's a trickster?" Crazy Horse said.

"What he will do is not illusion," Ghostwind said. "It will be real."

Crazy Horse studied Hall, who stood with his hands tied. He had tried to understand this odd Bluecoat ever since his arrival. He was still jealous and wanted him away from Ghostwind. But he had to admit, the man had great courage.

"Tell him," Crazy Horse said to Ghostwind, "that I will wager five ponies that I can shoot better than he can with his hands free."

"Are you certain?" Ghostwind said. "I told you about his life as a child and young man. You know he does not lie about anything."

"I want him to prove it," Crazy Horse said. "I want to see this trickster."

After Hall heard the translation from Ghostwind he asked her to pluck a feather from a wild turkey one of the hunters had brought in. At Hall's direction, she placed the feather upright in the ground some twenty paces away.

"Tell Crazy Horse I am going to show him something before my hands are untied," Hall told Ghostwind. "Then he can decide if he wants to go ahead with his bet."

Hall took the rifle from Five Bulls and cocked it behind his back. Turned sideways, he held the rifle behind him and aimed at the feather. Though it had been years since he had performed the trick, everything came back to him as if it had been yesterday.

Hall pulled the trigger and the top of the feather flicked off. All the onlookers gasped and covered their mouths with their hands. Even Crazy Horse stared.

The second shot cut the feather halfway down, and the third at ground level. The people talked and pointed. Many ran away. Hall gave the rifle back to Five Bulls, who studied the weapon as if it had been filled with magic.

"The spirits have given you eyes in your back," he said.

"No one can touch you from any direction, if you do not want it."

Crazy Horse untied Hall's hands himself. He gave Hall his own rifle and turned to Ghostwind.

"Tell him to use my rifle when he hunts. And have him give it back to me filled with good shots."

Ghostwind relayed the message. Other warriors were coming up to Hall, asking him to touch their rifles so that they would shoot with the great medicine. Hall noticed that most of the weapons were outdated, muzzle-loading rifles, many from the Civil War era. Some were even old Hawken rifles, from thirty to forty years ago.

"We cannot make the new bullets," Five Bulls told Hall. "We can mold the round balls for shooting, and use the powder, but it is hard to get the new bullets."

"You have to tell them that I can't make their rifles any better than they are," Hall said. "The shooting comes from me, not from the gun."

"Maybe you can hold a ceremony."

Hall looked to Ghostwind, who explained to him that her father was requesting that he call on spiritual powers to make the rifles shoot better. He would be paid in horses and riding gear.

"I don't know how to do that," Hall told Ghostwind. "I don't know that it's possible."

"I will tell my father," she said.

After Ghostwind had explained, Five Bulls left, disappointed. Hall asked her how he could be expected to change everyone's shooting ability.

"You have to understand that among our people we share our gifts," Ghostwind said. "If a man has medicine he can teach others, he will sell it or give it as a present. My people believe that your gift with the rifles is medicine that can be bought."

"I don't know anything about that," Hall said. "I hope it doesn't cause trouble."

"I hope not, too," Ghostwind said.

Hall spent the next two days hunting. He took three of the four ponies he had won and loaded them with deer and antelope. Many of the villagers, including Five Bulls and Red Bear, wanted to accompany him and watch him shoot. They hoped some of the great medicine would rub off on them. Hall insisted he be alone for the first trip out, at least until he knew how to make sign better.

But many of the warriors followed him anyway, keeping at a distance, marveling at his marksmanship. After watching, Red Bear and Eagle Wing would talk nightly about how Hall had gotten so many antelope.

The antelope had become skittish from hunting pressure and would speed off at the slightest hint of a rider's approach. Hall saw no reason to chase them. He left the horses picketed out in the open, one with a white flag on a stick tied to the saddle. He took a stand nearby and waited patiently. When the curious antelope returned to investigate the horses and the flag, Hall shot three of them, although two were on the dead run.

Hall eventually shot three more antelope and two mule deer. Though he saw a few wandering buffalo, he was not tempted. He would have to run a horse through the snow to get one. It would be hard on the horse and also on his injured leg, which was just beginning to feel good again.

When Hall returned, everyone cheered him. Ghostwind held Talking Grass in her arms, and Young Horse stood beside her, watching as Hall rode among the Cheyenne lodges, giving game to those who had children. He saved a large mule deer for Ghostwind and her children, and offered an antelope to Crazy Horse for keeping him in his lodge.

"I thank you for the offer, but I have plenty of meat,"

Crazy Horse told him in sign. "We will cook it along with other game in a feast tonight."

The talk throughout the evening was about Hall's marksmanship and hunting prowess. Hall ate and listened, not understanding a word, but interested in the methods used by the warriors to tell stories. They were very animated, acting out the parts of both Hall and the game he hunted.

Eagle Wing pointed at Hall often and told of the running shots at the antelope. He even acted out the scene in the village when Hall had saved Ghostwind and her daughter from the Bluecoats, as if Hall were actually one of their own people.

"This is a very unusual thing," Ghostwind told Hall. "Eagle Wing is asking that you be accepted as one of us. It's hard to believe this could happen so quickly."

"Why would he want this?" Hall asked.

"Likely because you decided not to fight him. He had made the challenge and then had stepped back. If you had wanted, you could have fought anyway and possibly killed him. He's grateful that you didn't."

Hall noticed Day Lily talking to Red Bear, her husband. "I know that Red Bear doesn't like me," Hall said. "That doesn't make it easy for your friend."

"Day Lily and I will remain friends," Ghostwind said. "I hope that Red Bear will change his mind, but he and my husband were war brothers."

Eagle Wing finished his story, and Crazy Horse called for silence so that he could make an announcement. "The council of Cheyenne elders has asked me to give you news. They have decided on a name for the Bluecoat who saved Ghostwind's life. He will now be called The-Trick-Shooter-With-the-Good-but-Angry-Heart. He will live among the Cheyenne people."

This met with general approval. Red Bear was obviously

unhappy, but it had been a decision made by the council, so no one could reject the decision outright.

"You have been accepted," Ghostwind said. "You are adopted as one of my people."

"That name doesn't fit me!" Hall told Ghostwind. "Maybe the trick shooter part, but not the angry heart."

"It's easy for everyone to see that the name fits you," Ghostwind said. "That doesn't mean anyone is judging you. Everyone knows that you have lived a difficult life. Just realize that you are now a different person. Maybe in time your anger will go away."

At first Hall had difficulty with the concept of such a drastic change. Throughout his entire life he had wanted freedom and a chance to be his own person. Now he was receiving that chance, and it seemed too soon. In but a few short days he had made his first contact with the Sioux and the Cheyenne, and had suddenly become a part of their society.

"I don't know what to do about all this," Hall told Ghostwind.

"Don't worry. Eagle Wing will help you through the ceremonies. Just listen to him."

Everyone gathered in the center of the village so that a ceremony could be performed and gifts given to Angry Heart in honor of his name. The people would call him Angry Heart for the rest of his life, or until he performed a deed that qualified him for a different name.

Before the naming ceremony, Hall's horse was killed, and his clothing was ceremoniously burned, so that nothing of his Bluecoat past might remain with him. New buckskin leggings and tops were given him. The clothing came from the Oglala people, as the attack had left the Cheyenne poor. This seemed fitting, for Angry Heart was now a man who could live among the Cheyenne or the Lakota, whichever he chose.

But Angry Heart was not yet a warrior. Everyone knew the day would soon come when he would have to prove his new allegiance by fighting against the Bluecoats, the people he was casting off. In time, when he had done significant war deeds, he might be asked to join a warrior society. To gain that honor, he would have to pass certain tests. As Ghostwind's father explained, no one doubted Angry Heart's physical strength and stamina; he had already proved them. But he had yet to prove self-discipline. And there were those who wondered if he could face his own people without breaking down.

"I have said before that my own people put me in prison once and now want me to go back there," Angry Heart told Five Bulls in sign. "It's in my best interest to keep away from them."

"We can see that your heart wants to live free," Five Bulls told him. "When it's time for the tests, there is little doubt you will pass them. You've already survived a great deal. The tests will only make you stronger."

During the feasting, Angry Heart was given many gifts. Though he felt honored, it bothered him that Red Bear had been joined in his disapproval by a good number of younger warriors and even a few of the older ones. There were also women, Day Lily not among them, who scowled at him from a distance. They did not take part in the ceremony or the feast, and a few of them spoke to the council about having Angry Heart sent away.

Of all the eyes upon him, Crazy Horse's stares were the hardest. They seemed to watch Angry Heart's every move, wincing whenever he came near Ghostwind.

"Don't let this bother you," Ghostwind told Angry Heart when he brought it up to her. "Crazy Horse respects me. That's why he agreed to allow you into his village. But he still isn't used to the idea that you and I are good friends."

"But he announced my new name," Angry Heart said. "I can see only one reason that he wouldn't want me to stay: you. Does he want you for his own?"

"He has a wife," Ghostwind said. "She has the coughing sickness. I don't believe he would take another into his lodge while she's sick."

"What if she dies?"

"Crazy Horse and I could never be united in that way," Ghostwind said. "He knows that, especially after the death of my husband."

"But it was I who killed your husband," Angry Heart said. "I don't understand."

"There's a long and complicated story I will tell you some time," Ghostwind said. "For now, just believe that Crazy Horse and I will never be man and wife."

"What about Red Bear and the others who do not approve of this?" Angry Heart asked. "Will they cause trouble?"

"We have to stay together, because of the Bluecoats," Ghostwind said. "The council decided to give you a name and welcome you, so that is the law. Anyone who causes trouble will be thrown out by the warrior societies, to live on his own. Everyone knows that."

"It doesn't stop them from protesting," Angry Heart said. "And Red Bear is the loudest. That makes me feel bad for you."

"Don't waste time feeling bad for me," Ghostwind said. "I have lived among a divided people from that snowy day in my childhood when I first entered the village. Even though I saved Old Bear's people from the fate of Black Kettle and his people at the Washita, there were those who did not trust me. Some still want me to go away, especially now that you've come."

"I accept the fact that I could be under suspicion,"

Angry Heart said. "But I don't understand why anyone would wonder about you."

"There are those who blame me for the coming of the Bluecoats you were with," Ghostwind told him. "I prayed every night on a sacred hill and learned what signs to watch for to tell when the Bluecoats were coming. But I missed the signs, and some of the people believe I did it on purpose. They believe I foresaw your coming, and that I wanted you badly enough to put everyone at risk."

Angry Heart stared. "They believe that you want me?"

"Yes, for a husband."

"Where would they get that idea?"

"It's a rumor that's been circulating through the village. Even if I wanted you, I could not take a husband for a while. I'm still in mourning. But some believe that I knew you would be with the Bluecoats."

"This is hard to understand," Angry Heart said. "Didn't they stop to think that the odds that you and I would ever meet are too great to calculate? Can't they understand that you or I, or both, could have been killed?"

"No, you don't understand," Ghostwind said. "I am considered a prophet, one who sees. Many believe that I knew all this would happen, but that you and I would both live. Because you are so unusual, they believe I saw you in dreams and waited for you."

"Is that true?"

Ghostwind thought a moment. "I don't know. But it doesn't matter now." She motioned toward the villagers who, accepting him, had formed a ring. "Go now and walk among the people. It's time for you to do that, so they can touch you and call you by your new name. You have become one of us."

PART III
Spring, 1876

TWENTY

It was the fourth day of the journey to Sitting Bull's village. Though the bitter cold had receded, the night temperatures dropped below freezing. Still, Angry Heart found the trip much more pleasant than the frigid ordeal he had faced with Ghostwind in reaching Crazy Horse's Oglala.

Angry Heart's past now seemed like another life that had blown away with the wind. Ghostwind and the Cheyenne people had pulled him into their world, where nothing earlier seemed to have any significance. There were times when he wondered if his head injury had been more serious than he had at first believed.

But Angry Heart realized the change that was developing within him would have come whether or not he had been injured. He had disliked marching with Crook's army and would have deserted sooner or later. His fall from a horse in a frozen Cheyenne camp was only the means that had delivered him.

Still, he realized he was lucky to be alive. The fall could easily have killed him, as well as a Cheyenne bullet or arrow. But he had been spared, and his headaches were subsiding, allowing more and more memories to return. Now he simply felt disconnected from the past, as if the person he had once been no longer existed.

Ghostwind rode up beside him. "You seem lost."

"I'm just thinking."

"That's good," she said. "Could it be that you're wondering about what has happened to you and how your life will change?"

"How did you know that?"

"It happened to me when I first came among Old Bear's people," she replied. "I was but a child of eight winters, confused, lost from my past. In many regards, I'm still lost from my past."

Ghostwind told of the amnesia that hid her childhood from her. She confided that she thought about her past daily, hoping her memories might return. But she had come to the conclusion that she might never know about her first eight years of life.

"If it serves me in this life, I will learn my childhood," Ghostwind said. "I'm not ashamed of anything."

"There's a lot in my childhood I wish hadn't happened," Hall said, "but I guess I don't worry about it. I just don't know what to expect from here on. I feel separated from anything I have ever known."

"A lot of things have changed for you," Ghostwind said. "Maybe you've come among us so that you can learn who you really are."

"What are you talking about? I know who I am."

"Then you were satisfied to live in prison, and to become a Bluecoat?"

"No," Angry Heart said quickly. "That's not what I meant."

"If you feel good about who you once were, then you must have no regrets about what you've done."

"I guess I see your point," Angry Heart said. "There's plenty about my past that I'm not proud of. I'm just telling you that all this is very new to me. It takes some time to adjust."

"You'd better work hard on adjusting yourself before we reach Sitting Bull's people," Ghostwind advised. "You're going to meet a very powerful man among the Lakota, a medicine dreamer of great courage and wisdom. You're a guest of my people and you will be allowed into the village; but you must impress Sitting Bull."

Angry Heart had learned from Kincaid that Sitting Bull's Unkpapa, the biggest of all the Lakota groups, had an intense dislike of whites. Though not as warlike as the Oglala, Sitting Bull's people wanted to be left alone and desired no contact with the white world whatsoever. "The less we are around them, the better off we'll be," Sitting Bull had said. "The *Wasichu* have no respect for themselves. Otherwise they wouldn't make war on the land and everyone else around them."

Angry Heart had been hearing about Sitting Bull ever since the journey to the Unkpapa had begun. Crazy Horse and his Oglala, incensed at the Bluecoat attack upon the Cheyenne, had already sent messengers ahead to tell Sitting Bull of their coming. There was no doubt the Unkpapa would be furious as well.

Angry Heart realized he was a *Wasichu* invading the Unkpapa domain. His acceptance by the Cheyenne and Oglala would do him no good. He would have to start over and prove himself once again.

"This will be another big challenge for you," Ghostwind said. "But you're very strong in spirit. You can face it and be victorious."

"What if Sitting Bull doesn't accept me?" Angry Heart asked. "Will they send me away?"

"Oh, no, they won't let you go and tell the Bluecoats where we are," Ghostwind said.

"But I wouldn't do that."

"I know that, but I'm alone in my feelings. No one knows for certain how the Bluecoats feel about you. They wouldn't take a chance on letting you go for any reason."

Angry Heart thought a moment. "So, I would be killed."

"You don't have much faith in yourself," Ghostwind said. "You should, especially after what you've been through."

"You didn't answer me," Angry Heart said. "If Sitting Bull disapproves of me, will I die?"

"Yes, very likely."

"So I'm pretty well trapped, is that it?"

"That's true. Very true. But like Crazy Horse, Sitting Bull is a fair man. He will know who you are by looking at you. He can read your very soul. Just relax and be yourself, as you were with my people and the Oglala."

"Maybe I could demonstrate my shooting ability," Angry Heart suggested.

"Don't do anything you aren't asked to do first," Ghostwind advised. "Sitting Bull must trust you before you are allowed to do even the slightest thing. Don't label yourself as dangerous right away."

"But Old Bear and Two Moon and Eagle Wing all think highly of me," Angry Heart argued. "That should mean something."

"I told you, my people are guests," Ghostwind said. "We must abide by the laws of the village, as the Unkpapa do when they come to our villages. Among the Lakota, Sitting Bull is supreme."

Angry Heart rode in silence, feeling totally helpless. He could see little difference now from being with the Army: he was bound. Should he decide to take his leave, he would face certain death. No doubt many young warriors would trail him until they caught him. At least with the Army, he would have had a better chance at escape.

"I don't see a lot of hope," Angry Heart said. "All I've ever heard from the Army, and now from you, is how much Sitting Bull hates whites. What can I possibly do to gain his respect? I mean, I wore an Army uniform. I don't stand a chance."

"You can show him that you respect us, and our way of life," Ghostwind replied. "But I'm afraid that will be hard for you. I've noticed that you feel discontented living among us, even with your new name. What is it you are trying to escape? Yourself?"

Angry Heart frowned. "I'm content with who I am."

"That's not how you act. Even my children can see it. They like you. They wonder at your feelings. Can't you believe someone would accept you for who you are?"

"There are a lot of people who don't want me here," Angry Heart said.

"There are more who do," Ghostwind pointed out. "And there are more who are coming to like you every day. Don't you believe you are a likable person?"

"I don't know," Angry Heart said. "I just feel out of place. Maybe I should just leave."

"If you really want to leave my people, you will have to prove yourself first," Ghostwind said. "Prepare yourself to become a warrior and offer to lead the way against the Bluecoats. To prove yourself in battle against your own people will impress all the leaders, and you will then be allowed to make your own choice about staying or leaving."

"I don't have any problem with that," Angry Heart said. "I have no friends among the Bluecoats."

"That is your only way out," Ghostwind said. "If you show enough courage, you might even be able to ride with the leaders, or become a leader."

"Will Sitting Bull and Crazy Horse want me to lead?" Angry Heart asked.

"Crazy Horse will not feel challenged," Ghostwind replied. "Sitting Bull is no longer a war chief. In the days before he was married and a father of children, he counted many coups against enemies. Now he's a medicine dreamer. He stays in the village and prays for the success of those fighting. He's a strong influence on their success."

"When I was a Bluecoat, I heard that Sitting Bull was responsible for the killing of a lot of whites," Angry Heart said. "We were told he and Crazy Horse were the worst Indians on the Plains. You're telling me that Sitting Bull isn't even a war leader?"

"Sitting Bull is a great leader of influence," Ghostwind explained, "but he hasn't led men into battle for a number of winters. The whites are afraid of him because of his wisdom and want to make him out to be bad. There is little truth in what the whites know about the Indian people."

Angry Heart remembered Grouard talking about Sitting Bull, saying he was getting up in years and shouldn't be considered a threat. Grouard wanted Crazy Horse. But a good many of the officers wanted to believe that Sitting Bull would lead the charges at them. As far as they were concerned, Sitting Bull was as big a target as Crazy Horse. The Army believed both must be subdued in order to control the Indian problem.

"I heard a lot about the fighting in this country ten years ago," Hall said. "That time the Army lost. They blame that on Sitting Bull and another chief named Red Cloud."

"Sitting Bull fought hard ten winters past, when the forts were built on the Bozeman Road," Ghostwind said. "So did Red Cloud. But these two men no longer fight, unless a village is attacked. All men who have gained status as warriors and are married with families can choose to stay out of the fighting. It is the young warriors who must gain honors before marriage who raid for horses and do battle."

"How long will it take me to gain honors and make everyone believe in me?" Angry Heart asked.

"I don't know," Ghostwind said, "but it is certain you should begin right away. Then, if you so choose, you can leave. There will be only one problem: even more people will like you and respect you. Though your skin is white, you will be considered one of the people. It will be hard for you to leave then."

"But no one will stop me?"

"No one will stop you. Unless you decide to stop yourself."

Sitting Bull's village covered a large open meadow near the head of a small stream that flowed into the Powder River. Blue Earth Creek, which flowed through the Blue Earth Hills, was a favorite campsite. To the east rose a large plateau whose sides were chalky white and surrounded by timber. "The whites call it the Chalk Buttes," Ghostwind said. "Indian people call it the Charcoal Buttes. The Lakota people make winter camp here often."

Angry Heart was struck by the sudden change of landscape, from rolling, sage-covered hills to this little forest popping up from the Plains. In the eastern distance he could see the territory known as the Black Hills, where gold fever ran rampant among the whites, the main cause of all the problems.

During the ride Angry Heart had heard the people talking about the Sacred Hills and how they had been pushed from them. Many of the young warriors wanted to go and take the hills back, but the older men cautioned them against foolish behavior. Banding together in large numbers was the only way to keep the Bluecoats from destroying everyone. Going off to fight in anger for a lost cause was a sure way to bring disaster.

A contingent of Unkpapa rode out to greet Crazy Horse and his party. They all frowned at Angry Heart and talked among themselves. As they entered Sitting Bull's village, Ghostwind told Angry Heart to remain confident, no matter what happened.

"It will be much the same as when you met Crazy Horse," she said. "Sitting Bull will test you."

"I don't think I can sign well enough to get by," Angry Heart confessed.

"Say nothing until I am given permission to translate for you," Ghostwind said.

They followed the Unkpapa escorts toward the center of the village. Already a number of Unkpapa were calling for Angry Heart's death. He didn't have to know the Lakota language to understand that.

Several Unkpapa warriors rode on both sides of the visitors, as a barrier against anyone who might start trouble.

"They are the village police," Ghostwind told Angry Heart. "They will keep everyone away from you. Sitting Bull must have given orders that you are not to be harmed in any way."

The shouting continued. Then a young warrior emerged from the crowd, leveled a rifle, and fired. The blast caused Angry Heart's pony to shy sideways; the bullet passed just in front of Angry Heart's eyes.

Angry Heart started to dismount, but Ghostwind stopped him. "Let Sitting Bull's police take care of it," she said. "He has committed a crime, and he will be punished."

"I wasn't going after him," Angry Heart assured her. "I just don't want to be a good target up here on this horse."

"Don't worry," Ghostwind said, "no one else will try to

kill you. That warrior will be severely punished. He'll be lucky if they don't kill him."

Angry Heart watched while the police took the warrior's rifle and whipped him with their quirts. The warrior tried to shield himself with his arms, yelling as the quirts opened cuts about his face and neck and along his arms.

"But surely some of the police must feel the same way he does," Angry Heart said.

"It doesn't matter," Ghostwind said. "Rules must be followed. An order was given not to harm you. Anyone who breaks that rule must be disciplined, no matter if the police feel the same as the lawbreaker. That's the custom."

Two of the village police rode to Angry Heart and stayed beside him until they had reached Sitting Bull's lodge. There the Cheyenne and Lakota leaders dismounted to greet Sitting Bull, who was emerging from under the doorflap.

Angry Heart and Ghostwind dismounted and their ponies were led away. Angry Heart stood as tall and straight as possible, feeling much as he had when standing before General Crook. But Sitting Bull was nothing like Crook, nor were any of the Indian leaders even remotely similar to Army commanders. They greeted one another in brotherly fashion, laughing and joking, with no formality. There was no visible envy or jealousy among them, only respect for each as an individual and Sitting Bull in particular.

Angry Heart tried not to stare. Sitting Bull, dressed in skins and wrapped in a multicolored blanket, stood nearly six feet tall. He was thickly built, with a large head and dark, piercing eyes. His hair, in two long braids with a single eagle feather, hung to his waist.

Sitting Bull gave no indication that he had even seen Angry Heart as he talked with Crazy Horse and the other leaders. Ghostwind told him under her breath to remain patient, that he might not be asked to present himself for a long time, possibly not until the next day.

"Crazy Horse has already told Sitting Bull that I'm here to translate for you," Ghostwind said. "When you're asked to speak, tell me in English and sign what you want me to say. But make no move until you're asked."

The Indian leaders continued to reacquaint themselves. Ghostwind explained that many of them had not seen one another for a number of winters. Then, after the greetings, the laughter died. Angry Heart knew the conversation had turned to the Bluecoat threat. It was a serious matter to be discussed at length. There would be a long council, Ghostwind said quietly, and a lot of serious decisions would be made.

Angry Heart's fear began to rise. He considered the possibility that Sitting Bull had already decided to have him killed. The leader still had not once looked him in the eye. As far as all the leaders were concerned, he wasn't even there.

Angry Heart leaned toward Ghostwind. "How long do we have to stand here?"

"Until we're asked to move," Ghostwind said. "To do anything else would be a grave insult."

"Why are they ignoring me?" Angry Heart asked.

"They want to see how you feel about being considered a lower-class person than they," Ghostwind explained. "I told you that you would be tested. Don't fail."

"I don't care about my status," Angry Heart said. "I'm concerned about Sitting Bull. What if he decides he doesn't want me around?"

Ghostwind spoke sternly. "If you think things should be easy for you now, you're mistaken. Your trials have only begun. Most everyone knows what's in your heart. You proved that by saving me and my child. You showed you are strong by surviving the ride to Crazy Horse's people. But now is the time to show what you are truly made of. If you want to become an equal with even the most ordinary of warriors, you will have to prove you know discipline. And you will have to show that you believe your body is not your own, but belongs instead to the Creator."

Angry Heart began to understand. Sitting Bull wanted to test his wisdom: how much he knew about the complexities of living as a human being, how much he knew about giving rather than receiving, and about accepting those things he had no control over. These were things that knew no boundaries of race or creed.

The test would be severe, Angry Heart knew. Sitting Bull's mere presence bespoke power and authority, and deep understanding. He knew truth and could tell if another knew it as well.

"He will not judge you, no matter what he thinks of you," Ghostwind said. "He's too wise for that. But if he believes you will not be good for his people, he will send you away, and he will not stop others from killing you."

"You don't seem worried at all," Angry Heart said.

"I'm not," she replied. "I know you very well already. You will be tortured, especially within your soul, but you will survive."

TWENTY-ONE

Ghostwind and Angry Heart took a seat outside the large, specially constructed council lodge. At times the voices from inside carried clearly out into the evening air. Ghostwind explained to Angry Heart that Old Bear and Two Moon were telling what had happened in their village the morning of the Bluecoats' attack. They were including everything, even Angry Heart's gun battle with the two Bluecoats to save Ghostwind and her child, and the encounter with Eagle Wing later.

Following the Cheyenne account, Crazy Horse then told his story of how the Cheyenne had come to his village. He told of questioning Angry Heart and witnessing his ability to shoot. He related Angry Heart's hunting success, and the Cheyenne naming ceremony.

"It's clear that my people's leaders respect you highly," Ghostwind told Angry Heart. "And I know that Crazy Horse respects you as well. But maybe not as much."

"Because of you?"

"That's possible."

"I think it's more than possible."

Angry Heart wanted to discuss Crazy Horse's feelings with Ghostwind, but a messenger suddenly emerged from the lodge and spoke to Ghostwind.

"Sitting Bull requests your presence," she told Angry Heart. "The messenger asks what your wish is. You can choose whether or not to talk with Sitting Bull."

"Yes, I want to talk," Angry Heart said. "Of course."

Ghostwind relayed the message. She and Angry Heart entered the lodge, where a group of Cheyenne and Lakota men sat around a low fire. Sitting Bull extended his hand, offering Angry Heart a seat directly opposite him. Ghostwind sat to Angry Heart's left.

Sitting Bull lit a pipe and puffed until the bowl glowed. He said prayers and made the offering to the four directions, as well as the earth and sky. He smoked again and passed the pipe to his left. When the pipe reached Angry Heart, he took it gingerly.

He had smoked cigars on occasion as a child and young man, but had never tasted anything so strong as this mixture. After coughing, he handed the pipe to the warrior on his left. When the pipe got back to Sitting Bull, the leader sat for a long time without speaking.

Angry Heart sat cross-legged, trying to relax. He was convinced Sitting Bull knew his every thought. The longer the silence remained, the harder it was to keep composure. Finally, Sitting Bull spoke.

"It is said that you can shoot like no other man. Is this so?"

When Ghostwind translated, Angry Heart answered immediately. "I've learned to shoot well. I cannot say that I'm the best, though."

"How many men have you killed with your shooting?"

"I've killed men in hand-to-hand fighting, to save my life, but I've never shot a man to death."

"It would be easy for you to kill enemies with a rifle. You wouldn't have to get close at all."

"I don't like to kill men," Angry Heart said. "It gives me a very bad feeling."

Sitting Bull studied Angry Heart. "Why did you learn to shoot so well?"

"I worked with a circus. I did it to make people pay money to come and see me. I didn't learn to shoot so that I could kill people."

"But the time has come when a lot of killing will occur. How do you feel about that?"

Angry Heart paused to think. "I've told you that I would kill to save myself, or those I hold dear to me. I believe there are times when killing cannot be avoided. But I don't look forward to those times."

"Would you kill to protect the Cheyenne and Lakota peoples?"

"The Cheyenne and Lakota peoples have saved my life. The Cheyenne have given me a name and a home. I am grateful. I would do what I must to protect them."

Sitting Bull relit the pipe. After more prayers and offerings, the pipe circled the council. Angry Heart smoked again, but did not cough.

When the pipe had completely circled the council, Sitting Bull began another line of questioning.

"Are you strong enough to face anything?"

"I've come through a great deal," Angry Heart replied. "I believe I could withstand most anything."

"Good. You will soon have a very strong test. It will come sometime tomorrow, when the Minneconjou join us. They are not far away."

"Will the test come from the Minneconjou?" Angry Heart asked.

"Yes, from one Minnecoujou only," Sitting Bull replied. "It will be a great test for you. Then we will see how strong you really are."

Angry Heart thought for a moment. Would he have to fight a prominent warrior? That made no sense. He looked to Ghostwind. "Will I have to fight one of the Minneconjou?"

"You will face one of them," Sitting Bull said, "but not for fighting. Your test will be much harder than any fight. You will be facing your past."

Angry Heart's mouth dropped. "Are you talking about my father? Is he among the Minneconjou?"

Sitting Bull nodded. "Your father, Shot-in-the-Throat, will come with his family. You will see him for the first time in many winters. It will be a hard test."

Angry Heart noticed everyone watching intently. Flooded with emotions, he sat as still as he could, then looked squarely at Sitting Bull.

"Tell him that he's right," he said to Ghostwind. "Tell Sitting Bull that tomorrow will be the hardest day of my life."

Angry Heart awakened to sounds of excitement in the village. He peered out of his wickiup to see people shouting and waving. Though light had barely broken the horizon, everyone was fully dressed.

Ghostwind yelled from outside the wickiup, "Hurry! The Minneconjou have arrived."

Angry Heart dressed and joined Ghostwind, who had sent Young Horse and Talking Grass ahead with their grandparents.

"They must have been traveling all night," Ghostwind said.

The Minneconjou were crossing the open flat east of the combined villages. Very shortly Angry Heart would be talking with his father, for the first time in so very long. His stomach was tied in knots.

"I don't know what to say to him," Angry Heart told Ghostwind. "I just can't greet him and make believe everything's fine."

"Of course everything's not fine," Ghostwind said. "But that's something you and he will have to discuss together. Tell him what's in your heart. That's the best way. Don't spoil the first time you've seen him in many winters."

"Actually," Angry Heart said, "I saw him just over a month ago, back at Fort Fetterman. But I didn't know it was him."

Angry Heart told Ghostwind about the frontiersmen who had come to Fort Fetterman with horses to sell, his father among them, and that night when Sergeant Buckner had molested the young Arapaho woman.

"My father and his friends came to help her," Angry Heart said. "They all thought I was to blame and were going to teach me a lesson. I came very close to killing my father and didn't even know it. A friend of mine who packs mules for the Bluecoats stopped me."

"You didn't know your own father?"

"It had been a long time since I last saw him. His hair was longer and he couldn't talk. I wasn't expecting to see him. They left, and neither my father or I knew each other."

"What did you think when your friend told you?"

"I was shocked," Angry Heart said. "I didn't think I ever wanted to see my father again. But I had almost shot him. Everything was very confusing."

"Your pain and anger are great," Ghostwind said. "It's time that you make peace with him and go forward with your life."

Angry Heart watched the Minneconjou approach the

village. "It's going to be hard to talk to him. I wish I didn't have to. I'm not ready."

"You're ready," Ghostwind said. "Just be certain you don't start yelling at him. I don't want any of them to have call to dislike you."

Ghostwind explained that she knew this band of Minneconjou very well. Her adopted father had been born among them, the son of an influential man, now deceased. She said that this band, under its leader, Lame Deer, was returning from the Fort Berthold Agency, where they had received their rations and traded for goods. They had left Sitting Bull's village in the latter part of March, when the weather had first broken.

Ordinarily, the bands would have remained separate. But news of the Bluecoats had arrived at the agency, and Lame Deer wished to rejoin with Sitting Bull's people for protection. Ghostwind was certain that news of a Bluecoat living among the Cheyenne would cause alarm.

"I'll be careful," Angry Heart said. "This would be a poor time to let my emotions get the best of me."

"That's why Sitting Bull asked you the questions he did," Ghostwind said. "He wants to be certain that you and your father make your peace. The slightest problem could cost both of you your lives. That would make your father's wife very sad. And it would make their son sad as well."

"Their son?"

"They have a boy of twelve winters. Tall Deer is big and strong for his age."

Angry Heart was speechless for a moment. "There are a lot of surprises, aren't there?"

"Surprises make the heart stronger," Ghostwind said.

Angry Heart studied her. "You said my father's wife would be sad if he was killed. How would you feel if I died?"

"Just don't let that happen," Ghostwind said. "Hurry and follow me. I see my aunt and your father."

Ghostwind was already hugging her aunt when Angry Heart caught up. Tall Deer was talking with Young Horse, and both of them were pointing at Angry Heart, who was now the talk of the newcomers. But Angry Heart's attention was focused solely on a man dressed in buckskins, wearing an ermine cap.

Angry Heart's father sat atop a gray pony, staring at him through piercing blue eyes. The scar on his throat was plainly visible, a discolored furrow that ran straight through his larynx.

With mixed emotions, Angry Heart watched his father dismount. The joy of seeing him again and knowing he was alive and well was tainted by anger and hurt. He remembered the vibrant delight that had always come when his father would lift him up and hug him, and tell him how much he had grown. As the memories flooded back, a deep pain rose from inside him and nearly brought him to tears.

Angry Heart's stomach churned as his father stepped toward him, his arms extended. Angry Heart offered only his hand to shake.

"It's been a long time, Pa," Angry Heart said in sign. He stood rigid.

Shot-in-the-Throat signed back, "You've learned the hand talk well. How?"

"Kincaid taught me first. Ghostwind has helped me a lot."

"You always were a fast learner." Shot-in-the-Throat looked him up and down. "You're a strapping kid."

"I was a kid the last time you came home to Missouri, Pa. I'm no kid anymore."

"You're right. I'm surprised you even came out to see me. I'm glad you didn't shoot me back at Fetterman."

"I didn't know it was you," Angry Heart said. "I had no idea."

"You didn't?"

"Of course not. Kincaid told me later."

"I didn't know you, either," Shot-in-the-Throat confessed. "When I learned who you were later, I couldn't believe it. I guess I should've known you'd make it out here one day."

"I wanted to come out with you, Pa. You shouldn't have left me back there."

"I went back to get you. They said you'd joined some circus."

"You went back for me?"

"I looked all over that country for you. I've always wondered what happened to you."

"No, you didn't go back."

"I surely did. You can ask Pine Woman. She'll tell you. I hurt inside for a long time when I got back out here. I wanted you with me."

"Then why didn't you take me with you in the first place?"

Shot-in-the-Throat moved from one foot to the other. "I couldn't. But I'll tell you about it later." He clapped Angry Heart's shoulder. "Let's eat something. We've been on the trail all night. We can catch up on everything later."

Angry Heart stepped away from him. "Why don't you go and eat? I need some time by myself." He turned and hurried back to his wickiup. He sat for a short time, his whole being spinning with emotion. Then he got up and left the village.

He followed the creek, his eyes brimming with tears. He fought them back. Water flowed under melting ice and meadowlarks sang of the coming spring. But he heard none of it, only the drumming of sealed sadness within him, bursting to get out.

Angry Heart found a small knoll next to the water and sat down. The sun flooded the hills, spilling pure light against the snowbanks that sprawled along the grassy slopes. Angry Heart looked into the distance, as far out as he could. There was no way to relive his life up to this point. It was too late for him to decide to jump from the Army ambulance he had ridden to Fort Fetterman and take his chances in the night cold. He wished he had, so that now he could be someplace other than here, possibly even dead, so that he didn't have to feel the intense pain that wouldn't let him go.

He heard footsteps behind him and turned to see Ghostwind.

"May I sit down?"

"Of course."

"Why did you leave the village?"

Angry Heart turned again to the distance. "My father has a family. He doesn't want me."

"Did he tell you that?"

"No, but that's the way it is."

"How can you be so sure?"

"Look, he has a wife and a son, and he's living his life with the Minneconjou. If he had wanted me, he would have looked until he found me."

"You're not being fair," Ghostwind said. "You don't know how long or how hard he looked for you."

"It couldn't have been that long. I wasn't that hard to find, with a traveling circus. There weren't that many, and we were among the biggest."

"You told me you never stayed in one place for more than a day or two," Ghostwind said. "If all the circuses do that, how would you expect him to ever catch up to any of them so that he could find you?"

"I was a trick shooter," Angry Heart said. "One of the best. People remembered me. He could have found me."

"Are you sure the people remembered you?" Ghostwind asked. "Or did they just remember your shooting?"

Angry Heart bowed his head and stared silently into the creek.

"Maybe to them you didn't have a face," Ghostwind continued. "Maybe it was just your shooting that they remembered."

"No! They remembered me! I know they did."

"Weren't there other trick shooters in other shows?"

"I was the best," Angry Heart said. "The best."

"You might have been the best, but he still didn't find you," Ghostwind said. "And I know that he went to look for you. Pine Woman told me. She cried because she feared that your father would stay among his people and not return to her. Then, when he did return, she cried because he hadn't found you. He stayed out in the hills for days, mourning you. He thought maybe you were dead."

Angry Heart turned to Ghostwind. Her eyes were filled with tears. "I didn't know," he said.

"You could have known, had you chosen to listen to him," Ghostwind said angrily. "You chose instead to be wrathful and to believe that he doesn't love you."

"I didn't say that."

"You didn't have to. Your actions proved it. You left him and came out here, making him feel very bad. Do you even understand how hard it was for him to go back and look for you? He can't even talk!"

"No, I guess I didn't think about that."

Ghostwind clenched her fists. "You make me very angry because you act like such a fool. He's your father. He can't help but love you."

"You're right," Angry Heart said. "Of course you're right."

"You meet your father and you spit on him," Ghostwind continued, more tears coming. "You don't understand what it's like not to know about your parents. Five Bulls and Mountain Water love me dearly, and I love them, but I would give anything to have my memories back and know who my real parents were. Maybe they're alive, maybe dead. I would love to know what happened to them. I would give anything."

Ghostwind started to rise and Angry Heart took her arm. "Please, don't go."

Ghostwind pulled away. "I have to go. I want to visit with everyone and be glad for the things I have. I don't want to be sad any longer or be around a man who is so angry he cannot see the beauty of life around him."

Angry Heart watched her leave. When she reached the village, he started back, then turned again and began to walk upstream, his emotions tearing at him.

He walked slowly, thinking about the things Ghostwind had told him. His father's search must have been very difficult. It must have been nearly impossible to communicate without the use of speech. He must have endured a great deal of ridicule.

Angry Heart felt a deep sense of guilt. Ghostwind had been right: he shouldn't have been thinking only about himself. Instead, he should have considered his father's feelings and what it must have been like not to find him. He must have thought there would never be another chance to see his son.

Angry Heart realized that by shunning his father, he was only hurting himself. He had wondered about his father for so many years, and now here was the opportunity to learn about the time that had been lost.

But what would he say when his father asked about the time after the circus—the year and a half in prison?

There was nothing to do but tell the truth. He had told it to nobody up to now, but it was time he looked it square in the face. The truth hadn't killed him, though it should have many times. What had helped him get through those years was the memories of his father's homecomings.

As Angry Heart remembered those times, it came back to him that he used to carve little wooden figures for his father to take along when he left again. Usually they were horses, with an occasional wildcat. Certainly his father would like one of them again. They could begin anew as they had known one another in Missouri.

A dense patch of young cottonwoods stood up a nearby draw, perfect material for carving. Angry Heart worked his way along the trail through a thick patch of wild plum and chokecherry. Magpies flew from large stick nests, scolding him for the intrusion. Two deer fled from hidden beds in old leaves. Then he reached the edge of the thicket and stopped, his mouth open.

The young cottonwoods were mixed with a number of older trees. From the lower branches of one hung the skeleton of a boy.

The remains dangled from the end of a rawhide rope, the neck twisted, the mouth open, the eyes nothing but hollow bone. Sparse and tattered remnants of clothing still hung from the ribs and backbone, as did strips of dried flesh and sinew. The coal-black hair reached well past the waist, no doubt having grown considerably after death.

Angry Heart turned and began to run. He fell and slid to the bottom of the gully, clawed at the bank until he regained a foothold and scrambled down to the river, his mind filled with the scene behind him.

No more than twelve or thirteen, the boy had committed suicide. Of this Angry Heart had no doubt. He could feel it, the terrible sadness, as if the boy were still there, his tortured soul seeking relief.

Angry Heart took a deep breath and looked back up the draw. He wanted to run until he could run no longer, but he knew it would do no good to run. He couldn't escape. It was as if the surroundings had suddenly changed to those of his own childhood in Missouri, and he was now standing at the edge of another draw, looking at the old oak where he had tried to hang himself that early morning after his father had left for the last time.

The knot had slipped and he had fallen to earth, spraining his ankle. For a long, long time the feeling of having tried would not leave him. With the circus, he had finally left it behind, meeting it again only in an occasional nightmare.

Now it was back. He sat and sobbed, holding his head, washing the thick layer of hurt from deep within himself. It brought him a sense of release, a feeling of having loosened some grip that had held him fast all his life. The bitterness seeped from him and drained off like old blood.

Angry Heart gazed toward the draw, where a raven was gliding into the top of the cottonwoods. It cawed loudly, and Angry Heart believed the bird was staring at him. It flew off, and he stood up, watching it glide lazily up the draw and over the ridge beyond.

"The past is dead," a voice inside him said. "Give it a decent burial. Live this day for what it's worth. Live each day that comes to its fullest."

Angry Heart started back toward the village. He realized that carving wooden horses and wildcats was no way to begin his new life with his father. He was now an adult and his father was middle-aged. Nothing was the same as before, nothing but the natural love they had for one another. That in itself was stronger than anything there was. It would certainly be more than enough to build on.

TWENTY-TWO

Angry Heart met Ghostwind waiting for him at the edge of the Cheyenne village. She said, "I shouldn't have talked to you that way. I should have left you alone. I'm sorry."

"You have nothing to be sorry for," Angry Heart said. "You gave me a lot to think about. Now I can see that I've been very selfish."

Ghostwind smiled. "No, you have a kind and giving heart, but you've been tortured inside for a long time. I'm glad to hear you feel better."

Angry Heart told her that he had looked into his past when he saw the boy's remains back upriver. Ghostwind listened with a startled expression.

"You found a boy who hanged himself?"

"There's not much left of him," Angry Heart said. "It must have happened two or three years ago."

"How do you know it was a boy?"

"I just felt it was. I don't know. I can't explain it."

"Perhaps his spirit is still there, and he spoke to you."

"It made me think about a lot of things," Angry Heart

said. "I've got to look forward from here on, not back-ward."

"It's too bad about the boy," Ghostwind said. "I don't know of anyone from our village who was lost that way. Perhaps he was from another Cheyenne village, or he might have been Lakota."

"Maybe you shouldn't say anything," Angry Heart said. "I wouldn't want to upset anyone."

"No, you don't have to worry about upsetting anyone," Ghostwind assured him. "If the child once lived in any of the villages here, his mother will give you presents and thank you. She would want to know. Even if the child is not from any of the people here, a medicine man will still take care of the remains. Prayers will be said for the restless spirit, so that it might pass on."

"I hope I don't see anything like that again," Angry Heart remarked.

"It happens sometimes," Ghostwind said. "What seems like the slightest thing can weigh heavy on a young person's mind. There were times when I was younger that I thought death would be better for me. But that's not a good way."

"No, it's not," Angry Heart said. "Everything gets bet-ter sooner or later."

Ghostwind smiled. "That's true. Let's go join the oth-ers. Your father will be glad you are back."

Though it was more difficult to face his father the sec-ond time, Angry Heart opened himself to whatever might happen and followed Ghostwind. He expected his father to shun him for having left. He felt he deserved this. Instead, his father opened his arms again and Angry Heart found himself spilling tears on his father's shoulder. Ghostwind and her family, along with many villagers, shouted their approval.

Angry Heart and his father decided to walk together to the top of the largest of the Chalk Buttes, where they could be alone and catch up on each other's lives. For Angry Heart it would mean a lot of work to release the pain and anger of his childhood. He would be hearing a lot of things he hadn't known, and it would surely bring the past before him.

The day remained open, with the sun shining the warmest it had all spring. Along the way, Angry Heart learned the answers to questions that had plagued him for many years. As a child, he had wondered what he had done to anger his father, how bad he must have been to make his father leave for such long periods and, ultimately, never to come back. As an adult, he realized that his father had left for reasons he couldn't possibly have understood.

Now, as he listened to tales of living free in a land that stretched as wide as the sky, he could better understand what his father had felt.

"Living out here made a lot more sense to me than what I knew in Missouri," Shot-in-the-Throat said. "I wanted you to see all this as a boy, but I didn't want to take you away from your mother. That wouldn't have been right. God knows I missed you so bad I couldn't sleep."

"Why didn't you take Ma and me both out here?"

"This wasn't a country for settled people," he replied. "Your Ma always needed things to be tidy and just right. The littlest thing out of kilter shook her up. I think that's what kept her sick all the time, so much worry about things you can't control. You remember how much we argued about things like that?"

Angry Heart could remember that his parents had argued a great deal. As a small boy, he had cried himself to sleep. As he'd gotten older, he'd hoped it would let up. But each time his father returned, the arguments would grow worse. He tried not to pay any attention, but they tore at him.

"The last time you left, I knew you wouldn't be back,"

Angry Heart told his father. "I ran after you. Do you remember that?"

Shot-in-the-Throat bit his lip. "I remember. But it would have killed your ma and me both if I'd stayed. We'd grown that far apart. I had to come back out here."

"Why did you wait so long to look for me?"

"I had to wait until I thought it was safe," Shot-in-the-Throat replied. "I would have feared for your life out here. You see, the Bozeman Road was open and there was a lot of fighting. There was talk that the Army was coming into all the villages, killing women and children and everyone. Custer had killed a lot of Cheyenne down on the Washita. Everyone believed he would be coming up into this country."

Angry Heart wanted to tell his father about the terrible dream in which he saw the warrior holding Custer's head. That could come later, after he had heard all his father wanted to say.

"And it wasn't just the U.S. Army," Shot-in-the-Throat continued. "A bunch of settlers banded together and raided a trading post. They killed the trader and his Minneconjou wife, and his three kids, just because they had Indian blood in them. I got myself shot in the throat during the revenge raid."

"One of the settlers shot you?"

"I don't know where the bullet came from. There were at least fifty of us, and we wiped out four homesteads. Killed the families and left them beside their burning cabins. There were four men in the last one. We were circling the cabin and bullets were flying everywhere. All I remember is feeling like my throat caught fire and falling from the saddle."

"I guess it doesn't matter much where the bullet came from," Angry Heart said. "What's done is done."

"It's done, and it changed my life," Shot-in-the-Throat

said. "I figured that to be a sign. I could go under at any time and never see you again. I vowed I'd go and get you just as soon as the trouble settled down. I wanted you with me right then, but I just couldn't take the chance. Do you understand?"

"As much as I can understand," Angry Heart replied. "It's not an easy thing to get over."

Shot-in-the-Throat smiled. "You're a strong man to admit that. You're a good man, and I'm proud to call you my son, even though I had little to do with it."

The two embraced for a long time, both apologizing for having hurt one another so deeply. Angry Heart felt a great load lift from his shoulders. "Show me the buttes," he said.

Shot-in-the-Throat led the way up the largest butte, telling the various legends of the tribes who used the area to camp and hunt. The Cheyenne and Lakota, allied and the two strongest forces on the Plains, kept everyone else away.

At the top, Angry Heart walked through old grass that reached just past his knees. Small green shoots were appearing among the thick stand of last year's crop, now cured to a deep gold.

"I'll bet the ponies would like to get into this," Angry Heart remarked.

"They'd like to, but they never will," Shot-in-the-Throat said. He told Angry Heart that neither horses nor buffalo could scale the largest butte. The thick vegetation had never seen grazing pressure. "There's not as much of this kind of grass down below," he continued. "The buffalo and the horse herds have hit the bottoms hard over the years, and other kinds of grass have taken over."

"How could the grass change?"

His father told him that the tall grass he was standing in was preferred by horses and buffalo, and was grazed down to the ground where it grew near the streams and rivers.

"I've watched this over the years," Shot-in-the-Throat said. "Along the rivers the choice grass is grazed hard all the time. Finally it dies out and other grasses and weeds come in, to fill the space. I've seen places that used to be full of grass that are now just cactus."

Angry Heart was impressed by his father's attention to detail. "You're seeing changes of all kinds out here, and it bothers you."

"It bothers me a lot," Angry Heart said. "But I don't see a thing that I can do about it."

Angry Heart walked with his father to the edge of the butte and scanned the vast distance, marveling at the view. The hills still held scattered patches of old snow, the last remnants of the blizzards of a week before. The patterns of white and brown, mixed with the gray of sage, spread across an eternity. He listened as his father went back to his early years in the west.

"I was nearly killed by the Minneconjou twice, but I had a good horse then and outdistanced them. I wasn't going to stay away, though. Not on your life. You see, I'd met Pine Woman in sixty-four, when I was leading a wagon train back to the States. We were stopped along the Platte and her people came along looking to trade with us. I was a sight older than her; she gave me a tailfeather from a bluebird. That meant she wanted to see me again."

It bothered Angry Heart to hear the story, even though his mother had passed on by that time. Already on his own, Angry Heart had been fourteen, a boy prodigy in the trickshooter's world.

"I don't mean to upset you," Shot-in-the-Throat said. "I won't discuss it anymore if you don't want to. It was less than a year later that I went back to Missouri and never found you."

"Ma was gone by then," Angry Heart said. "I guess you must have known."

Shot-in-the-Throat looked into the distance.

"How did you manage to marry Pine Woman?" Angry Heart asked.

"I brought the Minneconjou goods to trade," he replied. "I rode into their camp with a pack train of rifles. I dealt with them fairly and never gave them whiskey. They trusted me and I trusted them. After a while, I gave Pine Woman's father a good gun and two ponies. She and I have been sharing the same lodge ever since."

"I don't remember you being home much at all," Angry Heart said. "Did you ever tell me when you first came out here?"

Shot-in-the-Throat said he had traveled west even before he had met Angry Heart's mother. "The fur trade was about over when I first got here. When it died, I went back to Missouri for a while. I met your mother and you were born. But the fever of this country was in my blood. Then I was asked to lead a wagon train through the country. I couldn't pass up the chance to get back out here."

"You led people out here, and now you want them to go home?" Angry Heart asked.

"Crazy thing, isn't it? I brought those people in their wagons, just for an excuse to get back out here myself. Now I wish I'd never done that. The settlers, the Army, they don't appreciate this country enough to just leave it be. They can't be content to just live off it. No, they want to control it. They want to tear it up and ruin it, like they did back in the States. In time it'll be no different out here."

"This country's too dry for farmland," Angry Heart said.

Shot-in-the-Throat laughed. "If it's not so steep a mule would fall down, they'll put a plow into it." He waved an arm across the expanse. "They'll tear it all up, from here to hell and back."

"There's too many buffalo," Angry Heart said.

"Not for long," Shot-in-the-Throat said. "It used to be I could climb these buttes and see buffalo anywhere I wanted to look. Thousands of them. Now you see a bunch here and there. But the big herds are up along the Yellowstone, and north."

Angry Heart noticed small black lumps in the distance, some to the east and some to the north. But indeed they were few in number.

"The robe trade has taken a big toll in the northern herds already," his father continued. "It'll get lots worse. I hear from some of my friends who've been down on the Cimarron that the hide hunters have pretty well knocked the southern herd out. They're shooting them faster than they can skin them. They'd be up here, too, but for the Sioux and Cheyenne. They'll get here, though, in time. It won't be long until every last buffalo's gone. You won't see them."

"You think they'll all go? Why?"

"There's no good reason why, except Uncle Sam wants to get rid of the Indian. To do it, the buffalo have got to go. That'll break their backs, wiping out the food source. No other good reason than to just get rid of them so the Indians won't wander from the reservations. This land won't be the same without buffalo."

Angry Heart noticed his father's gaze drifting, his face pained, as if he just didn't want to believe it was really happening.

"You make it sound like a lost cause," Angry Heart said.

"It is a lost cause."

"Why don't these people surrender before all that happens?"

"There's something you don't understand yet," Shot-in-the-Throat replied. "When you're born and raised like these people, you'd rather die than sit in one place and fester. The mark of a warrior is to die in battle. Dying on a reservation of old age is dishonor. Crazy Horse and Sitting Bull, neither one will die of old age. Mark my words. You stay out here and live with these people very long, you'll see what I mean. This land makes you feel free. You don't want anything else."

Angry Heart had to admit that even during the cold campaign with Crook, he had developed an affection for the land. Some part of him had wanted to explore the mountains in the distance. Even though he hadn't come of his own free will, he didn't want to hear that what he was looking at would change and become what he had left behind.

"You brought a few settlers out here, but what makes you think everyone else is coming?" Angry Heart asked. "What could they want with this land? It's not near the same as Missouri, or points east of there."

Shot-in-the-Throat pointed west and then east toward the Black Hills. "There's gold on both sides of us, enough to bring a lot of folks out to glory hunt," he said. "Plenty will follow to farm and raise beef. There's discontent back where you came from. You know that. People want a new beginning. The government, the railroads, they see that. There's money to be made out here. Get rid of the Indians and send everybody west, that's their game. It's just a matter of time."

"Do you plan to stick this out and fight with the Lakota?" Angry Heart asked.

"I wouldn't have it any other way. If they'll let me, I'll fight alongside them until the soldiers are gone or I go under, whichever comes first. I love this land more than life itself. Give yourself time, you'll see what I mean."

* * *

Angry Heart slept fitfully that night, knowing that his father was right. The longer he stayed with Ghostwind and her people the harder it would be to leave them. He realized that he already had deep feelings for Ghostwind, feelings that he had been denying. Soon he would want to be around her all the time.

With the dawn he awakened to a crier announcing that the villages were to move. A great council of the four camps had met the night before and rules of order had been drawn up for the good of all the people.

Safety took priority. In better times, children would have been allowed to mix freely and ride with friends from other villages. Now all children were to stay with their mothers and not stray under any circumstances. Dogs were to be kept with their owners. Any found wandering would be dispatched with arrows.

Young Horse complained that he and Tall Deer could not ride together. "We haven't gotten a chance since the last warm moons. Maybe I can sneak back to be with him."

"The rules must be followed," Ghostwind insisted. "If you don't obey, you will lose all your privileges."

The procession was to be led by the Cheyenne people, for they had suffered the attack, and their warriors would meet any frontal charge with intense anger. They would send scouts ahead to watch for danger and to secure a good camping site. The Oglala would follow, then the Minneconjou, and finally the Unkpapa, the most numerous, to guard the rear against the Bluecoats.

The move got under way smoothly. Angry Heart marveled at the women's efficiency. They had the lodges down and packed and their children fed before the sun had fully risen.

Angry Heart was given a place with Ghostwind and her family near the center of the Cheyenne procession. There were nearly fifty Cheyenne lodges and just more than fifty

Minneconjou. Sixty Oglala lodges and a little more than seventy in Sitting Bull's Unkpapa village brought the total to more than two hundred thirty lodges.

Ghostwind told him that never before had the Cheyenne and Lakota peoples banded together like this. The large numbers made hunting and finding wood much more difficult, and there was so little grass that keeping the already winter-poor horses from getting weaker would be a challenge. A lot of things were happening that had never happened before because of the Bluecoat threat of total annihilation.

Though the trip would be difficult and the days long, the people felt safe together. The weather was open, and the birds' spring songs gave everyone hope of better things to come. Already there were a number of spotted foals among the horses, a sign of plenty and good fortune.

The sun shone, melting the snow down into grass that was bursting into small shoots of green. Tiny yellow flowers raced up the hills after the receding snowbanks, some bell-shaped and others open, with dainty round petals.

Yellow bells and buttercups. Angry Heart had learned their names as a child. During a stop for water he picked a few, seeing his mother's face in the palm of his hand. He found himself in the woods and fields of Missouri again, tagging behind her on a sunny spring morning, listening intently to her soft voice as she patiently taught him the names of various wildflowers. She knew them all, and they brought rare smiles to her face.

He could remember picking bouquets for her, to try to bring the smiles. Sometimes the smiles came, but just as often came tears and weeping. It made picking flowers difficult, trying to guess whether his mother would be glad or sorrowful.

The memory did not make him sad as it had in the past. That was behind him now. His concern lay only in taking the days one at a time. Many more of the Cheyenne were coming to accept him, as well as many among the Lakota. He could see that he had made inroads with Five Bulls and Mountain Water. His gift of meat had affected them greatly. Though neither had spoken of it, both would nod to him occasionally with slight smiles on their lips.

Young Horse and Talking Grass had both come to like him a great deal. Talking Grass would often leave her mother and ride with him on his pony. She would sit in front, her small hands holding the pony's mane, frequently turning to look up into his eyes and smile. Young Horse often rode up beside him to touch the scarred leg. "You must have special powers to heal so well and so quickly," he would say. "I want my legs to be as strong as yours."

Eagle Wing, who was on police duty, told him more than once to observe what was going on, so that he would know what his own duties would be when the time came. Many among the Minneconjou and Unkpapa had asked to see him shoot. But there was not enough ammunition to waste on spectator sports. In time, they would see what he could do.

The combined villages were joined in their first camp by seventy more lodges of Unkpapa from Fort Berthold and just over fifty lodges of Sans Arcs, the No Arrows Lakota people. The village moved in three days. A new camp was located along the headwaters of the next stream, where there was new grass and wood for cookfires.

The first evening, Angry Heart was taken to a council meeting presided over by Old Bear and Two Moon. The men talked fast, but Angry Heart knew that much of the discussion centered around him. He could think of no crimes he might have committed. The men were so stoic that he could not tell whether they were angry or not. Even out of council it was difficult to know when they were serious or joking. Only when someone smiled or chuckled could he be sure.

When the council had concluded, Eagle Wing took him aside and told him that his preparation to become a warrior would begin.

"I have been told to educate you," he said. "Is that good with you?"

"That's good with me," Angry Heart said, his heart pounding. "Is that what they were talking about?"

"That, among other things. You show some fear. That's good. That means you are not taking anything for granted." He pointed to a hill above the village. "I want you to meet me there before sunrise. The sun must not yet be up. Don't be late."

Word soon spread among the villagers that Angry Heart was to begin his tests. Ghostwind and Day Lily both assured him that he would succeed and become a trusted member of the tribe. Red Bear, seeing Day Lily talking to him, yelled for her to return to their lodge and confronted Angry Heart.

"I see that you're out to steal my wife," he said. "I won't have that."

Ghostwind glared at Red Bear. "That is no way to treat your wife."

"She is not to be making eyes at this Bluecoat," Red Bear said.

"You know better than that," Ghostwind said. "You have hurt her deeply. I will go and see if I can make her understand that you didn't mean it."

"I *did* mean it!" Red Bear called after Ghostwind.

"You had better be careful with that kind of language," Angry Heart warned him. "I know that among your people it is a great dishonor to lie."

"Are you calling me a liar?"

"I believe you want trouble, even at the expense of your wife. To me, that makes you a sad person."

Red Bear stared.

"I can understand that you miss Kicks-the-Fox," Angry Heart continued, "but hating me will not bring him back. Nothing can change what happened."

"I don't like having you here," Red Bear said. "I've made that no secret. I just want you to know that after tomorrow, the people will see that you cannot be one of us. You will fail, and you will be disgraced."

"That won't happen," Angry Heart said. "I don't know what I will be required to do, but I will succeed and go on to the next step. And the step after that. What are you going to do when I'm a warrior?"

Red Bear spat on the ground. "You might become a warrior in the eyes of the people, but to me you will always be the enemy."

TWENTY-THREE

Angry Heart rose in the darkness. Since he had not been told otherwise, he dressed as usual. Eagle Wing awaited him at the top of the hill.

"I wondered if you would come," he said. "Did anyone tell you what your test is to be?"

"No," Angry Heart replied. "Many have offered encouragement, but there is one who has told me he wants me to fail."

"Red Bear?"

"Yes, Red Bear. I cannot decide why he hates me so. I've told him I wish I hadn't killed Kicks-the-Fox. I don't understand it."

"You will learn that such things are not yours to understand," Eagle Wing said. "Each man is responsible only for his own actions. Each man must make his own way in life, despite what goes on around him. If others cause him to falter from his path, then he has problems within."

Angry Heart looked into the east. The sound of birdsong welcomed the first glints of dawn.

"You will face the sun the entire day," Eagle Wing

instructed. "You must watch the sun from the time it rises until it falls over the horizon on the other side of the sky."

"I have to watch the sun?"

"You do not have to keep your eyes open at all times. I'm not asking you to go blind. But you are required to face the sun. You may sit down, or you may stand. If you stand, you will be given higher honor."

"I will stand," Angry Heart said. "What if I fall during the day?"

"Then get right back up, if you are able. Do as well as you can. There will be many people watching."

Angry Heart took a deep breath. "What you're saying is that I shouldn't fall."

"If you cannot make it through the entire day, you can try again another time. It's up to you."

"How many make it through the whole day, the first time?" Angry Heart asked.

"The young men do it all the time," Eagle Wing replied. "But they have grown up differently from you. They have been preparing themselves since early childhood."

"I believe I can accomplish anything a boy can do," Angry Heart said. "It hasn't been easy for me up to now, but I'm still here."

Eagle Wing smiled. "You don't know what you're facing."

"You make it sound like a fate worse than death."

"Not worse, but similar. If you succeed, you will have gone through a death of sorts. You will be a different person this evening."

"Then I will survive, and you will find me a different person this evening," Angry Heart said. "Will you come up to get me?"

"You must make your way down the hill on your own," Eagle Wing said. "After the sun goes down, you will open your eyes and immediately notice the change in yourself. It will take time for you to adjust. Take as much time as you want. And remember, there will be many people watching you."

Eagle Wing left, and Angry Heart pondered the task ahead of him. An entire day must go by before he turned his face from the sun. He could not afford to think of the time involved; an entire day standing would tax him greatly. He could not allow himself to dwell on the incredible stamina he would be required to show.

As he kicked rocks away from a flat space and took his stance, Angry Heart decided to abandon all sense of reason as he knew it. What he was about to do defied any logic that he had developed during his lifetime. He realized that he must approach this with an open mind. Otherwise he would certainly fail.

Angry Heart took a deep breath and watched the sun peep up over the distant Black Hills, quickly rising to form a round ball of gold. He squinted at the sphere, wondering at its origin and how it managed to sustain its glow and intensity without fail each day. After a time he abandoned all thought patterns, realizing that the use of his mental faculties would begin to overpower his mind and would soon force him to turn away.

The sun rose higher and brighter. Angry Heart closed his eyes. Red light swam before his vision, a three-dimensional depth of bright scarlet that changed intensity rapidly and faded to soft gold. The color soothed him and released some of his fear. His breathing relaxed, allowing him to feel comfortable.

Angry Heart felt that the reason for his being here was not to concentrate on the sun, but by training his face in that direction to experience the life that was sustained by the Great Light. Without vision, he began to sense his surroundings far more deeply. Rather than just hearing and smelling, he also felt everything that was taking place around him.

Birdsong, rich and vibrant in the spring air, mixed with the humming of bees and flies. The coarse *kee-kee-kee-kee-kee* of flickers in the cottonwoods below echoed against the far-off whinnying of horses and the thumping of colts' hooves against the hillsides in running play.

Camp noises and smells from below came up to him as if he were in the midst of the morning activities. Wood-smoke and the scent of broiled meat filled his nostrils; the growling and yipping of puppies filled his ears, and from overhead came the cry of a red-tailed hawk.

Angry Heart concentrated on the hawk's call. A very good sign, he knew, for the Cheyenne and the Lakota both understood the bird to be a messenger, a bringer of news that the listener must dream on to understand. Crazy Horse talked of the hawk as a great medicine symbol. He wore a small hawk against the side of his head when he rode into battle.

The hawk's call faded and Angry Heart found himself drawn deeper into the unison of life around him. He basked in the experience, forgetting where he was or why he was there. He began to drift into the light, feeling as if he were floating inside himself. Myriad thoughts drifted past, scenes from his childhood, days and nights in prison, even glimpses of himself at Fort Fetterman. They came and went fleetingly, as if reminding him of what had once been, but was no longer.

Angry Heart's thoughts faded, and he found himself standing without any experience at all. The sounds and smells around him continued, but they no longer gave him any pleasure. They were just there.

The morning passed and Angry Heart's body began to tire. He kept his face toward the sun, moving his legs frequently to ease the increasing pain of cramped muscles.

By midafternoon he had begun to lose feeling within himself. His head felt detached from his body. His eyes seemed now to pull him within them, as if he had entered the organs themselves and was now swimming in the fluid. His eyes seemed to be turning, moving up and down uncontrollably. He felt himself pinned against the inside of an eye, spinning and twisting, as if trying to climb the pure white lining, slipping each time to fall back into the watery fluid that held him. He struggled for what seemed like an eternity, while the feeling of being trapped overpowered him and tested his mind to the limit.

The tension became almost unbearable. Though he hadn't done so since childhood, Angry Heart began to think about God. As a child, he had been certain God didn't care about him. Otherwise, why would He have allowed his father to go away and leave him? But he now realized that everyone suffered, that he was no different from anyone else. Perhaps others had suffered far more. Many of those with him in the traveling show had led complicated lives, and certainly those in prison with him had felt a great deal of pain and anger. Crook and the soldiers he had ridden with all suffered in one way or another.

And there was Kincaid. How could a man watch his family being killed and not hate for the rest of his life?

Angry Heart now understood Ghostwind's advice about humility. He knew these people lived solely in honor of a Great Medicine, as they called it, a Creator who had exclusive control of their lives. The earth and sky, all the elements, were controlled by this Creator. The very breath that came into their bodies *was* this Creator.

Angry Heart had never known humility. He had fought himself to make his life different, but his situation had only gotten worse. As hard as it was to admit, he couldn't ease his own pain, no matter how hard he tried.

Then he had met Ghostwind and her people, who seemed to understand his pain. These people had looked inside him, to the character within, and had urged him to become himself, to release the past and join them. It was difficult to grasp, yet he knew that he had been treated far better when he joined the Cheyenne people than at any other time in his life.

Angry Heart longed for darkness. But the sun had a good distance yet to travel. His mental and physical distress now began to peak. He wanted desperately to lie down and let the remainder of the day pass without him. But he knew that would be failure, and he wanted no more failures in his life.

Angry Heart once again turned his thoughts to God. He needed understanding where there had been none before. The desire to realize his situation overwhelmed him. He asked why he had been brought to these people and why he was on this hill; he got no answer. He asked whether or not he would survive with them; he got no response.

Controlling his urge to scream in frustration, Angry Heart asked that he be given the strength to endure, to pass this test and learn the things he must. He asked for whatever power he might need to make it through the remainder of the day. He no longer required understanding, for he realized all was beyond his understanding. He was willing to accept things as they were, without question.

Angry Heart was suddenly aware of someone yelling. Then realized his mouth was open. Instantly his feeling of being trapped eased, and the fluid he had been immersed in seemed to drain from around him. Everything turned a swirling blue, mixed with deep purple. Angry Heart felt as though he were part of the mixture, moving with the changes of color. He wondered if he was still alive, or had died and gone somewhere he had never heard of.

He willed that his hands come to his face. He suddenly felt tears pouring down his cheeks. His fingers felt separate from him, as if they belonged to someone else. All he could feel was the touch against his face; no attachment at all to his being.

At first he thought it might be an angel coming to touch him, or possibly Ghostwind taking pity on him. He dared not open his eyes to see. The sun's light would shock him and he would be finished. He must keep his eyes closed and his face toward the sun, which had now descended into late afternoon.

When he willed the fingers gone, the sensation of touch left. Again he felt himself floating. The light was almost white, clean and pure. He was aware that the sky was changing. The glow behind his eyelids gradually turned to darkness.

Angry Heart opened his eyes and immediately lost his balance. He slumped to the ground. He wanted desperately to rise, but his legs felt immobilized, as if they would never work again. He rubbed the muscles, feeling pain surge through his body. He lay back looking into the dusk above him, wondering if he was in the same place where he had begun the ordeal.

When he sat up, nothing at all seemed the same. His eyes, unable yet to focus clearly, seemed to pick patches of color out of the twilight. The ground felt different, the air seemed lighter, with a soft texture to it. The sounds around him were clear, yet the tones mixed together, in a harmony he had never before experienced. A bird flew overhead, singing the most beautiful song that he had ever heard.

From below came shouts of encouragement to get up and descend the hill. Ghostwind and her children stood in front of a crowd. Shot-in-the-Throat and his wife and son stood close behind her.

Angry Heart breathed deeply for a time. He stretched

and groaned until he managed to rise to his feet. A tremendous shout rose from below him. He took a few steps, feeling more and more confident. The roar of voices from below increased.

Now, with his eyes in clear focus, Angry Heart saw the waving and yelling Cheyenne people. He had passed his first test. A rush of pride and confidence coursed through him, and he walked to the edge of the hill to acknowledge the cheering. He turned a full circle, his face skyward, his arms in the air. The God he thought had abandoned him as a child had come to him, way out here, and had helped him through the day.

When he brought his arms down, he took a last look into the east, where the day had begun. A flaming glow of twilight shone across the hills and through the valley. A glint of light lingered on a single man standing beside a group of rocks on a nearby hill, a man wrapped in a red blanket with his arms crossed in front of him.

Angry Heart waved at the man. He started down the hill, confident that he had seen the faintest smile on the lips of Crazy Horse.

The council convened, and the combined villages moved to a campsite along the lower reaches of Powder River, where scouts had reported an abundance of new grass. Along the way they were joined by a small group of Blackfoot Sioux, a division of the Lakota with little influence.

The Blackfoot Sioux reported that the agency Indians who had never left were getting edgy. Rations were dwindling and unrest growing. The agents were telling the young men not to wander after game, even though their families were on the verge of starvation. Very soon the combined villages would be joined by other bands of Lakota and Cheyenne who wanted to live free and desired safety against the coming Bluecoat armies.

For the time being there was no cause for alarm. The scouts reported no Bluecoats anywhere near. The people settled in to allow the ponies time to foal and to gather strength. For the first time in many nights, the people began to venture out a short distance from camp.

Angry Heart was still adjusting to his experience on the hill. He now saw life in a better light, and knew that more of the people had come to accept him. Whether or not they liked him, they respected him. Even Red Bear looked at him differently.

"Everyone knows that to remain on the hill all day as you did was very difficult," Ghostwind told him. "You did not grow up learning the techniques of self-control that are required among my people. So you were not at all prepared for what you did. For you to persist shows strong character."

Crazy Horse approached him to say that he had not only been there in the evening, but had spent the day observing. "You went through many changes within yourself. You are not lacking in courage."

"I asked for help, and it came to me," Angry Heart confessed.

"You have learned a good lesson," Crazy Horse said with a smile. "We all must have help daily. You seem to be looked upon with favor. Maybe you can help us against the Bluecoats, and the time will come when we will fight together."

Angry Heart felt pride growing within him, yet he shuddered at the thought that he had almost given up. Things would be far different if he had. He wondered if the next test would be as difficult, or more so, and what he must do to prepare himself.

"There is no point in worrying about the next test," Eagle Wing told him when they discussed it. "Live each

moment as it comes to you. That is the best way to prepare."

Angry Heart spent an entire day with Eagle Wing, learning how to make a bow and arrows. "To me, these are more
reliable than the guns," Eagle Wing said. "If the powder
does not fire, you are helpless. I have seen that many times.
The bow is more reliable."

"You have to consider the range a rifle will shoot,"
Angry Heart argued.

"I don't care about range," Eagle Wing said. "A Bluecoat will have to hit me moving. I won't be still. You have
to be close to hit a moving target. Besides, I can shoot far
more arrows than bullets in the same period. Learn to
shoot a bow as well as you do a gun and you will have a
position of great power among my people."

Though weapons were important, Angry Heart learned
that the expert use of a good pony would keep him alive far
longer than his marksmanship. Eagle Wing insisted that he
spend much time on his ponies and develop the ability to
ride for long periods without tiring. Angry Heart found the
ponies testy, and realized he would have to learn a lot more
about horses than he presently knew.

"You'll never see a horse ridden any better than by
Plains warriors," his father told him one afternoon. "They
grow up on their ponies, eat and sleep on them. They can
ride under a horse's belly just as well as on its back. You'd
best be able to do it yourself."

"Can you?"

"You bet. I could hang with the best of them when I was
younger. I'm not required anymore. You will be."

Later that afternoon, Angry Heart witnessed a demonstration of horsemanship that stunned him. Eagle Wing
and a number of warriors, including Red Bear, had orga-
nized a game of tag. They were using a charcoal stick to
make a mark on any part of the body, chasing each other

up and down hills and across flats, riding in zigzag patterns that left Angry Heart shaking his head.

"I told you," Shot-in-the-Throat said after they had watched for a time. "Let's go back into the village."

"I'd like to stay and watch a while longer," Angry Heart said.

"You should come back."

"In a little while."

Shot-in-the-Throat shrugged. "Suit yourself."

Angry Heart settled down on a small ridge to watch. Eagle Wing had trained his small roan stallion to respond to various combinations of ankle and knee pressure. When a rider approached him with the charcoal stick, Eagle Wing would nudge the roan into various speeds, slowing and speeding up, turning quickly one way or another, usually leaving the pursuer frustrated.

So that none were overworked, the players changed ponies frequently. Eagle Wing got his fair share of marks when he rested his roan and the other warriors worked their better ponies. Angry Heart watched them all with wonder, seeing how they not only used their ponies in expert fashion, but also used their own agility to slip and slide around and so avoid the charcoal stick.

Once Red Bear, pursued by a younger warrior on a smaller pony, rushed up the hill at Angry Heart. He swerved off just a few feet in front of Angry Heart, who by then was on his feet.

Red Bear turned his pony back and approached Angry· Heart.

"You are a poor watcher. You frighten easily."

"I didn't know running at people on foot was part of the game," Angry Heart said.

Red Bear leaned over. "What do you know about the game? Why don't you get on a pony and join us? I will try and mark you."

Eagle Wing and the other warriors rode up. Eagle Wing asked Red Bear, "Why did you stop the game?"

Red Bear pointed at Angry Heart. "I challenged him to play. But he's afraid."

"I don't know my ponies well enough to play this game," Angry Heart said.

"No, you aren't a good rider and you're afraid," Red Bear said. "I don't think you could ever ride with us."

"I will get one of my ponies and show you differently," Angry Heart said.

Eagle Wing dismounted and stopped him. "Don't let Red Bear make you do something foolish. You can't ride like this when you aren't used to it. Nobody can."

"He's calling me a coward."

"If you do this, you will fall off. Then you'll be a fool. You don't have to meet his challenge now. There's plenty of time."

Angry Heart looked to Red Bear, who smiled with satisfaction and rode his pony off toward the village.

"I suppose he will tell everyone how he challenged me and I backed down," Angry Heart said.

"Let him," Eagle Wing said. "Everyone down there knows that he lost out here. He just wanted to find someone he could beat."

"I still don't like being called a coward," Angry Heart said.

"Why should it bother you?" Eagle Wing asked. "Have you forgotten everything you learned while watching the sun?"

"I'm just tired of him, is all," Angry Heart said. "He puts pressure on me. I killed his friend and he would like to see me dead."

"Red Bear is always going to dislike you," Eagle Wing said. "You will have to get used to that. If you let him, he will drive you crazy. He's just another test for you."

"You mean he's doing it to test me?"

"No, he's doing it to drive you away," Eagle Wing said. "You see, Kicks-the-Fox was destined to become a leader very soon. Red Bear had hoped to gain high office because Kicks-the-Fox was his friend. Now that will never happen and Red Bear will likely never amount to anything, unless he accomplishes something on his own. He wants to blame you for that."

"Whatever his reasons, I'm not going to allow him to shame me," Angry Heart said. "Before long, I'll be riding better than him."

Eagle Wing mounted his pony. "Maybe. Just remember that your development as a warrior is more important than your problems with Red Bear."

TWENTY-FOUR

L ate that evening, Angry Heart took one of the ponies Five Bulls had given him and rode a short way from the village. The pony, a stout dun named Mud, had an exceptionally long mane. It was only because of the mane that Angry Heart didn't tumble to the ground many times.

He would kick the pony into a fast gallop and lower himself down one side and then the other, but try as he might, he couldn't keep himself balanced against the pony's ribs. He slipped continually, nearly falling head first under the hooves, but saved himself with only handfuls of mane.

Exasperated and nearly exhausted, Angry Heart took a seat on the ground, holding the pony's reins. He noticed someone sitting on a red pony atop a nearby hill, watching him intently. Angry Heart knew the pony belonged to his father. The rider was Tall Deer.

Angry Heart waved the boy down. Tall Deer raced to a stop and jumped to the ground. "I see you're doing some riding."

"Are you making fun of me?"

"Oh, no. You hold on well. You're very strong. If I rode like that, I'd fall off."

Angry Heart stood up and stretched his aching muscles. Young Horse wasn't with Tall Deer, yet the two were usually inseparable.

"Where's Young Horse?" Angry Heart asked.

"He got in trouble for putting a frog in Talking Grass's food dish. He has to stay in the lodge for two days."

"I see," Angry Heart said. "For two days?"

"It wasn't just a little frog. It was *big*. I don't know where he found it. You don't see big frogs like that until the weather gets warmer. He was lucky."

"Some luck. He got himself into trouble." Angry Heart threw the reins over his pony's neck.

"Are you going to ride some more?" Tall Deer asked.

"No, the show's over for today," Angry Heart said. "Don't you tell anyone about this."

"I didn't come to laugh at you," Tall Deer said. "I was going to ask you if you wanted some help."

Angry Heart chuckled. "How can you help me?"

"I can teach you how to ride on the side and under the belly. Watch."

Tall Deer jumped on his pony. He raced three wide circles around Angry Heart, turning and twisting and rolling, performing every conceivable trick. Upon his return, he stood up on the horse's back and somersaulted off into a full circle dismount.

"What do you think?" he asked.

Angry Heart was speechless. "How did you learn to ride like that?"

"I've always wanted to be the best rider among all the Lakota people. I've been working at it."

"You've got a good start," Angry Heart said. "But how can you help me?"

Tall Deer jumped on his pony as easily as if he were

skipping down a trail. The pony stood motionless while Tall Deer draped himself over the left side.

"To ride on the side, you must lock your knee in the right place," he explained. "When you're first learning, you can't just hang your knee over the middle of the back and hope to stay on. You have to move up so that the back of your knee is locked against that little hump where the mane starts. See?"

Angry Heart took note. Tall Deer slipped from one side to the other, and then spun himself under the pony's neck to dismount.

"Now you try it."

"Your pony doesn't know me."

"Don't worry. That won't matter. He has good manners."

Angry Heart climbed on the pony and lowered himself over the side. Tall Deer showed him the correct position for the knee.

"Now just relax and hang down. You can't fall off."

Angry Heart groaned and frowned.

"I know, it pulls the muscles when you aren't used to it. But after you've practiced, you can ride like that all day."

"I don't know why I'd want to," Angry Heart said.

"All warriors can, if they have to," Tall Deer said. He helped Angry Heart position himself flat against the pony's side. "Brace your hand under the belly to help you hang on."

Tall Deer began to lead the horse. Gradually Angry Heart began to feel comfortable. He switched from side to side, locking his knee in place, leaning his chest into the pony's shoulder. As he loosened up, he gained the confidence to take his own pony and work. By nightfall, he could keep his balance on either side with the pony at a gallop.

"You learn quickly," Tall Deer said. "Before long, you will be as good as me."

"No I won't," Angry Heart said with a laugh. "I could spend a lot of time at it and never be the rider you are."

"But you can do many things that I can't," Tall Deer said. "They say that you can shoot guns like no one else alive. I would like to see that."

"Maybe someday I will show you," Angry Heart said. "If we happen to get some extra ammunition for the rifles, I'll give you a demonstration."

"Could you teach me to shoot?" Tall Deer asked. "I don't think I could ever be as good as you, but I would like to learn how, anyway."

"I could teach you," Angry Heart said. "But only if our father approves."

Tall Deer smiled. "I'm glad to hear you say that he's *our* father. I didn't think you had accepted me."

"You have to understand that all this has been hard for me," Angry Heart said. "I didn't even know if my father was still alive, much less married and raising another son."

"You have adjusted well to everything," Tall Deer said. "It shows that you are strong inside. I'm proud to call you brother."

Angry Heart put a hand on Tall Deer's shoulder. "And I'm proud to call you brother as well. I hope we can have many more days like this."

Tall Deer beamed. "We can have as many as you want. Let's race back to camp."

Angry Heart laughed. "No, you race back. I'll just ride. I'll be lucky to stay on sitting upright. Another day."

"Yes, and I'll hold you to it," Tall Deer said. He mounted and waved, then kicked his pony into a full run toward the village.

Angry Heart climbed onto Mud. Every muscle in his body cried for rest. He laughed to himself. A short while earlier he had felt shamed by Red Bear. Before long he would be riding better than Red Bear. If he allowed Tall

Deer to teach him, he would likely be riding better than most anyone else. Then he would ask Red Bear to play horseback tag, and Red Bear could see how it felt to be "it" all the time.

While on the Powder River, the combined camp grew considerably. Everyone was now calling it the Big Village. More Cheyenne, more Blackfoot Sioux, and a contingent of Brulé all came in on the same day, followed by fifteen lodges of Santee, who were Nakota Sioux, not Lakota, and hadn't gotten along with the Lakota for many years.

Sitting Bull allowed them to join anyway. "All allies of the Lakota people must come together," he told the council. "If we have strength in numbers, the Bluecoats will leave us alone."

The Santee had been unsettled since the uprising in their Minnesota homeland in 1862. They were a poor people, with ragged clothing, small lodges and no horses. Their goods were loaded on travois pulled by large dogs. They had settled in Canada to avoid persecution, but had found little solace there.

Having moved to northern Montana Territory, the Santee had received word of the Bluecoat threat from a band of Assiniboine, with whom they had allied. The two groups had been searching for the Big Village for more than a week.

Angry Heart continued to learn warrior ways from Eagle Wing, preparing himself for the inevitable confrontation with the U.S. Army. He tried not to think about it, for it would come very soon. Then he would have to fight as if he had been a Cheyenne all his life.

Sitting Bull had said many times, "I'm no agency Indian, and I can't live as the *Wasichu* want me. I am a free man." The many who followed him all agreed that to take away their freedom would rob them of their very lives.

"Their traditions are the center of their culture," Angry Heart's father told him. "To lose the right to make medicine and chase buffalo would be the end of them. It would be the end of me, for I can't think any differently now."

"There's a lot to be said about the way these people do things," Angry Heart agreed. "When I first got here, I thought the women did all the work and got no credit. That's really not it. I see them doing the camp work because they're in charge of their homes, not the hunting and the warfare. They have the more important responsibility of maintaining daily life, under any and all conditions. I see them as the honored members of society."

"An older woman who has helped raise many children has more honor than a war chief," Shot-in-the-Throat said. "Women here are considered like spring flowers. They are strong and weather cold and storms while bringing forth life and beauty. They know that it's the women who carry the generations. The hopes and future of the people come from the womb of the female. The children follow their mother's bloodline, not their father's. There's no argument about who's the more important sex here."

Angry Heart thought about how Ghostwind revered her children, and how she worked hard to be a good mother and guide them in the right direction. He saw that quality in most of the women, and realized that it explained why the children thought highly of themselves. He said as much.

"These kids can get kind of wild at times," Shot-in-the-Throat said. "But when they're asked to be quiet, you see them settle down right away. And you don't see their parents thrashing them with sticks and belts. You never see that. The only tears you see in children's eyes are when they have done something to hurt themselves."

Angry Heart thought about the attack on the village and the children, including Ghostwind's, who had suffered as a result. He told his father how the entire campaign had been fraught with discomfort and frustration. It was as if Reynolds had intended to right all errors and bad decisions during one fight on a bitterly cold morning.

"I didn't feel good about myself over that," Angry Heart told his father.

"When are you going to understand that it wasn't your fault?" Shot-in-the-Throat asked. "None of this is your fault, any more than it's mine. It's started, and it's gotten too big to stop. It's like having a thousand of those mold-board plows locked abreast, each one pulled by a team of six mules, just eating the ground for miles in every direction, on and on. You can't stop something like that."

Angry Heart knew that his father detested farming. That, more than anything else, was what had driven him out of Missouri and into the West.

"You can't tear people up like you do the ground," Angry Heart said. "There are those who will resist. It just won't work."

"The government already knows it won't work," Shot-in-the-Throat said. "That's why they're giving bounties on buffalo hides and letting crooked agents get away with their swindles. They want to get rid of these people. They won't just bow down to the white man. If they're not doing what they're told, the next step is to just wipe them out."

"But the government's already promised to let these people keep part of their lands," Angry Heart said. "When I was with Crook, I heard talk among the soldiers that the Lakota reservations were plenty large enough for them to roam and hunt on. They were guaranteed those lands by treaty."

"That was before they found gold in the Black Hills," Shot-in-the-Throat said. "That makes everything different, you see. There's treasure there, and it shouldn't belong to the Indians. Now the government is determined to take away a big chunk of land rights, treaty or no treaty."

"What these people need is good legal counsel," Angry Heart said. "Those treaties should be binding."

"What the government is doing," Shot-in-the-Throat explained, "is working to show that the Indians are breaking the treaties themselves, not the government. And on top of it, they're trying to get the Indians to sign their rights away voluntarily. It's all been planned."

Angry Heart was watching his father closely. He could never remember having seen him so angry, not even when he had talked about the plows tearing up the land everywhere. As a child in Missouri, he could remember his father talking often about the ruination that kept creeping westward. His father seemed to envision the plows moving like so many cavalry, working their steel teeth through Indian lands.

"The government is using a lot of tricks," Shot-in-the-Throat continued. "They make head chiefs out of lesser leaders who never had much influence among the people. The Lakota call them 'agency chiefs.' A bunch of politicians will come out and fill these leaders with whiskey and a few rations, and get X's on paper that they call signatures. Then they say they have the right to go out and kill those who won't honor the new contract. I tell you, the government can't do this and not expect big trouble. They're playing with fire."

"You see this all blowing up soon, don't you?" Angry Heart asked.

"You should know that better than I," Shot-in-the-Throat told him. "Look at what's happening. Troops are coming from everywhere, and this village is growing daily. Sooner or later the whole mess is bound to come together. There'll be a big explosion, all right, and a lot of men will die."

* * *

During the following days, Angry Heart thought about the discussions with his father, and about his own experience. His short time with the U.S. Army had told him that the white world wanted the Cheyenne and Lakota conquered as soon as possible.

Angry Heart's time with Crook's forces had made him realize that only the officers came from the higher classes of society. The rank and file had been pulled from among everyday laborers and the underprivileged. Largely uneducated men had been taught to follow orders to the letter, and taught that the heathen Indian had no right to normal life. These troops would put their lives on the line to prove their own worth in a society that thought them no better than servants.

Angry Heart was glad to be a part of it no longer. Though certain conflict lay ahead, he found himself more relaxed than at any time in his life. He had talked about leaving at the first opportunity, and finding his way farther west. But he realized life in the gold camps held no promise for him. Nothing in the society he had known before could ever satisfy him.

Now, for the first time since his father's departure, Angry Heart had come to enjoy the people he lived with. In the traveling show he had found little companionship; and with the exception of Kincaid and Morgan, he certainly had not felt friendly toward anyone in Crook's command.

Angry Heart realized that the Cheyenne and the Lakota would never give up their way of life. They sought only to exist as they always had. Their ways were simple, yet honest. They cared about one another far more than about their possessions.

The village was larger than any usual gathering. Despite the Bluecoat threat, the people enjoyed visiting and danc-

ing. Children played games and the young men raced ponies and held athletic contests. Young Horse and Tall Deer
made many friends and met distant cousins. Many were
greeting relatives they had never known or had not seen for
a long time.

The arrival of more bands of Cheyenne and Lakota
made it essential to move again. The combined camps
constituted the largest gathering in anyone's memory.
Nearly four hundred fifty lodges were dragged across the
divide and erected along the Tongue River, with more than
five thousand ponies scattered through the surrounding
hills. Even from a hilltop, the entire village could not be
viewed, for it strung along the twisting river for more than
five miles. More strength was gathered together than at any
time before.

As the first morning on Tongue River dawned, Angry
Heart was surprised to learn that the month of May had
arrived. He had been keeping track of the days, carving
little notches in a stick, but had not bothered to count
them for a while.

Angry Heart felt more comfortable. Many of the Cheyenne who hadn't liked him now considered him in a different light. The day watching the sun had convinced many
that he desired to be one of them. Red Bear still frowned
at him, but he no longer spoke of enmity.

Angry Heart had learned much from Eagle Wing and
Shot-in-the-Throat, but he found himself treasuring
Ghostwind's presence. She had become the center of his
thoughts. Her voice reached inside to fill him with a deep
calm that he had never known.

With Ghostwind's help, he had been working to perfect
his sign talk and begin learning to speak Cheyenne. He
struggled with the language, despite her assurances that he
had plenty of time and didn't have to be perfect. He wanted

to be able to speak to everyone and make them all understand him.

Angry Heart had decided to begin the new month by talking only in Cheyenne. After making an attempt to communicate with Mountain Water early in the day, Angry Heart went for an evening walk along the river. Ghostwind found him chucking stones into the current.

"Are you sick?" she asked.

Angry Heart rose to his feet and stared in surprise. "No. Why do you ask?"

"My mother thinks you're sick. She says you asked her for some beetles. She uses ground beetles in herbs to help certain ailments."

"Beetles? No, I wanted a spoon. *Hamesko,* I told her. Spoon. She told me to come back later. She would have something ready. I didn't think she wanted me to eat with her, so I left."

Ghostwind laughed. She formed her hand into a cup and began to scoop it to her mouth. *"Hamesko* means both beetle and spoon. You should have showed her what you wanted in sign, also. My people used to eat from scoops that looked like the shell of a beetle. It can be confusing."

"No wonder your mother looked at me funny," Angry Heart said. "She asked me to lie down and I told her I wasn't tired."

Angry Heart and Ghostwind laughed together. They fell into each other's arms, and their lips met. Ghostwind hesitated at first, then wrapped her arms around Angry Heart and drew him close. Their kiss lasted until the passion in both of them had risen strongly.

"I've wanted to hold you for a long time," Angry Heart said. "I guess since we first met."

"I thought you wanted to leave my people as soon as you could," Ghostwind reminded him. "What made you change your mind?"

"You."

"Me? I haven't asked you to stay. I haven't said a thing."

"No, I mean I don't want to leave you. I don't want to leave Young Horse and Talking Grass."

"None of us wants you to leave." Ghostwind took his hand and began to lead him farther from the village.

"Are you certain about this?" Angry Heart asked. "I don't want to break any rules or bring you dishonor."

"I can see no dishonor in being with the man who will be with me the rest of my life," Ghostwind said. "Come with me now and say nothing more."

TWENTY-FIVE

They discovered a trail that led through a thick cottonwood grove. After a short walk they stopped in a small
meadow filled with grass.

"Do you really want me for your husband?" Angry
Heart asked.

"Yes. I've felt this way since the morning we reached
Crazy Horse's village. As strange as it sounds, I knew you
had come to live with me. I felt it so strongly."

"I've wanted to ask you for some time," Angry Heart
said. "But I thought it was too soon, and I thought I would
be insulting you."

"I know what you thought," Ghostwind said. "Now you
know what I've been thinking."

Angry Heart pulled Ghostwind close and began kissing
her. His lips trailed along her neck, while his hands slipped
under her buckskin shirt. He found the rise of her breasts,
working gently until the nipples had grown taut.

Ghostwind moaned with pleasure. Angry Heart's touch
brought a desire she had never known before. She pulled
him down over her and ran her hands along his strong

shoulders and back, then came around to his stomach and released the knot holding his buckskin pants.

She guided him into her and they both gasped. His strong surges took her breath away. They held one another tightly, two people whose desire for one another had been growing for many days.

When Angry Heart began his spasms, Ghostwind felt her own passion rise to a peak. She cried out, an overwhelming satisfaction flooding her being. Her fulfillment was entire.

"You are a master at lovemaking," she said as they lay together.

Angry Heart laughed. "I was going to say the same thing to you. I've never felt anything like that in my life."

"Have you had a lot of women, to do it so well?"

"Actually, I've been with just one. I didn't even know her name."

"You didn't know her name?"

"Oh, she called herself Sadie, or something like that. It wasn't her real name."

"Kicks-the-Fox was my first and only," Ghostwind said. "I always knew we weren't quite right for each other. But we had children together."

"Young Horse and Talking Grass are very special children," Angry Heart said. "I never used to think I'd want children of my own. They've changed my mind. We've become close friends."

"They see you as more than just a friend," Ghostwind said. "I know for certain they would welcome you as their new father."

"I would think that would be hard for them," Angry Heart said. "Considering that I killed their father, it would seem they should hate me. Yet they don't."

"They never have," Ghostwind said. "I told you that children have an understanding about life, something deep within them that is given by the Creator. We seem to lose that connection when we become adults. We don't see that the Creator knows what is best for us. If we are to die, then that is what's best. My children know that."

"Are you saying that your children have seen this before?"

"Yes, they have," Ghostwind replied. "Three winters past, we were camped with another band of Cheyenne. Warriors went out to raid a nearby Shoshone village for horses. But there was a fight."

Angry Heart noticed that Ghostwind was speaking as if the event had just happened. As she talked, she was feeling pain for the people involved.

"That day a warrior named Cloud killed his best friend, a warrior named Calling Bull. Calling Bull was mixed in among the Shoshone, fighting, and Cloud shot him by mistake. Yet Calling Bull's children never hated Cloud for it. They knew he didn't mean it. They even helped Cloud get through his time of mourning."

"I don't know if I can fill the vacancy left by their real father," Angry Heart said.

"You don't have to," Ghostwind said. "They see you as a man with a good heart, who will love them and provide for them. After you gave them your food that night, Young Horse asked me if you had given up your chance to heal your leg properly. They thought you would be crippled for life by giving them the food that was meant for you."

"But I had already eaten a lot. My leg was going to heal fine."

"They didn't know that. They felt that you were willing to sacrifice yourself for them, to make amends for killing their father."

They continued to talk about their future. Marriage would not take place for a while, possibly not until the end of the warm moons. Ghostwind was still considered in mourning and would be until her hair grew out and the cuts on her arms and legs were totally healed. She could not even begin to gather things that a wife might use.

Angry Heart would have to prove himself a warrior before he could ask for Ghostwind's hand. He would have to own more horses, so that he could give at least three to Five Bulls, and he would have to show that he had faced danger and had survived with honor. There was no telling how long it would take for him to count coup in some way.

"You will have to risk your life before we can share a lodge," Ghostwind said. "But I'm not worried, for I've already watched you do that in my dreams."

"What did you see?" Angry Heart asked.

"I saw your face, lined with war paint, and Bluecoat horses passing in front of you. I don't know when or where this happened. But it was in the future, for you haven't had your medicine vision yet."

Angry Heart knew a medicine vision would tell him his animal helper and the correct way to paint himself for protection in battle. He might even learn a song or a certain dance to perform before facing danger. He had yet to meet his animal protector and know what the Powers felt about him.

Eagle Wing had told him about visions and had said that he was ready to seek his own power at any time. "It will be hard to do for a while, though," he had said. "The village moves so often. You should be out fasting and praying in the hills a period of four days. We don't stay in camp long enough."

"I know who you are now," Ghostwind added. "I cannot tell you about this now, for you will learn. But I have seen you in my visions since first coming to Old Bear's village."

Angry Heart stared while Ghostwind told him that their union had brought them as close together as two people could be in the flesh, and that it had also united them spiritually.

"When we joined and held one another," Ghostwind said, "I began to feel things I hadn't understood until now. The visions, the signs that have come to me for a long time, they have all been about you. I know you cannot understand, but you will in time."

"Can't you tell me some things about this?" Angry Heart asked.

Ghostwind kissed her finger and pressed it to his lips. "Don't worry about it now. There is plenty of time for that. We must hurry back to the village. We've been gone a long time."

On the way, Ghostwind and Angry Heart talked about their plans, and about the fact that sooner or later the Bluecoats would find them, and fighting would begin.

"My people believe that it is an honor to die in battle," Ghostwind said. "You have already learned not to fear death. Now you must see for yourself how the Powers work in this world through the worlds beyond. You will learn to enter those worlds and know things for yourself."

Angry Heart stopped Ghostwind. "I have a problem understanding that. How can the worlds beyond influence this world? And I don't know what you mean about entering the other worlds."

A voice from a hill above the trail addressed Angry Heart. "You cannot know about any of that until you have lived the way we live. That will take some time."

Startled, Angry Heart and Ghostwind turned to see Crazy Horse, wrapped in his scarlet blanket, looking down at them. He descended to the trail.

"I've been trying to find you, Angry Heart," he said. "It's getting late in the day."

Angry Heart fumbled for words. "We went for a walk."

"I see. You nearly missed your chance to prove your

courage. How would you like to steal some Bluecoat horses?"

"Bluecoats are near here?" Angry Heart asked.

"Scouts came in not long ago to report a Bluecoat camp at the abandoned fort called Peace, up on the Elk River. There are Crow scouts with the Bluecoats. There will be plenty of ponies."

"Is it Three Stars Crook?"

"No," Crazy Horse replied. "The scouts say it is the big leader from the west, across the divide from Elk River. He is One-Who-Limps, the Bluecoat chief named Gibbon.

While on Crook's campaign, Angry Heart had heard other soldiers talking about John Gibbon. Although a colonel like George Crook, Gibbon was also addressed in his brevet rank as General. He was the main commander of the Montana Column.

Gibbon was a discerning and thorough commander, keen on detail, not given to rash decisions. He paid close attention to order and, unlike Crook, was not inclined to anything other than military affairs.

A specialist in artillery, Gibbon had command of the Seventh Infantry. Like Crook, he relied on Indian scouts and guides, but he didn't have Crook's patience with them. "He don't think much of the Indian ways," Kincaid had said. "He expects them to behave like white soldiers. That will never do."

Angry Heart thought about his good friend and hoped Kincaid had decided to forget his vendetta against the Sioux. The last person he wanted to meet on the battlefield was Kincaid.

"What do you know about this place called Fort Peace?" Crazy Horse asked Angry Heart.

Though few of the soldiers had any knowledge about Fort Peace, Kincaid had known a great deal and had shared his information.

"I know it's at the mouth of the Bighorn," Angry Heart told Crazy Horse. "I understand it was started sometime during the last warm moons by a Crow agent and some of his business partners to trade with the Crow. I suppose it's a big fort by now."

"You know some about it, and I know the rest," Crazy Horse said. "The Bluecoats have always wanted the Crow to fight with them against us. They promised the Crow many things to do this. But this fort was not very good and the Minneconjou made it hard for them by killing some wolf trappers. One-Who-Limps sent a smaller chief to take the agent and his people out of there."

"I heard they were looking for gold from there," Angry Heart said. "If they had found it, these lands would have been like the Black Hills."

Crazy Horse's face clouded with anger. "You know this to be true?"

"I know the white man," Angry Heart said. "They all want gold."

"Sitting Bull and the other old chiefs say it is not good to start trouble with the Bluecoats," Crazy Horse said. "I respect their feelings, but I believe we cannot back down any longer. It is time that One-Who-Limps and his Bluecoats leave the Elk River and go back across the mountains."

Angry Heart knew that Crazy Horse was challenging him. "I'm ready to go anytime," he said. "I want to live as your people and the Cheyenne do. I don't like the society I was born into. I will never like it."

Crazy Horse nodded. He was looking back and forth from Ghostwind to Angry Heart. "Good. I'm glad you're eager to show your courage. Sitting Bull is holding a council and will address all young men who want to go." He turned a hard stare toward Ghostwind.

"Is something wrong?" Ghostwind asked him.

"I guess it's not wrong," Crazy Horse said. "The two of you have been gone for a long time. Everyone knows that you want each other. When the time is right, I will be the first to congratulate the two of you." He then looked hard at Angry Heart. "But first you must prove you are worthy of this woman. I can tell you now, it won't be easy."

As the sun set, the village leaders convened in council about the attack on One-Who-Limps at Fort Peace. The leaders hoped this encounter with the Bluecoats would send an important message: We are not anxious for war and do not want to kill, but we want you to stop chasing us in our own country. Leave us alone, and we will be of no harm to you.

Nearly sixty young warriors, mostly Cheyenne, had gathered around a big fire outside the council lodge. The Cheyenne were eager to strike back at the Bluecoats for the attack of two weeks past. Many of the people were still suffering.

Crazy Horse would stay behind to help guard against Bluecoats coming from the south and east. Two Moon would be the main war leader.

Angry Heart and Eagle Wing waited anxiously with the others outside the council lodge. Finally the leaders emerged and Sitting Bull addressed everyone.

"We have decided that it is important to go against the Bluecoats and take their horses. But we should do nothing else."

Rumbling began in the crowd. There was obvious disapproval among the young warriors. Sitting Bull noted it and continued.

"To draw first blood would anger the spirits. *Wankantanka* knows the Lakota people and also the Cheyenne. We should do nothing that will bring anger to the Creator. However, if we are to take the offensive, let us steal their horses. But do nothing else. That will leave them without a means to follow us."

A young Minneconjou war chief named Rides Far asked to be heard. He rose, tall and lean, with a woodpecker tied into his long hair. He argued that the Bluecoats would never back down.

"The Bluecoats will never leave us alone," he said gruffly. "If we take their horses and do not kill them, they will only find more and we will be forced to fight them anyway."

"Besides, the Crow are scouting for them," another warrior said. "We should teach them a lesson they won't forget. Then they won't be back."

There was cheering among the group of dissenting warriors. Sitting Bull raised his hand for silence.

"How many times have we said that over the years?" he asked. "We kill their people, they kill ours. Back and forth. All the dying, yet no one stays out of the other's lands for very long. I'm getting tired of it. Besides, someday they'll see that the Bluecoats really aren't their friends."

Everyone was silent. The firelight danced against faces wondering at Sitting Bull's words.

Eagle Wing explained to Angry Heart that many of the people were surprised to hear Sitting Bull discourage fighting the Crow. "Many of his war scars are because of them," Eagle Wing whispered. "But he is aging and getting tired. He doesn't want to see a lot of people die."

Rides Far broke the silence. He addressed the audience with fervor. "We shouldn't worry about the Crow. They want to kill us all. Everyone knows that. They and all the Bluecoats should have their hearts cut out."

The young men cheered again. The elders looked at one another. When the cheering had died down, Sitting Bull made his final comments.

"I have seen days of war and I know I will see more. My

heart is sad that we cannot all agree. But what my heart wants does not always come to pass." His eyes scanned the crowd, letting the words sink in. "I believe in defending our people, but I don't believe in going out and starting trouble. We are many all together and the Bluecoats would be foolish to attack us. Let them see this and leave our lands."

Sitting Bull waited while the crowd cheered. "I know that many of you younger warriors want revenge against the Crow for old fighting. Maybe so. But this is not a good time. It is more important to stay together and be strong. Wait for the enemy to come to our village. Then we will fight if need be. But better to watch them open their mouths in wonder at our great numbers. Watch them turn and leave, with no fighting."

After more cheering, Sitting Bull's face grew hard as stone. "Young men, I tell you it is important not to look for blood now. I know that any Lakota warrior who kills not in self-defense will see darkness. If you go out to get One-Who-Limps with blood on your minds, you are bringing great danger upon yourself and your families. This camp cannot be filled with hatred, or *Wankantanka* will turn the other way. Listen to my words. I have spoken."

A heavy silence fell over the crowd. Rides Far looked down, as did a number of warriors eager to fight. Angry Heart learned from Eagle Wing that the intertribal warfare had gone on for generations, and that the younger warriors had always carried on the tradition of avenging family deaths at the hands of enemies.

"Now that the Bluecoats have come, everything is changing," Eagle Wing said. "Sitting Bull wants everyone to forget the past and try to live in peace. He is a peace chief, and he wants what he believes is best for his people. You will see now that Sitting Bull has power. What he wants will be done."

Two Moon rose and spoke. "All who follow me will do

as Sitting Bull has asked, for the council has decided. If any of you wish to kill, then stay back here and defend the villages. Otherwise, come and take ponies for our herds."

Angry Heart and Eagle Wing joined the warriors going with Two Moon. A number of young Minneconjou gathered around Rides Far and talked among themselves.

"He will no doubt lead a war party of his own," Eagle Wing told Angry Heart. "Sitting Bull and the other elders will not try to stop him. Everyone has to make his own decisions in life."

The raiding party would leave that evening. Warriors hurried to prepare themselves, taking only enough clothing for survival. Everyone was to take one pony and enough food for three nights. A camp would be made some ten miles upstream from Fort Peace. From there, half the raiders would go the remaining distance on foot.

The warriors would gamble to see who got the honor of stealing the horses. Not everyone could go; too many would make discovery by the Crow scouts that much easier. Those who remained behind would act as backup, in case the Crow and the Bluecoats gave chase.

Everyone knew the importance of succeeding. They could not fail, for that would give the Crow and the Bluecoats confidence. They must get all the ponies, or as many as possible, so as to demoralize them and send them back where they came from.

Angry Heart knew he and Eagle Wing would be among those going after the ponies; that had already been decided. This was Angry Heart's time to prove himself, and everyone would be watching to see how well he performed.

Shot-in-the-Throat and Pine Woman joined Ghostwind and her parents. Young Horse and Tall Deer crowded in front of everyone. They all looked on as Angry Heart prepared for his first raiding party.

Angry Heart fought for composure. When Five Bulls

gave him a rifle and he dropped it, Ghostwind commented, "If you can't hold onto that, and you an expert, how can you hold onto an enemy horse?"

"I'll settle down," Angry Heart told her. "I don't do this kind of thing every day."

"No one does," Ghostwind pointed out. "Not a one of our warriors has ever been on a more important raid. It is doubtful that our people have ever been given a more important mission."

Angry Heart noted that Ghostwind had referred to the Cheyenne as *our* people. They weren't just *her* people any longer. In her eyes, he was a member, just as if he had been born in one of the villages.

"I have no doubt you can do it," Shot-in-the-Throat said. "I've never seen you fail at anything you were determined to do."

Angry Heart asked Young Horse to select a pony. "It will bring me good luck if you pick him," Angry Heart said.

"Would you let Tall Deer help me?" Young Horse asked. "He is your brother and he would bring just as much good luck to you. Probably more."

"That's a great idea," Angry Heart said. "Now I'll have twice the luck!"

Young Horse and Tall Deer hurried out to the herd and brought back Mud. Tall Deer was smiling. "You can show the Crow how you learned to ride. Don't forget to tell them who showed you."

"I wish Tall Deer and I could both ride with you," Young Horse said. "I would give anything to see you count coup."

"I will do my best to count coup for you," Angry Heart told Young Horse.

"Bring back a pony for Young Horse and myself," Tall Deer said. "If you can only get one, give it to Young Horse."

"I'll get you both a pony," Angry Heart promised.

Eagle Wing and a number of warriors were mounted and waiting. Ghostwind took a step forward as Angry Heart jumped onto the buckskin. She could not say good-bye as a wife might her husband, but she reached out and Angry Heart took her hand.

"Be careful," she said. "I know you will succeed, but be careful."

Angry Heart joined Eagle Wing and the other warriors. His blood raced as they fell in behind Two Moon. Never in his life had he felt this way, not even before his most daring shooting exhibitions. There had never been anything to match this night. He would succeed, he told himself as he rode and whooped with the others through the darkness. He would take ponies from the Crow, and he would be that much closer to proving himself a dignified warrior of the Cheyenne nation.

TWENTY-SIX

"They have no wolves posted to watch for enemies," Eagle Wing said in a whisper. "Not even a single campfire burns." He laughed. "It will be a good night for taking ponies."

No guards whatsoever, Angry Heart thought to himself. How could it be? Tents and wagons indicated the fort was occupied; but it was difficult to believe it was a military camp.

Angry Heart and Eagle Wing lay on a ridge overlooking Fort Peace, with thirty other raiders. Two Moon lay next to Eagle Wing, staring down in silence. He had said just that morning that a dream had come to him. In the dream there had been many horses and many Crow warriors standing in a circle crying.

"They were crying because they lost their horses," Two Moon had said. "We will be successful."

The ride to Fort Peace had been uneventful: a full night and most of a day riding, and a short rest in war lodges built along the river. The ten-mile walk from camp had taken them half the night. They had journeyed with caution, two scouts moving ahead just under the surrounding ridge tops. Not once had the scouts barked like the coyote, the little wolf of the Plains. They had seen no enemies; there had been no danger.

The lack of fresh pony tracks along the trails indicated that the Crow scouts had not been east along the river. They likely had gone straight south in their search for signs of a village. If so, they had gone looking in the wrong place.

Angry Heart looked into the night sky. Broken storm clouds rolled before the moon. They had hoped for a rainstorm and total darkness. But they would have no need for such cover.

Everyone was elated. The talk in camp the day before had been about the danger that they would certainly face. Angry Heart had spoken often about the sentries that had been posted in force during Crook's campaign. He had told them what to look for and how the sentries were placed. Gibbon would certainly be taking strict precautions.

"It makes no sense," Angry Heart told Eagle Wing as they prepared to descend the slope toward the fort. "Why would they leave horses and mules with no guards?"

"They must think our village is a long way from here, or that we've gone back to the agencies," Eagle Wing replied. "They've been in camp for many days and have grown soft."

"That's good for us," Angry Heart said.

"Don't relax until we're back at the village with the horses," Eagle Wing advised. "Anything can happen."

Angry Heart followed Eagle Wing down the slope. The two of them had been chosen to scout the grounds and find the horses, as part of Angry Heart's training as a warrior. They would scout the fort thoroughly and report to Two Moon. Then the raid would begin.

Angry Heart moved cautiously behind Eagle Wing

down a little draw filled with shadows. The moon shone intermittently through the clouds, bathing the rolling hills in a diffused white light. Close to the fort, Eagle Wing turned and whispered, "You have to learn to breathe right. I can hear you plainly."

Angry Heart was aware that his heart was thumping. He was trying to hold his breath, but his lungs cried for air and he gasped.

"Are you too afraid to do this?" Eagle Wing asked.

"No, I can do it."

"You cannot go ahead with me until you've calmed yourself," Eagle Wing insisted. "You'll awaken every Crow and Bluecoat in camp."

"I'll admit, I'm a little nervous. The success of all this rests on us, you know."

"All the more reason to relax," Eagle Wing said. "I want you to sit down cross-legged."

"What?"

"Hurry and do it! We haven't much time."

Angry Heart complied. Eagle Wing instructed him to close his eyes and bow his head. "Listen to your breath come out," he told Angry Heart. "Just listen as each breath comes out."

Angry Heart tried to concentrate, but thoughts raced through his mind, pictures of adolescence when he had stolen chickens or loaves of bread to survive, times when he had fought to keep himself alive.

"Empty out your mind," Eagle Wing instructed. "Make it as black as the night."

Angry Heart tried, but he was too anxious. More scenes filled his mind. He looked up at Eagle Wing. "I can't relax."

"You can if you will," Eagle Wing said. "You don't have to be a rabbit."

"I'm no rabbit," Angry Heart said.

"We'll both have to run from here if you don't relax," Eagle Wing said. "Close your eyes."

Angry Heart took a deep breath and let his chin fall against his chest. Eagle Wing asked him in a low, soft voice to imagine a hawk circling in the sky on a lazy summer afternoon, rising and sinking with the wind, over the winding, twisting big river.

"Can you see the hawk?" Eagle Wing asked.

"Yes. But it's not high in the sky. It's flying lower, and fast."

"What does it look like?"

"It is medium-sized, with bars of white on long, pointed wings."

"Does it like to glide and soar in fast circles?"

"Yes."

"Oh, you were made especially for this raid," Eagle Wing said. "Yes, you are special. You can see through the hawk's eyes, can't you?"

Angry Heart had calmed down. "Yes, I am the hawk with the pointed wings. I can see the river."

"You can see more than just the river," Eagle Wing said. "You can see everything below. You glide and drift anywhere you want. You go up into the sky and sail down, making whooshing sounds. It feels very good to do that, doesn't it?"

Angry Heart began to feel the warm sensation of relaxation. "Yes, it feels very good."

"Now you're gliding through the afternoon," Eagle Wing continued. "It's getting later, much later. Nightfall has come and you are gliding toward the fort. You can see where a group of horses is being held for the night. There is no fear in you."

"There is no fear in me," Angry Heart said.

Eagle Wing continued to speak low and soft. "I'm glad you are with me, Nighthawk."

"Nighthawk?"

"Yes. You are a nighthawk, the glider hawk with the white-barred wings. He does not sit in trees very often, but he's very good at hiding on the ground. Nighthawk lands, and you can't see him until you step on him. Nighthawk speeds through the darkness and shares the lower skies with Owl."

"Nighthawk sees well at night," Angry Heart said. "I can see very well at night."

"Then you can see where the horses are. Show them to me."

"I will show them to you."

Eagle Wing gently touched Angry Heart's shoulder. Angry Heart took a deep breath and smiled. "I feel light."

"You are light. You're Nighthawk. Take me to the horses."

Angry Heart led Eagle Wing closer to the fort grounds. He felt unusually calm, as if he were walking above the ground. The idea that he could die did not cross his mind. He knew that he would make no noise, and that the two of them would bring success to the others.

Angry Heart stopped near an opening in the trees. The river ran just below, rippling softly. The water was low, as the hard winter and the unseasonable cold of a few weeks before had held back the spring thaws.

Eagle Wing noticed Angry Heart staring at the river. "Do you feel the horses?" he whispered.

"Yes, they're near."

Eagle Wing crouched, his fingers touching the ground. "Tracks, many of them. This is where they water the horses. Where do you think they keep them at night? In the hills behind the fort?"

"No," Angry Heart said. He led Eagle Wing to the river's edge and pointed to a small, tree-covered island not far from the bank. "The horses are hidden over there. I'd bet anything on it."

The crossing was easy. The water was cold but only waist-deep, the bottom sandy and even, with no snags or dangerous holes. On the island, they covered themselves with mud to diffuse their smell.

"These horses don't know us," Eagle Wing explained. We don't want to scare them."

Angry Heart and Eagle Wing counted close to thirty head. The ponies rested peacefully, barely bothering to notice Angry Heart and Eagle Wing, who crouched, looking for guards.

On their way back across the shallows, Eagle Wing remarked, "I can't believe our luck. We must hurry back and tell Two Moon."

In a short time, the entire raiding party was on the island. The ponies were quickly and quietly led into the water, and riders swam them down river a distance before bringing them out. Eagle Wing and Angry Heart stayed behind with Two Moon and five other warriors who wished to raid the fort grounds themselves and take what they could from the sleeping Bluecoats and their Crow scouts.

"Remember," Two Moon told everyone, "we must not kill, even if we are attacked. Just try to get away. We did not come to draw blood."

Each of the raiders selected a particular section of the camp to penetrate. Angry Heart decided upon a grouping of tents and wagons along the river.

"This is your chance to gain even more honor," Two Moon told Angry Heart. "Walk softly among the tents and take something. We will all do it."

"You will be on your own this time," Eagle Wing told Angry Heart. "But I know you will do well. You're a night-hawk."

Angry Heart slipped along the edge of camp, still unable to understand why there were no sentries. He couldn't believe that an infantry campaign could be that different from the cavalry. Even though there were not nearly as many horses, there was the safety of the men to consider. If they had come for blood, Gibbon and many of his troops would have died in their beds.

Just ahead, a horse snorted. Angry Heart stopped and rubbed dirt and mud over his face and arms. He moved forward cautiously. A horse and a mule were tied to picket pins, lazily eating oats from a wooden trough.

Angry Heart wanted to laugh. He couldn't have found anything better to take. He thought about looking for weapons, but decided it was too risky.

After cutting the picket ropes, Angry Heart led the horse and mule down to the river and along a trail out from camp. He led the horse and mule to the top of the hill. Soon the rest had all returned. Everyone had gotten something: a coat, a saddle, a bridle, something of use. But no one had gotten more horses.

" 'Nighthawk' certainly fits you," Two Moon told him. "Eagle Wing was telling me how you found the horses on the island. You have gained great honor this night."

For finding the herd and then stealing another horse and a mule, Angry Heart was to be given five ponies of his choice. Three would go to Eagle Wing. Two Moon would take two for himself, and the others would be divided after gambling among the rest of the raiders.

Dawn was breaking as the raiders joined those waiting with the horse herd. Four miles from Fort Peace, the celebrating began. Never had a horse raid gone so easily. Two Moon commented that he could now tell his people that he had walked in a Bluecoat camp without being seen or touched.

"And it's fitting that we have another naming ceremony when we reach the village," he told everyone. "The man we have known as Angry Heart has learned to soar with eyes that see in the darkness. He has helped us with a great victory. It's fitting that he be called Nighthawk."

Eagle Wing and the other raiders cheered. "You are no longer Angry Heart," he said as they rode through the night. "You have a name that is befitting a warrior. Now you must continue to live up to the name."

The entire community anxiously awaited the return of Two Moon and the raiders. Many were already arranging their finest clothes in preparation for the victory celebration.

But not everyone was so optimistic. Ghostwind looked on as Pine Woman comforted a young Minneconjou woman. Her name was Fawn-That-Goes-Dancing, Pine Woman's niece of sixteen winters. The young wife, mother of two small boys, was in tears because of her husband's decision to go against Sitting Bull's wishes and fight the Bluecoats.

"Rides Far is thinking about glory and not about what's best for all the people," Fawn was saying. "He will get himself and the others in trouble."

"Maybe he will change his mind," Pine Woman said. "Even now Sitting Bull and the other leaders are holding council. Maybe they will stop them all from going."

Fawn, a strong young woman who usually saw the best in everything, was beside herself with grief and worry. She stared out into the evening sky, where the sun was approaching the horizon.

"No one can stop Rides Far," she said. "As sure as the coming of night, he's made up his mind to go and take revenge for the death of the horse raiders."

"But he doesn't even know if the horse raiders were caught or not," Pine Woman said. "It's foolish to go on a revenge raid when there's no reason for revenge."

Ghostwind had been listening intently, biting her lip at

times. The thought of losing Angry Heart bothered her deeply. Though she felt confident he would return, she still did not like to hear anyone talking about revenge raids. She had seen the two of them in her dreams, living happily together. She didn't want to think that harm could come to him.

She thought about the night he had ridden off with Eagle Wing and the others, shouting and yelling as though they had already triumphed. As she had watched him disappear into the darkness, she had remembered her feelings the night Kicks-the-Fox had left. That night, she had been worried; but even though she had been married to Kicks-the-Fox for many winters, she had never developed the feelings for him that she already had for Angry Heart.

Ghostwind touched Fawn on the shoulder and said, "You should dry your eyes. There is no need for a revenge raid."

Fawn stared at her. "How do you know this?"

"I am confident they will all return safely."

"She's a seer," Pine Woman told Fawn. "She's a prophet like no other."

Fawn's face lit up. "Then you don't believe my husband will meet death, either?"

Ghostwind felt her abdomen tighten. Feelings she had never known enveloped her, filling her with sadness. She suddenly felt dizzy.

Both Fawn and Pine Woman noticed her reaction. "What is it?" Pine Woman asked.

"I don't know," Ghostwind said. "I've never had this feeling before. It's as if I am dreading something terrible to come. I can't understand it."

Fawn's eyes filled with tears again. "Are you seeing my husband's death?"

"I can't say that your husband will die. I don't know."

"You *have* to tell me," Fawn insisted. "I must know. Tell me what you're seeing. Please!"

"I don't know what I'm seeing," Ghostwind replied. Tears then filled her eyes. "I just don't know."

Ghostwind got up and hurried away. Pine Woman called after her. Ghostwind turned, her heart aching with a pain she couldn't comprehend. Fawn and Pine Woman caught up with her.

"What is bothering you?" Pine Woman asked. "I've never seen you this way before."

"I don't even know what to say," Ghostwind replied. "I've never felt like this before. I don't know what it means. I have to pray."

"What about my husband?" Fawn asked.

"Whatever I'm feeling has to do with more than just your husband," Ghostwind said.

"You can't go off into the hills," Pine Woman said. "There may be Bluecoats near."

"I must," Ghostwind said. "I must speak with the Powers. It's very important."

"I won't stop you, then," Pine Woman said. "Do you want me to tell your mother?"

"Just tell her that I went to pray, and not to worry," Ghostwind said. "I have to go now, and find the top of a hill."

Ghostwind hurried from camp, climbing into the hills above the river. A warrior on guard duty stopped her and asked her where she was going.

"Please, I must go to that hill." She pointed to a rocky knoll nearby. "You can see me from there. I will go no further, but I must pray."

The warrior consented. Ghostwind gathered sage wood and climbed to the top of the knoll. As darkness descended, she built a fire. Her hands shook and her mind raced, something she could not remember happening since childhood. She had no understanding of what was happening to her, except that the dread was growing stronger.

Ghostwind raised her hands to the sky and sang her prayers. She watched the smoke spiral into the vast open above her. She closed her eyes and let her body move in a slow, steady, side-to-side rhythm.

Her dread would not leave her, yet she could see no pictures. Nothing came to her but a swirling mass of dark colors, swimming and running together. She persisted, swaying her body until she lay down upon the ground, held within a deep trance.

The mass of dark color suddenly became a twisting river that she was viewing from above. The current ran a thick and murky red, churning and boiling its way through a country where spring had given way to a hot, dry summer. There were no singing birds, no bellowing buffalo, no signs that life had ever existed. The only movement was the frothy red current of the river.

Ghostwind gasped as the river suddenly began to change. The water grew even darker. Hands began to appear from below the surface, reaching, grasping for something to hold on to. But each one slipped back below the surface.

As the hands reached out of the water, many things were happening simultaneously outside the river, things that she couldn't see. She heard yelling and screaming, men crying, horses in the labor of hard running. Though she had never witnessed one, she knew these to be the sounds of a terrific battle.

Ghostwind felt deep dread and sadness overwhelming her. She wanted to scream, but her mouth wouldn't open. Then, in an instant, the crimson river rushed up at her. She felt engulfed, drowning. She fought the feeling, but could do nothing to free herself.

In a desperate effort, she reached out of the frothy water. She felt a hand take hers and pull her from the river.

She lay on her back, her eyes closed, the sounds of battle all around.

Open your eyes, Ghostwind. You must see!

Ghostwind had never heard the voice before. It was commanding, *Open your eyes!*

Ghostwind struggled with fear. She reached out again and felt the strong hand clasp hers. Her eyes opened and she looked up into a vast sky filled with fire. The fire rolled through the clouds, exploding them into showering flame. Tongues of blue lightning licked everywhere, as from the mouths of giant snakes. All the while, the screaming continued.

Horrified, Ghostwind continued to stare at the sky. A terrible smell overpowered her, making her want to vomit. The smell reminded her of the gases that rose from the deep pools in the Stinkingwater River, where the hated enemy, the Shoshone, lived. But the smell was much stronger, like that of decaying flesh.

As she watched, Bluecoats poured from the flames, turning and twisting, their uniforms falling off to reveal naked white bodies. They fell toward her, their faces etched with the most intense terror Ghostwind had ever seen. They fell all around her, their bodies exploding upon impact with the ground.

Soon there were piles of Bluecoat body parts everywhere. The stench was overpowering, yet she could not move.

Finally the sky began to change. The flames gradually turned inward and clouds reappeared, not white, but dark and roiling. The sadness within Ghostwind returned as a massive wailing began, erupting from above and all around her.

Rain fell from the sky. She turned her face upward and let the water fall, touching it with her fingers. Its taste was salty, like tears. The Creator was crying.

TWENTY-SEVEN

Ghostwind sat for a long time with her face raised into the storm. Tears streamed down her cheeks, mixing with the rain. The wailing in her head continued, bringing sharp pain. She lifted her hands to the sky and prayed that her vision would not become real. She asked that the wailing and the rain both cease, so that there would be no need for sadness. But both continued.

Ghostwind rose unsteadily to her feet. Dizziness overpowered her, and she fell. She came to her knees and waited for the dizziness to pass, then rose again and began to wander over the hill, feeling totally lost. She believed she was searching for her people, hoping they were not all gone. It seemed she was the only living person anywhere in the world.

As she continued to wander, the rain fell harder. The wailing continued at a high pitch, and the sky darkened into night. Unable to see clearly, Ghostwind felt as if the ground were moving under her. She slipped and feil, striking her head. Unconscious, she rolled down a slope and came to rest at the foot of the trail.

Sobbing uncontrollably, Ghostwind awakened in the arms of her mother. Young Horse and Talking Grass were also there.

"You're alive!" Young Horse said. "We've been worried about you."

Confused, Ghostwind looked around. Nothing was as she remembered it. The rain had ceased and there was no wailing, only laughter and gaiety coming from the village. Mountain Water and Pine Woman looked on with concern as Young Horse and Talking Grass asked her more questions.

"You got hurt badly, didn't you?" Young Horse said. "Can you walk?"

"You needn't worry about me," Ghostwind replied. She rose unsteadily to her feet. "Go and wait for me in the lodge."

"What happened on the hill?" Young Horse persisted. "You fell down and rolled to the bottom. You're covered with mud."

Talking Grass was hugging her mother. "Why are you crying?" she asked. "What happened to you?"

"I was unhappy, but I'm better now," Ghostwind said. "Please, both of you, no more questions. Go and wait for me in the lodge. I will be with you very soon."

"Hurry," Young Horse said. "The raiders have returned and everyone is celebrating."

When her children had left, Ghostwind turned to her mother. "Have the raiders returned safely?"

"Yes," Mountain Water said. "Not a one was hurt, or even bothered. Everyone is rejoicing!"

"What?" Ghostwind asked. "Isn't everyone crying?"

Day Lily and Pine Woman approached. They had heard about Ghostwind's fall from Young Horse and Talking Grass.

"What happened to you?" Day Lily asked.

Ghostwind took a moment to gather her thoughts. "I've seen something terrible. I don't fully understand it."

"You don't need to worry about the raiders," Day Lily said. "Everyone came back safely, with many enemy horses. Angry Heart gained many honors."

"Angry Heart is in a ceremony now," Pine Woman added. "His new name is Nighthawk. He wanted you to be there, but we told him that you were praying on the hill."

Ghostwind started forward, holding her head. "I need to see my children."

"Don't you want to see Nighthawk at the celebration?" Day Lily asked.

Ghostwind stopped. Her face was twisted with grief. "How can everyone be happy with what is to come? There is nothing to celebrate."

The women all looked at one another.

"What are you talking about?" Mountain Water asked.

"I have seen terrible things, Mother. You cannot begin to understand." She held her aching head. "Something awful is going to happen. It will be the worst battle ever fought."

"Haven't you heard us?" Mountain Water said. "The raiders have returned with many Crow ponies. Not a shot was fired. Everyone is happy."

"What?" Ghostwind asked. "No shots were fired?"

"Oh, no!" Pine Woman said. "The Bluecoats and the Crow slept like babies."

Ghostwind turned her face to the sky. Tears streamed down her cheeks.

"Tell us what happened to you," Day Lily said.

"I had a vision that I have been trying to explain," Ghostwind said. "Where's Fawn-That-Goes-Dancing?"

"She's in her lodge," Day Lily told her. "She doesn't feel like celebrating. Rides Far led a war party of young warriors out yesterday."

"Then it is as I dreamed," Ghostwind said. "All is not well. There is no reason for the celebration."

Mountain Water and Day Lily helped Ghostwind begin walking again. "When you get some rest, you will feel better," Mountain Water said.

"Mother, I cannot feel better!" Ghostwind snapped. "As long as there are thoughts of war, there is nothing to celebrate. Someone must find Rides Far and the war party, and have them all come back to camp. They cannot stay out."

"Maybe there will be no Bluecoats for Rides Far to find," Pine Woman suggested. "Without horses, maybe the Crow have gone home. Then the Bluecoats will leave also."

"No," Ghostwind said, "the Bluecoats will not leave. There are too many. They are coming from all directions."

"How can that be?" Day Lily asked. "None of the scouts have seen Bluecoats. Red Bear has been scouting to the east. He has seen no Bluecoats."

"It doesn't matter," Ghostwind said. "It is already happening. It has begun, and no one can stop it."

"What has begun?" Mountain Water asked.

"The end," Ghostwind said. She closed her eyes. "It is the beginning of the end."

The Big Village moved up the Tongue to Wood Creek, where the Cheyenne celebrated the successful raid. Everyone talked about Nighthawk. He had gained the most honor and had brought back the most horses. As promised, he gave Young Horse and Tall Deer one each, being careful not to give one a much better horse than the other.

The second evening in camp, Nighthawk accompanied the two boys to the edge of the village, where they raced a number of times. Neither could beat the other convincingly.

"How did you pick two horses so evenly matched?" Young Horse asked.

"Eagle Wing and I raced them a few times on the way back to the village," Nighthawk replied. "They are very good horses. You should both be happy."

"We are most happy for you," Tall Deer said. "Especially since you will be taking Ghostwind as your wife."

Young Horse was smiling as well. "After tonight, you will be my father."

"What do you mean?" Nighthawk asked.

Tall Deer pointed. Five Bulls approached, smiling, demanding three horses from Nighthawk. "Old Bear and Two Moon have just come from council with other elders. They told me that my daughter can build a lodge for you, if that is what you wish."

"Take any three you wish!" Nighthawk said with delight.

"No, there are two you cannot have!" Tall Deer said with a grin. He and Young Horse jumped on their ponies and raced away.

Five Bulls laughed. "I'm too old to stay on ponies like that, anyway. Did you get an old, tame mare?"

In the village, Day Lily and Mountain Water were talking and laughing with a number of other women. Pine Woman and Shot-in-the-Throat were there, as well as others from the various Lakota villages.

A council had convened and word had already reached everyone's ears. Nighthawk had gained sufficient honor to marry. The women who had gathered were already building a lodge that would be filled with presents.

The feasting and dancing lasted most of the night. Day Lily, who had been sewing secretly for more than a month, presented Ghostwind with a finely beaded white antelope dress. Ghostwind wore it with pride. She rode Nighthawk's buckskin through the village, while everyone cheered.

Ghostwind's emotions ran high and low, back and forth. She was elated at having Nighthawk for her husband, but the feelings brought on by the visions lingered, threatening to ruin her evening.

She decided to ask the Creator for help. Something so special as marriage could not be tainted with anguish.

After her parade ended, Ghostwind hugged her mother, Day Lily and Pine Woman. Immediately she began to feel better. Her warmth grew to elation and she began to laugh with the other women. Young Horse stood holding his new pony, beaming with pride and joy. Talking Grass whispered in her ear that she was glad to have a new father, especially one as special as Nighthawk.

Everyone seemed happy for them. Even those who hadn't liked having the Bluecoat in the village were congratulating her. To them, a man whose name changed twice in less than a year's time was very powerful. It was a good sign; it meant that the entire Big Village had power. And it meant that if the Bluecoats insisted on fighting, they were going to have a hard time.

In the eyes of the Cheyenne and Lakota, and all the others in the village, the Bluecoats had lost their best fighter. Nighthawk believed in freedom and had brought his medicine to the Cheyenne. When the real fighting began and the Bluecoats saw him charging down at them, they would all run in fright.

Crazy Horse, who had wondered if Nighthawk could prove himself, had joined in the naming ceremony, and now nodded with approval at the marriage.

"I know you will think this strange of me," Crazy Horse told Nighthawk, "but I'm glad for this marriage."

"It does sound strange," Nighthawk said. "At times I felt you wanted Ghostwind for yourself."

"For a long time I did want her," Crazy Horse admitted. "But I went into the hills, while you were gone raiding

One-Who-Limps. There I had a vision that told me to concentrate entirely on stopping the Bluecoats. I saw the hailstorm that I often see, and listened to the voice that came down to me. I learned that if I want victory over Three Stars Crook, I cannot be thinking about Ghostwind. I have a wife. My vision said one is enough. My life has already been damaged by wanting women I shouldn't want. I cannot go against the Powers that talk to me."

"It's good that you're telling me this," Nighthawk said. "I was concerned that you would always dislike me for marrying Ghostwind."

"I cannot dislike you," Crazy Horse said. "I tried, but I cannot. I don't understand you, for you are more like our people than your own. This I have never seen before. It has told me a lot about skin color and looking inside instead of outside every *Wasichu.* I guess you are not all the same after all. I'm glad for it. You will be good for Ghostwind."

"Thank you for your kindness," Nighthawk said.

Crazy Horse handed Nighthawk a small round stone and told him to wear it behind his left ear. "I have a stone behind my right ear. When we fight together, we will share powers."

Nighthawk stood dumbfounded while Crazy Horse walked off into the night. To get such a charm from someone like Crazy Horse was unheard of. He would find a way to tie it into his hair and never lose it.

Nighthawk quickly got used to life in the lodge with Ghostwind and her two children. They waited on him, bringing him food and other items, just so that they could smile and get a hug from him. They even helped their mother pluck the hairs from his face, so that his beard would be gone and he could wear paint like the other warriors.

Everyone in the Big Village knew of Nighthawk. Because of him, the raid on One-Who-Limps at Fort Peace had been a success. As a result, other raiding parties left to find other Bluecoat camps. War dances came with every sundown. Everyone wanted a share of the glory.

Despite protests by Sitting Bull and other peace chiefs, war parties came and went from the Big Village. Ghostwind rejoiced with Fawn-That-Goes-Dancing when Rides Far returned with his war party. No one had been hurt among his group, and they boasted that they had held One-Who-Limps at bay with his Bluecoats at Fort Peace. One-Who-Limps could not cross Elk River, the Yellowstone, as long as they commanded the hills on the other side.

Others said that a small command of Crow and Bluecoats was scouting the area south of the Elk. The Crow were being cautious, though, and would not bring the Bluecoats too close.

With the knowledge that they held a far superior power, the people of the combined villages went about their usual daily tasks. Hunting parties brought in fresh game, and the women dried meat and dug roots from the hills. Children played and roamed about the camps, always aware that Bluecoats were around, but never hiding in fear of them.

Camp moved cross country toward the Rosebud River, stopping at two locations near Elk River. At the second site, Nighthawk took part in a major buffalo hunt, killing nine. He downed three with a bow and arrows given him by Eagle Wing. The first one killed, a huge bull, nearly gored his dun horse, Mud. But Nighthawk stayed on. Leaning over the side of his pony, he had placed three arrows into the bull's chest.

In return, he showed Eagle Wing how to aim down the barrel of his rifle, while a number of warriors watched. Most of the warriors held their rifles against their right shoulders, but aimed across the sights with the opposite eye, throwing off their aim.

"Aim down the sights with the same eye as the shoulder

you shoot from," Nighthawk advised. "It gives you a straight line of sight."

Some of the warriors caught on, others didn't. But all admired Nighthawk for his abilities and his willingness to teach others. Nighthawk had done everything any Cheyenne warrior had done except fight an enemy hand to hand. Everyone knew that would come before long.

With plenty of meat drying, the Big Village crossed over to the lower Rosebud River. Soon the huge horse herds stripped the grass, and people moved farther upriver. After two more moves, the people settled along the river where the valley widened considerably. Here the grass was lush and plentiful, and there were more buffalo nearby.

It was in this camp that Nighthawk challenged Red Bear to a game of horseback tag. Red Bear quickly declined. He had been watching Nighthawk practicing trick riding. Nighthawk had learned well from Tall Deer, his brother, the young horse tender who everyone knew would someday be the premier rider among the Lakota people. Red Bear knew he would lose and face ridicule. It was far better to back off and retain some dignity.

Nighthawk did not humiliate Red Bear by calling him a coward. Instead he invited Red Bear to hunt with him. To the delight of both Day Lily and Ghostwind, Red Bear accepted. They returned with five elk. Ghostwind and Day Lily took the hides to make war shirts for the two of them.

While Nighthawk basked in his glory by day, Ghostwind fought the return of her dreams. Since reaching the Rosebud, she would often awaken at night with a start, disturbing Nighthawk. Yet she never spoke to him of her vision, nor to anyone else. Day Lily asked her about it frequently, as did her mother and Pine Woman. She told them she was not ready to discuss it. They hadn't cared to hear the truth the night of Nighthawk's return, so they likely wouldn't ever believe her.

Ghostwind knew Day Lily was afraid of dreams and never discussed them. But it puzzled Ghostwind that her mother was not as concerned as she. Mountain Water usually took her very seriously. Perhaps her mother couldn't envision a defeat with so big a village to draw warriors from.

After a time, Ghostwind prayed again to the Creator for relief. Each time she even thought about her vision, she was overcome with fear. She wished she could forget it; but the images and the feelings remained with her day and night. Going into the hills to pray and search for meaning hadn't helped her. In fact, she felt she might never go into the hills alone again, not after what had happened at the second Rosebud camp.

She had seen many large red owls streaming from a grove of dead pines. Never before had she seen a red owl; she knew such a bird did not exist. They had come from the Other Side, and she wanted no more to do with death.

Still, death wouldn't let her go. She would take late-night walks, so intense were the visions. Often they were of the same roiling, bloody sky and river water, and of hands grasping. At other times the sky would darken and the whirling clouds would come down, straight at her, until she would jump awake in her robes.

Her walks most frequently took place just after midnight. Then one night she slept until just before dawn, when another bad dream awakened her. She left the lodge and began to walk along the river, noting that the sky overhead was filled with swollen black clouds.

Usually the fear left her during her walks. This time it increased. As she stared at the clouds, she realized that her death visions were coming, in part, from her childhood. She remembered seeing the same kind of clouds just after falling down the hill. The blow to her head had opened up her memory.

As dawn broke, Ghostwind noted a faint green in the

churning clouds. She remembered seeing clouds like that as a child in Colorado, where she had lived in a small cabin with her parents. Her mother had been Cheyenne and her father mixed-blood, Cheyenne and white. Until now she hadn't remembered anything about either of her parents, or about that terrible morning.

The whirling cloud she now remembered had sent a huge death spirit funneling down from the sky, killing both parents. It had been a freak storm in late fall on the Colorado Plains. Such storms usually came only in the spring. But the autumn had been unusually warm and wet, with many thunderheads building morning and night. Death spirits had descended from the sky often that year.

Ghostwind could remember the night it had happened. It had been just before dawn. The air had been very still just before the death wind. Fear had awakened her, and she had gotten up from her bed to look outside. The clouds had been roiling and churning overhead.

She had stood transfixed with horror as the funnel had descended. The small trading post had been torn to fragments.

Something had struck her in the head and she had awakened between two felled cottonwoods, with no idea what had happened to her. It was as if she had just been born, with no name and no identity.

Nothing had been left of the trading post. There had been no bodies. None of it had made sense. Her only reality had been that her head hurt terribly and she was alone.

Ghostwind stood on the bank of the Rosebud, remembering and crying. A flood of images came back to her, including a loving father and mother who had done all they could to make her happy. No one could have asked for better parents, yet they had been taken from her. And she hadn't been able to remember until now.

Ghostwind felt someone watching her and turned to see Crazy Horse standing near a tree.

"I will leave if you wish," he said. "I came to see if you needed help."

Ghostwind walked toward him. He watched her with intense curiosity.

"My memories of childhood have returned," she told him. "I am seeing everything."

"Why are they returning now?" he asked.

"Some days ago I fell and hit my head," she replied. "I was praying while Nighthawk was gone. I fell down the hill the night he returned."

Crazy Horse continued to stare. "I heard from your friend, Day Lily, that you saw something very bad that night on the hill. Can you tell me about it?"

Ghostwind told her story, trying to relate it to the churning storm clouds that had triggered the memory of the death spirit. Crazy Horse was more interested in the images of naked Bluecoats, and hands reaching from a bloody river.

"You have received a very strong message from the Spirit World," Crazy Horse said. "How many know about this?"

"I tried to tell my mother and some of my friends when Nighthawk returned. But they believed my head was hurt and that I was seeing things that weren't real."

"What about Nighthawk? Does he believe you?"

"I haven't told him. I don't want to disturb his happiness."

"You had better tell him," Crazy Horse advised. "He should know, so that he can prepare himself for what's coming."

"Is there any way to stop this?" Ghostwind asked.

Crazy Horse looked into the dark sky. "No, it's been too long coming. Too many bad things have happened." He turned to Ghostwind. "Do you know why you are being told these things?"

"I have no idea," Ghostwind said. "As you know, I've seen death's coming before. I believed those times that the village should be moved. But this time I feel there is no escaping it. When I was a child, the death spirit came down and killed my parents. I awakened just in time to save myself. But myself only. I feel that way now."

"We talked before about your memories," Crazy Horse said. "Do you remember? It was the night Kicks-the-Fox saw us together and became angry."

Ghostwind nodded. "I remember that night. You told me that my memories would return when the time was right. My memories have returned, but I don't know what that means."

"I think you have seen a very bad fight," Crazy Horse said. "I think it is a message of many deaths. But how does it happen that you remembered your parents and your childhood at the same time?"

"It was the sky," Ghostwind replied. "I saw it flaming, and then I saw it black and churning, as it is now. It broke open the memory of my parents' death. Death is certainly coming again. But I don't know if it's coming from the sky."

Crazy Horse was staring at the storm clouds. They were moving out from camp, toward the east. "I have also felt death spirits coming into this valley. But my power comes from the sky, so I don't feel them coming for me. Yet death is coming from all around. Death will take many. I hope it will be the Bluecoats."

"Death is coming for many Bluecoats and many Indian people alike," Ghostwind said. "And I know it won't be long from now."

PART IV
Late Spring, 1876

TWENTY-EIGHT

Jordan Kincaid held his arm up against the snowy blasts.
It was the first of June, and General George Crook's
renewed campaign against the hostiles was into its fourth
day. The grassy trail that led north to the Bighorn Mountains was covered with white.

Kincaid wondered if Hall hadn't been right about this
land: there was no season other than winter. He had
thought about his lost friend many times since the beginning of the expedition, remembering the bitter cold and
gnawing hunger they had endured together during the last
campaign. Hall's end in the Cheyenne village was still a
shock. St. Patrick's Day had now become a holiday to be
avoided.

Though he hadn't been with Reynolds and Egan, Kincaid had pictured the fight many times, still believing that
Hall had died at the hands of the Cheyenne. He wondered
if they had tortured him throughout the night, and if they
had left him in the same condition as the Crow they had
found hanging in pieces from a cottonwood. He doubted
that he would ever know. But now he wanted revenge
against the Cheyenne as well as the Sioux.

The only one he could discuss his feelings with was Zack Morgan, the packer who had also come to know and like Hall. Kincaid could talk with Morgan about Hall, but not about the battle itself. Morgan declined to discuss Reynolds's attack; he believed it would bring bad luck to the present campaign.

There was one other along who Kincaid wished had been left back in the Cheyenne village instead of Hall. Sergeant Arlan Buckner had recovered from his wound, and his disposition was even worse than before. He had been given a medical discharge but had chosen to remain with the command. Though not officially on the rolls, he had been assigned to Captain Guy V. Henry's Third Cavalry. Formal reenlistment papers would be processed after the campaign.

Buckner took every opportunity to tell Kincaid that Hall had gotten what he deserved. "It was get cut up by the Cheyenne or die at the end of a rope," Buckner kept repeating. "I would have preferred to see him hang, but knowing that his bones are strewn all over the prairie does my heart good."

Kincaid had wanted to end the harassment once and for all. But he knew the consequences would be severe. The Army took care of its own, no matter the circumstance.

But when the time was right, Buckner would get his due. When the campaign was over, Kincaid would have nothing to lose. Buckner would answer to him for a lot of things. But for now, it was more important to keep his thoughts on the campaign.

Crook had designed the campaign to succeed where the first one had failed. He would take the same trails into the same country, but with a stronger force this time. More than thirteen hundred officers and enlisted men had begun the march up the old Bozeman Road. Wagons and pack mules heavily laden with supplies accompanied the command.

Though the general had mixed feelings about it, five correspondents from major national papers had come along. Crook had not been happy with the coverage after the Reynolds fight the previous March.

After his winter campaign, Crook had filed reports destroying the careers of Colonel Reynolds and the other officers under his command at the Cheyenne village. He wanted no more problems, just results. And he wanted them without question from his men. They would follow his orders to the letter. He was confident that he would return victorious this time.

Kincaid had no idea of Crook's strategy. He was not alone in this. No one, not a single officer, not even his adjutant and close friend, Lieutenant Bourke, knew the battle plan they were following, if any. All anyone knew was that they were marching up the same trail as before, headed for the vast country between the Bighorn Mountains and the Black Hills.

Crook looked no different than before, in his worn coat and floppy hat. His beard had grown considerably; he braided the two forks and taped them back out of the way. Lieutenant Bourke, with a long mustache, had taken to wearing similar attire. Together they looked like two sportsmen who had been on the hunt for a number of weeks.

For this campaign Crook rode in an Army van, a number of rifles at his disposal for shooting game and, he hoped, Indians. A large black gelding was tied to the back of the van. On occasion, Crook would burst from the van and ride to the top of a knoll, where he would sit his horse for a few moments, or sometimes a long while, staring out over the country.

Crook hadn't changed his silent, eccentric ways, nor had he changed the manner in which he led men. But not everything was the same as before. The general had cut his scouting party to just three: Frank Grouard, Big Bat Pourier, and one other named Louis Richard. They were expected to coordinate with Indian allies, en route from the Crow and Shoshone tribes, in locating the hostile villages. Crook's command and the allied Indian forces were to unite against the hostiles.

Kincaid had been disappointed. He had not been given a position as scout, but was once again packing mules and giving advice without gaining any acclaim. The general seemed to have forgotten their discussion after the Reynolds fight. Many times he had felt like telling Crook he should get his information from his head scout, Grouard, if he thought the man so knowledgeable. But Crook liked to talk about Hall, and kept Kincaid coming back.

"Private Hall could have been a standout in this army," Crook had said more than once. "He no doubt would have risen through the ranks. I was looking forward to personally pinning some bars and stripes on him."

In the general's mind, Hall would always ride with the column. Though no one had actually seen Hall killed, everyone believed him dead. Yet Crook had refused to list him among the missing, saying, "I wouldn't be surprised if he escaped. Maybe he made it over west and is now with Gibbon. We could be reunited with him soon. Wouldn't that be fitting?"

Kincaid had never fully understood Crook's affection for Hall. It couldn't be solely the general's strong remembrance of Hall's deceased uncle. No, it had to reach deeper than that.

Kincaid had always believed the general had secretly wished for a son whom he could usher upward through the ranks of the U.S. Cavalry. Married but childless, Crook must have longed for someone to carry on his name and reputation. Hall was someone whom Crook could feel fond of and protective toward, yet Hall had never responded to him.

Kincaid had gotten closer to Hall than Crook had, and Kincaid now saw that as a possible reason for Crook's behavior toward him. Everyone knew the general kept his word, yet Kincaid was not a scout, as he had been promised. Still, Kincaid never brought the issue up. Their discussions would center around Hall briefly, then branch out to cover the Sioux and Cheyenne forces and where they might be. Kincaid told Crook more than once to watch the buffalo. "You see riled buffalo, you know they've been hunted. You see them grazing peaceably, there's been no one bothering them."

When Kincaid talked about how to read the country, Crook most often ignored him. Crook fancied himself a superior outdoorsman and hunter. He believed he could tell when buffalo were nervous.

Kincaid realized that he was not taken seriously. For whatever reason, Crook had decided that Grouard was the man to rely on. Kincaid learned to tolerate the general's indifference, because he wanted to learn what he could about Crook's battle plan. If Crook had none, he wanted to know that as well.

Attaining his long-sought revenge was all that kept Kincaid marching with the column. To him, this expedition had so far proven a greater fiasco than the first, and there had as yet been no encounter with the hostiles.

As the following days unfolded, Kincaid began to believe that Crook was flying blind, and wondered if they all might soon be joining Hall in the land of the dead. With the storm subsiding, they reached Fort Reno the following afternoon, only to learn that their Indian allies cared little about fighting. A detachment sent ahead by Crook to meet the allies had been waiting in the snow for nothing.

The Crow had sent word that they had no time for

chasing the Sioux. Large herds of buffalo were near their villages. Obtaining food was the priority. In addition, it was rumored that most of the Shoshone had backed out and the remaining force was having trouble getting through the mountains.

It seemed there would be no Indian allies to strengthen the force. Kincaid knew that without the allies, there would be no force at all. Crook realized this as well, but he could not turn back. Another failure would ruin his military career. He would march until he found the hostiles and he would fight them no matter the odds. This was his last chance to polish his tarnished reputation.

Crook had already gone to great lengths to strengthen his command and give himself every edge. Before the campaign had begun, the general had sought help from those Sioux who had chosen not to join Sitting Bull. At both the Red Cloud and Spotted Tail agencies, his requests for scouts had met with flat refusal. Many had wanted to kill him and would have if it hadn't been for the large force of soldiers. Instead, the Sioux had later taken their wrath out against a lone mail courier.

Kincaid had wondered at Crook's asking the agency Sioux to betray their own brothers. They had their share of disagreements, but they couldn't be expected to side with the hated Bluecoats.

Now it appeared there would be just three scouts and a lot of unskilled soldiers against the strongest cavalry ever assembled. Crook was beside himself with anger and concern. He ordered his three scouts out to try to talk the Crow into changing their minds. The snow had melted, and the sun was out again, making traveling much easier. They would rendezvous in a week at the forks of Goose Creek, near old Fort Phil Kearny.

Kincaid said nothing while the general took the front of the column and acted as if he knew the country. He followed the trail correctly as far as old Fort Phil Kearny; but after passing Fetterman Hill on the fourth morning, the general promptly led his command off in the wrong direction.

The command spent the remainder of the day talking about Fetterman Hill and the December battle in 1866 that had wiped out the well-known commander and all his men. Shortly after, the fort had been abandoned and later burned by the Sioux. That evening the clouds opened up and the command bivouacked in mud, dejected, fearful, and nowhere near the Goose Creek rendezvous site.

During the following day's march, the men talked about being lost and how many Sioux there were, while the general hunted buffalo and fished the streams for trout. Crook ordered camp at the mouth of Prairie Dog Creek on Tongue River. Everyone was certain Crook thought he was on Goose Creek. But the general never commented.

Kincaid and Morgan unpacked and ate their meal nervously. "Not a good place to be," Morgan remarked. "Too many memories here from last winter."

"You keep talking like that and you'll bring trouble on us," Kincaid said. "Just don't think about it."

But everyone was thinking about it. The next day a soldier from the Third Cavalry accidentally killed himself with his own revolver, making Morgan even more nervous. The funeral was presided over by division commander Colonel Guy V. Henry. As taps sounded, Morgan was all for telling the general that moving camp would be the best thing for everyone.

"I'll tell him, when the time's right," Kincaid said. "You have to handle Crook a certain way, or he won't listen to a thing. You do it right, and you've got him in the palm of your hand."

Though the men remained fidgety and the atmosphere tense, Kincaid would not approach the general or suggest that he might turn back. More days passed while the general continued to hunt and fish and explore the area.

Many of the men settled their nerves by playing whist or making checkerboards. Books and newspapers were read to pieces. Others took to fishing or walking the surrounding hills; anything to break the strain. Everyone was certain the hostiles were watching, waiting for the right opportunity to engulf them.

A group of miners joined the camp, eager to help drive the hostiles back to the agencies. They were traveling from Montana to the Black Hills and had heard that crossing the Tongue and Powder River country was suicide.

Most had fought in the North–South conflict and could shoot better than the soldiers. Some had hunted buffalo before trying the gold fields and carried the big Sharps Sporter rifles, one of which Kincaid won quickly in a poker game.

Crook welcomed them with a hearty meal. He was happy to have volunteers. Spirits rose further when two mail couriers from Fort Fetterman brought news that just under a hundred Shoshone warriors had crossed the mountains to fight the Sioux. They were under Washakie, an older and highly respected leader.

Talk of battle arose once again, and then the camp was ambushed by a roving Sioux war party. Kincaid and Morgan took cover with the others as the tents were cut to ribbons by bullets streaming down from the rocks above the river.

Return fire poured back at the Indians, but the warriors were too high in the rocks, and the bullets were ineffective. Crook ordered out a detachment of cavalry, and the war party vanished. During the entire fight only two soldiers received wounds, neither serious. But a number of horses were badly wounded and had to be destroyed.

Though it couldn't be proved, Morgan believed the war

party had been led by Crazy Horse himself. "You know he told the general not to cross Tongue River," Morgan told Kincaid. "He's making good on his word."

"I don't think it was Crazy Horse," Kincaid said. "Otherwise there would have been a thousand warriors with him. I'd bet it was just a raiding party. They'd rather steal horses than fight."

"But they'll fight us before it's over," Morgan said.

"That's what we're here for," Kincaid said.

That evening a courier told Kincaid the general wanted to see him. Kincaid crossed camp to Crook's tent and announced himself to Lieutenant Bourke.

Bourke entered the tent, then came back out and held the flap aside for Kincaid. Crook was seated cross-legged on a bag of provisions, studying a raven's egg. A card table served as his desk. He pointed to a box of ammunition.

"Have a seat, Kincaid."

Kincaid sat and watched Crook study the egg and toy with his braided beard. After a moment, Crook leaned over the card table and handed the egg to Kincaid.

"Can you believe such a large, ugly bird comes from something that small and pretty?" Crook asked.

"Can't say that I've ever thought about it much," Kincaid said, handing the egg back.

Crook placed the egg on the card table and watched it roll toward him. He let it roll off, then caught it. He amused himself that way for several moments.

"Was there something the general wanted?" Kincaid asked.

"I climbed a big pine this morning," Crook said, ignoring the question. "I got to the nest and found this single egg. Cold as a winter stone, it was. No mother to warm it. Why do you suppose that happened?"

Kincaid smiled. "I can answer that easily. We're not supposed to be here."

Crook frowned. "I don't understand."

"It's this way, General. Crows, ravens and magpies are messengers to the Other World. The Indians all know this. If one of those birds abandons a nest, you know for certain there's soon to be trouble."

Crook stared at Kincaid. "Do you really believe that?"

"I know it to be true."

Crook studied the egg again. He held it tenderly to his breast, as if incubating it himself. "I know you've been disappointed in not being able to scout. But I have a reason for my actions."

"I don't need any apologies," Kincaid said.

Crook's eyes narrowed. "I'm not apologizing, Mr. Kincaid. I'm offering you a different position. Would you care to hear me out?"

"Yes, General, I'll hear you out."

Crook cleared his throat. "I'm aware that you've lived among the Shoshone. Do you know any of them who might be coming to join us?"

"I know Washakie," Kincaid replied. "He's their main war chief. I expect I'll know some of the others, too, though they were kids when I lived with them. I can't say if they'll remember me."

Crook continued to hold the egg against his breast, occasionally peeking at it. "Oh, if they ever knew you, they'll remember you, Mr. Kincaid. No doubt about that. Can you talk to them about fighting? I mean, can you get them riled up against the Sioux and Cheyenne?"

"I won't have to say much, General," Kincaid said. "If they were mad enough to cross the mountains, they'll be ready to fight."

Crook tossed the egg up and caught it. "Good. I'm going to have a big party for them when they get here. I want you to welcome them. I want you to show them that we are very glad they've arrived. Do you understand?"

Kincaid nodded.

Crook tossed the egg up again. "I'm afraid the Shoshone are all we've got. I haven't much hope left that Grouard and the other two made it to the Crow village. It's been too long."

Kincaid didn't speak. He knew the general had gotten lost and had led the men too far east. It was even possible that Grouard and the others had brought the Crow back with them and were now searching the country. Had the general asked Kincaid to guide, they would have camped at the mouth of Goose Creek, as had been planned.

"Well, Kincaid?" Crook said. "Are you willing to help me welcome the Shoshone?"

Kincaid cleared his throat. "Listen, General, we're never going to meet anyone here. We've got to move camp to Goose Creek."

Crook frowned. "Where are we now?"

"Prairie Dog Creek, sir. We've got to head back west, into the foothills."

Crook's frown deepened.

"You took the wrong trail back at Fetterman Hill, General. We're too deep into Sioux and Cheyenne country. The Shoshone will turn around if they don't find someone near old Fort Phil Kearny. We've got to go back to Goose Creek."

"Couldn't you go back and bring them here?" Crook asked. "After all, we're closer to the hostiles now. There's no sense in backtracking."

"You don't understand, General," Kincaid said. "The Shoshone will want to make war medicine before they start fighting. They won't do that here. They'll turn back!"

Crook stared at the egg. "You make a hard stand, Kincaid."

Kincaid pointed to the egg. "You should listen to the raven."

"It's saying we should turn back to Goose Creek?"

"That's what it's saying, General. Loud and clear."

"Very well," Crook said, "we'll listen to the raven. We'll go up to Goose Creek."

TWENTY-NINE

On Goose Creek, Kincaid himself began to worry about the arrival of Grouard and the other scouts. Perhaps, as Morgan had suggested, the scouts had had to ride deep into Crow country to recruit warriors. No one wanted to think they wouldn't make it back.

For a number of days there were no scouts, no Crow and no Shoshone. Crook sent a detachment to old Fort Phil Kearny to see if the Shoshone were waiting there. The detachment reported no sign of any Shoshone or of Grouard and the two scouts.

After a day of rain, the sky opened to sunshine. Kincaid and Morgan scouted the nearby country for Sioux and Cheyenne war parties. Crook diverted his worried mind with more hunting and fishing trips, along with short excursions after butterflies and more bird eggs.

One of the soldiers made friends with a burrowing owl and brought the bird to camp as a mascot. The owl took the name Sitting Bull and sat on the ground stoically while the men fed it scraps of meat.

Morgan and Kincaid watched a soldier get bitten while

trying to pet it. The soldier wanted to shoot the bird, but others stopped him.

Morgan took it as a bad sign. "I don't fancy having an owl in camp," he told Kincaid. "It's bound to bring death and bad luck."

"So far our luck hasn't been all that good," Kincaid pointed out. "Maybe it will bring a change for the better."

Morgan stared at the owl. "That's a bad joke, Kincaid."

"Loosen up, Morgan," Kincaid said. "I've never seen you this jumpy before."

"I've never felt this way before," Morgan said. "I don't want to go on."

"You can't turn back. You'll run into Sioux for sure."

"I'll take my chances," Morgan said.

"Just stick with it," Kincaid said. "When this is over, I'll take you wherever you want to go."

Morgan's eyes brightened. "How about you help me build a cabin in Montana?"

"Sure," Kincaid said. "We'll be neighbors."

Morgan laughed. "Neighbors. Yeah, neighbors."

One day ran into another with no sign of Grouard or of the Shoshone. The men who weren't out from camp played cards and read. Some took to horse racing. But the best horses had been killed or injured too badly to race. Though there had been no human mortalities, the sudden attack on the Tongue had taken its toll.

After nearly two weeks, and to Crook's relief, Grouard and the other scouts arrived with nearly two hundred Crow warriors. Grouard reported that he and the others had worked a long time to persuade the Crow to send warriors. They all knew about Gibbon's command on the Yellowstone and what had happened to his scouts' horses.

The Crow had their doubts about fighting, as they believed the Bluecoats knew nothing about Indian warfare.

During a council with Crook they pointed out that he picked bad camping locations and couldn't even find his way to Goose Creek, the agreed rendezvous. They believed if he was having that kind of trouble already, the future could only hold worse.

After a long council, Crook and his officers persuaded the Crow to stay. While the warriors were building war lodges, Kincaid found Grouard rubbing down his pony.

"What happened?" Kincaid asked. "It sounds like they want nothing to do with this."

"I had a real hard time with them," Grouard confessed. "We got back here, and no Crook. So we went on down to Tongue River. When the Crow saw the dead horses from your fight, they were sure you'd been beaten back. They were ready to turn tail then, but we talked them out of it." Grouard spat into the grass. "Things had better come together, or we'll lose them. They don't like warring alongside soldiers, and I can't say as I blame them."

"I don't know why you stick with this," Kincaid said. "It can't be for the money."

"There's not enough money to pay for riding with fools," Grouard said. "But like you, I have my reasons. You know that it's no secret, I want Crazy Horse. And by damn I'm going to have him!"

Kincaid thought about Grouard's remarks, remaining quiet throughout the evening meal. Morgan commented on his silence.

"I'm worried Grouard will get us into trouble," Kincaid said. "He's the one who led Reynolds into that Cheyenne village on St. Patrick's Day. Grouard should have known where he was. He knows Sioux from Cheyenne. He's the one Crook should have written up in his report."

"You're just sore because you're not a scout," Morgan said.

Kincaid's eyes narrowed. "Are you saying you think Grouard knows this country better than I do?"

"No," Morgan replied, "but it won't do no good to get riled about Grouard. He wants Crazy Horse, and so does the general. That's what holds them together so tight."

The next morning, Crook called Kincaid for another meeting. The general was sipping coffee, much more relaxed than he had been for two weeks. He studied a map laid out on his card table.

"We've got the start of a strong force here, Kincaid," he said. "We'll find that village and we'll give them their due." He laughed.

Kincaid studied the general. "You're lucky the Crow didn't turn around and go home," he said. "You about lost them."

"But I didn't lose them," Crook said with satisfaction. "They've decided to fight with us. How it turns out in the end is what counts."

"Well, you'd better hope the Shoshone get here soon," Kincaid said. "We still haven't got enough allies for a successful campaign. There's too many Sioux and Cheyenne, and they're defending their wives and families."

"And we're defending the United States of America," Crook said. "That's what counts, and that's who'll win this."

Crook finished his coffee and turned his full attention to the map. "Do you want to go out and find the Shoshone? I'll double your pay."

"Give them another day," Kincaid suggested. "If they don't show up by this time tomorrow, they've all turned back. None of them will be coming."

"Surely they'll want to fight," Crook insisted. "This is their chance to gain a lot of glory."

"Maybe they have the same feelings as the Crow about

fighting with soldiers," Kincaid suggested. "They don't fight the same way."

"Maybe they should learn," Crook said. He thought about his remark and added, "Heaven forbid they should!"

From outside came yelling and whooping. Bourke stuck his head in. "General, the Shoshone have arrived."

Crook burst from the tent, then came back inside momentarily. "Well, Kincaid, come on. I want you to greet them. Then we'll have a parade."

Kincaid followed Crook to the parade grounds, where the Crow and Shoshone were exchanging war songs. The Crow joined the Shoshone and the groups rode together in a large circle around the camp, shouting and waving banners and flags and rifles.

Crook and his officers had held council and now exchanged formal greetings with the Shoshone leaders. Washakie told Kincaid that he was glad to be gaining revenge against his old enemies, the Sioux and Cheyenne. But he was not certain that he could follow a Bluecoat's commands. "None of them understands us," Washakie said. "They don't understand how we fight."

"I will tell the general that you are glad to be here, but that you will lead your own men," Kincaid said.

Crook heard the translation and frowned. "Tell him I must have a commander working with him," he told Kincaid. "That is a regulation."

"Have all the commanders you want, General," Kincaid said. "Just let them fight the way they know how. We'll all be better off."

After the council, the warriors paraded their war articles and told of past battles against the Sioux and Cheyenne. Then a feast began. Crook saw to it that coffee and sugar, biscuits, butter and venison, and a dessert of dried apples was placed before the new guests. A similar feast had been prepared the evening before, welcoming the Crow.

Kincaid spotted a nephew among the Shoshone who had grown from a small boy into an impressive young warrior. Kincaid wouldn't have known him except for the circular scar on his left cheek where, as a boy, he had fallen on a knife.

Kills-in-Snow was tall and well muscled. He wore three streaks of red paint across his forehead and one across his chin. He possessed a Springfield .45 carbine that he kept in excellent condition.

"Yes, I do remember you," Kills-in-Snow told Kincaid. "You were the one who helped me find my mother after my accident with the knife. I will always be grateful."

"I see you've become a warrior," Kincaid said. "Now you can help me avenge the death of your aunt, and your cousins."

"You had better teach the Bluecoat chief how to fight in the right manner," Kills-in-Snow said. "No one is certain of him."

"He fought and won many battles against Indians to the south," Kincaid pointed out. "He's proven himself a good leader."

"This is different country and we are all different Indians," Kills-in-Snow said. "Three Stars Crook cannot bring his victories into these valleys and have the Cheyenne and the Lakota give up so easily."

"No, it won't be easy," Kincaid said. "But we'll do what it takes to win."

"Yes, we will do what it takes," Kills-in-Snow agreed. "But I'm not so sure about Three Stars Crook. Maybe he should be following instead of leading."

"Hear me, my people, I have something to say to you. Please, all of you, listen well. It is important."

Sitting Bull stood before an enormous crowd of mixed Lakota and Cheyenne people. He held his body steady, though his eyelids drooped from exhaustion. One of the Unkpapa subchiefs offered to help hold him up. Sitting Bull refused; he must stand on his own to give this message.

"As you all know, I have danced the sacred dance to the sun, and I have given of myself to *Wankantanka.*" He held out both arms, lined from wrist to shoulder with dried blood. Fifty slivers of skin had been removed from each. "I have given of myself so that my people might have food for the coming cold moons and also safety from the Bluecoats. *Wankantanka* has heard me and has given me a vision."

Ghostwind sat next to Nighthawk. Both listened intently. Though this Sun Dance had originally been planned for the Unkpapa, Sitting Bull's experience had caused alarm throughout the entire Big Village. Everyone wanted to hear Sitting Bull's words. Ghostwind wondered how close the great leader's vision had been to her own.

"It is important that you listen to me and do as I ask," Sitting Bull said. "It means the salvation of our nation." He stopped and looked at all the faces. Total silence greeted him. Every soul was fixed upon his message.

Sitting Bull's voice never wavered. "I have seen death, both for the Bluecoats and for the Lakota and Cheyenne people. I have seen many Bluecoats falling into our camp, upside down, like so many grasshoppers. *Wankantanka* gives them to us because they have no ears. They do not listen to our pleas for peace. They want only war. That is what they will get.

"But their bodies must not be touched! We must leave the spoils on the battlefield. Do not take their horses or guns! Leave their clothes alone. Do not touch them! If we take the belongings of the whites for our own use, it will prove a curse to our nation. Hear me, my people. I have spoken."

As Sitting Bull turned toward his lodge, loud discussion broke out among the people. Ghostwind looked at Nighthawk, her face filled with fear.

"Now do you understand what I told you?"

"I never doubted what you told me," Nighthawk said. "It just seems so terrible. I wish there was some way to avoid it."

"You know the Bluecoats as well as anyone," Ghostwind said. "Their world is one of war."

"How well I know that," Nighthawk said as they came to their feet. "How very well I know."

Camp moved farther up the Rosebud, while hunting and scouting for Bluecoats continued. After Sitting Bull's vision, life did not go on as usual. Children stayed close to their mothers, never wandering. The camp police grew very strict, keeping order without mercy. All thought now of the people as a whole; no one could do anything that jeopardized others without severe punishment.

In the middle of June, the Big Village settled on the banks of Great Medicine Dance Creek, known to the whites as Reno Creek. Scouting parties returned almost daily with reports that One-Who-Limps and his Bluecoats were moving slowly and cautiously toward them from the north. From what the scouts said, Gibbon was forty to fifty miles away.

On the sixteenth of June, a hunting party returned with news that the upper Rosebud River to the south was black with Bluecoats. And Three Stars Crook had brought a great number of Crow and Shoshone warriors to fight with him.

One of the hunters, a warrior named Wooden Leg, remarked, "We will have a hard time with our old enemies, the Crow and Shoshone. But the Bluecoats don't know this land, or how to fight here. There are a great many, and some of them are trying to ride pack mules. They fall off and everyone laughs. They will be too stiff and sore for fighting."

Some saw the remark as a joke, but most were very serious. Now was a time of life or death for the people. Even while the elders held council, the younger men, under Crazy Horse, painted themselves for war. In fact, Crazy Horse had begun preparing his Oglala warriors even before the hunters had returned.

Some said it was because he had spent two whole days staring at the sky, and that he had seen a vision. He knew what he must do to save his people. Before Sitting Bull had called the council of elders, Crazy Horse had already left to fight the Bluecoats.

Sitting Bull sent criers through the villages, urging everyone to stay back and think of the old and the very young, who could not defend themselves or run from an attack. It was most important to defend the people against Bluecoats coming from other directions. One-Who-Limps could arrive at any time. He might even have joined with the hated Long-Hair Custer and his Bluecoats, whom scouts had seen advancing toward them from the northeast.

The criers implored the younger warriors not to attack unless the village was threatened. "Do not shoot up your ammunition until it is really needed. Wait, and we will fight all together as one," they would say. But no one was listening.

There was panic in the Big Village as nightfall descended. Already many of the women had packed their families' belongings and now awaited orders to take down the lodges and move. But there was no place to move any longer. It was time to drive the Bluecoats away.

Fighting men from every village hurried to pack their war bags. Horse tenders rushed to the herds and brought back the best ponies. Each warrior would take two, so that they could be changed during the battle.

Nighthawk had come from his lodge and was talking with Eagle Wing. Shot-in-the-Throat approached and wished Nighthawk good luck.

"You're going to learn what it's all about," he said. "Stay low. I want to see you back here alive."

Nighthawk looked into his father's eyes. "There's a lot to life I'll never understand, Father. But I do know that I belong with these people, not my own."

"These *are* your people," Shot-in-the-Throat told him. "They're my people. Fight bravely for their cause and we'll feast in celebration tonight."

Young Horse and Tall Deer arrived, each holding one of Nighthawk's ponies.

"I wish I could go and tend your ponies," Tall Deer said. "Father says I'm too young. Maybe in another winter."

"When you're ready," Nighthawk said, "I will be proud to have you help me."

"You know how to ride," Tall Deer said. "Show the Bluecoats what you've learned."

Young Horse couldn't hold his tears. "I know you will fight with honor," he said. "I want you to come back."

"I will come back," Nighthawk promised. "You stay with your sister and mother. I will return with the others."

Mountain Water suddenly arrived to fetch Young Horse. "Plans have changed," she said. "You will stay with your grandfather and me, not your mother. Don't ask questions. Just come along."

Without saying a word to Nighthawk, she took Young Horse by the hand and led him away. Tall Deer stood back with Shot-in-the-Throat as a number of women came forward to their men, each one leading a pony. Ghostwind was among them.

"We've come to help with the horses and the wounded," she said. "Day Lily and others are going also.

Please, don't ask me to stay behind in camp. I cannot. I must be with you."

"I won't ask you to stay back," Nighthawk said. "I'm glad you've come. I know the danger, but I'm still glad you're going to be with me."

Nighthawk mounted his buckskin. Ghostwind rode one of the ponies Nighthawk had given her father. "He says it will bring luck," Ghostwind said. "He is usually right."

Day Lily rode next to Red Bear. They joined Nighthawk and Ghostwind. Red Bear extended the tips of his fingers and Nighthawk touched them.

"I was wrong about you," Red Bear said. "Today I will be proud to fight alongside you."

"I will have the same pride," Nighthawk said.

The Cheyenne gathered. Two Moon and other prominent men would lead. All seemed to know that this battle would be the most important of their lives. If they could not drive the Bluecoats back, their people would be in grave danger.

More Lakota and Cheyenne warriors rode out joining to number more than a thousand, riding through the darkness toward the upper Rosebud, where their lives would change forever.

THIRTY

Kincaid awoke with the first reveille. It was three A.M., June 17th. Though the mule packers and the miners wouldn't be leaving until around five, he could never sleep once camp had begun to break.

Morgan, who was even more jittery, had taken to saying the Lord's Prayer at least three times a day. He was sitting in the light of a new fire, his head bowed into his hands.

"Our Father, who art in heaven . . ."

Everyone had his own way of dealing with the stress. Many wrote letters, though they knew the chances of sending them were slim. Couriers had not been able to get through from Fort Fetterman, nor had anyone come in from anywhere else. Likely the Sioux were blocking all trails. Crook's force seemed cut off from the rest of mankind.

Kincaid and Morgan drank coffee and chewed on bacon and hard biscuits as the infantry readied for departure. The column was to move quickly and find the huge village the Crow and Shoshone kept talking about. Time was of the utmost importance.

To travel faster, Crook had ordered the wagons and excess supplies left behind at Goose Creek. Each soldier had been issued forty rounds of ammunition, and everyone had been given a mount for faster travel, even the foot soldiers. They had fought to stay on unbroken mules since leaving Goose Creek.

The first few days had kept the doctors busy treating severe sprains and bruises from the kicking and bucking mules. This unskilled riding had caused the Crow and Shoshone to respect Crook and his men even less. They had grown weary of laughing and had taken to filling their time with buffalo hunts and horse races. Even stripped down, Crook's force moved so slowly that the Indian allies had time to scout ten to fifteen miles ahead and still return to camp at night before everyone had arrived and had settled in.

"I don't like being strung out like this," Morgan told Kincaid. "If the Sioux get to us, they'll surround us and split us into little groups. We won't stand a chance."

"I hear you," Kincaid said. "But there's no other way it can be. We can't move as fast as the cavalry. If you want to know the truth, I'd rather be right where I am than up with the cavalry. We stand a lot better chance of holding Indians off than they do."

"Maybe so, but the Crow and the Shoshone are our best bet," Morgan argued. "We're just damn lucky they're along."

Kincaid couldn't argue that fact, though many were now cursing their presence, including Crook. They did not respond to orders or follow instructions of any kind. Kincaid's nephew, Kills-in-Snow, said that the white commanders gave orders just to have power. "There is no good cause in what they do," Kills-in-Snow said. "Once in a while they're right. But not very often. So why listen to them?"

The Indian allies did their reconnaisance before daybreak and knew by sunrise whether or not they would meet enemies. As always, they left just after the first reveille. They knew their enemies operated the same way. If there was to be a battle, it would start early.

Just after five A.M. Kincaid and Morgan moved out with the others, watching the dust rise in front of them. For days the men had complained about the endless rain and cool weather. Then the rain had stopped and the skies had cleared, leaving the open ridges and bottoms exposed to a merciless sun.

After three hours of marching, a messenger rode along the line announcing that Crook had bivouacked in a narrow valley just ahead. Most of the packers decided to stop where they were and rest for a while. Crook would likely be fishing for the remainder of the morning, giving them plenty of time to catch up. Kincaid and Morgan decided not to rest and led their mules ahead.

When they reached the little valley, they found Crook and his forces eating breakfast. They had forgone eating earlier to catch up with the Crow and Shoshone, who were shooting in the distance.

"They must be hunting again," Morgan remarked. "You'd think they'd get tired of just shooting all the time."

"Gives them a sense of accomplishment for the day," Kincaid remarked. "Lord knows they're bored out of their wits traveling at this pace."

Sergeant Arlan Buckner spotted Kincaid and Morgan playing a game of whist with a group of cavalrymen. "Why aren't you men with your group?" he asked. "You have no business taking up time with these men."

"I didn't see where it said that in the regulations," Kincaid remarked.

"You'd best go find an officer to protect you," Morgan added. "You'll get yourself in a pickle if you keep badgering us."

Buckner opened the flap of his holster, but Kincaid was on his feet before Buckner could get his revolver out. He slammed a fist into Buckner's face, sending him sprawling. Kincaid turned to the soldiers watching. "I'm going to teach him a lesson. Will that bother anyone?"

"Give him a punch for me," one of the soldiers said.

"Go ahead and kill him," another one said. "He's caused more grief than the Sioux ever could."

Buckner lay on the ground, dazed, fumbling for his revolver. Kincaid pulled the pistol away and stuck the barrel in Buckner's face. "I've had all I can stand of you. Give me a good reason not to just blow your head off."

Morgan stepped forward. "Don't take it too far, Jordan."

"Why not? The world would be better off."

Buckner's eyes were wide with terror. Kincaid continued to glare, shoving the barrel into Buckner's nose, bloodying it.

"Look ahead!" Morgan suddenly shouted. "What's going on up there?"

Everyone stood up to see a contingent of Shoshone warriors riding full speed down into camp. They were yelling, "Lakota! Sheyila! Many of them!"

The shooting in the hills north of the valley had intensified, though no one had paid much attention. Now it was evident that the Indian allies were not enjoying a buffalo hunt, but were defending the camp from a charge by hostile forces.

Kincaid threw Buckner's pistol aside. He and Morgan fell in with Captain Henry's cavalrymen. Orders were being shouted from all sides and confusion overtook nearly everyone in the command. Finally, as the shooting drew ever closer, Kincaid and Morgan took positions in a skirmish line of mixed infantry and cavalry that stretched for more than a mile along the valley bottom.

"This is what we come for," Kincaid told Morgan. "Get your shooting eye ready."

Morgan wasn't listening. He was reciting the Lord's Prayer.

"The time has come," Crazy Horse told Nighthawk. "Your day to become a full warrior is here."

Nighthawk sat atop a hill with Ghostwind beside him. Eagle Wing and Red Bear sat their ponies, along with nearly fifteen hundred Cheyenne and Lakota warriors who had come to drive Three Stars Crook back to Fort Fetterman.

Nighthawk felt his stomach turn upside down. Sweat broke out on his forehead. The feeling that had come when he had ridden into the Cheyenne village that cold St. Patrick's Day had returned. This time it was far more intense.

Already some of the younger warriors were two hills over, riding back and forth in front of a skirmish line made up of Crow and Shoshone warriors. Runs Far, the energetic young Minneconjou warrior, had led a force into battle early. Rifles popped in the hot morning and shouts echoed through the hills.

Crazy Horse pointed toward the fighting. "Three Stars made his scouts wear red cloth on their arms, so that his Bluecoats could tell them from us."

"That will make it easier for us!" Nighthawk said.

"Hau, hau!" everyone yelled.

Crazy Horse had already prepared himself for battle. He wore only a breechclout and a calfskin cape. A single eagle feather hung from the top of his loose hair. Sunlight gleamed off war paint that had been splattered like hail against his face. A long knife hung from a sheath at his side, and a .44 Winchester rifle, model 1866, lay on the ground near his pony.

"This day has been a long time in coming," Crazy

Horse continued. "It was bound to happen, even though the Bluecoats left the forts along the old Bozeman Road. I always knew they would return. No matter the treaty papers and the promises, I knew they would return to try and take this land as their own."

Crazy Horse began to sing a war song as he prepared his red pinto for battle. He bound the horse's tail with thin rawhide and painted the sides and shoulders and rump with various symbols, including a full handprint, which meant he had fought hand to hand before and had won. Splotches of white paint dotted the pony everywhere, and a circle of red enclosed each eye.

When he had finished, Crazy Horse tossed dust over his pony's back and blew a root powder into his nostrils, invoking a spirit of strength and endurance. Then he jumped on and sat still, as if falling into a trance.

Nighthawk had painted red and yellow stripes across the shoulders and hips of his buckskin. He now prepared himself in the manner of his vision with Eagle Wing three months before. With a mirror in one hand, he applied three bars of bright yellow paint crossways along each cheek, from the nose back to the jawline. Three bars of red crossed his forehead, with a single, thicker stripe of red trailing down from his lower lip, over his chin, ending at the base of his throat.

His hair, which had grown down over his shoulders, hung loose. The body of a nighthawk, caught, dried, and given him by Eagle Wing, was tied into his topknot.

Eagle Wing watched with satisfaction. "You look more like one of us than we do. You will become a true Cheyenne warrior this day."

Nighthawk reflected on the words. He looked into his mirror, staring at a face that seemed foreign to him. Everything about him, even his eyes, seemed to belong to another. In just three months he had become an entirely different person.

"Do not think of yourself as a stranger," Ghostwind said. "See yourself instead as turning into the real you, the person you were born to be."

"*Hau!*" Eagle Wing said. "Ghostwind is right. When I challenged you to fight in the snow of our burning village, I saw you as you are now. I saw you as the strongest man anyone could face in battle."

"*Hau!*" Red Bear agreed. "The strongest!"

Nighthawk handed his mirror to Ghostwind and checked his weapons. He carried a Henry .44 repeating rifle, and a Colt Navy .44 in his waistband. While a good many warriors had chosen bows and arrows or lances, many others had rifles, some newer and some very old.

They carried everything from single-shot Springfields and cap-and-ball revolvers to lever-action Spencers, Henrys, and Winchesters, which fired modern cartridges. Some even had the big Sharps rifles used to hunt buffalo; Nighthawk had seen them carried by the packers with Crook. Any kind of firearm that had ever been taken or traded from the whites was in use, including the muzzle-loading Hawkens of the fur trade.

Though ammunition was not abundant, the warriors did not worry. As with arrow-making, some warriors had begun to specialize in reloading empty shell casings in exchange for favors from those warriors getting the ammunition. They had learned about guns and ammunition from traders and from men like Shot-in-the-Throat, who were doing what they could to help the Lakota and Cheyenne keep their homelands.

The last thing Nighthawk did was to draw a rawhide rope tightly under his pony's forequarters and take a wrap around each leg. This would enable him to hold tightly to the horse and maneuver and shoot without fear of falling off.

Eagle Wing and Red Bear were both ready to fight. As did many of the warriors, they wore cartridge belts criss-crossed over their chests, and coup sticks within quivers on their backs. Many warriors carried medicine shields as added protection. Painted for battle, they raised their rifles and shook them, then screamed into the sky.

Nighthawk brought his rifle up and yelled with the others. Crazy Horse came back from his trance and turned to Nighthawk. His eyes appeared glazed over.

"Do you have the stone I gave to you to put under your left ear?"

"It's been there since the day you put it into my hand," Nighthawk said. "It will always be there."

"Good," Crazy Horse said. "We will carry our medicine into the battle. Do you fear death?"

"It is a good day to die," Nighthawk said.

"Ah, but you will not feel death," Crazy Horse said. "You will see it and you will smell it. But your spirit will remain with your body." He looked around at the warriors gathered. Tears fell from his eyes. "It will not be so for some of my brothers. I wish there was a way to save them."

"A lot of lives will be saved if this battle does not take place," Ghostwind said. She pointed to the valley floor. "The wild roses, and the other flowers of blue and yellow and white. They will die this day as well."

"It cannot be helped," Crazy Horse said.

"Yes, it can," Ghostwind argued. "Turn everyone around and ride back to the village. Form a line around the camp. When Three Stars sees the numbers, he will turn and leave."

"No, he will wait for the other Bluecoat leaders to come," Crazy Horse said. "Then they will have us on all sides. Do you want our women and children to die?"

"I don't want anyone to die," Ghostwind said. She looked into the cloudless sky, where a searing red sun rose toward the zenith. "But I have already seen the death that is coming."

"There must be fighting today," Crazy Horse said. "You know it, and I know it. What has been started must be finished."

"No, it is only beginning," Ghostwind argued. "All our children will feel the impact of this day."

"We will all feel the impact," Crazy Horse said, "from this time forward."

Nighthawk looked across the hills, where the younger Lakota warriors continued to race back and forth in front of the Crow and Shoshone line.

"We've talked many times about how to fight the Blue-coats," he said to Crazy Horse. "Do you have a plan?"

"It's time that we surprise the Bluecoats and fight the way they do," Crazy Horse said. "We will break into large groups and charge at them from many directions. We will try to separate them from their horses. We will charge all at once, then fall back so that they charge us. It won't be just a few warriors going at them to count coup and gain honors. We will fight as one whole nation bound together."

Nighthawk was reliving his vision of fighting together with Crazy Horse. He could see himself painted, as he was now, riding with the other warriors. This battle would fulfill his vision. The Cheyenne and Lakota would fight in detachments, charging at Crook's men from many directions. This would be very different from what Crook and his officers were expecting.

"You will ride with your leaders among the Cheyenne and I will lead the Oglala and any of those who wish to follow," Crazy Horse continued. "When it is finished, we will exchange war stories."

Crazy Horse was preparing to ride when he saw a young

Lakota warrior running on foot along the bottom just below. His horse had been shot out from under him, and a group of Crow and Shoshone were whipping him with quirts. Nighthawk fell in with Crazy Horse and the two rode down with other warriors to stop them.

The Crow and Shoshone scattered, but stopped a ways distant and raised their weapons in challenge. Crazy Horse made sign for them to go home, that he wanted only Blue-coat blood. They yelled their defiance even more loudly.

Crazy Horse ordered that no one pursue them. Everyone would attack at once later. He then turned to the young man, who sat on the ground in tears, his face and back covered with whip marks.

"Why didn't you stop and take your pony's bridle when it was shot?" Crazy Horse asked. "Why did you show the enemy that you were afraid?"

The young warrior hung his head in shame, his arm shielding his face.

"Find another pony and go home, Jack Red Cloud," Crazy Horse said. "I warned you not to wear the eagle medicine headdress. It has brought you bad luck, and now you have lost it to the Crow. It was not yours and you should not have been wearing it."

An Oglala warrior offered his extra pony and Jack Red Cloud jumped on. As the young man rode away, Crazy Horse explained that Red Cloud, the young man's father, had once been a great leader. Now he was despised by many Lakota.

"Old Red Cloud gained much honor when he stopped the *Wasichu* from using the Bozeman Road," Crazy Horse explained. "But that was many winters past. Now he does what the *Wasichu* ask. They give him silly presents and call him chief of all Lakota people. His son is too much like him."

Another large force of Lakota warriors arrived to join

Crazy Horse, all of them whooping war songs. Crazy Horse touched Nighthawk's fingers with his own. "I am going to fight. Good luck, my friend. Keep your wife away from trouble."

When Crazy Horse had left, Nighthawk and Ghostwind followed a leader named Dull Knife and four hundred warriors to a hill that rose above the valley floor. Eagle Wing and Red Bear got their rifles ready, as did Nighthawk.

Below, Crazy Horse and his Lakota forces hurried to assist Runs Far and his warriors. Crazy Horse led a charge directly into the Crow and Shoshone lines. After intense fighting, much of it hand-to-hand, Crook's Indian allies were pushed back into the Bluecoats, who were forming long skirmish lines.

The Bluecoats had been divided into three main groups. One group had made it to a high formation of rocks overlooking the valley, while another was making a stand along the Rosebud. Nighthawk could see Crook retreating atop his black horse with still more men toward a high hill overlooking the valley. Forces of Cheyenne and Lakota were riding toward the back of the hill, hoping to cut the general and his troops off before they reached the summit.

The battle began in many places at once. The Indian allies engaged Sioux and Cheyenne forces on different fronts, while the divided commands worked to unite on Crook's hill. Lines of infantry used their long-barreled Springfields to keep the charging warriors from coming too close. While they reloaded, the warriors would turn and charge again, driving the Bluecoat lines back. Then they would turn, and the Bluecoats would give chase.

Nighthawk and Ghostwind watched the battle for some time, while the younger warriors groaned in agitation. Yet Dull Knife kept his forces in check for a long time, waiting for an advantage.

Finally it came. A large force of Lakota had succeeded in breaking one of the lines along the bottom, near the creek. The Lakota were changing horses on the far side and the Bluecoats were retreating up a small hill. It would be a perfect chance to push the Bluecoats back into the Lakota forces on the other side.

Nighthawk sat fighting the butterflies in his stomach, awaiting the signal from Dull Knife to charge. Ghostwind remained back with the other women, holding the horses. Her face was lifted to the sky.

Finally, Dull Knife nodded and a chorus of screaming voices filled the air. Nighthawk leaned over and kicked his pony into a full run down the hill, riding headlong into a battle that would change history.

THIRTY-ONE

Nighthawk leaned over the side of his pony, aiming his rifle at the blur of blue in front of him. He realized if he hit anyone it would be sheer luck. Shooting from horseback was far less effective than from the ground.

Bullets and rifle balls sang and buzzed through the air. A bullet nipped a section of mane from Nighthawk's pony. Though warriors fired wildly on all sides of him, Nighthawk waited to shoot. He wanted to be as sure as possible of his target.

The blue line broke ahead of the charge and Nighthawk rode through without even firing. As the warriors turned their ponies for another charge, the Bluecoat line had re-formed and rifles were pointed, awaiting the order to fire.

Dull Knife turned his warriors, not wanting to begin another charge with tired ponies. Knowing this, a group of Shoshone rode at full speed toward the retreating Cheyenne forces. They fired heavily, and Nighthawk saw Red Bear's horse go down.

Nighthawk turned his pony and rode back. The Shoshone were screaming, racing to be the first to count coup. Red Bear was struggling to get out from under his fallen horse. Nighthawk reached him just before the Shoshone. Nighthawk jumped to the ground and aimed his rifle. Bullets zipped past his head and puffed dirt at his feet. He fired, then levered another round into the barrel and fired again. Two Shoshone warriors pitched from their horses and the others scattered.

Nighthawk helped Red Bear from under the pony. Red Bear spit blood; a bullet had sheared his upper lip away.

"My knee is torn. Save yourself."

"I'll get you on my pony," Nighthawk promised. Bullets again started to tear up the ground around them.

Nighthawk dragged Red Bear to his buckskin, then turned to meet another Shoshone attack, dropping a warrior at a good distance. The others turned away with their hands over their mouths, marveling at his marksmanship.

"You shoot with the strength of ten," Red Bear said. "It's good that it was you who came down to get me."

Bullets continued to whiz by them as Nighthawk lifted Red Bear onto his pony and swung up behind.

"Hold on," Nighthawk said. "We're going to charge them."

"No!" Red Bear begged. "Don't be foolish."

"It's our only hope," Nighthawk said.

Nighthawk wheeled his pony around, his rifle aimed directly at the line of Shoshone. Seeing this, and wanting no more casualties, the Shoshone retreated. Their medicine was no match for Nighthawk's rifle.

On the way back up the hill, Nighthawk rode past one of the fallen Shoshone and leaned over, touching the body with the barrel of his rifle, counting coup. When he reached the top of the hill with Red Bear, he was greeted with loud cheers.

"You have gained great honor," Eagle Wing said.

"You've become even stronger than I thought you would."

"I'm proud of you, my husband," Ghostwind said. "But you will have to share your honor with another. While you were saving Red Bear, a woman was down on the other side of the hill saving her brother."

Nighthawk learned that a Cheyenne leader named Comes-in-Sight had fallen when his horse was killed. He hadn't been hurt like Red Bear, but his sister, a woman named Buffalo-Calf-Road-Woman, had ridden down and risked her life to save him.

"Buffalo-Calf-Road-Woman has performed a deed that will be told around campfires for as long as the Cheyenne people are alive," Ghostwind said. "There are warriors saving one another everywhere. It is not often that you see a woman with the courage to race her horse into battle."

"It will be a good day for all of us," Eagle Wing said. "We are fighting strongly. It will be a hard battle and it will take a long time to win. But if we're patient, we will drive the Bluecoats away."

Red Bear was on the ground, holding his knee and spitting blood. Day Lily was trying to stop the bleeding.

"I want my other pony," Red Bear said. "I'm not content to just drive them off. I want to kill them all!"

"You stay back with Day Lily and me," Ghostwind said. "You did well today, but now you must wait and fight another time."

"Yes, wait for another day," Eagle Wing said.

Red Bear looked up to Nighthawk. "I owe you my life."

"We will fight together again," Nighthawk promised. "I will bring back a Crow pony for you."

"Don't do anything foolish," Red Bear said. "You've done enough for me already." He pointed. "Everyone is gathering to charge the Bluecoats again. Thank you, my friend. Go and fight bravely."

* * *

Kincaid ran with Morgan toward a formation of sandstone rocks. Captain Henry's company was spread out, racing for cover before another force of Cheyenne or Lakota could cut them off. The company had narrowly missed being pushed into a deep ravine, where the hostiles would have destroyed them.

Henry was moving his men as fast as possible. They had orders to join a commander named Royall and with his forces make their way toward Crook's hill. Word had come by courier that Crook had divided the command and needed everyone remaining to keep the hill.

Crook had sent Captain Anson Mills with a detachment to ride downriver and attack the village. No one knew just where the village was, but Crook had decided that it couldn't be far and had ordered Frank Grouard to lead Mills and his troops past the big bend of the Rosebud.

Mills had been anxious to go. He had been the most successful commander of the day, driving Cheyenne and Lakota forces back time and again. Some of the hostiles believed his medicine as strong as many of their own leaders', and avoided him. Had there been more Bluecoats like him, the battle would have been a hard one for the hostiles.

But Crook thought the battle was going too slowly and that Mills could do more good by attacking the village.

Henry had received the word by courier. Kincaid and Morgan heard the news as they reached the rocks and took position.

Morgan was breathing heavily. "How does Crook think Mills is going to take that village with what few men he has? We need everyone we've got right here."

"Nobody has ever known what's in Crook's head," Kincaid said. "If I get out of this, I'm quitting the outfit. This is crazy."

"You mean it?" Morgan asked.

"Damn right. I've been thinking. I could kill a thousand

Sioux and it wouldn't bring my family back. I'd be better off to find a quiet spot in the mountains and build a cabin. I don't need any more fighting."

"That sounds good to me," Morgan said. "We'll be neighbors. How's that sound?"

"We'll be neighbors," Kincaid said. "Just keep shooting straight for now. We'll get out of this. Soon we'll be neighbors."

Kincaid and Morgan sat in the rocks with Henry's men, ducking hostile fire and awaiting further orders. The barrel of Kincaid's rifle was searing hot, but he was still able to fire and eject shell casings without any trouble. Morgan and many of the other soldiers hadn't been so lucky.

Morgan cursed as he struggled to pull an expanded shell casing from his Springfield. "I'm going to toss this thing," he said. "I'd do better with a slingshot."

"Let the barrel cool down and then tamp the butt end against the ground," Kincaid said. "That will loosen it enough so you can pull it out."

"I ain't got time for that!" Morgan yelled. "I just ain't got time!"

Kincaid couldn't argue. When the hostiles were charging, every man needed to shoot as fast as possible. But most had single-shot Springfields, and most everyone was having trouble with them. The battle had lasted more than four hours, and it seemed as if the Sioux and Cheyenne had just gotten warmed up.

Early in the battle Kincaid saw that Crazy Horse had adopted a new strategy. Time and again the hostiles had charged the lines, then had turned in retreat. The mounted cavalry would give chase, only to find that the hostiles had circled back and were attacking the weakest points in their position.

Though the battle had been continuous, neither side had prevailed. Attacks and counterattacks had used up a great deal of ammunition, but there were relatively few casualties on either side.

Kincaid knew that would soon change. The hostile fire had almost ceased, indicating that they were mounting their strongest attack yet.

"Why aren't we advancing?" Kincaid asked. "What's Henry waiting for?"

"Royall's moving into position to cover us," Morgan said.

"We can't wait for that," Kincaid said. "There's not enough time."

Kincaid and Morgan would have to cross the open with the others to the next hill to join Royall's men. There the horses would be brought up. Once mounted, Royall's and Henry's forces could ascend to the ridge where Crook had made his headquarters. But they would have to move soon or be caught between two forces of hostiles grouping on either side of them.

The hostiles had been trying all morning to reach the horses and mules secured in a ravine behind Crook's lines. If the hostiles could succeed, they would effectively dismount the better part of the Bluecoat force and have them surrounded.

Kincaid yelled in rage. They had been sitting in the rocks too long. The Cheyenne and Sioux had massed, and were simply waiting for the right moment to attack.

Captain Henry rode along the lines, yelling for everyone to begin the advance to the next hill. Many of the men were balking, reluctant to leave the rocks for the open. Sergeant Buckner rode through the men, whipping them with his quirt.

"Get moving, you stupid bastards! Get out there, I say!"

As Bucker approached, Kincaid swung his Sharps around and cocked back the hammer. "Don't come near me, Buckner. I'll drop you like a stone."

Buckner's face flamed with hate. "Get moving, Kincaid! And get these men out there with you."

When Buckner had left, Kincaid pointed to a line of Shoshone forming to meet the Sioux and Cheyenne forces. The men cheered and formed a line that spread out from the rocks, down through a creek, and back up toward the next hill. Captain Henry rode back and forth along the line, shouting for the men to hurry, as the Shoshone were too few to stop the hostile charge.

"We're in no-man's-land now!" Morgan yelled. "God, I'm tired."

From the ridges and hills on either side, warriors descended like a wave of rolling thunder, their horses grunting and pounding the ground. They passed in front of the line, their painted, screaming faces at point-blank range. The gunfire was so intense and so close that the horses squealed from powder burns.

Arrows and bullets ripped through the lines. Horses and men filled the air with screams. Kincaid leveled his rifle and fired blind at the vague form of a warrior riding headlong through the boiling dust just in front of him, never knowing whether the bullet had struck anything. Troops shouted, "Hold the line! Hold the line!" while wave after wave of Sioux and Cheyenne descended upon them.

Suddenly there was a break in the charging hostiles. The line began to move. Kincaid reloaded on the run, bumping into a soldier no older than eighteen, on his knees crying for his mother, an arrow through his stomach.

The air cleared momentarily as the hostiles regrouped along the hillsides. Henry yelled for his men to advance, stopping frequently to urge dazed or wounded soldiers back into line. Kincaid looked for Morgan and saw Arlan Buckner riding his horse toward him, his pistol cocked.

Another wave of hostiles charged. Buckner fired just as

Kincaid ducked. The bullet creased Kincaid's back and he straightened up, screaming at Buckner.

Buckner's horse reared, throwing him off into the oncoming hostiles, who rode over him, shooting and swinging war clubs. Buckner tried to stand and was struck full in the back with a war club made of knives.

Kincaid knelt behind a fallen horse until the attack subsided. As the hostiles again changed ponies, Kincaid searched the line until he found Morgan. Henry and the other officers were once again yelling for the men to advance toward the hill.

"I can't go no further," Morgan said. He dropped to his knees.

"Don't stop now!" Kincaid yelled. "We have to get across!"

Morgan began to vomit. "This heat's too much for me. You go on."

Kincaid took Morgan by the arm. "You get to your feet! I'm not leaving you here."

"I ain't going to make it, Jordan," he said. "I can feel it. The end's come."

"Damn, here they come!" Kincaid yelled. "Put your rifle to your shoulder!"

The hostiles once again swarmed down. Kincaid fired and Morgan fought to load his jammed rifle. Men screamed and fell while others broke and ran. Kincaid saw Captain Henry's head snap back as a bullet tore through his face.

Henry's horse bolted and the captain fell. Crow and Shoshone warriors engaged the hostiles, who were trying to count coup on the fallen commander. They fought hand to hand on horseback and on the ground, screaming, churning the grass and flowers to dust. The hostiles were finally driven away from Henry's prostrate form, and a doctor rushed to aid him.

Kincaid turned toward a warrior who had fought off two Shoshone and was mounting a buckskin pony. The warrior leveled his rifle as Kincaid brought his Sharps to his shoulder.

Kincaid held his fire, as did the warrior. The two stared. For an instant, Kincaid thought he knew the man. He thought he knew the face. But there was so much paint and long hair. And so much dust. How could he know him? But he did.

A cavalryman and a Sioux rode between them, fighting hand to hand. The cavalryman fell and the Sioux rode off. When Kincaid looked again, the warrior and the buckskin pony were gone.

Dazed, Kincaid turned and rejoined the line. The warrior had been the same size as Hall, the same build, with the same dark hair. And the warrior had stared just as hard at him.

Kincaid looked to see if he could find the buckskin pony. It was useless. There were too many hostiles and too much dust.

Someone shouted at Kincaid to get into line. The troops began advancing again, but Morgan was not with them. Kincaid turned back to find him.

Morgan was on his knees. His right arm hung limp. The top of his shoulder had been blown away and his left hand held the shaft of an arrow that protruded from his ribs. He was sobbing, mumbling the Lord's Prayer.

Kincaid broke into tears. "Morgan! For God's sake, get to your feet!"

Morgan's eyes stared straight ahead. Kincaid tried to lift him. Another soldier grabbed Kincaid by the arm.

"He's gone, cain't you see? We've got a chance to make it! Hurry up!"

Kincaid turned as two screaming warriors charged them from behind. Kincaid and the soldier rolled to the ground, Kincaid turning and firing up into a painted face. Kincaid heard a pistol report and a shout of triumph from the other warrior. He ran to the other soldier and found him kicking and jerking in a death spasm, his face all blood and black powder.

Kincaid yelled and started to run. He remembered Morgan and turned just as a Sioux warrior leaned over the side of his pony and slammed a huge rock war club into Morgan's face. Two others jumped from their ponies and drove knives into Morgan's body.

Fighting shock, Kincaid raised his rifle and killed one of the warriors. He felt a hot, stinging sensation against his cheek and reached up to feel warm blood. In an instant he had turned and was running, screaming, "Morgan, how could you! We were going to be neighbors! We were going to be neighbors . . ."

THIRTY-TWO

C rook's hill was deserted. After six hours, the battle had ended when Crazy Horse had given the signal to withdraw. Enough had been done this day. Many had fallen, and the Bluecoats had been stopped.

The battle had shaken Ghostwind to the depths of her being. She had witnessed so much death. Many Bluecoats had fallen, and a great many Crow and Shoshone warriors had also died. But the losses had been greatest among the Cheyenne and Lakota.

Though the counting was not complete, more than a hundred warriors had been killed or wounded. It disturbed her that the valley had become so sad, as if the very ground were weeping.

Though the fallen men on both sides had mostly been removed, the air still smelled of blood and death. Dead ponies littered the hillsides and bottoms, drawing ravens and magpies from everywhere. The roses and other flowers were all gone, smashed into the dust. Nothing here would ever be the same.

The Lakota said that some of their brothers lay up the

creek, close to the Bluecoat camp. They would have to leave them until the following day and hope they hadn't been disturbed.

Nighthawk had been helping to build travois for the wounded Cheyenne and Lakota warriors. Many were singing their death songs. Three Stars and his Bluecoats had tasted defeat, but it had cost a great deal. Many young warriors had passed on. There would be much sorrow in the Big Village.

Ghostwind knelt beside Rides Far, unable to help him. He had ridden through charge after charge against the Bluecoats, only to be struck in the final run. Blood seeped from two bullet holes in his stomach, through his fingers and into the trampled grass.

Ghostwind held his head up while he spoke. "I lived a good life . . . and I found the best wife a man could want in Fawn-That-Goes-Dancing." His face was contorted. "I hope her life is good."

"Save your words for when you see her," Ghostwind said. "We will take you back."

"I will not see her again in this world," Rides Far said. "My relatives have come for me. They are gathered around me." He began his death song.

Nighthawk arrived with a travois. He and Eagle Wing loaded Rides Far while Ghostwind stood facing a breeze that swept through her hair. In the distance lightning snapped from a bank of dark clouds that hovered over the Wolf Mountains. Rides Far reached out and Ghostwind took his hand.

"Tell Fawn that *Wankantanka* loves her. He will take care of her and provide for her." He arched his back and uttered a muffled cry. A rush of air poured from his lungs and he lay still.

Tears formed in Ghostwind's eyes. She crossed his arms over his breast. "Rest well. I will tell Fawn that her husband fought bravely. She can be proud that you died a warrior's death."

Nighthawk and Ghostwind started back toward the village, with Eagle Wing and just under fifty Cheyenne and Lakota warriors. Day Lily and Red Bear had gone back earlier with others who had been hurt. Ten warriors lay on travois, three of them now dead.

Ghostwind continued to grieve for Fawn-That-Goes-Dancing. Besides her loss of Rides Far, her father and two of her brothers had fallen. She would be in mourning for a long time.

Nighthawk pointed down toward the river bottom. "Maybe some of us should stay. There may be more fighting."

"There is no use in fighting any longer," Ghostwind told Nighthawk. "We have no more food. The ponies are spent; the ammunition is gone. Everyone has fought a long time, and too many have been killed or wounded. No one can win the battle this day."

"I believe you," Nighthawk said, "and I think Crazy Horse feels the same way. But Three Stars believes he can still win the day. He wants the Crow and Shoshone to lead him to the village."

Ghostwind looked out to where the Bluecoats were riding in double lines behind the Crow and the Shoshone. They were headed toward a canyon just past the big bend of the Rosebud.

"Crazy Horse and his warriors have just entered the canyon," Nighthawk said. "Many of the Lakota are waiting there for Crook."

"Three Stars would do well to turn around," Ghostwind said. "He's lucky to be alive. If it wasn't for the Crow and the Shoshone, he and all his Bluecoats would now be in the Spirit World."

Nighthawk stared at the Bluecoats in silence. Ghostwind had heard him tell of meeting his friend, Kincaid, on the battlefield. Either one could have shot the other. Somehow neither had fired. It had been a shock to Nighthawk, one he would not easily get over.

As they rode on, Eagle Wing and the others made up for Nighthawk's silence, talking endlessly about the battle and what they had seen happen. Most of them were certain they had accomplished Sitting Bull's vision, for there was a story circulating that Three Star's black horse had been shot out from under him.

Those who saw it said that the horse jerked forward so violently that Three Stars was flipped head over heels. It sounded to them like the falling Bluecoats of the vision. Now that he was headed into the canyon, they were certain that he would die and fulfill the prophecy.

Ghostwind was not so certain. She did not have the feeling that enough Bluecoats had died, nor enough Cheyenne and Lakota. Her vision had been very intense, as if the entire sky had burst into flame, igniting everything into violence.

She was certain of this when Eagle Wing and a number of warriors rode to a hilltop. They watched below them for a time, then returned excitedly.

"The Crow and Shoshone are turning back," Eagle Wing reported. "They will not ride into the canyon. Three Stars is angry and wants to go. The Grabber is telling him to turn back and wait for another day."

"Let him go into the canyon," a warrior spoke up. "It will be his last day in this world."

"He won't go," Nighthawk said. "Frank Grouard, The Grabber, wants Crazy Horse badly. But even he won't take a chance. They'll all turn back."

"Then we have certainly won the battle," Eagle Wing said. "We have driven them from our lands."

"Yes, we have won," Nighthawk said. "Three Stars will never admit it, but he's been beaten."

"There's a lot of daylight left," Eagle Wing commented. "If everyone wasn't tired of fighting, we could have killed them all. Then One-Who-Limps would have left. All the rest of the Bluecoats would turn and run from our lands."

Nighthawk said there were too many Bluecoats coming from all directions; it would be impossible to drive them all away. But he couldn't be heard over the shouting. The warriors were all yelling together that they could wipe out all the Bluecoats.

"If they return, we will finish what we started," Eagle Wing said. "We will end it for them."

After the yelling had subsided, Ghostwind spoke. "There will be another time and more Bluecoats to fight, that is certain. Many more will die. But maybe the next time, the Bluecoats will all die."

Kincaid sat on a bluff, watching the sun fall over the battle-field. A short distance below, Kills-in-Snow and a number of other Shoshone buried their dead in caves and under rock outcrops. The Crow were doing the same thing else-where in the valley.

Kincaid had buried Morgan himself, even while the fighting still raged. He had carried Morgan down to the creek and had interred him in a patch of wild rose. He had wanted to be shot, to see the end, but no one had even noticed him.

When he had finished, he had walked to the hill where he now sat, vowing never to fight another battle. He wanted no more of his quest for revenge against the Sioux or the Cheyenne.

Kincaid turned as a messenger rode to the crest of the hill, leading a horse behind him. "The general wants to see you," the messenger said. "I brought you a mount."

"Tell the general I'm in no mood for his company," Kincaid said.

The messenger stared. "What?"

Kincaid lurched to his feet and waved his hat. "You heard me! Git on out of here! Scat!"

The messenger released the horse he had led up the hill and rode away at a gallop. Kincaid caught the horse and mounted. He turned to the west and began to ride.

He had no concerns about anyone coming after him. The hostiles had fought long and hard. They were guarding the village and mourning their dead. They wouldn't be out for some time to come.

Crook wouldn't send anyone out. He certainly still feared Crazy Horse. Kincaid could see no reason for the general's wanting to see him, and he was in no mood for more bird eggs. The last thing he wanted to do was ride back to Fort Fetterman and listen to Crook plan another campaign. He never wanted to have anything to do with the U.S. Army ever again.

Near sundown Kincaid reached the base of the Bighorn range. A dark cloud rumbled overhead. Kincaid sat his horse under a large pine and watched small hailstones bounce against the ground.

After the storm, he shot a deer and butchered it. He built a fire and cooked a large cut of tenderloin. In his bedroll, he sighed and closed his eyes. Men and horses filled his mind. Gunshots. Screaming. He opened his eyes and looked into the heavens.

But the stars were little comfort. The day would remain with him forever. He would never forget losing Morgan and seeing the others fall around him. He would never understand how he had remained alive. Somehow he had survived with but a few crease marks.

Kincaid resolved that time would help him. The days would pass. He would ride deep into Montana and build a cabin near a mountain stream. He would stay up there for a long time, and he would always think of Morgan as his neighbor. Maybe after a time he would begin to see life in a different light.

But no matter if the scars all healed, there would be one vision that would forever remain: the young warrior who had stared at him through the heat of battle and hadn't fired. Private Mason Hall, painted red and yellow, naked except for a breechclout, had become a Northern Cheyenne. He was certain of it. He had never been more certain of anything in his life.

Kincaid was also certain he would learn the reason why. After the fighting was all over, and there was certainly more to come, he would find Hall. He wasn't worried about Hall not surviving; men like Hall couldn't die. He would find a way to search Hall out.

When that day came, he would clap Hall on the back and say, "You know how to take care of yourself, don't you? You had me worried there for a time. You'd better come up to my cabin and tell me all about this."

Kincaid turned in his bedroll. For the first time since Reynolds had returned from his attack on the Powder River, he smiled. He took a deep breath and closed his eyes. The night had finally turned peaceful.

Ghostwind rode with Nighthawk and her two children along the trail toward the Greasy Grass. The Big Village was moving. The police were vigilant. No one was allowed to wander anywhere.

There was little discussion as they rode. The various camps had broken early in the day, leaving behind a single lodge where a lone warrior rested. His relatives had decided that his journey across should take place in the camp he had left to fight the Bluecoats.

This first morning after the battle, Ghostwind had

many things on her mind. She had left the lodge early to talk with her spirit helpers. She had built a sage fire and had prayed. Again she had seen the red owls, confirming that her terrible vision had not yet come to pass. The worst battle was some time in the future.

On her way down the hill she had become nauseated. At first she had believed it to be the result of all the tension. But her mother had stopped her and had touched her abdomen with a smile.

"You and Nighthawk have not wasted any time, have you?" she had said.

Ghostwind had wanted to argue. It wasn't possible; she couldn't be with child already. But she was. Her mother had been able to tell beyond a doubt. Older women knew about such things, even upon the moment of conception.

She hadn't told Nighthawk. As they stopped to water the horses, she decided there would be no better or no worse time. She sent Young Horse and Talking Grass to be with their grandparents and turned to Nighthawk.

"I'm going to have a child," she said.

Nighthawk stared. "Are you certain?"

"I was sick this morning. I wondered then. My mother told me as we broke camp that she had been noticing a change in me. It's very early yet, but she can tell."

Nighthawk took her in his arms. "That's wonderful. This is the best news I've heard in a long time."

"I'm worried," Ghostwind said. "I know this should be a time of great happiness, but I'm afraid for us and for the child. Many bad things are coming."

"We can face whatever is to come," Nighthawk said. "I'm certain of that."

"You don't understand. The bad times are going to last many winters. I already have two children who are facing hardship. I don't know if it's fair to have a third."

"Are you saying you want to lose the baby?"

Tears formed in Ghostwind's eyes. "I don't know what I want. I only know that it will be very hard for little ones during the coming moons. Harder than it has ever been."

Nighthawk was well aware of the various herbs that brought about abortion. He had seen women using them. Each had their own reasons, and no one interfered. He felt that Ghostwind was reacting to the battle of the day before.

"Fights like that are very rare," he said. "I believe the worst is behind us."

"No, the worst is yet to come. I know this. And after the worst, I don't know what will happen."

"We'll all make it through," Nighthawk said.

"Maybe, but for what good reason?" she asked. "I have talked to those who live at the agencies. It is a life worse than death."

"The Creator gives life for a reason," Nighthawk said, "and takes life for a reason. You're the one who told me that. I should have died many times, but I didn't. I believe that I lived to share my life and my happiness with you, no matter where we are. Having a child together is the greatest happiness, isn't it?"

"I just don't want my children to suffer," Ghostwind said. "I don't want any children to suffer."

"Maybe there is a balance," Nighthawk suggested. "Life is cruel and also wonderful. We have to accept all sides. Isn't that what your elders say?"

"Yes, that is what the elders say," she replied. "It's not for us to understand, but to accept and to do the best we can."

Ghostwind and Nighthawk embraced for a long time. Young Horse and Talking Grass returned. Ghostwind told them she would soon be giving them a new brother or sister. Both hugged her tightly, and Young Horse began to dance around.

"It will be a brother, and I will teach him all I know. He

will be a famous hunter." He began to compose a song he would teach the baby.

"I have a different song," Talking Grass said. "I need a sister to share my dolls with."

The village began to move again. As they rode, Ghost-wind thought of the many times she had been told to listen to the children, and the many times she had told Night-hawk to listen to them. She listened now and it filled her with new hope.

Young Horse and Talking Grass continued to discuss the birth and whether it should be a boy or a girl. Though the shock of the previous day's battle was all around them, they focused on the thought of new life. Having a new brother or sister would be a special gift. It was new life that showed the Creator's love.

Nighthawk thought of his days as a child. Missouri was a long way away, a place he would likely never see again. He could never have dreamed of his life now.

His memories of prison were far distant, even more so than his time with the traveling circus. He thought of his days with General Crook's command; they also seemed very long ago. Even the battle of the previous day now was distant, a memory sailing like a raven into the clouds.

One memory, though, would burn. Kincaid's face would be a part of his life until the day he died. He wished that he might see the man again, but he didn't hold much hope. Yet he knew very well that nothing was impossible.

As the children laughed, Nighthawk realized the only truth to life was in living for the moment. Each moment he had with Ghostwind and the children was to be treasured. He had never known such freedom before coming to the Northern Cheyenne.

Perhaps Crazy Horse was right: the future might already be in form. And Ghostwind was always right in what she saw in her visions. But no matter what lay ahead, Nighthawk believed they would survive.

Together they would live the days one by one, meeting each new sunrise with reverence, watching the last glow of evening with quiet hearts. He had found his place in a strong land, and there he would spend his last days, whenever they came, for he believed in the words of the elders: nothing lasts forever but the earth and sky.

AFTERWORD

The fight on Powder River and the Battle of the Rosebud were the earliest confrontations in what is com-
monly referred to as the Great Sioux War of 1876—if war
can be called great. One week after the Rosebud, on June
25, 1876, the infamous Little Bighorn Battle took place,
the end for George Armstrong Custer and nearly three
hundred soldiers of the Seventh U.S. Cavalry.

The Battle of the Rosebud has taken second place in the
history of the Sioux War because of the disaster that befell
the U.S. Army at Little Bighorn. However, historians are
quick to point out that the Rosebud fight brought a new
insight into the mind of the Plains Indian warrior.

Before the Rosebud, soldiers expected warriors to fight
in their traditional manner, charging singly or in small
groups at will, with no real structure to their battles. That
changed at the Rosebud. Crazy Horse's forces were
grouped in legions and sent to strategic locations. Many
believe that had it not been for the Crow and Shoshone
forces fighting with Crook, the Rosebud battlefield would
have looked much like the Little Bighorn a week later.

As a result of the Powder River and Rosebud battles, General George Crook had to work hard to maintain his status in the Army. A bitter struggle developed between Crook and Colonel Joseph Reynolds stemming from the Powder River fight, bringing court-martial for Reynolds and other officers involved. The Army was at war internally, as well as with the Sioux and Cheyenne.

The Battle of the Rosebud led the Sioux and Cheyenne to believe that the Army would leave them alone. That was not to be. From this point of view, Little Bighorn can be seen as a battle of ultimate frustration for the Indian people. They were being chased against the terms of their treaties, and had no recourse but to make a stand. Protecting their homes and families, the warriors gave no quarter to this enemy who seemingly cared nothing at all for human values.

Though victorious, the fight on the Greasy Grass, as the Indian people called it, marked a terrible downturn for the Plains tribes. After this tragedy, the U.S. Army began an all-out assault on the Sioux and Cheyenne nations, hunting them mercilessly until each and every surviving band was under close reservation guard.

My next novel, yet untitled, details the events on the Little Bighorn and their aftermath. The months and years after that terrible day will be seen through the eyes of Nighthawk and Ghostwind, along with Crazy Horse and Sitting Bull, leaders whose strength kept their people from total despair.

This novel follows the Sioux and Cheyenne in their journeys and their conflicts with the relentless U.S. Army forces, and details Sitting Bull's retreat into Canada to avoid further bloodshed. The new tale ultimately ties in with *Song of Wovoka*, my novel of the Ghost Dance religion and the Battle of Wounded Knee.

It is my hope that these tales express my belief that

intercultural and interracial conflict is detrimental to the human race. War and suffering exact a tremendous toll on the human spirit. We are all sent by the Creator to live together; it is our challenge to be friends and brothers, not enemies. In the words of the Lakota Sioux people, *Mitakuye Oyasin*—"We are all related."

—Earl Murray
Yellowstone River Valley
Laurel, Montana
March 1993